Salvation on the Blade

Zhi Wen

Translated by Qiao Di

Published by New Generation Publishing in 2025
Originally published in Simplified Chinese by New Star Press Co., Ltd in 2017

Contents © Zhi Wen 2025

Print ISBN 978-1-918291-92-6
Set in Times.

 New Generation Publishing

www.newgeneration-publishing.com

Zhi Wen is a Beijingese lawyer, who set up the offender profiling association entitled "Zhi Wen•Crime Research Office" in 2004.

Qiao Di, Master of Translation and Interpreting from Peking University, is a certified CATTI Level 1 translator and an expert member of the Translators Association of China. With over a decade of experience in translation between English and Chinese, she is a proficient translator and the owner of several translated works from fiction to popular science books. She is now working with several famous publishing houses, including CITIC Press Group and the New Star Press, and possesses expertise in the translation of subjects involving news reporting, marketing, and advertising, with a total volume exceeding one million words. She also teaches translation and is the author of the textbook *How to Translate: Learn About the Basics in Three Weeks*.

Contents

Chapter I
The by-blow

The morning fair under Jimen Bridge was a traditional Beijing one: the ancient city gate, woods, Xiaoyue River, and vendors peddling around with hawking, everything you can expect to find in a fair. Only the city gate was restored, litter were scattered everywhere in the woods, a stinky smell came from Xiaoyue River, and vendors no longer sold drinks like Douzhi and groceries like cloth scraps, their long rhythmic cry turning into bargaining with diversified accents. The 21st century was creeping in, and Beijing, where I have lived for thirty years or more, seemed to be standing on the other side of a faint haze, making me familiar as well as strange at the same time to its presence.

Be it familiar or strange, however, the churning in my stomach was real in the morning haze. I forced my way to one of the vendors for my breakfast."A set of Jianbing[1] please. No Baocui, and one more egg." said I with my hands deep in the pockets and my shoulders hunched.

"You either buy everyone a set or leave yourself starved like us all." snuffled my leader, his voice coming through the earphone, raging in my head. "Is Team Two ready? Less than two minutes! Come on! Cao Fa! What are you doing there, standing like an idiot? Walk around and keep alert! Have you finished checking the Heyan area? ...

"Team Two ready."

"Team Four ready."

"Team Nine split. Zhang Qi and I are moving along the east bank up to the north. Nothing special."

---

1 Jianbing, or Jianbing guozi, a kind of pancake with eggs, vegetables, and deep-fried dough sticks or Baocui (crispy deep fried crusts) rolled in, is a popular street food and breakfast especially in Beijing, Tianjin and neighboring Hebei province.

"Got visual on someone suspicious at the entrance of Tunnel Seven. We are moving in."

"Van Two can be seen from the south slope! Move it elsewhere!"

"Team One report! Nothing special in Tunnel Two. Our radius is overlapped with Team Two at the buffer zone of Tunnel Three. Please rearrange."

"Some vendors are spatting with customers in the middle of the north end. Team Four, send someone to see."

"Van Two, do not move forward! Go back 30 meters."

"Team Four report! The one selling long beans is bickering with the old lady. He is pushing her. Oh my god, her son is now fighting with him. Zhou, come on and stop them!

"Director Bai, Jimen Bridge station has our men checking around the outside. They reported a call from 110, saying there's a fight in the site and asked whether they should come to deal with it ..."

"Tell them no. If there's a complaint, tell the inspector to come and talk to me ..."

Squatting on the bank, I was gulping my breakfast while reading the newspaper in my cellphone. The sizzling hot eggs and cheap chili sauce made me achingly pleasant, compared with whom the chaos in my earphone was nothing – I've long been used to it anyway. In the newspaper, someone forced a superstar to marry her, otherwise her father would commit suicide, despite the fact that the superstar didn't know her at all. The ones who supported her were calling for the legislation to protect fans' welfare, which I was also in favor of. Carina Lau, Rosamund Kwan Chi-lam or Charlie Young, who doesn't like those beautiful actresses? Wait, did that mean there's finally a chance to legally and legitimately realize my dream after all these years? But the only problem was, why wasn't the girl herself the one who committed suicide, but her father? Even though she couldn't marry the superstar, it was also good to do something to promote the legislation process.

After the front page, more fun to see. Some parents called up a bunch of people to batter the teacher only because the kid late for class was asked to review the misbehavior in writing. Seeing this, I was so shocked that I even went back to double-check. Yes, the parent thought that a written review is surely the restoration of feudalism. Besides, a boy stabbed his grandma to death only because he was not given the money he wanted to go and play in the Internet bar, and his parents said the grandma was an actual Shylock. Most dating shows have turned into the auction of sex deal, but the easy girls were praised on the Internet as the brave ones who weren't afraid of speaking out their mind ... I was so grateful that I was living in such a wonderful world, with everyone free to do anything in the relics of morality.

After my breakfast, I took out a cigarette and glanced at my watch when a serious female voice from the van completely cleared out the communication. "Attention! The ATM is coming in. All units, move in! I repeat! The ATM is coming in. Move everybody, move!

The deep voice from Director Bai came in afterwards, "Stay alert, guys! Keep your eyes on him! Acting Squad, remember to keep your distance!"

I lighted the cigarette up unhurriedly, got up on my feet and rubbed my numb legs. Stepping down from the stairs, I left the bank and forced my way into the crowds, to the largest roundup in Beijing ever since the millennium.

It was because of a kidnapping three days ago. The hostage, Cai Ying, 28-years-old, is the wife of Dong Ji, an "insectaholic" without any proper business. At the time of the kidnapping, he was collecting some crickets in Ningyang, Shandong province, showing no concern at all to his wife's suffer. He wouldn't even come back but for his father's personal order on his immediate return.

That day, Cai Ying was taking a walk outside at six o'clock in the evening. According to the nursemaid, Ms. Jin, she accompanied Cai Ying out and went to the convenience shop by the west gate of the housing estate community for four batteries for the remote controller. It took her no more than two minutes to get the batteries and when she came back, Cai Ying was gone. "At first I thought she went home by herself, or took a walk elsewhere with some neighbors, so I came straight home to wait. But almost two hours had passed and she didn't came back. I went out to find but where should I start with? I was really burning with worries, and then Mr. Doing Sr.'s call came in ..."

The kidnapper directly called the only one with the ability to pay the ransom – Caiying's father-in-law, a famous magnate in real estate in Beijing. The call was blunt and simple. "I have your daughter-in-law here with me. Tell your son to come with three million RMB in cash in a woven bag. The day after tomorrow, 17th that is, at seven o'clock in the morning under Jimen Bridge, I'll meet him there. Tell him to take your phone and I'll let him know the exact place to put the money. The moment I got the money, I'll let her go. Don't you dare to call the police and you'll never see her again."

Having it verified from Ms. Jin, Mr. Dong Sr., an experienced hand, made a prompt decision and told her, "Call Dong Ji at once. Tell him to come back in no time. Do not call the police."

However, his decision was not precisely carried out.

She followed his first order and called Dong Ji at once, but Dong Ji didn't react much after getting the call. From his bustling background, he may be bargaining with some cricket catcher and only replied, "I'll come back next week. Tell the old man to call the police! What do we pay so much tax for? Where is the government? What is the government doing there!" But for the second one, she didn't follow, not because she believed what Dong Ji had said, but from her limited experience, the old lady, who came to Beijing to earn a living since young, chose to believe the police to deal with the issue.

But the above mentioned, no matter kidnapping or magnets, were not what made the case so important to be supervised by the City Bureau.

This morning, the reason why the Deputy Director in charge of criminal investigations of Haidian Branch Bureau was on site, together and almost two hundred police officers from the Criminal Investigation Division, was only because of Cai Ying – she was a nine months pregnant mother and due to deliver any minute.

The moment the case came out, people who are related and unrelated, who give orders and implications, who come to help and hinder – all relevant authorities came out to give directions in turns. What a real sensation!

Mr. Dong Sr. was almost driven crazy. "Cai has done the obstetric ultrasound and that's a boy! One child one generation for four consecutive generations, that's the only hope of the family. Don't get in my way. I just want to pay the ransom and get her back! I don't care what you do as long as she's back. If anything happens to my baby, there's nothing you can do to make it up!"

Dr. Xu, associate chief physician from Haidian Maternal & Child Hospital verified his saying. "Cai Ying is indeed with a boy. She is healthy and so is the baby. The expected date of confinement is this weekend. We don't know whether the kidnapper masters the skill of natural labor. But even if he does, the place, devices, temperature and sanitary conditions ... they are all problems he has to deal with. The newborn baby is very vulnerable. Under such circumstances, he may not survive even delivered successfully."

The Criminal Investigation Division of Haidian Bureau replied. "We have to handle the case according to the law. But we can assure you that we will put the hostage's safety in the first place. We also hope that you can cooperate with us and tell Dong Ji to come back as soon as possible, and prepare the ransom if possible ..."

The technical team reported the next morning. "According to the surveillance footage from the Public Security and Traffic Administration Bureau, there were 71 vehicles passing both ways outside the west gate ten minutes after Cai Ying's disappearance. Thanks to the help from all branches and divisions, last night, we have narrowed down the suspects into a white Jetta, plate number EY5786. This car is the asset of a car rental agency located outside the 3rd West Ring Road and was rented out yesterday. The man renting the car is named Shi Zhan, who was born in 1972 in Qinghai province. After researching his background, we have known that he left the Chinese People's Armed Police Force (PAP) here in Beijing in early 2001 and took the job as a driver afterwards. After that, he resigned to be an informant for some debt collection & recovery agencies. He has an older sister who stays with his parents in Qinghai and has no relatives here in Beijing. After Cai Ying was kidnapped, we have dialed his phone but it was powered off. We also went to the apartment he rented and found no one there. According to the nursemaid Ms. Jin, Shi Zhan had come to Cai Ying several years ago. Cai Ying then said they came from the same place and he was coming to borrow some money. But the background research for Cai Ying shows that Shi Zhan was her ex-boyfriend and they broke up after he attended the army. Rumors also tell it was Cai Ying who broke up with Shi Zhan because she wanted to marry Dong Ji for his money, but it is to be verified. Since the two of them know each other, we believe even if Shi Zhan's got the ransom, there is still a big chance that he would kill the hostage..."

The next afternoon, a patrol officer from Zhichun Road station reported, "About one o'clock in the afternoon, the white Jetta was found parking in the southwest of Dayuncun crossing, Zhichun Road, Haidian District. There was no one in the car, and the keys were left there. Black hairs were found on the back seat. The hairs were not long, greasy, with dandruff spotted around the root. Samples have been sent to the medical examination center in Haidian Branch Bureau to conduct DNA matching ..."

The technical team from the Criminal Investigation Division of the City Bureau provided technical support. "According to the analysis from Dr. Yuan Shi, consultant in criminal psychology, the suspect is a criminal with organizational abilities. Since this is a kidnapping case, the suspect must have at least one partner. Shi Zhan's experience of being trained as an armed police enables him a certain ability of counter-reconnaissance. He may be armed and there must be a fixed secret place to keep the hostage which may be around Zhichun Road or between Zhichun Road and Jimen

Bridge considering the victim is pregnant. Although the suspect used a rental to commit kidnapping, there's also a chance that he himself owned a car which, according to his past experience, may be an off-road vehicle of dark colors similar to the color of his clothes ..."

The Secretary of Judicial and Law Enforcement Committee of Haidian District also called. "Mr. Dong is an entrepreneur of exemplary character in our district. He not only makes great efforts in boosting the non-commercial housing market and helping to control the market price, but also handles properly some of the most intractable displacement issues. For such an outstanding taxpayer, we must protect the safety and security of lives and property of him and his family with might and main, or the credibility of the country and government will melt into thin air! This case must be solved in no time and the safety of the hostage must be secured!"

The Criminal Investigation Division from the city bureau also emphasized in the teleconferencing. "There is no need to address the importance of this case ...... Saving the life of the hostage is not only the responsibility of our policemen, but also critical to how the public would view the harmonious society. Safety, that is! The security of the capital! If we cannot even protect a pregnant mother, how can we guarantee the security of a city! Listen guys, if this case is failed, not only the Ministry of Public Security will hold us accountable, the city bureau, the victim's family and the society will all come to us and hold us responsible as well! By then, you will be ashamed even to wear this uniform!"

2

Dong Ji was shaky when he walked into our sight, taking the woven bag. He was tall and fair in complexion, with a side part hairstyle and a belly bulging front out of phase which made him look like a gourd. I was looking askance at this good-looking young guy with a small belly, as if seeing a grasshopper walking on two legs.

"ATM's phone is ringing." The Acting Squad was reporting in details.

"Captain Zhao, why are you not at Tunnel Six? Please keep your post." said Cao Fa, who always wanted to make some trouble for me whenever he could.

"He's picking up the phone. Direction center, please locate the signal." seemed to be Cui, who should be monitoring on some high ground eastward."

"Captain Zhao, would you ... would you come back a little bit?"

requested from those dastards in my own team.

"The locating has been started ..." Jiang Lan from Van Two reported.

Director Bai from Van One was giving orders, "Put ATM's phone on the line."

Bai's orders have been carried out immediately. We now could hear them, but the quality was not good. I even doubted whether Jiang had put the loudspeaker of the monitoring line right on the microphone.

"Where, where are you? How am I suppose to give ..."

"Walk on my instruction. Don't look around! Keep forward! ... ... Did you call the police?"

"No, we, we didn't ..."

"..."

"Hello? I, I said we didn't ..."

"Wait! Stop! Turn right ... That's fucking left! Yes. Did you see the Wonton stall on the south? The one with two tables? One is empty and the other is vacant. Now there's a man sitting there ..."

"Yeah, I see."

"..."

"Hello? Hello?"

"Go find a place to sit ..."

"Signal Located! The signal is right under Jimen Bridge. He's here!"Jiang's voice cut in all of a sudden. Come on! Now that the criminal was talking about "Wonton stall", not a more general "breakfast stall", he must be in the crowd!

He was right next to us.

"Acting Squad, stay focused! Follow everyone who is making a call. The suspect may be quite close to our ATM ... Zhao Xincheng! Go back to your Tunnel Six!"

Bai was the only one I would listen to in the whole division. Now that the leader was asking, I've got no other choice but to go back to where I should be. Anyway, Tunnel Six, the place my team was in charge of, was right to the opposite of the Wonton stall where Dong Ji was. I could still have visual on him."

"Hello? Hello? Is this where I should leave the money? Hello?"

"Hello?"

"Hello? I've already sit down. Hello?"

"..."

On the other side of the phone, Shi Zhan gave no answers.

I suddenly had a bad feeling.

"Target discovered!"

The Acting Squad was a little bit slow. I have noticed him on my way to Tunnel Six: Around 15m on the right behind Dong Ji, a lot of people are surrounding a stall selling fish. One of them was a young man in a dark green coat, browsing around for the fish, but with a phone in his right hand all the time. His age and physical features seemed to match Shi Zhan's since we could only find an ID photo before he attended the army, too young for us to identify.

And he was now holding his phone, not talking.

"Keep your distance. Don't alert him." Bai's arrangements came quick. "Stay focused on him. We don't need that many people on the ATM side, focus on the suspect. Acting Squad, come closer. Everyone else, stay put."

The green coat's mouth was moving; at the same time, the phone call continued –

"Push the bag under the table. Unzip it, open it, right. Did you have breakfast? Ask for a bowl of Wonton. Are your rich people used to this humble and cheap dish? Take a note from the bag if you don't have money. This one is on me."

"Err ... Ah? I ...

"..."

"Hello? Do you want me to buy a bowl of ..."

"Put down the bag and get out! The moment I get the money, she's all yours!"

The green coat put his phone in the pocket, focusing on the fish.

Knowing not what to do, Dong Ji stared at his phone and wondered a while. And then, he stood up and walked quickly to the main road.

Bai's deep voice came through the earphone, "Acting Squad, leave the ATM, focus on the Safe. Officers on the outside, stop the ATM."

Everything went all right so far. There were many plans prepared. According to our analysis and instructions from Dr. Yuan from the City Bureau, the kidnapper wouldn't operate alone. The man who showed up on site may be Shi Zhan, or his partner. We would follow whoever came to collect the money to locate the hostage, and then, the SWAT Team would come in to rescue and capture.

But something was wrong.

Shi Zhan was a former armed police and worked as an informant for a debt company. Would he blow his cover just like this? The signal location was right, and the call showed he was right on the spot ... Did he really believe that the Dongs didn't come to the police? No, there must be something wrong. What did I miss? There must be some details right in front of my eyes but I didn't see.

"Someone is approaching the Safe!"

"The target has bought something and is moving west along the road."

"Target Two confirmed: Female, short fair, short and thin. The target is around forty years old, wears a ocher sport suit with an obvious Nike mark on the back. She is sitting on the place where the ATM sat on and looking down at the Safe."

"She is looking around. Acting Squad, keep your distance."

Was she his partner? Why bothered to come to the scene if someone else was coming to collect the money?

"Target One enters into Tunnel Five. Keep your cover guys. Let him pass."

"Target Two is leaving with the Safe. She didn't eat anything. She just collected the money and go! Observation post, ID her location! ID her location!"

"Tailing plan activated. Van Two follow the Safe, report all possible routes. Others stand by. All that in Tunnel One to Tunnel Four, get together on your buffer zone and move to the target route."

No! There must be something wrong! But what was it?

"Boss, don't move out! There's something wrong. Team Six Zhao Xincheng Report! Don't move out! ..." I cannot continue. I haven't figure out what the problem was myself.

Bin, I wished you were here.

"What's the problem?" Bai asked right after my report.

"Something, something is wrong, boss. It's just not right ..."

You were always saying: I could see all that you have seen. But I didn't see anything! Or, I saw them, but I didn't know what I have seen ...

"What's the problem! No more bullshit! Other suspects? Come on!"

Calm, calm ... What did I see?

"Boss ..." I tried to slow down like Bin to buy me some time to think. I saw the last two officers of the Acting Squad going out of my sight to the direction of Target Two. I saw the the swarm in the morning fair, the scattering litter, and the golden clouds on the eastern sky. I saw my men looking at me, an old lady in red walking pass me pulling a trolley. I saw the groceries and vegetables she bought from the morning fair: green peppers, tomatoes, potatoes, garlic bolts, leeks, apples ... no long beans.

I said to myself, "No long beans ..."

"What did you say?" Not only Bai, maybe all that wearing earphones were confused, but the fact seemed to dawn on me –

Bin, I saw them. I really saw.

"No long beans because of the bicker, which leads to the fight, which means there should be police on site five minutes after they call. But there was no police on site because of our arrangements. So..." The police calls, phone calls, Wonton, the green coat, the ocher sport suit – all became clear. "Boss, our cover has been blown."

For a moment, Bai didn't say anything. And then he gave a decisive order. "Everyone goes back to your position! Lockdown the scene! Tell the City Bureau we are requesting backup from Xicheng Branch to protect on the outside. Acting Squad, stay closer! Focus on the targets! What's going on, Zhao?"

His choice was not only because he trusted me, but more on the importance of the case – this is so important a case that he'd rather believe what I said.

"Shi Zhan is straight to the point when asking for the ransom, but talks a lot on the site and talks hesitantly and incoherently. He is trying to match up what Target One is doing. The phone call Doing Ji receives is not from Target One. It is a two-man act. He pretends to be the old lady's son to fight with the vendor selling beans to cause a sensation in order to let someone call the police. Or maybe he's the one who's calling the police. Normally, police should be on site in five minutes. But we stopped them, which exactly reveals the truth that he is under our surveillance." I kept my voice low and watched around alert. "So, Shi Zhan may suspect an ambush even before he calls Dong Ji. He played us. Target One may not be even related to the case."

"Then how about Target Two?"

"Probably no. Shi Zhan asked Dong Ji to put the bag there open. Who won't be attracted by such a bag of money? What he has to do is to follow whoever takes the money. When he's sure about not being followed, he could find some nook to take it back. Now he must have discovered there's so many people following that two targets. So I believe we have completely blown our cover."

Complete silence in the channel.

Bai was quite calm. He started to rearrange at once. "The ones who monitor high grounds, tunnels, overpasses, and river mouths, stay where you are and wait for backup. All police who patrols along Xiaoyue River, get together with the Acting Squad, and divide the morning fair crowd into groups according to the violent repression plan. Others on the outside, move inwards to control all other escape routes besides roads ... Hold on, everybody! Backup from the Social Order, Patrol Forces, and Xicheng Branch is on the way! From now on, no exit under Jimen Bridge. Take down and search everyone in this morning fair!"

In an instant, the communication channel became much more noisy than the morning fair.

"Target Two is taken. The Safe is secured."

"Target One is taken."

"Citizens pass by Tunnel Four. Already intercepted. Can we show our IDs?"

"When will the Acting Squad arrive?"

"Vehicles from the police station is jammed on the southeast of the bridge. Our men has left the car and is heading to the south-to-north one-way road."

"Acting Squad hasn't arrived yet. There is about to be a public disorder. Request to divide into groups immediately to separate the crowd."

"Go back. Build a buffer zone."

"Too many people in Tunnel Three. Back up needed!"

"Director Bai, can we identify ourselves?"

"Van Two is in position. All units, you may show your ID."

"This is Bai Yinshang. Keep all exits shut. Take them if needed."

"Communication is a mess. Acting Squad requests for an exclusive line. Hello? Hello!"

...

The lockdown led to immediate disorder.

In Tunnel Six which my group was in charge of, many people were arguing with the plainclothesman. Some of the unlicensed vendors even tried to rush out pulling their trolleys, or took the goods and ran out.

Was this old lady the one used by Shi Zhan. Didn't seem to be. Maybe just an ordinary old lady who didn't buy long beans. ... But where was Shi Zhan?

The effect of separation was very limited. Bai was always in favor of people. If he knew this early, he would encourage all units to come out on site.

Shi Zhan was monitoring Dong Ji quite close when he was on the phone. Maybe he took one of the high grounds? No. That would be the only fly on a pane of glass – just too obvious.

An encouraging piece of news came form the communication. "Men from the Social Order arrived!"

A sudden conflict broke out in the south for unknown reasons. Team Two was calling for backup in the communication. The Acting Squad was running there and the people controlled by them was pouring into every exit, then stopped by the backup from the Social Order.

He must have find some safe spot to observe. But where was it? Our men were everywhere. There was no such spot at all.

Backup from the Patrol Forces have also arrived.

Crying and cursing, the crowd was swarming in from south to north, which meant the Acting Squad had lost control of them.

I tried to run to the bank to avoid the crowd, but was taken in half way. An old man was shoved down. The bag of eggs in his hand were stamped into trash in an instant. I elbowed my way down to him ...

How was he able to do that? Bin, tell me. How can he ever get the chance?

The old man was not heavy, but it was difficult to hold him in arms and get out of the crowd. I was hustled here and there in the horde, punch-drunk. A young man in white sweater walked pass me, the paper clip on the collar shining under the sun – an identification mark of all our men.

You were always saying that I'm a hairsplitter, that I'm always driving to dead ends. Am I waking to the wrong direction now?

"Hey! Give me a hand!" I called him aloud. He turned back, his eyes clearly lingering on my collar and earphone for a moment, and nudged his way out of the crowd. He took the old man and said, "We can't stay here. We'd better move outside."

Shi Zhan made his phone calls right under Jimen Bridge next to Dong Ji – under the surveillance of countless trained eyes. How can he do that?

After hustling our way out, we put the old man on the side of the road. The young man asked gently, "Did you hurt?" Only by then did I realize that the back of my left hand was bleeding, and my little finger swelled up to the size of my thumb.

I wedged my earphone back and said, "How is he, buddy?"

"He said he has a pain in the chest." He looked around and said, "How's your hand? We don't know whether there's something wrong to his heart. We'd better find someone to give us a hand and take him out."

Since there was no safe spot to find, then unless ...

Much too noisy here, so is the communication line. I said something to the direction center and didn't get any answer. "I stay, you go out to find someone to help." I pointed to the direction of Tunnel Six. He nodded, patted me on the shoulder and got on his feet. Before his leaving, I added, "You work really hard, buddy. Where did you find that paper clip?"

Unless he has found a safe cover.

And then, I brandished my nightstick.

After the case, many people, including Bai, asked me, "How did you know he was Shi Zhan?

I have made up a variety of explanations. For example, if he wanted to make the paper clip more obvious, white clothes was not a good choice; or he was just looking miserable and fierce; or his earphone was for a cellphone, not police gear, so on and so forth.

However, what makes me identify him in that exact second was my pure instinct.

It's like when I was questioning suspects when working at the Interrogation Office, none of them can successfully lie to me. I could not tell whether they've got any weird facial expressions, actions or eye contacts, but I did know, they were lying.

The fact also proved my judgement, or luck. No exceptions.

On this point, Pan Xuejing, my newly wedded wife, and also my colleague from the Interrogation Office, said, "He is just as rash as this, counting on the connection with Director Bai and Professor Han, fists moving before head. I really don't know what to do if he really hits one of our own."

He Jingcheng, the medical examiner, and also one of my best men in the Criminal Investigation Division, said in a more blunt way. "He is just being impetuous, moving in when it seems to go wrong. How could he even have time to think in such chaos!"

Bing's comment was more like a joke. "Yes or no, the nightstick would tell anyway."

I knew I was not sure, so the first hit was not strong. Even so, that guy staggered for a few steps. He turned back with one hand pressing on his shoulder, eyeing me fiercely.

All right. Now we both got it.

Shi Zhan kicked back instead of running away. What? So cocky being a retired armed police? You will know who's the boss in a second. "Police!" I grabbed his left leg and thrashed the nightstick on his knee. He was really tough. Without a sound, he bounced high and his right leg hit right on my chest. I stepped back and loosened my grip. At the same time, he turned over, got up on his feet and ran into the crowd like a lame rabbit.

All criminals were alike, even the most ferocious ones. When they had no other options, they could fight the police but when there was a chance, running was always their first choice.

I couldn't beat him to death. The hostage's location was counting on him. I avoided his head and hit at his arm. Wanted to run? How could you run with broken legs!

It seemed that he had an eye on the back. He squatted a little bit and leaned ahead, lifting his leg and hitting my right shoulder. My nightstick got off, but I have taken his left leg. The push and pull cost his balance. I lowered my position and gave him a suplex, throwing him back like throwing a cement bag. Before he was down on the ground, he locked my neck with the other leg. I didn't get off and was dragged onto the ground.

Stall him! The backup I called should be here soon!

Falling down at the same time, whoever got up first won the game. But I didn't even think about that. What I should do was to stop him from getting up. This guy moved fast, pummeling his fist all over me. I covered my head with my arms, one of my legs twined onto his waist and the other kept booting his broken knee. He got my idea soon enough to try to break off my leg. I spared a fist and gave him a hard swing. Even though it was not a good one, it still turned over his left ear. What an idiot! My score of weighted squats would just scare him to shit!

"Captain Zhao!"

"Over there!"

The first backup has arrived.

Bleeding along his neck and half of his face, he looked rather hideous and howled like a trapped animal. Before I took my fist back, his elbow was pressed on my neck. A sudden assault on the neck bought him a few seconds and just at that moment, he kicked me out.

I got up on my feet with the support of my right hand, and the next second, Song from Team One fell into my arms, bleeding from his mouth and nose. I put him aside and saw Zhang Qi fell down in front of me, hands on his stomach. In a few seconds, there was only Cao Fa standing in front of Shi Zhan, shaking and bluffing. And suddenly, Cao Fa pulled out a gun ...

Damn it! Who authorized him that gun! Type 54 penetrated too well to be used in such a crowded place!

"Move!" I cried and rushed between them. Shi Zhan had clear scruples about me and turned around to run away. I chased after him only to find that he collected something, a man to be exact, on the ground and hurled to me.

It was the old man who had a pain in his chest.

I rushed a step to hold the old man in arms and was welcomed by Shi Zhan's sound kick, falling back right onto Cao Fa. I got up, and Shi Zhan was already nowhere to find.

I helped the old man to the roadside, turned around and snatched Cao Fa's gun, along with a fist that would beat his shit out. "Report from Zhao Xincheng! The suspect has escaped to the southeast. We got citizens hurt and our men as well. Where is the goddam backup!

"High ground Three report! The suspect has jumped into Xiaoyue

River."

"High ground Two report! Visual on the suspect!"

"River Team Two report! The suspect is diving into the river ..."

"This is the Bai. Xiaoyue River has run dry. I want eyes on all docks and sewage outlets. Let him swim!" Bai's confidence was well-founded. We've got Xiaoyue River under full surveillance. Escape through the water like in the films and TV series? No way.

"River Team Three report! The suspect took a breath and dived in again."

"River Team Four report! The suspect surfaced and dived in again. Such a long breath!"

...

No one expected that this was the last time Shi Zhan was ever present in our sight.

There were 425 officers involved in this operation. 1529 people were controlled on site, in which 291 were vendors. 7 citizens were hurt and 15 officers. After inspection, 3 were ex-buglers, 1 was an ex-robber and 9 were once involved in fighting. 2 were once behind bars because of whoring, 1 was once on the run and now captured because of theft, 1 was accused of unjustified enrichment and several were found illegal operation. But none of them was involved in the kidnapping.

With the help of Xicheng Branch, the above inspection was done before noon. At the same time, technical team found the reason of Shi Zhen's disappearance on site – a secret sewage outlet lower than the waterline, outside all blueprints and emergency plans. Divers from the City Bureau found traces of Shi Zhan along this sewage pipe and also discovered the hotel that violated the regulations of urban planning and environment.

Before going to report to the City Bureau, Bai left a parting shot, "What the fuck! Go burn that hotel!"

I held in detention before the boss came back for very simple reasons: Shi Zhan ran away right under my nose was the primary one, and there were also others like absent without leave, disobey of order, fighting with colleagues, etc.

In the afternoon, Direction Bai came back. All leaders from every division, department and squad were asked to attend the meeting. As the leader of the Eastern Area, I was also summoned to the conference room and saw Cao Fa, wrapped like a mummy on his head, was sitting at the able.

"Four hundred versus one and let him go. What the fuck!" roared Bai, holding a cigarette one hand and a lighter just the shape of a gun the other. He pointed the "gun" right to Cao Fa. "What are you doing here with a mummy head? Go back and have some rest! Do you have anything special to report?"

Deliberately, he didn't look at my direction, whining like an beaten dog. "No ... I ... We ... What I want to say is that we have to find more witnesses and search his escape route ..."

"What's wrong with your head?" Bai cut in, knowingly asking the question.

"Err ... Err ... That was Zhao ..." murmured Cao Far, with no idea why Bai was asking something he already knew.

Pointing me again with his "gun", Bai asked, "Why did you do that? For what reason?"

"Because he took a gun into the scene and pulled it out in the crowd," I shrugged. " Rumors may also scolded me for private revenge or something."

Bai's cellphone rang suddenly. He picked it up and said hello, his face showing that it was surely a telemarketer. "Thousands of RMB a month, what do I have to buy your sea-view house?"

He hang up impatiently and stared at Cao Fa. "A gun? Who authorized you that gun? Did you register in the depot?"

Cao Fa, too afraid to look back but having no idea where to put his eyes on, had to look down on the ground and answered, "Yes."

"So it's one of our commander's authorization then. Now that he has registered, I wouldn't bother to ask. Whoever authorized that gun, hand in your review and reassignment application to me after the case is closed." Bai lighted his cigarette by pulling the "trigger". "And for you, Cao Fa ..."

He reassigned a commander with the excuse of a gun. All of us were holding our breath, including me. We all scared he would pull out a M134 to light up his next cigarette just like Arnold Schwarzenegger.

"With hundreds of our men and you took a gun? So scared of death? If so, why do you choose to be a cop! Why not shoot him down with your gun! Catch him to save you from this trouble!" Bai clicked the surface of the table with his "gun". "Cao Fa, you are an experienced hand. The time you spent here is even longer than me. Asking you to take off the uniform and go seems to be too much. It is not that I cannot let you be here, but a leader like this is absolutely not qualified ... So, I'd say, you'd better save your position for someone more qualified. Where there is short of hands, there will be the place you'll be. Which one of you want one more hand?" The last question was for all of us.

No one answered. It was not only because the one fired by the current leader is a trouble for anyone else, but also because of his way of doing things. A tippler and lecher, a coward and a troublemaker. The vice captain, his only friend, now could not even save himself, let alone gave him a hand. Others? They were happy to see it.

"Boss." I raised my hand and said, "I've got an internal officer on maternity leave and a field detective retired due to illness. I'll have him."

"You?" Bai glanced me like an eagle. "Is this some compensation after fight? OK, I have no problem. Just have to see whether the victim himself got anything to say."

I glanced at Cao Fa and didn't say a word. He was smart enough to know that there was even not a chance for him to go down to the station. If he didn't take my offer, he would have to go forever. Although the bondage covered his eyes, I can still felt his hesitation and embarrassment. After a while, he nodded slowly.

"That's settled then. Let's make it clear. Zhao Xincheng, you are way too rash this time. Are you the only fighter in the division? Then how would you let Shi Zhan go? Go write a review and apologize to Cao Fa in the next team meeting. Pay his medical fee. Cao Fa, here's nothing for you. Go home and have a rest. Collect your things and report to Zhao."

After Cao Fa was gone, Bai pulled another cigarette, pointed his "gun" and said to the rest of us, "Shi Zhan has run and the hostage is now in extreme danger. The City Bureau has an emergency plan. Let's go with that."

3

Beijing covered a large area with millions of people. If Shi Zhan just disappeared into the crowd, there was no way to find him. The criminal profile[1] made by Dr. Yuan Shi was sent from the City Bureau: the suspect cooperated with others to commit this crime; they owned a vehicle (an off-road vehicle of dark colors) and lived in fixed (maybe temporary) location (along Zhichun Road to Xueyuan Road); they could be armed and with a certain counter-reconnaissance ability; they were well-connected, maybe got informants inside the police; they lived a regular life, had a slight of

---

1 Criminal Profile, also known as Criminal Profiling or the Profiling of Criminal Mind, is a behavioral and investigative tool that helps investigators to profile unknown criminal subjects or offenders. It is described as a method of suspect identification which seeks to identify a person's mental, physical, personality characteristics, and also family backgrounds based on things done or left at the crime scene to help narrow down scopes and solve cases.

Obsessive-Compulsive Disorder (OCD) and liked to wear dark clothes ...

Speaking of Dr. Yuan, he was a rising star in the criminal inspection field. It was said that he had obtained a Doctoral Degree of Criminal Psychology in Clayton University[1] and was sent to Quantico, the FBI Academy, to study behavioral science. Participated in the capture of several serial killer, he was praised as the Chinese Legend in Criminal Psychology field in America. Early this year, he left the US to came back to Beijing despite the money and position they gave him and joined the City Bureau to help establish and improve the technical support system in criminal investigation. He was currently the Criminal Psychology Consultant of the Technical Team in the City Bureau, member of the expert team in the city's Evidence Identification Committee, director of the Academy of Forensic Science, and a member of the Council of Physical Evidence in Criminal Justice of the Supreme People's Court.

And in terms of criminal profiling, Haidian Branch definitely took the lead in involving such a new technical approach in criminal investigation. The former consultant was Bin's father, Han Songge, Criminal Psychology Professor in Renmin University of China. Professor Han was such a knowledgeable person with so many works. He was modest and down to the earth, earning public praise in the bureau. Later on, he was invited to Huairou District People's Procuratorate to be Deputy Chief Prosecutor and left the work of criminal profiling to the support of Technical Team in the City Bureau.

Of course, in the division, it was known to all, including Director Bai, Professor Han's comrade in arms, that the technical support from Professor Bai counted more or less on his son, Bin and Bin's workshop – Fingerprint. Bin is a criminal profiling lover, which made Professor Han quite pleased. The composition of the workshop was complicated, with personnel from the police, the procuratorate, the court and the judiciary, and also lawyers, prison guards and civilians. Xuejing, He Jingcheng and I were all key members. Although after Professor Han's leaving, the workshop became a complete non-governmental institution, it still developed well, with website, columns, theme cafe and all. However, at the moment that the workshop is thriving, Bin, showing no hint at all, took back a "little" girlfriend and, without rhyme or reason, quit his position as the leader, leaving the entire workshop to He Jingcheng and me.

---

1   There is no such university in the world. It first originated from a famous Chinese novel *Fortress Besieged* by Qian Zhongshu (Ch'ien Chung-shu) and is used to refer to some illegitimate foreign degree qualifications or academic institutions.

Professor Han has left and so has Bin. But Dr. Yuan soon came and gained a firm foothold by solving several tough cases in a short time. Anyone who got to know his legendary techniques would say in compliment, "Really professional! Just like a miracle!"

I have experienced Dr. Yuan's profiling once in my life. In that case, Dr. Yuan fixed the suspect into a small scale: male from a certain region, 20-30 years old, short and thin, a migrant labor from other provinces. The suspect was unmarried, living alone and had no criminal record. He may be wearing dark blue jeans and oxford shoes without shoelaces. According to the profile, we have researched the region for an entire week, and finally got him in a demolition site through an informant. The suspect, Liu, was not only in accordance with the profile, but more amazingly, was wearing dark blue jeans and brown oxford shoes!

Bin laughed out loud after he learned this, "Brilliant! This one is almost as good as James Brussel[1]. He's really got something."

The contingency plan started in the afternoon was basically based on Dr. Yuan's profile. Twelve units started to explore the field along Zhichun Raod to Xueyuan Road successively. With the help of the Public Security and Traffic Administration Bureau, the Social Order Division checked every single off-road vehicle in the main road and big parking lots in Haidian District. Since the vice-Commander of Eastern Area asked for sick leave after the meeting, Bai ordered me to take the Eastern Team to search all 109 hospitals in Haidian District. But until 9 o'clock in the evening, nothing was dug out.

At 9 o'clock, I called Bai in the van. "Boss, we cannot just fool around like this."

The other side of the phone was noisy. "What's up?"

"In addition to the illegal clinics, there were 109 hospitals in our district, in which 9 belongs to the military, 10 are primary A hospitals and 90 are secondary and community ones. My men aren't even enough to cover these places. And hospitals are more for Cai Ying, the pregnant mother. If Shi Zhan doesn't care about her, he doesn't have to go to the hospital. A pharmacy is well enough for him to deal with his wound. Do you know how many pharmacies do we have?"

"All right! Stop the bullshit!" Bai's voice suddenly became clear. "What

---

1 In 1975, James Brussel, a psychiatrist in Greenwich, has profiled the suspect to the details such as "wearing a double breasted blazer". And the suspect, George Mestesky, changed into a double breasted blazer after taking off his pajamas. The case was then regarded as the best example of the support of profiling to criminal investigation.

do you want to say?"

"We are searching from the wrong side. The suspect has a military background. He knows, more or less, the operation mode of the inspection procedures and he will not show up under the current circumstances. We'd better start from his escape route, the place he went ashore ..." As I was speaking, I suddenly realized there was complete silence on the other side of the phone. At first I though the line was off, until I heard a sigh from Bai.

"How long would the hostage usually live after kidnapping if the kidnapper was not intended to keep her alive?"

I understood what he meant. "Theoretically, two to four days, which means tonight at most..."

"If the mother is gone, so is the infant."

Bai could punish Cao Fa for his mistake, and was also to be punished when he made one.

"The current plan is the direction from the City Bureau. Technically, it is all good."

Only time didn't wait. It seemed that Bai wouldn't want to put all his hope on the contingency plan of the City Bureau.

"Zhao, you worked with me from local stations and all the way through criminal inspection, interrogation and social orders. You have experienced all different divisions. Do you know why I transferred you here after I came to criminal inspection?"

Yes, I do. Because I'm the one you can trust the most.

"Boss, what's the order? I'll follow your lead."

Orders from the City Bureau could not be violated. If we wanted to do it in our own way, Bai needed to have some conclusive evidence.

"Let Zhang Qi take the lead. You go and find where Shi Zhan is. Don't play hero, report to me anytime. Once you've got proof, I can send backup." Just in an instant, Bai was the old tough Bai again. He said, "I don't care who you turn to, what strings you pull and what troubles you make. Just get me the suspect!"

"Right on it!"

On the southeast of Jimen Bridge at the gate of Wuliang Hotel, He Jingcheng was waiting for me.

The moment he caught sight of me, he asked, "You didn't call Bin?"

I waved my phone at him. "I did, but his phone is powered off." Bin took his girlfriend to travel in the south and didn't send even a word back.

I connected my earphone and asked, "Hello, Jiang! You got me?"

"Very clear! Captain Zhao, did you arrive at Wuliang Hotel?" We've all stayed up late for several nights but Jiang Lan's voice was as energetic as usual. How nice to be young!

"Yes, I did. You were at the center, right? Connect a line to He Jingcheng's phone." I gave He a sign to let him put on the earphone.

"Oh, my! It gets out of line to set up a line if you aren't in action. You'd better cover my ass if the boss asks."

"It is not if the action is directly authorized by Director Bai." I had no time to comfort her and directly asked, "Did you get that evidence South Team found in the hotel?"

Seeing me not in the right mood, Jiang answered at once. "Just arrived. The hotel is now closed. If you want to get in, I'll tell the local police to cooperate ..."

"Not now. Tell me the results from the Technical Team and what the South Team have found."

"Technical Team has traced the footprints and discovered the suspect entered from the back door. The surveillance camera got him entering the staff fitting room and coming out in two minutes, changing into staff uniform. – Mr. He, you've got too much electrostatic noise on your line. Hang up and I'll reopen it for you. – Since he's been wounded on the head and lame on the right leg, he was remembered by several staffs and security guards when he left from the front door. – He, is it OK now? Can you hear me clear? – On 7:26 in the morning, the surveillance camera on the front door got him leaving. After going around the neighbors, the old lady from the newstand opposite the hotel said that she saw a young man in the hotel uniform faltered away from the door and went north to Jimenqiao North, which is the region Dr. Yuan had circled.

He shook his head and said, "We've got the outside controlled and the roadblocks set. He cannot just walk away."

"Will it be the bus?" Jiang cut in. "The crowds on the bus can provide effective cover."

"He has so limited ways of going out. Walk? Then he'll be dead. Ride a bike? He won't be able to with a wounded leg that can barely walk. As for the bus, the crowd can help him hide but the chance to be spotted has also increased. And bus is too slow to get away from the controlled region." I shrugged and said to He, "We have the region from Xueyuan Bridge on the 4th Ring Road to Xizhimen Bridge on the 2nd Ring Road all under control. Such a large area, how can he get away in such a short time? Taxi? Or driving by himself? It's half past seven in the morning. The road is so jammed ..."

"How about subway?" He pointed to the south, the way to Xizhimen Subway Station. "The subway is basically on time, which means free from the traffic jam. There are thousands of people on the subway and he can just disappear into the crowds. There are so many stations on a subway line and it can take him almost everywhere. And the closest subway station is on the south border of our radius..."

"Brilliant!" I didn't save my complement and asked loud, "Jiang ..."

"Already inform the Public Security and Traffic Administration Bureau and Beijing Subway to get me the surveillance tape of Dazhongsi Station, Xizhimen Station and Jishuitan Station. The latter two are jurisdictions of Xicheng Police. I cannot coordinate across districts..."

"Good! We are on our way. Report to Director Bai and ask the help from Xicheng Branch and local police station. Tell him it's my request." I pulled out the door and said to He, "Working in medical examination center for so many years and still an associated medical examiner? Why not come to criminal inspection to work with me? With your expertise and hunch, you'd move up to vice-Commander by now."

The moment I stepped into Beijing Subway, Xuejing's voice popped out in my earphone. "Cheng, why didn't you tell me you don't come home?"

I was startled and asked, "Xuejing? You went to the division?"

"No, I was at the north yard[1]. The breakfast is done and I was waiting for you but you didn't return. I was a little boring and tidied up the apartment, watered the flowers and got the turtle fed. And now I'm prepared to go back to the office for some extra work."

"Err ... I did forget to give you a call. But you didn't call me either."

"It's you who said do not call you when you're working."

"Excuse me, Captain Zhao. Do you need an exclusive secure line to talk with Ms. Pan? ..." Jiang joked.

"Thank you but no. That won't be secure in the least way. Sorry, sweetheart. It's just crazy today and I forget about telling you all this. Someday ... no, just tomorrow or the day after tomorrow, as long as the case is settled, I'll go to the north yard to apologize. I promise I'll take you your favorite flowers and we'll go have a big dinner ..." Girls are just like that. In front of others, especially other girls, the more you care about her, the happier she will be.

"All right. I didn't blame you anyway." Xuejing seemed to be a little

---

1 The old Interrogation Office. After the inspection and interrogation merged into one, the Interrogation Office has been incorporated into the Criminal Inspection Division as a subordinate institution.

shy. "I know today's not going well. Someone told me you hit the suspect and also one of our own. What happened?"

"Nothing important. I'll talk to you later, OK?"

"OK. Only you and Mr. He? Did Han Bin come back? Yang asked me whether you would need some help."

Yang Yanpeng? What was this son of bitch doing here? Yang was Xuejing's classmate in junior high and was self-regarded as the lifelong admirer of Ms. Pan. He joined the workshop when Bin was the leader, but who he was after was known to everybody. I've argued with Bin about his stay and insisted that I would definite get him sacked after I took the lead. But Bin's reply was quiet and calm. "He was once working in the Ministry of State Security. Maybe one day, you could use his help."

But at present, he was just a little boss of a research agency around the corner. And he was buzzing around my wife all day long, just like an annoying fly!

He Jingcheng's advice was simple. "Bin must have him chosen for a reason. You'd better go with it."

He was right. Although I disliked Yang and was annoyed by his attitude to my wife, I could not just sack him without Bin's approval. It was a delicate issue concerning interpersonal relationship.

"I don't need him. You stay away from him!" Although I knew the our talk was on public line, I could still not hold my temper.

Xuejing seemed to titter a bit on the other side. "Look at you! So childish every time I spoke of him. What's the matter with you and him? Well, he told me that the City Bureau had given Director Bai so much pressure. If the hostage is killed, the he will definitely lose his job."

I had to admit that son of a bitch was really well-informed. But what Xuejing said was also what annoyed me most. "Don't listen to this bullshit! I got to go and check the surveillance. I'll talk to you around." I turned to He and said, "let's go."

He Jingcheng pulled off his earphone and teased, "One more sentence, I'll go apply for a separate secure line for you ..."

Since we had to go behind the City Bureau's back, Bai must have pulled some personal strings with the leaders in Xicheng Branch to get us the backup. Dozens of people stared at the screen until 3 o'clock in the morning and finally discovered that the suspect took the subway from Jishuitan Station. After checking the surveillance footage along the route, we found that he got off at Fuchengmen Station.

It was only several stops away between these two stations, but where he got off was already outside our radius.

"Go! Let's find him."

Jiang advised hesitantly. "We have wanted posters posted online around 9 o'clock yesterday, but until now nothing came back from Xicheng Police. Should I check the surveillance cameras around Fuchengmen Bridge again?"

Having the whole case reviewed along the way, He Jingcheng gave his own advice. "It's OK to check the surveillance again but not very helpful. What we did must have occurred to the suspect's mind. Suppose he knows out playbook, he will try his best to avoid the surveillance cameras. Taking a subway is a forced move. But now he is outside our radius, he will not let himself exposed easily."

"But Fuchengmen Station is just several stops away from the radius. Since he's already got on a subway, why not take a few more stops?" I disagreed. When I checked the surveillance footage, I found out other details. "Non-residential areas like Fuchengmen in downtown area cannot possibly be his nest. And he didn't know whether the police was out there after him. As long as the wanted posters are posted, all policemen in Beijing will try to dig him out wherever he stays. He couldn't possibly choose the sewage in Wuliang Hotel by chance. This is his planned route to escape. He is both well-planned and flexible. So he must have a focus getting off at Fuchengman Station."

"The security footage in the subway shows that he's still bleeding on one of his ears. Your punch really hurts." He Jingcheng also noticed what I said. "Hotel uniform and bleeding wound, he is easy to be recognized. He needs to clean his wound and change clothes and his appearance."

"So, it's time for us to take a chance." I parked the car to the northwest of Fuchengmen Bridge. "He needs water and clothes, which means restrooms and clothes shops. So ..." I pointed to the Hualian Shopping Center located right beneath us. "A shopping center would meet all his needs."

He Jingcheng looked around and said, "This really is the closest shopping mall outside the radius along the subway. But does it even open when Shi Zhan got off?"

"Did you see in the footage?" I was banging on the door while speaking. "The big billboard in the subway waiting hall says there is a celebration for BHG Group from 15th to 17th. All subsidiary shopping malls will have discounts and run 24 hours a day. This is the only choice after he got off."

Before I broke in, the security guard went out to open the door with his sleepy eyes. With no time to spend on the introduction and all, I directly showed him my ID and called loud, "Open the door! Get me your manager!"

Luck was on our side. Around 8 o'clock in the morning on 17th, Shi

Zhan came into our sight on the security footage of the mall. He first went to the restroom on the first floor and then staggered to shop in the sports shops. He had taken a complete new look with a pair of Pepsi shoes, a Nike pullover and an Apple jeans he bought. Before the payment, he ran out for about 5 minutes, probably to the ATM to get some money.

He Jingcheng became pretty tired if he didn't get some sleep around midnight and now, he was talking to Jiang with a tired voice. "Hello? Yeah, check all ATMs in the vicinity. Find out the card he used."

"There are 4 ATMs around the mall and 32 transactions between 8 o'clock to 9 o'clock. 24 of them was to withdraw cash, but none of the cards is registered to Shi Zhan's name. I got no one to ask for the security footage at this time of the day."

I turned around and snapped to the nervous manager. "Tell your cashier and financial manager to get up. We need their help."

After checking with the cashier, Shi Zhan has spent 1780RMB that morning in the mall. Paying in cash seemed to be safe, but the transaction will still be recorded.

"There were 11 cash withdrawals over 1500RMB. According to the suspect's walking speed and the time he came in and out of the shopping mall, the ATM in the west of the mall should be the one the suspect went to. So three of the ATMs, altogether 9 transactions can be excluded and that will leave us two. I've checked the two credit cards and found out they belong to Liu Wenxian and Zheng Bai respectively. The withdrawal are both 2000RMB."

"Well, Jiang. You know what to do."

"Yeah, I'm already on it. The two credit cards were never reported loss and I am researching for the background of their owners. ... Can the Ministry change a faster server? This one is as slow as a snail!"

I checked my watch and said, "Cross check the names with Shi Zhan's file."

"Yeah, I'm checking it right now. Liu Wenxian is ... Zheng Bai is an armed police! He is now serving in the same place where Shi Zhan used to serve!"

"Go check every transaction record on that card, especially the ones close to the case. Does this Zheng Bai has a place to live here in Beijing? I want all his background information. Get someone to visit his family and coordinate with the troop he serves to ask him for his relationship with the suspect."

"Captain Zhao, I cannot..."

"Get me Director Bai."

Bai's voice was still powerful, without the slightest of fatigue. "What's the matter?"

"Boss. I'm almost onto him. I need backup from the division and coordination from the City Bureau."

"Go ahead."

"On the day of the case, Shi Zhan used one of his comrade's credit card. This person is a serving armed police. If we want to question him, we have to coordinate through the City Bureau ..."

"No other options?"

"Unless the suspect is too careless to leave a trace on the credit record."

"Will that man be his partner?"

"Don't know yet. I need at least two teams' backup. I got a feeling that I was hitting him close."

"Go find Zhang Qi. You'll have all Eastern Team under control. I'll talk to the patrol team and let them send two cars to meet with you. If you really bump into him, you'll have to need guns."

He Jingcheng patted on my shoulder and said, "Results from the transactions records. From 10th till yesterday, there were five transactions. All happened in a Wumart supermarket and a Golden Elephant Pharmacy around Wuluju in the 4thWest Ring Road.

"Boss, we've got a range. Wuluju Bridge on the 4thWest Ring Road. Let the Eastern Team, the patrol team, and all backup meet me there. " After I hang up the phone, I looked at He and we ran to the gate.

Jiang asked me on the way, "Captain Zhao, I've heard that Mr. He and you are in charge of that profile workshop, aren't you? The boss sent you guys to deal with this. Does that mean he has doubts about the profile that Dr. Yuan gave?"

"I don't know what his meant, but profiling just doesn't suit this case."

"Why? Did you just ..."

"When do you see us profiling the suspect?"

Jiang was totally unexpected to my question. Seeing her embarrassment, He Jingcheng explained immediately, "Profiling is just a supportive approach with limited effects. Most of the profiles help in narrowing down the research range and finding out some features of the suspect. In this case, we've already know who the suspect is. There is no need to profile him. And Shi Zhan is well-equipped with counter-reconnaissance ability, profiling from cold statistical results doesn't help much."

"But the profile from Dr. Yuan depicts quite well. Is it helping in finding the suspect?"

"His profile is fine. It's just we don't have that much time." I stopped He from further explanation. We don't have time, energy, or obligation to enlighten everyone on criminal profiling. "Get me the backup team."

Move of every team would first be sent back to me. Bai was really tough, and bold. He not only violated the directions from the City Bureau to get me all the manpower, but also get some helping hands from Shijingshan Branch. Of course, I knew that he and the leader of Shijingshan Branch graduated together. Actually, coming from a well-connected family, Bai had quite a few personal strings to pull inside the police department. Leaders from the Ministry to every Branch Bureau, everyone can show him some kindness.

The boss asked me where to start the research after arrival. My advice was simple. Manpower is the basic move. In such a community with complicated residential components and poor management, what we need most was the help from our informants.

The so-call informants, or nark in some movies, were the ones who brought us information. There were criminal informants and social order informants. The criminal informants, or CI, were divided into two categories, "Red CI" and "Gray CI", referring to those law-abiding citizens and pilferers respectively. Such informants were difficult to cultivate, but more effective than undercover agents. They were the frequent sources for the police to crack a case. An outstanding detective, me for example, would have connections with scores, or hundreds of informants.

Soon, news came from the Criminal Investigation Division of Shijingshan Branch. Someone from a hair salon around Zhongcun village, southwest of Wuluju Bridge, reported that a man looked like our suspect rented a cottage with a yard in No.12, Row 4 several days ago, taking a pregnant woman with him.

"I'll be right there, boss!" I was on the east of Wuluju Bridge when I heard the news. "How much time do I have?"

"Zhongcun village has been locked down. We cannot wait for you. The boys are preparing to move in." Bai's voice seemed tight, meaning he was really nervous. "Come here anyway. You may be lucky enough to hear about the takedown on the way. Good job, this one!"

The positive comment from the boss finally relaxed me. But only for five minutes.

An upset voice from the takedown team came through the line. "Captain Zhao ..."

I was driving and the voice made my hands trembling in spite of myself. "What's wrong? Did the hostage get killed?"

"Well ... You'll have to come to see ..."

I stepped hard on the gas.

No. 12, Row 4 was a real small one, whose only room was less than $15m^2$. There were nothing much on the inside, only a table, a bed, a simple clothes closet and scattering litters.

Only that all of these were covered with a film of crimson.

Being a police for so many years, I have seen so many horrifying scenes. But I had to admit that this one was much too overwhelming.

I really didn't know how Bai could still keep his calm. He was right here, giving orders. "Don't touch anything. The technical team is on the way. I'll report to the City Bureau right now. Let me know once the technical team find something."

I stood at the door, in a daze. After a while, I asked He jingcheng, "How much ... blood do you think is there?

"At least one liter. Or more." He peeped in time to time instead of looking at me. "There is no more than 4 liters of blood in Cai Ying's body, or less considering her situation. Now, this may go worse."

Jiang was still on the line and gasped at our conversation. "A loss of 25% of blood will lead to death ..."

"Yeah. So now we've got a room of blood and a missing pregnant mother who has lost one forth of her blood. Who's got constructive ideas? I'm on all ears!"

He Jingcheng stopped me with one of his palm down, reminding me to calm down. "There is no body on the scene. Some of the blood hasn't congealed. The hostage ... It shouldn't be long before they leave."

"Got a two-kilometer control radius from the scene. Orders from the City Bureau asked Shijingshan Branch to work with us to explore the outside."

"Anyone saw him leaving?" I asked.

"The interview team hasn't got message back. We've got our men to check the surveillance camera around Wuluju Bridge. Director Bai just informed us to continue as per normal procedures and wait for new orders."

"Who is the informant from Shijingshan Branch?"

"Ah? Which one?"

"The one tells us the location of this place. No matter who he or she is, I want information."

"Wait for a second," He Jingcheng pulled off his earphone and asked, "What do you want to do?"

"I don't know." I closed the circuit and dialed out. "Now the hostage may be dead – at least one. Bai may lose his job. I have to do something ... anything. I have to find somewhere to wedge in."

The cold digital female voice told me that Bin's cellphone was still powered off.

I took a deep breath and reopened the circuit. "Did you get me the information?"

"Shijingshan Branch refused to provide the information. They only said that if you want to check, you can contact their Captain Liu. The phone number is ..."

"Fuck!"

Actually, the reply was normal enough. No policeman would give out his own informant. It's not about connection or friendship. Informants are valuable assets for all police. In such issue, every policeman is mean.

Upon leaving the apartment, I passed over the technical team. "He, you stay here with the technical guys. I'll go find someone to talk."

He Jingcheng took gloves and shoe covers from the technical team and answered, "OK. Don't be reckless. Call me if you need."

Some hair salon in Row 4? There were altogether two hair salons in Row 4.

The so-called salon on the east end had no name on the sign. I knocked and a middle-aged women opened the door. After checking my ID, she leaned on the back of a chair and asked, "What's the matter, young man?"

I pointed outside the flickering alarm lamp and asked, "Did you know what happened?"

"Fuck off!" Maybe because she didn't have time to wear any makeup, her face looked like a withered eggplant, dry and wrinkled. "What?! I've got my residential permit here."

"How many people in the salon in the west? It seems to be a little larger than yours."

"Four or five. Go find it yourself." She picked up a cigarette packet but found nothing in there, and threw it hard outside the door to show her disappointment. "That's a real brothel. That old crap had a bunch of girls sleeping with the guests as well as himself. Maybe one day he'll be sleeping with his own daughter ... "

"Excuse me." I took a white-yet-colorful towel from the heater and left her my half packet of cigarette. "Thank you."

Coming out of the salon, I talked around, making sure they were all our men.

"Close the west exit. Find someone to guard the salon in the west." I ordered.

I took a torch from the car and wrapped my right hand with the towel. Coming near the door of the salon, I knocked the glass door open with the end of the torch and opened it from the inside. After all these, I broke in and shout, "Police!"

The outside room, which looked like a real hair salon, was empty. Some strange yet alluring voice came from the inside. I went straight in, tripped a little by a chair, and bumped into a middle-aged man rushing outside. He was wearing as less clothes as his hair and got a belly as white as pure lard.

I didn't give him the chance to talk. Pinching an artery on his neck, I took him back inside with no sweat. There was a large bed in the room. As the torch light swept around, faces of three naked girls came into my sight, suspended and terrified.

I lowered the torch and said, "Put some clothes on."

And then, I took the man outside. Upon getting out of my hand, the old crap slumped on the floor out of great astonishment. I pulled him on his feet and asked, "Are you the informant?"

"No! No! My mistake, officer! My mistake ..."

I asked one of our guys to keep an eye on him and went back to the inside. The three girls have already dressed themselves and turned the light on. I took out my ID, comforted them a little and said to one of them in red, "Get a coat. Come outside to stay with your boss."

And then, I said to the girl in green, "You, go outside."

The old crap was freezing at the door. I came out and yelled at him, "Stay put!" and then turned to the girl in red. "We need to ask you about something. You will be questioned by a female police and if you are under age, we'll need your guardian to be here."

I spent five minutes to educate the girl in green about the same things.

At last I came inside. With the door closed, I said tenderly with a low voice, "My name is Zhao Xincheng. I'm with the Criminal Investigation Division in Haidian Branch. Thank you for your help. Your source didn't give you out, I found you by myself. It is about two lives, a mother and her child. I only came to you with no other choices. I hope you can help me."

That girl was sixteen, seventeen at the most, just like Bin's girlfriend, pale and slim. In my eyes, she got a certain characteristic of an informant that she was too young to hide.

She just sat there, her face as dull as dead. After a while, she uttered several words in a reluctant voice. "Thank you, officer."

"I need you to answer several questions. I hope you can tell me the truth. It is not only to help us, but also to save two lives ..."

During the questions, the girl suddenly lifted her head, her eyes confused.

It was my phone ringing. There were a set of zero on my phone screen – that is the communication channel.

I waved at her and picked up the phone, "Hello?"

It was Jiang on the phone. "Captain Zhao, Shi Zhan is calling the hostage's family. Do you want me to ..."

I rushed through the door at the car and shouted, "Get me in!"

When I cut in the line, the best part was on.

"Ten million!"

"Yes. Ransom doubled. That's the cost of you calling the police."

" 可……这么短的时间…… "

" 好好想想你的孙子。 "

"Think about your grandson."

"Grandson? Did she deliver the baby? How is the baby?"

"Ten million RMB, all in cash. Cut it in five shares. Four million sent to two different places in cases, I'll give you the address; and the rest six million in three woven bags – just like last time. Five hours later, which is ten o'clock in the morning, your son will take two million to the west gate of the Temple of Earth; you take two million to the lobby of the New Beijing Poly Plaza; and the last two million will be taken by your nursemaid. The location is the parking lot in Beijing West Railway Station."

"Wait! I need time to pool the money ..."

"Don't you dare to cut in again! Remember, first, four million must be sent out before ten o'clock; and second, to the police who are listening, if I see any of you in any one of the three locations, the deal is canceled. I'm able to tell you from the crowd yesterday morning, so am I today. But you can still try to see whether the stoke of luck is on your side. The moment I got my money, you'll have the woman and the baby, but whether they will live to that moment depends on your luck."

"Wait, wait for a second. I, I didn't mean to interrupt you, but that's a lot of money. It's quite difficult in such a short time to ..."

"You can borrow the emergency fund from the government. Take it easy. The police couldn't be able to bear the responsibility if the baby is dead."

"But..."

I saw He Jingcheng frowning on the front passenger seat.

"Director Bai, this is Zhao Xincheng. I request to talk with Shi Zhan. Let Jiang put me on the line."

He Jingcheng turned at me out of astonishment, silently saying, "Are you crazy?"

Bai couldn't believe what he heard either. "What did you say?"

"Locating the signal still needs less than one minute. Shi Zhan must have known that. Believe me, boss. He'll hand up any minute. Put me on the line!"

Bai didn't ask further. He said to Jiang, "Put him on the line."

There was a short "bee – " coming through the earphone. I took a deep breath and asked in a low voice, "Sorry buddy. How's your knee?"

Mr. Dong Sr. uttered a short "Ah" and became silent in an instant, probably pulled off by one of our men.

After two seconds, Shi Zhan answered, "You?"

"Yeah, it's me. I won't talk bullshits. You are running out of time because of all the sensation you've made. Now, it's not Mr. Dong who leads the call. It's me. If you want to talk, come and talk to me. My phone number is 1391175××××. You can hang up and call me by another phone. I will wait for ten minutes and after that, there's only radio hotlines you could turn to."

The phone was hang up.

Bai couldn't help but titter out of tension. "Are you fucking trying to kill the hostage or kill me?"

I tried to make myself calm. "Believe me, boss. He'll call. Jiang, get my phone on monitor."

Bin once said, as long as the suspect was not insane, he would put committing the crime his first priority. Shi Zhan's goal was to get the ransom. So as long as we had the ransom in hand, we had the call.

He JingcHeng murmured alongside. "He sounds a little bit different this time."

Bai puzzled. "In what way?"

I agreed with He. "He's been talkative. Yesterday's hunt and research in Wuluju both show that he's doing this alone. So why did he pull out five ways to deliver the ransom? He wants to separate us. He wants to redirect us. But in today's call, he said nothing about killing the hostage or words alike. It is abnormal. After all, the hostage is his only card to play."

"So where did this abnormality come from?"

"Maybe it didn't occurred to him that we've got him under radius so fast, or maybe the hostage is dead. If she's not delivered the baby before death, he'll have nothing to issue with us."

Or maybe, we've lost both the mother and the kid. There's no one for the suspect to kill.

"There's no body on the scene. Can we confirm Cai Ying's death?"

He Jingcheng coughed a little and answered. "I've just checked the scene with the technical team. There were many fingerprints and large amount of blood from Cai Ying. According to our initial estimate, the loss of blood in Cai Ying's body was up to two liters, which means half of the blood in human body... The blood is not splashing around. Taking this into account, and also the amniotic fluid, the medicine and tools for cleaning, sterilizing and staunching, we think it is possible that Cai Ying was not killed but died of obstructed labour. As for the new born baby, based on the current information, we cannot confirm his living, or death."

I suddenly remembered one thing and asked, "Boss, how about the City Bureau ..."

Bai didn't answer, just making a cold voice through his nose.

Then The phone rang.

"Hello?"

"Go and collect the bodies!"

For one second, my heart almost jumped out.

And then, I, controlling my trembling, said in a cold voice. "OK. Where's the place? Take your time and run."

After several long seconds, Shi Zhan laughed. "You pretend well. Scared to shit, hah?"

Sweating in my balled fists, I answered, "Shi Zhan, if you want to talk, prove me the kid is still alive. Or I'll go."

"You are monitoring this line, right?"

There's no need to lie on this one. "Yes. What?"

Several baby cries came out through the line.

He Jingcheng whispered, "Jiang ..."

Shi Zhan was back on the line and said, "Now, what's your point?"

"The time limitation you give is certainly not enough. Mr. Dong cannot pool that much money in such a short time and the government would way beyond bankrupt if ransom loan were to be permitted. Since the alive is more expensive than the dead, I'll cut you a deal. Let's say, six million. Six million, for the alive.

On the other side of the phone, Shi Zhan was clearly shocked. It took him several seconds to answer back. "Are you really a fucking cop?"

"The handover locations are too many, you cannot cover them yourself. We can easily monitor all postal lines, be it mail or cargo, which means ten million is not possible in the first point. It's no use to play such a trick. You

33

don't have to handover Cai Ying, that will do you good. If we cannot find the body, it's quite difficult to prove her death. So even if we've got you in, as long as you are tough, we may not be able to pin her death on your head."

Shi Zhan started to talk fast. "What's your angle?"

He Jingcheng patted me on the shoulder and gave me a thumb up – the child is still alive.

"My angle is that we can save the postal service. Six million, I'll see to the delivery by your time, location and people. There will be none of our guys within 200m radius in each of the three locations; but outside the radius, we won't spare any effort to take you down. I know it's wasting my time to say this, but I still want to warn you that you have to figure it out – you won't make it this time.

"First rule! No police!"

"Turn to the radio hotline, you idiot!"

"You don't want to stall me, do you?"

"It still takes two minutes to locate you! Don't pretend to know everything! I'm telling you this is the best offer I can give you. If you don't take it, then go ahead kill the hostage! One death or two, I've got my eyes on you anyway. We've met and know each other, Shi Zhan. Your life is a hard one, and I show you my respect. But you want to take the money? You have to do it my way."

He seemed to murmur something to himself and then asked, "What's your name?"

"Zhao Xincheng. Remember this one. It's good for you to know the one who get you behind bars."

"You have a call on this one?"

"How can I speak directly to you without authorization?"

"Zhao Xincheng! Keep your word. With in 200m radius, ..."

"You can kill the hostage if you see any police with the radius. 200 meters! You have my word. But keep in mind, only 200 meters."

"OK. I believe you. That's a deal then!"

The conversation brought up an inevitable discussion from different parts. At last, it was Bai who cleared the line. "Shut up if you cannot give constructive ideas!"

Jiang said with a timid voice. "I think Captain Zhao is right. The suspect does avoid the issue of killing the hostage. But we've tests on the audio. It says the cry of the baby was ..."

"He's got the kid. He will be at the Temple of Earth." With no time to spend on details, I asked Bai, "Boss, I've made the deal. What do we do next?"

"Three locations. How would you know he'll be at the Temple of Earth?"

"The New Beijing Poly Plaza is a building. He cannot go out after taking the money. Even if he's got 200m safe radius, it's still hard of him to escape if we have the outside fully controlled. As for Beijing West Railway Station, the crowd seems to make it difficult for us to monitor the site; however, with so many surveillance cameras, it is also easy to trace and control. If we got the station all under surveillance, the parking lot will turn to be his nightmare. Only in the Temple of Earth can he escape on different routes. There's not enough surveillance cameras on that location and there's so many people. If we presume the suspect is working alone, this is the best choice he's got."

"Ten million was bargained to six million, and now he's got only one third to take. That's not a good deal." Bai teased me.

"He wanted three million yesterday for two living people. Now he's only got one, a 30% discount would serve him well. Of course this is just my personal opinion. I totally agree that we should get the three locations all under control just in case."

"Liu Qiang take the Northern Team and Zhao take the Eastern Team. You two are in charge of the west gate of the Temple of Earth. Sun Tao, you take the Western Team to Beijing West Railway Station, and the Southern Team is with we to New Beijing Poly Plaza. Leader of every team, take charge of all arrangements on site. I want plans in writing before seven o'clock, and get together and ready to go before half past seven. At eight, everyone goes in to know the area. I will ask the City Bureau to send backup from each branch and division. If you're short of hand, go find some from the Social Order, Patrol Force and Interrogation Office. Go to the local stations to ask for people if needed. I don't care. My requirement is simple: within the 200m radius, none of you can show up; outside the radius, not a single inch can be out of control! The communication line to the direction center is clear at all times. Communicate any minute."

"Boss, no one on this site?"

"Let the technical team send someone. Well, He Jingcheng is here, right? The medical examination office should step out of this roundup."

"Director Bai, I'm short of hands ..."

"Stop the bullshit! We won't be ants on a hot pan like this if it weren't your deal! 200m meters? Why don't you think with your toes first before cutting the deal. How many people do we have in the whole division!"

"Right, right. That's it boss. I've got an informant to ask. Plans will be ready before seven ..."

"Zhao Xincheng!"

"Yes!"

"If the mother is gone, take me back the kid."

"Right, sure. I will."

Fifteen minutes to ten.

Standing with two of my man and He Jingcheng, I stood at the overpass, overlooking every tree and flower outside the west gate of Temple of Earth.

"This is Van Two. Dong Ji's car is approaching Andingmen Bridge South. Will be there in five minutes."

"Got it." I pinched on the bridge of my nose to refresh up a little bit. "Listen everyone! Stay alert!"

He Jingcheng wasn't used to late nights. A whole night of stay up made him an outdated film star who didn't wear any makeup.

Seeing him staring down the bridge, I prodded him in the ribs and said, "Hey, what's wrong? Come on, the boss won't blame it on you."

"I think Cai Ying must be dead. Bai has to bear the responsibility sooner or later. It's not for him to blame me."

"Come on pal! It's almost about time!"

"Yeah. You are saying like the suspect will definitely show up."

"I have explained my reasons. And that Dr. Yuan from the City Bureau has already agreed after his analysis. You can disagree with me, but you can't disagree with the expert, right?"

"Yeah, I agree. But the whole world can think about this, except for the suspect?" He glanced at me and said, "All of you think this is best location to escape out of the three. But you see, hundreds of policemen down below. Even if he can have the money from Dong Ji, where could he run to?"

"If he went to Poly Plaza or the West Station, he'll get worse."

"He has completely lost the call when talking to you."

"Oh my! My dear fellow! I was really guessing at that time. Only until later did I confirm that he won't kill the hostage."

He looked at me, suspiciously. "What's your secrets?"

"The informant from Wuluju offered some useful information. Of course, it's just my bold guess ..."

"Report from Van Two. Dong Ji has arrived. He is approaching the scheduled location."

"I'll talk to you later. Don't get down." I told one of my guys to stay to keep him safe and said through my microphone, "This is Zhao Xincheng. Everyone from the Eastern Team, keep your distance! I repeat, keep your distance! How about your side, Commander Liu?"

"All good."

I walked along the overpass all the way to the east and checked every spot of our men. "Where's Dong Ji now?" I asked the observation post.

"Dong Ji's car has just pulled over 200m east of the fixed spot. He has just got off the car."

"Van Two, move out. Acting Squad, follow him up."

"Acting Squad is in position. Nothing special around him. Commander Liu, he is about to approach the radius."

Dong Ji crossed below the overpass.

"Report from the observation post. Dong Ji has entered the radius. 100m from the scheduled location."

I stared at my watch.

"This is Liu Qiang. Acting Squad, you may leave. Others, move along with Dong Ji. Keep you distance at 200m."

"Dong Ji has arrived at the scheduled location. Acting Squad, tell him to stop."

Two minutes to ten. Perfect timing.

"Everybody stay alert! Report every three minutes."

I looked over to the other side of the overpass where He Jingcheng is. No, there's no point of attacking or seizing him, I thought.

"Team Two report. Nothing especial."

"Team One report. All good."

"Backup is in position. Nothing special."

One minute past ten.

"Team three report. Nothing special."

"Team Nine report. All exits of the Temple of Earth has been temporarily closed."

"Team Four report. All good."

It didn't occur to me that Shi Zhan would show up on the scene on time like an Omega, but I did wonder how could he manage to find a way out.

"Direction Center, this is Region One. No visual on the target. How about the other two?"

"Roger that. The same with Region Two. No reports from Region Three."

Three minutes past ten.

"Zhao Xincheng requests to talk with all regions. Direction Center?"

"Can't do that. Region Three just reported that due to an entering train, the nursemaid was hustled down by the crowd. She may have sprained her ankle and the suspect didn't show up. Nothing special happened."

"Team Seven report. All good."

He Jingcheng was walking to me, seemingly wanting to say something.

I looked at the guards to stop him. He was not working the fields. I couldn't take the risk to let him inside.

"Team One report. Nothing special."

"This is the observation post. Dong Ji is moving!"

"This is Liu Qiang. All people, move along with Dong Ji. Acting Squad! Find out what he's doing!"

Seven minutes past ten.

"He bought a pocket of cigarette at the newstand. Already tell him to go back to the spot. What the fuck..."

"Observation post report. Dong Ji has gone back to the scheduled location.

"Xincheng," He Jingcheng's voice came through the communication line. I turned around and saw him talking to me through a communicator from one of the patrol police, the overpass between us just like the Milky Way with the two of us being the Cowherd and the Weaver Girl[1]. He was saying, "We are ..."

The communication line was a little bit crowded. Liu Qiang was giving orders. "The target may be stalling to find the opportunity to move in. Keep alert everyone! Don't lose your position! We have to be prepared for a tough battle on this one!"

"A suspected target is discovered! Due south, male, crew cut. He is wearing a black jacket, green cargo pants and black sport shoes, with his hands in his pockets ..."

I stopped and searched for a while, and flinched at the sight of the target. That was not Shi Zhan.

"Team Four report. The target is really close to me. He is staring at Dong Ji."

No response from the communicator. Apparently Liu Qiang was as hesitant as me.

He Jingcheng's voice came again. "Xincheng, did you hear me?"

"What?"

The suspect is looking at Dong Ji. Is he Shi Zhan's partner? I thought to myself.

"The target is not Shi Zhan. He is already in the radius and heading to Dong Ji. Shall we take him down?"

"I've just said that we've still go with plainclothes on this one..." He Jingcheng was talking to me through the communicator.

---

1   The Cowherd and the Weaver Girl is a Chinese folk tale, which tells the love story between the weaver girl, symbolizing the star Vega, and the cowherd, symbolizing the star Altair. Their love was not allowed, thus they were banished to opposite sides of the heavenly river, symbolizing the Milky Way. Once a year, on the 7th day of the 7th lunar month, a flock of magpies would form a bridge to reunite the lovers for one day.

"The target is approaching Dong Ji. Shall we take him down or not?"

"This is Liu Qiang. Don't move. Let's see if he's coming to collect the money."

All of a sudden, I wanted to know what He Jingcheng was about to say. But in a moment, I figured out most of his words.

"The target is definitely heading to Dong Ji. He has just ... He is beating Dong Ji and Dong Ji is down! Oh, fuck! He's got a knife in his hand! Dong Ji is down!"

What they described through the communicator was happening right under my nose. All right, now the rest of He Jingcheng's words were clear enough.

Liu Qiang acted promptly. "Move in everyone! Get him down!"

Scores of plainclothesmen dashed into the scene. Such a chaos in the line.

"The target is taken down!"

"Separate the crowd. Get the car here!"

"Dong Ji is bleeding on his leg! Call an ambulance!"

"Where is the bag with the money?"

"Captain Zhao! What's next?!"

...

This was his way out.

I strode down the overpass and called, "All attention! The target has shown up! Dark green clothes with the woven bag in hand. Moving west along the road. He may have the identification sign with him, but he's not with us! Acting Squad! Go intercept that man with the bag!"

He just found any thug to stab Dong Ji and pretended as one of our guys to take the money. It turned out our mufti-functional medical examiner has noticed that he planned to play the old trick.

That was his way out.

"Got visual on the target! Get him down!"

"Police! Stop there!"

...

In an instant, Shi Zhan found out his cover was blown and ran quickly to the road, limping.

This time, it really became a sandplay. "Team Eight, Team Ten, close the road from both way. Backup team, take him down in the front."

Two of the backup team intercepted him. Shi Zhan dumped the bag into one of them and wanted to kick out on the other. Before he could make his move, another of our man controlled his leg and tripped him over. In an instant, the following Acting Squad rushed in one after another and pressed him tightly down on the ground. At the moment I strolled over, more than twenty people were around him and several of them was cuffing him.

"Direction Center, report from Region One. The suspect has been taken down. I repeat, the suspect has been taken down. Doing Ji was hurt and sent to the hospital nearby. No other casualties. No loss of the ransom. No visual on the hostage." After reporting to the center, I took off my earphone and asked my men to pull Shi Zhan on his feet.

Maybe scratched on the ground, his forehead was wounded, a streak of blood running down his cheek. He looked at me, with a cold smile, and squeezed between his teeth my name.

"ZHAO! XIN! CHENG!"

"Right! Perfect! You've got my name right. That's good. I've told you to remember it ..." I wiped the blood on his face with my sleeves. "Where's the hostage? The mother and the kid, I want both of them. Alive or dead."

He just stared me, speechless, his smile getting more and more weird.

"You're working this all by yourself. You can't take the kid with you, can you? Where did you leave him? A newborn baby couldn't be left unattended at all." Stepping front, I was almost whispering by his ear. "Even a vicious tiger won't eat its cubs, Shi Zhan. You are that tiger, aren't you?"

4

Shi Zhan winced a little when he heard this and then relaxed gradually.

That girl was scrupulous. She told me when Shi Zhan went to borrow a washbasin, he was nervous yet with a little excitement. Ex-boyfriend went to borrow some money? Come on! I have long been suspecting this. A wild dog and a caged bird, there must be some sexual relationships.

I searched him thoroughly and found his cellphone and wallet with several hundreds of cash, two credit cards and several invoices.

"Your death is not for me to decide, but I can save your son."

Seeing that he wasn't in the mood to talk, I shifted to a tone of teasing. "You know, no matter how frequent you have been dating with Cai Ying, she's still the daughter-in-law of the Dongs. To be frank, we even don't know whose child the baby is. Now take us to the kid, I can ensure you a paternity test in case that you would be executed at last. I'll let you know the result. How about that?"

He smiled finally and answered, "No, but thank you."

Anyway, the suspect has been taken down. I've already fulfilled my duty and we couldn't question him on site. "Take him back." I put on my earphone and gave my orders. "Drive all cars here. Clear out the scene. Let's go home."

"Captain Zhao, this is Jiang. Emergency report from Region Three."

"What?"

"When Region Three was clearing out the scene, they discovered a dark green Cherokee in the parking lot. The plate number is ... Anyway, it is Zheng Bai's vehicle we are searching for. In the car, they found ... Oh my! The kid is right in that car!"

"Perfect!" I caught up and patted Shi Zhan on the shoulder, laughing. "All right, man! This time it's a complete lost ..."

"Wait for a minute! Captain Zhao, they just reported ... the kid ... When they smashed the window open, the kid's already ... already ... Well, the medical examiner has claimed his death and the reason may be dehydration and anoxia.

I stood frozen.

Shi Zhan looked at me and asked anxiously, "What happened?"

It seemed something was pressed tight on my chest. I suddenly realized that I was a real idiot.

"Let our men in Region Three stay where they were, and get me Director Bai."

Case summary, case report, technical identification report, medical examination conclusion, autopsy report, and record of inquires ... After reading the entire case file, the clock has run past 24 hours. I stretched myself and went to the Director's office to see whether Bai was still in that office, and ask for leave for half a day.

Before leaving, I went to find Jiang. "Anything to fill me in?"

Jiang Lan was a typical "new type of police". She's a beautiful young lady with hair dyed into light red, transparent lipstick and raspberry perfume. She's also got all the passion to handle everything carefully.

"Shi Zhan's phone is completely clean. He deleted all of them. The technical team have spent a whole morning recovering the data. But the device ran down before they could retrieve much.

I saw dozens of evidence bags lining up on the desk, Shi Zhan's phone and sim card in one of them. Some papers were put under the bag. I took them out and saw some phone numbers and text messages. "How did the evidence end up with you?"

"The technical guys are coping with their devices. All those bags and things, I couldn't find a place to work."

I recited one of the numbers several times and was ready to leave. Upon stepping out of the door, I thought of something else and asked, "When will they fix their device?"

"Don't know. It looks pretty bad. I'd say it'll be good they'll finish it by dusk."

I lifted the sim card from the evidence bag without anyone's notice and put it in my pocket. "I'll be away for a while. Call me if anything happens."

Stepping out of the flower shop, I placed all the things on the back seat, switched the sim card into my phone, put the earphone, dialed the number and started the engine.

After several dial tones, to my surprise, the phone was picked up.

What a great surprise.

I said with a deep voice from my throat, on purpose. "Hello?"

Nobody answered.

Impersonation failed. I gave up and said, "Hello Ms. Cai."

"..."

"This is Zhao Xincheng, the one who caught your lover."

"..."

"I'm just calling to tell you that, as you wish, the kid has died."

"..."

"And all the people you used, Shi Zhan and Ms. Jin, they have all been caught."

A faint but heavy breath came through from the phone.

"Shi Zhan does love you so much. Or he won't be willing to plot and play the decoy voluntarily. I don't know what did you do to contact Ms. Jin but when she knew the whole story, she showed great sympathy on you. It's a real pity that she trapped herself in by working with you to play the swap in the West Railway Station ..."

The breath was getting clear.

"Right. Sympathy and love cannot lead to success. No matter how well they treated you, I won't be surprised if you sold them out."

"..."

"I just don't understand, why won't you let the kid go?"

"..."

"I know he may be a mistake, but he is your child. You gave birth to him. Where is your humanity?"

"..."

"Take it easy. This phone is not monitored. It doesn't have to be when it comes to you. The local police have discovered your trace – some coach to Yangquan city after you got out of the train in Baoding city. Believe me, they will find you soon.

I heard some hisses through the phone. Was that a breath or a sigh?

"You want to know my advice? My suggestion is that you get off from that coach and wait for the police to come. The evidence from that cottage in Wuluju shows all the blood in that house comes from your difficult labor. There wasn't a piece of record in any of the hospitals in Beijing, which means you haven't received proper treatment. Lose nearly half of your blood and still can walk this far? You should be listed in Guinness Book of Records. I'm not a doctor but you should know that if you are not properly treated in time, you may die at any moment. Come to us and make a confession, that's the only way you would save your life – at least for a few more days."

Silent again.

"OK, that's it. To someone like you, I have nothing more to say. Two million, the ones you sold out, the kid you killed, they only worth more than two million, don't they? ... But even so, they are better than you."

Now, complete silence.

"Cai Ying, you, don't worth even a penny."

When I hang up the phone, it was barely even one forty. But at the time, what I didn't know was that at two o'clock in the afternoon, Acting Squad from the Criminal Investigation Division of Baoding Bureau of Public Security intercepted a coach with a plate number JiCxxxx at about 120km on highway G107 from east to west. Reports showed that Cai Ying was leaning on the chair, holding a huge woven bag. She was found dead less than half an hour ago. In the woven bag were the swapped two million.

Xuejing had fine, delicate figure and looked just charming in a slim fit gray blouse and a plain belt on the waist. Her long hair was bundled into a pony tail at the back and the pink skin of hers provided a perfect foil of her big and shiny eyes. The first sight she saw me, she smiled slightly as usual and asked, "Why did your phone power off?" But her eyes were glancing at the rose bouquet in my hand.

I knelt down and heaved the bouquet high. "My beloved Mrs. Zhao, in order to fulfill my promise, I have asked for leave and come all the way to pick you up. I deliberately had my phone powered off ahead just in case to be called back. Please my love, do forgive me."

She beamed at me and happily took the flowers. "Thank you Mr. Zhao. Your effort is much appreciated. You may now stand up and come with me."

I jumped up and held her waist. "Come on, honey! Let's go for the afternoon tea. I've already made reservations at the South Beauty[1] this

---

1 A fine and exquisite restaurant noted for cuisines featuring southern China.

evening. We'll have dinner there together."

"Hey, watch your hands. I'm still at work..." She chuckled and gave me a light push. "Come to the office and let me finish my files first."

"What! I'm holding my own wife! Anything wrong with that?" I teased loud on purpose. "Well, I've been in the field for more than 70 hours. With two suspects taken down, I haven't slept for a minute! Is it wrong to relax a little bit and enjoy my life with my wife? What do you say, guys?"

The passers-by were all my former colleagues. They just get together and laughed.

"Yeah! That's right!"

"I got your back, buddy!"

"I want to dine at South Beauty too!"

"Take me with you guys! Take me!"

"Let's go find Director Yu and ask for leave!"

...

Xue Jing was flushed with all the banter. She dragged me into her office and closed the door to keep all their jokes outside. "Yeah, you're really good. All people in the Investigation and Interrogation, you're the most wily one." she teased, "I heard that you've done a lot in solving the case. Now, Bai would count on you more, wouldn't he?"

"He may or may not keep the position. Who knows?" I threw myself into a chair and asked, "I remembered you had a day off today?"

"Yeah, I did. But thanks to my husband, we now have Shi Zhan and the nursemaid Jin Guilan in custody. They are short of hands and I only come to help. It's all right. It won't take long. Speaking of the suspects, I really cannot understand what Cai Ying did. If she's going for the money, why would she do this since she's already married into the family."

I shrugged. There must be something hateful in the pitiful, and vice versa.

"I've just heard from Qin Feng in Team Four that Shi Zhan is really tough. He won't admit until now that it was Cai Ying who had planned all this. The armed police has questioned Zheng Bai and learned that it was he who lent the credit card and the car to Shi Zhan out of pure free will. But he didn't know what Shi Zhan was plotting."

"He's being that generous? Without asking anything?"

"Rumors tell that it's just because Shi Zhan was his comrade in arms. Oh, the military men ..."

"What the fuck? Oh my! There couldn't be any affairs between those two, could they?"

"Well, did you know? After Shi Zhan knew the kid was dead, he almost cried his heart out. The whole office could hear his crying. I don't have the

ID report yet. Did you see in the division? Is that ... really his child?"

I've just switched my own sim card back when I was confused by her question. "Why bother to care about this? This is not your case."

She leaned over, pulling my arms, and continued to ask with a typical gossip excitement that belongs especially to women. "You've read the files? Whose kid is that? Dong's or Shi Zhan's?"

"Neither. Actually ..." I heaved a sigh, lifted my head with great guilt and teased, "Actually, this is my son. Sorry, honey. It's totally wrong for me to do this with other women ... Well, let's go home and make some babies tonight ..."

"You naughty boy!" She took a file case, pounding on my head and laughed. "Who's going to make babies with you ..."

The phone was ringing. I picked it up as I was laughing and asking for her pardon. "Hello?"

Jiang's voice came through, sounding like she was going to cry. She truly did. The loss of evidence must have scared her to death. It was an mistake that could cost her job.

I started by soft comfort and told her in a mysterious way that the sim card was taken to the Evidence Identification Center in Renmin University to analyze. It was secretly authorized by Director Bai and had to be kept a secret since it concerned the position of the boss. If she didn't believe me, she could go and ask the boss himself. But I would send the sim card back before five o'clock. She didn't have to worry about that.

Actually, the connection between me and Bai, or Bai and Professor Han from Renmin University,or me and Professor Han's son, Bin – all prevented Jiang from checking the truth of my saying. At last, she calmed down and promised that she won't say a word about it.

Xuejing saw me hanging up the phone and teased, "Bully the girl again? You are a true liar. I have to be prepared ..."

I was shocked. How did she know I was talking nonsense?

"No reason. I just know. That's why I'm your wife." She didn't even try to hide her complacency. "Go back to return the evidence. You have Bai to cover your ass, but don't drag Jiang into this. She's just a girl. ... Oh, and cancel you reservation tonight. When you powered off, He Jingcheng called me to hang out together at the Fingerprint tonight."

Fingerprint was a cafe Bin ran with his friends and also the location of the workshop. It was on Zhixinqiao Bridge South.

"Who will be there?"

"Like old times."

Oh, Bin has come back.

Chapter II
False Evidence

1

Fingerprint was temporary closed today for stocktaking.

After dinner, Bin, He Jingcheng and Zhang Beitong, Bin's partner, were sitting with me as usual at a table close to the electric fireplace at the back of the hall, chatting, smoking and talking with a cup of coffee in hand. And all the girls — my wife Xuejing, He's wife Jingjing, and Zhang Beitong's Korean wife were sitting at the bar counter, playing a Korean card game called Go-stop.

Han Yichen, Bin's "little" girlfriend was sitting by Bin's side quietly as usual, naturally blending into the background of the whole scene. Yichen was born with a reticent face, not ugly but not beautiful at all. Her features were delicate but not impressive. She was wearing a light gray woolen jacket with butterfly sleeves, a turtleneck white knitwear, light brown bell bottom pants and a pair of soft leather ankle boots with low heels.

Yichen's family name was the same with Bin's because she was officially registered as the adopted daughter of Professor Han, which meant she was the younger sister of Bin. But they were basically two generations. Yichen was from a orphanage in a small frontier town called Pianma in Yunnan province. In the year 1999, when I haven't known Bin for long, he took then nine-year-old Yichen back to Beijing. Being a child with infantile autism ever since she was born, along with a slight delusion of persecution, Yichen was quite difficult to communicate with. Bin, who then was nearly 30 years old, was the only person that could come close to her and communicate.

Due to the reasons above, Bin took Yichen with him for the past seven years. They ate and lived together, thick as thieves, and gradually developed something more than kinship. Serious as he is, Professor Han loved his son so much that he chose not to intervene their obviously incestuous affection. Actually, Bin has never admitted the relationship between his sister and him in public so we, as his friends, have never asked. This was some tacit knowledge among us.

Speaking of Bin's romance history, He Jingcheng, who went to the same university with Bin, had once told us that Bin had a girlfriend when he was in college but they broke up before graduation. More precisely, it was that girl who broke up with Bin because she waned to emigrate abroad. Her move broke Bin's heart so much that he took an overdose to commit suicide. But apparently it didn't work out. He Jingcheng found out his plan and broke in to take him to the hospital. There, he was saved. After graduation, Bin left Beijing for several years for travelling. When he came back, he was able to walk out out from the past and started a new life, but still remained single until Yichen came. So, hearing that he's started a relationship with his own sister dozens of years younger than him, we all heaved a sigh.

It was Bin who took me into the field of criminal profiling. After he left the workshop, I was still fond of asking for his advice about cases at hand, although, apparently, he loved Yichen more than criminal profiling. Actually, I was well aware that to seek advice from him was just my dependence on him, as the moment I saw him when things didn't go right, I could go straightly clear — just like a conditioned reflex.

The first half an hour of our chatting was normally my monologue. I talked about how Cai Ying's case was full of complications and ended in a unexpected way and how Cai Ying deserved that ending; and that the plan from the City Bureau was a complete disaster and my worries about Bai's unknown future.

"There were indeed certain flaws in the plan of the City Bureau, but who is going to take the responsibility is still a problem." said He Jicheng. I didn't know whether he was to comfort me, but he continued. "Yang told me that the profile from Dr. Yuan Shi was originally a reference, but some mid-level leader from the City Bureau took it directly as the core evidence for the case — probably from the point of supporting Dr. Yuan. I've heard that they were doing some internal accountability work at the moment."

His mention of Yang's name upset me from the beginning. "Where did his information come from? Is that reliable?"

"Reliable or not, Bai is still in office. Much rumors as it is, not a single move from the City Bureau is seen and the suspect actually matches the profile from Dr. Yuan."

It was true. Dark off-road vehicle (a Cherokee), a temporary residence (a cottage in Wuluju), partners (altogether three people involved in the case), certain social connections (comrade in arms), counter-reconnaissance ability (entering into the controlled radius alone and walking out intact once), dark clothes (dark green coat when arrested) ... Apart from the circled research area, Dr. Yuan almost hit all the points. I had to admit that his profile was quite precise when the result was to be taken as the only consideration.

"Does that mean, even if the City Bureau has to find someone responsible, the one to bear the brunt should be the one who approved the contingency plan?" I glanced at Bin.

Bin was about the same size as me but with darker skin. Among all the male creatures I knew, he was that kind of guy who would pay attention to his appearance. He liked clothes within the same color range — blue, black, gray and brown to name a few; he would go with a watch less than 10,000 RMB, a phone within 1,000 RMB, a necklace no more than 100 RMB and a packet of cigarette about 10 RMB, which, based on his income, was fashionable and affordable. As for the classic BOSS perfume and some expensive and quality scarf with no tags, they were only some secret symbols of yuppies.

At the moment we were talking, he was sitting in the sofa at the corner and listening to our conversation with a serious yet somewhat blank face. But that was Bin. If there were only one person to talk to, he would give him an intent gaze as if talking with that one was the only thing he would pay attention to in the world. But if there were more than two people, he would bisect his gaze and distributed them equally. I bet if he had the chance to lecture in a pyramid scheme, all his sources would think that they were intently and passionately looked at. Of course, they could never be sure about that.

He Jingcheng shook his head. "It's hard to say. After all the child is dead. Leaders from our division cannot just walk away clearly. The problem is, if they blame Bai on this and got him sacked, who would be the one to take it over? Ever since Bai came here, our close rate has been ranking the top three among all bureaus. With everyone listening to him in the division, being his successor would be a tough job."

"When I was returning the sim card, I heard of several other cases. A woman died at Changxin Building, and a skeleton was dug out around Banjing Road, the victim not identified yet. If you ask me, Bai was not like to be sacked at this moment and no one is willing to take over his job."

"What are you talking about?" Xuejing popped out and said.

Zhang Beitong put down his cigar, which, from my point of view, matches a lot with his strong figure, pony tails and beard, as well as his field vest and jack boots. A slight smile emerged on his ferocious face. "We were listening to Zhao about the case he just solved. Quite interesting."

"Oh, don't listen to his bragging. ... Well, as for the kid, whose child is he? Dong's or Shi Zhan's? You haven't tell me for there were interruptions this afternoon."

Everyone likes to gossip. Hearing this, He Jingcheng and Zhang Beitong were both looking at me, curiously. Bin bent forward to reach a cigarette on the tea table and Yichen moved a glass ashtray toward him a little.

A DNA test was done to the corpse during medical examination. But Bai pulled the test report out of the case files after he took a look at the report. Fortunately, I was among the few who had happened to catch a sight of the report.

"How can I know when they didn't run the DNA test? But we can simply guess. I'd say half-and-half, either Dong's or Shi Zhan's."

Xuejing was a little disappointed. She started to think romantically with her logic that didn't change at all from school. "Well, I guess it was Shi Zhan's, judging from his total grief."

He Jingcheng didn't take part in the medical examination. As a usual conservative, he said, "I'd say they should have run a DNA test. Now Cai Ying has gone, nobody knows."

Zhang Beitong was merely taking this as a story to tell after dinner. "She was a real good one with two lovers at both ends. I'd say maybe she didn't even know whose child it is.

Things got interesting from here. I asked Bin, "What do you think?"

At first, I thought he didn't heard me, but he then turned at me and said, "There's no need to guess. I know who the father is."

Everyone turned to him, wondering whether he have some inside news to share. I was staring at him too, reviewing whether it was what I said that gave me out.

He paused a little and said with a low voice, "It was me."

We boys all took a serious look at the same time. Xuejing almost believed us for a few seconds until Yichen laughed out, which was rarely seen. Then Xuejing realized he was only joking. She complained out of embarrassment, "Even you are joking with them ..."

We all laughed. As we were talking and laughing, my phone buzzed in my pocket. I took it out and picked up, "Hello? Who's that?"

Bin looked at me with a smile, the left corner of his mouth tightened a bit.

He knew! I was sure that he knew who the father is.

"Bai Yinshang, Deputy Director of Haidian Branch, leader of Criminal Investigation Division. Let Zhao Xincheng, the one who didn't read phone numbers, answer the phone!"

"Ah, Boss! I'm sorry ..."

"All those music and giggles, where are you playing?"

"Bin's workshop. We're hanging out. I thought I've asked for leave."

"Han Bin? Is his father there too?" Bai has always got along well with Bin's father.

"He's not here. What's the matter for calling, boss?"

"Stop the bullshit! New cases here, don't you know? Get back at once!"

"Right on my way!"

Bai's order had destroyed my attempt to enjoy a romantic night with my wife. After our party, I let Xuejing drive home to have a rest. Bin and Yichen lived around Renmin University. They could drop me off on their way home.

Bin pulled off the door and let Yinchen go into the front seat.

I asked him, "How did you know?"

He turned back and looked at me, his face covered in the shadow of the trees cast by the street lamp.

"I mean, you did know, didn't you?"

He passed across the car and uttered a short laugh.

I wouldn't be surprised even if one day Bin told me that I was the son of Charles Augustus Lindbergh Jr. coming back from that kidnap or that he knew the real assassin who killed John Kennedy. I only cared about how he had drawn that conclusion. "You have seen the report? Or some details in the case? I knew because I have seen the report. How did you know?"

Bin put his hand on the handle and turned to look at me. "Lift the evidence secretly to call Cai Ying. You are really playing an Robin Hood."

"I hate those to sell others out. She sold out all the ones who loved her."

"Yeah."

"So I was just taking the chance to let myself feel good."

"So you hid some of the facts behind and deprived her of the only chance to get others' understanding and sympathy."

The night wind chilled through my back.

"Is there any need to call me in for a such a simple case?" It was already three o'clock in the morning when I stepped out of Changxin Building to take a smoke.

Bin was woken up by my call from sleep but seemed sober. "Finished?"

"Yeah, I've got my boys out to search for the suspects."

"..."

"Err ... Did I just wake you up? I'm sorry about that."

"That's all right."

"Then what's the silence for?"

"Since it's you who call me, I suppose that you have something to say to me."

"Yeah, I was just ... I was profiling on scene so I don't feel that concrete. So ..."

"I'm listening."

"Here is the case. Chi Shanshan, design director of Anderson Design, was raped and killed at ten past eleven at night the day before yesterday. The surveillance camera shows that she went to the underground parking lot after working alone in her office that night. She left the elevator at ten past eleven but didn't show up in the surveillance camera in the parking lot."

"The victim was 29 years old and 1.75m tall, an attracting beauty. But apparently, she ..." I paused deliberately.

Bin continued. "She was not the victim of high risk."

"Correct. She was single and lived with her parents. When she didn't come back home till midnight, her mother called her cellphone and her office, but didn't get any answer. Her father came to Changxin Building to find her. The guard took him to the parking lot and saw her car was still there. Then they checked the surveillance camera and found she was indeed heading for the parking lot. Her body was found in the stairwell from B1 to B2, which is outside the radius of surveillance camera. She was not dumped there. That was the primary scene."

"I'll spare the autopsy report. Briefly, the victim was kidnapped after she stepped out of the elevator. The suspect took her to the stairwell and striped her off, but left her underwear untouched and raped her from the back. From the blood on the scene, it's estimated that the there were at least three knife wounds on the victim, which were shallow and not fatal. The last wound was stabbed horizontally from her sternocleidomastoid on her left chest, cutting off her trachea. The wound shows that the killer was stabbing from her back. My opinion is that the killing happened at the same time of raping and the killer was holding the knife with his left hand. And coincidentally, the victim happens to be left-handed. Hello? Are you still with me?"

"Yes."

"We found some semen in the victim's vagina. Some suspicious hair and clear blood fingerprint were also discovered on the scene. ... Overall, the killer has left plenty of traces that can be used in comparison. My profile is like this: male, age unidentified, tall and strong, and left-handed. He knew the victim for a long time and has sexual fantasies towards her. He knew Changxin Building well and was equipped with counter-reconnaissance ability, but was lack of criminal experience. Maybe this was his first time to commit a crime. He is a normal man who loves girls."

"I knew that these are not very practical. But based on the scene, if there's someone who knew the victim for a long time and knew the building well, he must be within in the range of the victim's friends, colleagues and workers in Chaingxin Building. My boys were searching from that direction before I arrived. I searched the victim's belongs and found that one of her earrings went missing. The surveillance camera shows that she was wearing it in the elevator. It's possible that the killer has taken it for a souvenir. And I've also found that in her handbag, there's a waterless car wash membership card of on-site service for a month."

"And?"

"I told my men at once and they started to check that card. From that card, we found the boss of Jie Yi Carsales. He was sleeping when we found him. From his information, we found out that the man providing on-site service was called Du Yang, male, 39 years old. Du Yang comes from Shangdong province, unmarried. He is about 1.8m tall and left-handed. We don't know his address yet but know that he doesn't like to hang out with his colleagues. He is very cautious at work with few mistake, quite an ordinary person. But he didn't show up at the company yesterday and didn't called for leave. We've dialed his phone but it was powered off, which means he went missing. All his features go with the profile so we took him as the primary suspect on our list."

"OK. Sounds reasonable."

"So ... What's your opinion?"

"Nothing."

"Come on, man! Don't you even have a slight piece of advice? What's this 'nothing' for? An compliment? An encouragement?"

"I was neither on site nor see the body. I didn't even read the files. What do you want me to say?"

"But ..."

"But you've told me the whole case and your profile, your deduction and conclusion. I understand what you've told me and didn't find any problem."

"Which means I can leave and wait for them to bring me the guy? My profile is helpful?"

"Profiling is nothing but a supporting approach in criminal investigation. It is enough to be helpful in finding the suspect among the crowd."

Bin had said that the conclusion of profiling must meet three requirements. First, it has to be helpful in finding the suspect. Second, it has to be concrete. And third, it cannot lead to any specific person. That means:

First, the conclusion of criminal profiling should be something like gender, age, height, residential address, occupation, education background, religion, sexual preference and family members. These are the features that can help the police to identify and find the suspect. Conclusions like whether the suspect is a person with antisocial personality disorder, or whether he or she suffers from Asperger's syndrome can be saved. This is really not helpful in actual investigation. Imagine there are 100 suspects standing in the front, who knows which one of them has been sodomized by some of his male relatives which leads to passive-aggressive personality disorder? This kind of "high-end" profiling seems to be good, but it may not be even helpful in academic research, let alone practical in actual investigation.

Second, profiling relies more on deduction, not imagination. Guessing and suspecting are not even possible. Deduction means proof, evidence. It is in need of presumption and premise, as well as real and practical logic, which means precise and reasonable cause links with sound and concrete conclusions as well. It is not possible to say a suspect has OCD when the victims is found to have six wounds in the six floor of a building at June 6th, and then assume the suspect is a neat freak or an admirer of Satan or disabled with an extra finger. This is a complete assumption, maybe suitable for films and children's books.

Third, although criminal profiling can cover the mental and behavioral features of a suspect, maybe physical as well, it still cannot be 100% precise. Life is not a math function. It cannot be calculated. It is full of coincidences and accidents. It will not develop strictly according to scientific development and crimes will not be committed by the book. A chopped body doesn't mean the suspect is medical related, or a butcher or meat vendor. That people like this form the list of primary suspects doesn't mean that others are not suspicious. If mistakes are made on this one, the real suspect may take the chance and run.

I held the phone at hand, pondering from the beginning to the end about which one I have broken. Bin said to me tenderly, "You're tired. Go back to the office and have some rest."

"But I'm afraid of ..."

"You are the leader of the workshop, and the pioneer of the bureau. Get yourself a little confidence."

"Would you like to check on the case if you've got time?"

"No, and I don't want to. What I can see, you can see as well."

"When I really see it, there is only a dead kid."

"You've done your part on that one."

"How I wish you were there."

"Like I said, you did well. If I were you, I couldn't even save the kid as well."

"You can ... you can. Bin, the kid is dead."

"There are so many things in the world that are up to nobody. Millions of police working diligently for several days cannot save the kid, neither can a flash of enlightenment in someone's head."

"I've made so many mistakes. I respond so slow. You wouldn't ..."

"No. Cai Ying, Shi Zhan, you and me — we are all doing things according to the best approach in our mind, and doing the right things in our perception. That's it. You've done it well, Xincheng. You've done your part."

"I feel sorry for the kid."

Bin was silent for a while. And then he said, "No, you are just feeling sorry for Shi Zhan."

I began to regret about not telling him the truth.

"The most fortunate thing for a man is that whether a woman is in love with you, you can love her either way. So Shi Zhan is the only person to know whether he is really happy in his relationship with Cai Ying. Only he himself knows that."

Then, what's the most unfortunate thing?

Bin didn't tell.

2

"You have a call." Bin waved at me outside the boxing ring.

I loosened my body and nodded to the man opposite me. "Wang, you're good."

Wang Rui, who has been playing with me for dozens of rounds here, was the new training partner here in the gym. After work, besides hanging out with friends, my favorite thing to do was to go boxing in the gym in the bureau. Last year, the rear services has been reassigned into branch bureaus and all coaches and training partners should be recruited publicly from outside the system. Coaches were easy to find, but training partners were clearly not. After all, training partners were the ones who have to fight with the our policemen in person. Few people would be competent for the job since only in Baidian Branch, I have seen hundreds of training partners come and go. Actually, that was normal enough since all officers in Haidian Branch, no matter social orders, patrol, interrogation or criminal investigation, would come here and have a try. You know, we field officers got tough fists. Male officers were like this, so were female officers. In Haidian Bureau, even internal officers like Jiang Lan and Xuejing, who are not so good at boxing, can fight over some of the training partners.

And as for me, I was the person the training partners don't want to see at all.

When I was at college, I majored in Police Management, not specializing in field work. But all these years have passed and those tough guys from Criminal Investigation would unconsciously feel painful on some of their old wounds when they heard my name, Zhao Xincheng. I had altogether 28 fights at school and won 27 of them, including 15 knock-outs. The only failure was the final round at the graduation game.

And after work, I haven't lost once.

I run to the ringside. Biting the cord open, I took off my puncher with my teeth and took the phone. "Who's that?" I asked.

"Your office."

I toweled off some of my sweat and put the phone by my ear, glancing at Bin teaching Yichen. He was showing her the standard straight punch, swing punch and hooked punch. He has never fought with anybody, even with me. But both his pinkies was suspiciously short, thick and out of shape and he's got really fine muscles.

"Hello. Who's that."

"This is Cao Fa. Director Bai is asking for you. We've got Du Yang."

But Bai is calling me for another case.

"There a skeleton dug out in a construction site on Banjing Road. Did you know that?"

"Yes. Are there any cultural relics dug out together?"

"No one would take you as a dumb." Bai's unexpected temper startled me a lot. "Go and find Jiang Lan to get the file. The case is yours."

"What? But the raping case in Changxin Building has just had a suspect identified ..."

"What?! Afraid of being cast aside? Nobody wants your case! The skeleton in Banjing Road has already been identified. It was a very important figure in the District Committee. At present, it is our top priority and had aroused the most attention from the City Bureau.

I was really doubtful that this was some side-effect from the Shi Zhan case. The City Bureau might be still assessing his working ability.

"This is a cold case with very limited evidence. You have to have it figured out. If there's something you need, come and talk to me. As for the suspect, find me an answer in three days."

"No problem."

When Jiang was handing me the file, she said, "We have identified that the body was dead and here's the information."

The body was dead? I was teasing to myself. What else could it be? How did you graduate from your elementary school?

After the reading the file, I finally understood why she said that. The body was dug out from the green belt construction site in the north-to-south pathway of Banjing Road. It was intact and skeletonized. The structure of pelvis showed that it was a female and she had died for more than five years. Officers have found a slivering ring on her left ring finger, corrugated gold necklace on her neck, several coins and a set of keys. After the identification of what she had left and the cross-reference of the missing people in the neighborhood, the body was identified as Wang Xianping, former vice-President of All-China Women's Federation, Haidian Branch. She was reported missing in July 2000 and was declared death in December 2005. The coalesced wound on the left leg of the remains could match her medical record, which also provided supporting evidence.

Her occipital bone has been smashed and that meant she was murdered by others. No murder weapon spotted on scene.

Anyway, this time, her death can be finally and concretely confirmed.

According to the record from local station, Hao Jianbo, Wang's husband, reported on Dec. 5th, 1999 around eleven o'clock that she didn't come home for the whole night after leaving her office. Considering her position and social influence, local station immediately sent out police to search along her commuting route but failed to find her. After their research, they found out that Wang had left her office to the north of Zhongguancun Hall. She then got on a bus and got off at Huoqiying Station. As usual, Hao Jianbo would ride his bike from his office — Beijing Municipal Intermediate People's Court No. 1 and picked his wife up at Huoqiying Station. And then, they would go back home — Gongnan Community at Sijiqing Bridge South.

It was windy that day. Hao arrived at the station around six o'clock but didn't see Wang. He waited for about half an hour and left, thinking his wife had walked home. He didn't see her along the route and she was not at home. Hao cooked some meal for her daughter in a hurry and went out to look for his wife again.

But to anyone's surprise, Wang Xianping, the 31-year-old woman and mother, just disappeared into thin air.

Oh my god! Cold case with a skeleton? No murder weapons, no evidence, even the surroundings have completely changed. We cannot even identify the first scene! I was almost sure that Bai was playing me.

"Go and find me maps about the scene around 1999. The more detailed the better." Although I didn't know where to start, I have to find somewhere to wedge in. "Cao Fa, take your team to interview the neighbour. See if you can find something on living conditions, traffic or roads, or anything else. Report everything you can find when you come back."

Cao Fa didn't answer back and took his team to conduct my orders. Jiang murmured, "Map? Where can I find you maps around 1999?"

"Bureau of Planning, Construction Committee of the District, Public Security and Traffic Administration Bureau, labor contractors, community offices, the elders in the neighborhood ... I don't care who you reach to. Get me the maps tonight! And, contact the policeman in charge of the case, and I want background information of all family members of the victim. You can have Team Two to help you. Anyway ..."

Jiang gave me a helpless face. "Yeah, I know. You'll have it before tonight."

"Hey Bin, having dinner at home?"

"Yeah, what's wrong?"

"Ahh, the thing is ..."

"Coming for dinner? Welcome. Coming to talk about your case? Bye."

"Hey, hey! Dude, you know me well. The boss had dumped me with a deadly cold case. Would you just see me walk into my miserable life? No, I know you wouldn't ..."

"I'm not a policeman, and didn't get paid from the police department either. That's not my obligation. You said it's a cold case? A case the police cannot even solve the case, you are counting on me? A lawyer? Are you kidding me?"

"I'm not saying I'm counting on you to solve the case. You can just consider it ... as taking a walk with your dude. Bai gave me three days to solve the case. It's nothing for me if I cannot find any clue, but definitely something not for him. You don't want to help me? That's OK. But that's Bai. Sure you want to help him right? You know, he's got a lot of pressure from the City Bureau ... Well, what's the sigh for? ..."

...

At the gate of Shuguang Police Station, the first sentence after Bin saw me was "You are such a rascal! You are really my buddy."

I looked at him with a joking wince. "This is the file. Please do me the favor and take a look."

Bin didn't take it. He just said, "Divulge case file under investigation. This is a real malpractice."

"You've read case files before." I argued back.

"That's under the authorization of the Bureau to help my father on a summary. It was legit."

"Come one, man! Don't be like this. My pants are on fire."

"Yeah, wait for your eyebrows are on fire."

I was about to continue my persuasion when an officer came out and called, "Zhao Xincheng?"

"Yes."

"The meeting is over. Our Director Zhou is waiting for you."

The one who was in charge of Wang Xianping's case was Zhou Hongruo, the current director of Shuguang Police Station. Zhou Hongruo was not at all famous inside Haidian Branch, but was putting on so much airs. Jiang Lan had already spoken to them about us coming, but when I arrived, they just told me to wait outside as they were having a meeting, leaving me standing and waiting for more than 20 minutes.

"Nice to meet you, Director Zhou. I'm Zhao Xincheng. Jiang Lan had told you about us coming, right?"

"Of course. I was in a conference. Sorry for your waiting. Come on, have a seat." Zhou Hongruo pointed to the sofa and let us sit.

To my surprise, sitting opposite me was a female director.

Zhou Hongruo was about 40 years old with a white face and two big eyes. Her eyes didn't blink very often, which makes me feel that I was stared by some aliens. Few middle-aged policewoman would looked good in the police uniform, but she was one of them. Her chubby figure turned into a good-looking one in the uniform, making her a typical model of uniform demonstration.

"I'm coming for the case in Banjing Road ..."

"We've sent you the files, right? I was then the deputy director in charge of social orders. This case was under my jurisdiction. All files were sent through my hand. Anything you want to know, just ask me."

"Right. What was the place like around 1999?"

"Full of construction sites. All wastelands. The commute route of Wang Xianping, Banjing Road for now, was not a proper one. If you can be sure that the skeleton is her, the first scene must be around."

"Will it be ..."

"There was no road in that place. Cars cannot even move in. The murderer cannot kill her in other places and moved her here. I'm telling you, young man, Wang Xianping must be died on her way home after work on December 5th.

"So the research radius ..."

"I can't say there would be any radius. On one hand, it didn't occurred to us that she was murdered at that time, and on the other, there were so many the migrant workers around that place. If we can find the body then, it may be possible. But now ..."

"But her husband ..."

"We all know that families are the primary suspects in missing cases. If we go through the timeline, we can find from the conductor that Want got off at about six o'clock that night. It's estimated that she didn't see her husband and took a shortcut home due to strong wind. And they just missed each other. Her husband said that he waited for her until half past six and went home along Wang's commute route. Their daughter Hao Meng confirmed that her father arrived home before 7 o'clock, cooked some meal for her and then went out. That's almost half past seven."

"But this cannot prove ..."

"Well, let's take it like this. It takes at least half an hour to walk from Huoqiying to Gongnan Community along that road, which is Banjing Road now, maybe more than 40 minutes considering the strong wind that day. Wang was murdered half way. The spot she was buried was 20 minutes away from Huoqiying Station. Commit the crime, move the body, dig and bury, if it was Hao Jianbo who murdered his wife, it would take him more than two hours to finish all the work. He won't be at home at seven even if he met his wife at half past six."

"But he can ..."

"Go back home first and then come back to dig and bury? No way. He won't be at home until ten o'clock at least. I was patrolling there with my team at half past nine that night. Nothing special happened. And then, around eleven o'clock, Hao came to the station to report the case. No one would be so stupid that he called the police before dealt with the body, right?

"Are you so sure that ..."

"Of course. I've paid much attention to this one. Hao Jianbo and Hao Meng have been questioned for several times. The kid was definitely not lying. And the last time when I spoke to Hao Jianbo, he was worried and sad, almost crying his heart out. I've seen a lot of crying, I can tell whether it is true or not. I've observed him carefully, it's not fake. He was really worried. Wang was murdered, that's true. But the suspect was not his husband."

"But early the next year, he applied to the court that ..."

"Generally speaking, the families of the missing tend to avoid the fact, right? But this one is not. I've always been paying attention to the case, afraid of missing any important evidence. So I went to the court the moment I knew Hao Jianbo was applying for the declaration of missing. It turned out that he's really got a reason, which makes his action acceptable, or reasonable, at least."

I finally grasped a chance to ask a complete question. "Why?"

"People from the court told me that Hao Jianbo, a judge himself, was very frank when he applied for the declaration, or helpless if you asked me. Their daughter Hao Meng was ten years old, but was suffering from congenital cardiovascular disease and wasn't able to go to school. The only way to cure her was heart transplant surgery, which was 20,000 yuan by then. Hao and his wife were all ordinary workers with monthly wages. How can they afford that much amount of money? Wang Xianping's mother has died and her father was in hospital for cerebral cancer, more like a vegetable. The diagnosis from the doctor was that he could only live for no more than one year. Now you see."

See what?!

Behind me, Bin nodded slightly.

When I stepped out of the location station, I directly called Jiang Lan. "What's real estate escrow? What's the problem with Wang's property? Didn't I tell you do check Wang's family background?"

"Wang's parents have to two properties, a big one and a small one, all in Chaoyang District. Her parents didn't leave any will so the legal inheritors were Wang Xianping and her elder brother Wang Qianxiang. They seemed to be not getting along with each other. In order to prevent Wang Qianxiang from disposing the two properties, Hao Jianbo had to apply for a declaration of missing to preserve one of the properties. And of course, the property preservation should be done after the death of Wang's father. And also, it can help Hao identify himself as the escrow agent of the property during the time his wife went missing. This is an issue of civil law."

I picked up some useful information among Jiang's legal terminologies. "So Hao has obtained the inheritance of his wife through certain legal approaches."

"In early 2000, Hao sent the application of missing declaration to the court and after the period of advertising, which is half a year, in July the court declared Wang Xianping's missing. At the end of the same year, Wang's father died of cancer. Her brother reached an agreement with Hao Jianbo about the inheritance — Wang Xianping would have the small house and the big one belonged to Wang Qianxiang. Hao Jianbo stared to manage all the property of his wife. And in December 2005, the court had passed his application and declared his wife's death, which started the inheritance process of Wang Xianping's property. The first inheritors were Hao and their daughter, which means that by the end of 2005, Hao had legally controlled all his wife's property.

"Which means that Hao Jianbo was the one clearly benefited from the case."

"Until here, I did think Hao Jianbo is the primary suspect. But after Team Two's interview, they told me that since Wang and Hao married in 1995, they lived a really happy life. Even if they knew that Wang Xianping wasn't able to deliver a child ..."

"What? Hao Meng is not their biological child?"

Bin laughed alongside me. "Of course not, or when the children died before their parents, the parents' biological grandchild would naturally have the right to inherit the property. If Hao Meng were Wang's biological child, Hao didn't have to go to the court for those declarations. Why does he make himself so suspicious?"

Right, I've got a famous lawyer by my side!

I nodded at him to indicate my understanding and continued to ask Jiang. "They lived a happy life? Real happy or fake?"

"I suppose ... it's real." Jiang hasn't married or had a boyfriend. She didn't know what a happy marriage would be like and answered hesitantly. "Their colleagues, relatives and friends, even neighbors are all talking like that. And it's said that Hao rode a bike to pick up Wang Xianping at the subway station since the first day they fell in love, all the way until Wang's missing. Seems romantic enough to me."

"Is Hao Meng really their adopted daughter? Or the illegitimate child of Hao Jianbo?"

"She was adopted from one of Wang's remote relatives in Shanxi Province. The procedures are intact and legal."

"Hao Jianbo took Wang's property. Will he still bring up the child from Wang's family?"

"Ah! That's the vital part. The moment he inherited Wang's property, the house that is, he entrusted it to an agency to sell. From the record in the Real Estate Administration Bureau, the house was sold for 420,000 odd yuan. Hao then quit his job and took her daughter to Auckland in New Zealand. They went to the Greenland Hospital for heart transplant surgery. It's said the medical fee was up to nearly 500,000 yuan."

He spent all the money? I continued to ask, "Why go abroad?"

"I don't know. But the hospital, the Greenland Hospital that is, hasn't got a single case failed in heart transplant surgery. None. If you ask me, I'd say he really cares about the child."

"I need to talk to him. Give me his current address."

"I don't have his address. He was living in New Zealand since then. Hao Meng was sent back China and lived with her grandparents. She is now an elementary school student. You can go and talk to her."

"Why taking to her?"

"Asking for how to contact her father maybe. And also, the boss asked me to tell you that we need someone to officially announce Wang Xianping's death to them. Director Bai asked you to do that."

What the fuck.

Hao Weiguo, Hao Jianbo's father, heaved a long sigh. "Jianbo was really miserable. In the years Xianping went missing, people talked a lot. They gossiped about her eloping, or about Jianbo marrying her for her money. But we parents knew him the best. He, he was just taking the girl from Wang's family as his own."

Ever since I stepped into the house and told them about Wang Xianping's death, Hao Meng had done nothing but weeping, tears running down her cheeks silently. Her grandparents just sighed one after another, making me quite uneasy to stay in the room, let alone saying anything.

The moment I met with Hao Meng, I was aware that she was not the biological child of Wang Xianping and Hao Jianbo. More exactly, she was not that kind of child born in cities. 16 years old as she was, she was really short, her dark cheeks tinged with blush. When she sat down, the bowlegs of her became more obvious, not a eye-catching girl in every sense. In contrast, her small eyes with too short a distance between them comforted me the most, as it made the her weeping not that much delicate and touching.

I turned to Bin for help.

But he was looking at Hao Meng.

Noticing I was looking at him, Bin turned to me and hinted at me about leaving.

I hesitated a bit, stepped forward a little, turned around and then turned back, and finally, I waled close to Hao Meng and patted on her shoulder. "I'm sorry for your loss. I promise that I will find the one who killed her. You have my word."

The minute I stepped out of the door, I started to complain about Bai's asking me to do this.

Bin was calm enough and comforted me. "Someone has to do it."

"I know. But I still have to have someone question them. I didn't get Hao Jianbo's contact information yet. What do you think?"

"Congenital cardiovascular disease leads to unbalanced hormone secretion. She has a clear developmental disorder."

I was quite upset. "Let's go. We've got some killers to catch."

It was almost midngiht when we arrived at Kunyu River. I called Jiang, "Connect Han Bin into the line. Tell them to have a team standby." Then I turned to Bin and asked, "Did you get the basic information of the case I've just told you?"

Bin was making a phone call.

"Hey, man! Don't worry about your girl. Jiang cannot connect you in if your line is jammed."

He hanged up the phone and turned back, his black eyes shining. "I'm calling your love rival."

"Yang Yanpeng? What the fuck! Why are you calling him?"

"I asked him to check something. He'll contact you when he gets an answer. Well, I'm not supossed to be the one who's doing this."

"What ... Are there any information that a police cannot find? What's him doing here! Jiang! Have you finished or not!"

"Mr. Han, connect your earphone when you're ready. I can see all your calls and I can transit them to you. Captain Zhao, results came back from the insurance company. Wang Xianping didn't buy any commercial insurance before she died, and Hao Jianbo was not the benefactor of any insurance. Do you still suspect him?"

"Yes. The better a husband he is, the more suspicious he may be." I waved my ID to the guarding police. "What was the burying place like in 1999?"

"Wasteland, maybe ... The maps I found are too general, more than the hand-painting one in the case file."

"And the people around?"

"Most are construction workers, and some residents. There were also some students from the universities in the east renting here."

Bin was squatting beside the pit. He took the photos of the skeleton and asked, "What's the motive?"

"She has all her accessories, which means it's not a robbery. What Jiang has said and our research show it wasn't Hao killing his wife for the inheritance or the insurance money. Then it may be revenge killing, or rape and murder."

"Captain, do you know we cannot run tests of sexual assault on a skeleton?"

"Don't cut in. What do you think, Bin? Is it for revenge or for sexual assault?" I followed him and asked, "Never heard that she's got any feud over anybody."

"None of them seems to be reasonable according the current evidence." Bin was holding the photo in his hand, a slight aroma diffusing from his wrist. "Only one wound was found on the skeleton?"

"Yes. Shallow wounds cannot be identified on the bones. For example, shallow wounds caused by a knife cutting open the artery. It is fatal, but cannot be seen on the bones. "

"Maybe this was not the first scene. There was no Banjing Road in 1999, right?"

"No, there wasn't."

"Any traces like fingerprints on the bone?"

"No way."

"Any witness?"

"No."

"It's simple then. You can tell Director Bai right now that this is a cold case. Miss Jiang, you can disconnect me now. Thank you."

I was totally astounded. Before I could collect my thoughts, he walked away.

The moment I got his meaning, I ran to his SUV, dashed into the car and unplugged the key before he could reach it.

My rudeness upset him very much. "What are you doing!"

"What are you doing! Just strolling around? Don't play with me, dude!" I really lost my temper.

He was not angry at all. "There's not any evidence. Even if you catch the suspect, you cannot convict him. There's no point to continue."

"We'll talk about conviction later. I'm now focusing on finding the suspect. I will find him! I gave the kid my word that I will find who killed her mother. You can't make me break my word."

"I make you break your word?" Bin asked back, looking a little bit annoyed.

I knew I was being unreasonable, but I couldn't help it and didn't know what to do. I was just annoyed with myself.

"Xincheng, you know well that the case cannot be solved. We all know that." He pushed the door open, cold and moist air by the river coming in. "Few rapers would commit a crime in such a windy day. Despite the harsh environment, the hormone just cannot reach the point of committing a crime — of course there will be accidents, but that's very few. Her husband and her child are basically clear. Then there's only her brother, who is right under your investigation. But it's not beneficial at all for him to murder his own sister only for a house worthy of 400,000 yuan. The reason why Hao Jianbo was picking up his wife from work may be more on safety concerns other than their love. The person you what to find is probably the same type of murderer in the raping case in Changxin Building.

A stalker who has long been tailing the victim, an assassin and murderer.

"I was living close to Renmin University when I was young, not far from here. The neighborhood is not a safe place. Plants, construction sites, people from the suburbs ... You want the profile? All right, here's mine. The criminal is male, which is obvious. Age range cannot be identified. It's all possible from 20 to 50. He may be single or divorced. He was living or working in the vicinity. I prefer the latter or Director Zhou may have noticed him. The victim doesn't belong to high-risk victims. It was dark when the crime was conducted, but not midnight. So why did the criminal assault the victim all of a sudden? That's very suspicious, or rather, there are other possibilities. What places did the victim and her husband pass on their way home? A plant? A construction site? Who are the ones that the couple meet regularly? These may be helpful, but if you go through this line, there are so many people waiting for you to talk with. People like that are migrant workers going from place to place. After all these years, are they still in Beijing for you to investigate? It's hard to say. Now there's no crime scene, no murder weapon, no blood, no fingerprint and no NDA ... Apart from Wang's skeleton, there's nothing."

I had nothing to say but look at him, expecting, more or less, a sudden flash of enlightenment.

"If you ask, I can tell you that the suspect may be short and skinny, but I didn't have any proof. He may suffer from depression, but it's not helpful to the investigation. He may be timid and petty, but it's out of pure guess. Are these the information you want to know? Go and ask any kid who has read some books about profiling, he can give you more." And at last, he reached his hand out to me and said, "Key, please."

I had no other choice but give him the key, reluctantly. "What did you let Yang Yanpeng check?"

"Only an uncertain guess. He'll contact you when he find something." Bin pointed to the door, which means I should get out of the car. "Oh, I do have something to tell you and it's the only thing I can tell you. Maybe you have probably noticed too that the murderer didn't left any signature[1], and the wound on the skeleton didn't show that it was a planned crime, which means it, to a large extent, would not be a serial crime. The murderer may not kill again."

He Jingcheng had explained to me that the wound on Wang's occipital bone was resulted by a passive hit. Active moves such as knocking, striking and beating can be excluded. This told us that probably, the murderer was not taking a weapon with him when he committed the crime, which meant he was not planning to kill.

But I knew Wang Xianping's death was no accident.

I was standing for half the night by Kunyu River after Bin had left. It was too dark and cold. Few people were there to admire my somber and handsome silhouette. And when the sun rose up and more people showed up in the area, I have already be in sound sleep in my car.

The Western Team found Wang Qianxiang. He has been running antique business for decades, with millions of property in his bank account. He was not even in Beijing when her sister went missing. Learning the death of his sister from the police, he just said impatiently, "Did the court already announced her death?"

Hao Jianbo's residential phone number was obtained from Hao's family. But the phone was not answered even if dialed for dozens of times. After talking with his family, we have learned that Hao Jianbo was often out, selling home appliances in New Zealand. It's normal that the phone calls were not answered. Every month, he sent living fees and tuition to his daughter. While we were asking about these information, his parents were asking, repeatedly, when they can hold the funeral for their daughter-in-law.

In the afternoon, a big process was achieved.

---

1 A signature, also known as the offender's signature, is a unique ritual of serial killers when committing crimes. There's a similar conception called MO, Modus Operandi in Latin, which means the method of committing the crime.

There were altogether two construction sites around where Wang Xianping went missing from 1999 to 2000 — a paper mill and a waste disposal facility. Their intact staff lists were still under investigation. Now we only knew that there were 92 people working in the paper mill and 17 in the waste disposal. 51 of them were male, 20 to 50 years old and were either single or divorced, among whom 8 were under investigation, 3 were about to be investigated and the rest 40 were nowhere to be found. I cannot imagine the situation after we found the intact staff list. That would be the start of our nightmare.

I called Xuejing when it was close to dawn to tell her that I have to work late that night. Before I could say a word, she started to complain. "Cheng, I won't be able to come home tonight. The case in Changxin Building, you know, that Du Yang is in under interrogation. He, he just doesn't tell! I'm about to piss off. Zhai even wants to beat him ..."

Good! Her words saved my effort. "With the blood fingerprint and DNA test, he won't be able to get off even if he doesn't tell." I said.

"The result of the DNA test hasn't come out yet. The point is that the fingerprint is not his. He must be working with someone. So my boss Liao told us we must let him tell anyway."

I was confused. The criminal who involved in sexual violence usually do not share their "prey" with others. At least for the rapers who kill their sexual fantasy targets like Du Yang won't work with others.

I decided to go and have a look. Maybe I could get some inspiration. "Don't worry. I'm on my way to meet you."

Du Yang was black and thin. His arched back, his slouch in the chair and the black circles around his eyes caused by lack of sleep made him shorter than he originally was, unlike a man of 1.8 meters tall.

At the door of the Interrogation Room, Xuejing warned me repeatedly. "Remember to keep your temper. You cannot just beat him down even if he annoys you, or force him to confess. Can you promise?"

I gave her my word. "No forced confession. No beating and fighting. I will question him by the rules."

Actually I knew it well. To deal with people like this, forcing was useless. As long as he told, he would die. He's not that stupid.

My approach was — dinner first.

I didn't treat him with the the humble dish from the holding cell, nor the everyday meal in the canteen of the Interrogation Office, but the stir-fry bought from restaurants outside — Pork Ribs stewed in Brown Source, Mapo Tofu and Fried Potato, Eggplant and Green Pepper.

Xuejing was sitting by the door and eating the hamburger I bought for her, moaning with a low voice. "Why does he get better dish than I do?"

Food was good. Cuisines were better. People tends to get drowsy after a feast because the brain doesn't get enough blood as more blood goes to the stomach while digesting. On the contrary, keeping the suspect hungry has every limited effects in lowering people's willpower, maybe more effective in clearing their mind. So the first step to get him tell was to get him physically relaxed. The effect was immediate. Xuejing started to feel sleepy and I knocked her on her forehead in no time. "He's still there! Come on!"

Step two. Stuffed and wanted to smoke? Sorry that's now allowed. The food was a little salty and wanted to drink? Sorry that's not allowed either. Feeling tired and wanted to get some sleep? Sorry, no naps in the Interrogation Room. That is to keep the suspect uncomfortable, annoyed and uneasy.

Step three. Enclosed environment, depressed atmosphere, and tension, tiredness and sleepiness— he's already stepped into my trap. Now there should be me someone to give him a push, and I, Zhao Xincheng, was that push.

I started by talking around. He was wordless as before, but I didn't care. I just talk by myself, making him confused, the more the better.

At the same time, I was observing his reaction. Theoretically, the more the police knew, the less they would say. Although asking for the case was the goal, questioning the suspect was its premise. The police should find out what the suspect cares for, pays attention to and worries about based on his background, living experiences and personal characters, and hence made him tell. Actually, a direct question was to be clearly avoided in an interrogation, but Xuejing told me that they've already tell Du Yang about the Changxin case and I didn't have much time. So I have to ask specific questions which were, in fact, very passive moves.

As I was talking, I suddenly asked directly, "Did you go to Changxin Building in the evening on 18th?"

Du yang must be waiting for me to ask the question, but also panicked a little when I asked.

"On 18th, you should be in Changxin Building to wash a car for a client, right? Do you know who the client is?"

Du Yang still remained silent, only nodding a little.

"You didn't go to wash the car. What did you do?"

He swallowed slightly. I stared at him, keeping an eye on all changes of his muscles."

"You are left-handed, right? It's said the left-handed are all smart. You

68

must think that if you tell, things get worse. But do you think keeping silent will walk you away safely?" Browsing the case files on the table, I asked, seemly unfocused. "Are you from Jimo, Shangdong province? Shangdong guys are tough ones from the ancient times. Qinqiong in the Sui and Tang Dynasties, Wusong in the Northern Song Dynasty — all tough guys. Why are you such a coward?"

He was sitting there with two leg apart, pointing his toes to different directions, which means he didn't agree with what I said.

"What is a tough guy? Live on his own! Make some big money if you are really capable. Small is OK. At least it can get you a chance to get a woman. But now, without money, you just go ravishing. If you ask me, I'd say you were lucky enough to be taken here as soon as we got you. If you were put into a holding cell, you won't be able to be intact to sit here. People like you are just the kind of public enemy that would be thrashed every time you came out under the light.

Du Yang started to massage his neck. This was a way to release his tension by kneading the carotid artery.

"Well buddy. What's your difference with a woman apart from you balls? You've got balls to commit a crime but don't have the guts to take responsibilities? Do you know why you've never be liked by a girl? It's not because of the short thing down there, your arched back, your stinky teeth, or your fake outfits!"

Feet clenched, shoulders shrunk, he was sitting there, licking his lower lip. The effect was good.

"It's because you don't have any guts ..."

He started to breathe quick and disordered.

"It's because you are a woman with a penis! You don't have the guts to admit what you've done. Having interrogated so many people, I have never met a single one as timid as you! Any shrew can do better than you!" I lowered my voice a little, which seems to be my habit when I start to tell lies. "I'm telling you, you don't have to say anything. I won't listen. Now we've got fingerprints, DNA results and witnesses ... plenty of evidence to nail you down. I was about to give you a chance to be a real man, but now, you don't deserve that chance."

After these words, I closed the file in my hand, stub the cigarette out and started to collect things on the table, slowly and deliberately.

"Oh, I forget to tell you. When you get to the holding cell, you'd better pay more attention." I continued to cheat him out of sudden inspiration. "Do you know what they do to guys like you? The boss there will order his men to press you down, take off your pants and tied a thread on you penis, one twist after a another, really tight. And then, people would flick your penis which, you know, has a cavernous body inside that will congest when stimulated enough. So after several flicks, it will stand up and be strong." I tried to appear to be joyful when saying these words. "And then, the boss would come near you, in person, take the thread and pull hard. Oh my! Flesh and blood! How good it is!"

Along with my last sentence, the defense mechanism in his heart, which was weaker as time went on, immediately collapsed.

"I, I'd tell. I tell you all. I, I didn't think about that. She, she promised me in the beginning. But, but when I went in, she was too dry inside, but complained about me to be short. I was pissed off, couldn't control myself. She didn't cry out or scream and I thought she's OK with that. But after that, she, she said I gave her too little. We had a deal before! I gave her all my money but she's just not content. She ..."

The first two sentences told me something was wrong. Was this the case in Changxin Building?

Du Yang finally looked up, tears all over his face and sticky fluid running down from his nose. "She said she'll call the police. I knew she ... I knew that ... Officer, this was my first time. Please help me. This was really my first time. You got to help me! Officer!"

Glaring at his eyes, I was way more than disappointed.

"Take it easy. Zhai, record his confession." I stood up and headed to the door, down in the mouth.

Xuejing pulled in, grabbed my arm and lowered her voice. "Cheng, the DNA results came out ..."

"I know." The self-mockery on my face must be more than embarrassing. "I know it's not him.

On the third day, all people from Eastern Team were working in desperation. To know what had happen on the scene was impossible. Interviewing and researching for related people were just measures to keep some theoretical hope. And when I got the two staff lists for that two construction sites in 1999, more than 500 strange names just killed all my delusions.

This was a cold case. A real one.

We didn't get the right guy for the Changxin Building case and lost our direction. And for this case, I didn't have any direction. I even didn't know how to report to Bai.

Just at this moment, Yang Yanpeng called me.

Knowing that I didn't get along with him, he didn't say much in the phone. "I've done the research. Where do I send the results to?"

After half an hour, I was holding a pile of files and even wanted to kiss him right on the street. May be it was because that was Bin's request, he found whatever he could find in details and plus what I have known, a comparison diagram appeared in my head. Bin's uncertain direction was now my only hope, maybe Bai's, too.

After getting into the car, I asked him once again to make sure. "Can you be sure about this phone number?"

"The source is reliable. Whether you can get an answer depends on you luck." Apparently not expecting my attitude good as this, he was a little bit surprised. "New Zealand is four hours earlier than us. Now they are almost six o'clock in the evening. If you want to dial, you'd better be quick. Oh, and don't forget to add the area code 00649."

I took out the IDD card I just bought from the newstand and began the charging process. "Did Bin know about what you have found?"

"I've told him and he said directly give it to you."

"What did he say about this?" Listening to the dial tone in the phone, I waved the files to him.

"He said that when you saw, you can understand."

The phone was picked up. I put my index finger on my lips to keep him silent.

"Hello?"

"Hello. Is that Mr. Hao Jianbo?"

"Err... Who's that?"

"This is the Investigation Division of Haidian Branch Bureau of Beijing Municpal Bureau of Public Security. My name is Zhao Xincheng. A couple of days ago, your wife was found in Banjing Road. To be exact, it is the body of your wife was found. The one that has been declared death by the court in December 2005."

"How ... how could she ..."

"Mr. Hao. On December 5th, 1999, you went to pick up your wife at the station but didn't get her. She was then murdered on her way home. I won't ask more details since the time is so limited. We now know that the murderer should be some staff from Bei'an Paper Plant on that road, which is now reorganized into Bei'an Fuda Paper, LLC. Employees in that company have changed a lot, which causes so much trouble for our research. So ..."

I have no choice but to trust my instinct. "Please tell me. Who did that?"

Total silence from the other side of the phone.

The silence told me that my instinct hit the right point.

"I want the name of that murderer. Just a name. Hao Jianbo, I've

71

promised to your daughter that I will take the murderer down. Now tell me that name. For your daughter and for your late wife, and for yourself as well! I know you saw him. Tell me the name!"

After a long silence, the phone was hanged up.

I felt all my blood was rushing to my head. Knowing not what to do to let it all hang out, I could only got out of the car and walked back and forth. Yang Yanpeng was right beside me. Seeing my anxiety, he advised, "I knew someone in Auckland. I can try to contact this Hao Jianbo through them. But, you know, I cannot assure that's all legal and the cost should be ..."

Save your impractical idea! I have so many to deal with! I thought to myself and called back to the division. "Can we find the Embassy in New Zealand ... the Consulate-General in Auckland to help us?"

I supposed Jiang must have been puzzled a lot because her answer came back after several seconds. "Why the embassy? Do you have to go abroad for the case?"

Bai's response was more direct. "I'm asking you to find the murderer of Wang Xianping, not to turn a homicide case within the district into foreign affairs! You can solve it, that's good. If you cannot, that's also accepted. Man proposes, god disposes. Just try you best."

Telling Yang Yanpeng to go back, I asked all my men to search for the employees of Bei'an Paper Plant. When Cao Fa came to report, he asked, "Captain Zhao, are you so sure about the searching radius? Is the suspect really on the list?"

I was so annoyed that I didn't even want to answer him.

From what I have known, Hao Jianbo changed his living residence three times from late 1999 to early 2006. And then, he moved to Wudaokou in 2001, Fangzhuang in 2004 and Gaobeidian in 2005, all due to his own decision and paid by himself, one time further than the other to his working place. And at the same time, Bei'an Paper Plant also moved to Wudaokou in 2001 due to road construction, Fangzhuang in 2004 due to reorganization and dismissed many employees the same year due to bad management.

Hence, I came into a bold conclusion, which is also Bin's uncertain direction. Hao was watching the murderer all the time.

On December 5th, 1999, it was probable that Hao saw his wife was murdered on his way looking for her. After the murder, as a judge who knew well of civil laws, Hao, apart from his grief, was clearly aware that Wang Xianping's death may cost Hao Meng her life since once the inheritance right was lost, he could not possibly afford Hao Meng's medical fee. So he concealed the fact of his wife's death and let the murderer go.

But he must have seen the face of the murderer, or at least, he knew that the murderer was an employee of Bei'an Paper Plant. So he spent years to move between places to places and followed the murderer who should be among those people dismissed by Bei'an Paper Plant in 2004 and moved to a place around Gaobeidian to work in 2005.

Now the reaction of Hao Jianbo verified my deduction.

But what now?

北京洛成塑膠製品有限公司，蘇震。

名字不陌生，我在北安造纸厂的职工名单上见过。

My next call to Hao Jianbo was not answered. With the manpower at hand, it was impossible to finish all the interviews before tonight. While I was considering whether to call Hao's phone number until he answered, a short message in traditional Chinese popped up on my phone:

Su Zhen, Beijing Luocheng Plastic, LLC

This was not a strange name. I have seen on the staff list of Bei'an Paper Plant.

I pointed at Cao Fa. "Call the Eastern Team together. Follow my lead!"

Although I said repeatedly to the workshop manager that we were just coming to ask Su Zhen some information, that in order not to make him so worried, our identities had to be kept secret and that he can make any small excuses to take Su Zhen to the duty manager's office, the manager was still looking so suspicious when he stepped out of the door. However, it didn't matter at all. The coming backup has got all entrances and exits controlled. I just didn't want to make a spectacle when arresting the suspect.

In less then five minutes, Cao Fa, who was watching at the door glanced at me and dashed to the side of the door along with Zhang Qi.

Su Zhen was coming.

I signed to the duty manager to sit tight behind the desk and turned against the door, my head lowered.

Along with the sound of pushing the door, the room was in an uproar. Fighting, falling, screaming and grating of the cuffs ... and then came a loud shout. "Police! Don't move!"

God help those who help themselves. I looked at my watch and called the boss. "Boss, I've got the suspect, a former employee of the former Bei'an Paper Plant."

Turning around, I patted the duty manager on the shoulder and waved the stunned workshop manager away. Cao Fa and other boys pulled the suspect, already cuffed, up to his feet. I walked close to him and asked, "What's your name?"

Bai seemed astonished, asking with a surprising face. "Is he the murderer?"

Su Zhen was more than 40 years old, short and a little bald. The pockmarked face of him, which resembles the surface of the moon, was now pale as dead, more like the surface of the moon after snowstorm.

Staring at his straight eyes and trembling body, I couldn't help to laugh and celebrate our victory.

After escorting him into the car, I ordered Cao Fa. "Don't give him time to make up any stories on the road. I have a call to make. You and Zhang Qi come first to get him confessed. Any weapons? Put them on the driving seat in case being accused of forcing the suspect. Take the record book and ink pad with you. Close all windows and doors while working. Bad influence if someone sees."

Cao Fa was not very willing. "But ... what if he doesn't confess?"

I answered impatiently while dialing. "What are you doing? Are you a policeman with trained interrogation skills? Just take off your uniform if you cannot do you job. The Director is waiting for us to go back. Get me the confession before I come back and you get the first prize, or you'll have enough time to find a new job. I'm not the one who shelters!"

Cao Fa was under my lead so he had no choice but to follow my order. Speaking ill of me, he took off his watch and got into the car. I knew him well. People like him were all sophisticated and cunning. If I was not tough enough, he wouldn't make a slight of effort.

"Hello, Bin. Dinner at home?"

"Not yet. What's the matter this time?"

He sounded much alert. I laughed out. "No, nothing. I was about to invite you couple for dinner."

Bin uttered a short laugh through his nose. "No free dinner under the sun. What are you up to this time?"

"Look at you! I just want to thank you. The case is solved."

"Hao Jianbo did see, didn't he?"

"Yes. The suspect's name came from him. Su Zhen from Bei'an Paper Plant. We've just taken him in."

"Are you sure?"

"Yes."

"Did he confess?"

"Not yet, but in a minute."

"That's really good luck. Congratulations!"

I had to admit that my luck wasn't bad at all. "Well, thank you. But why did you ask Yang to check those. You must have noticed something long before. Why didn't you tell me? And you told Yang to check for you. Why didn't you just tell me to ..."

"That's how you thanked me? Well, you can save your dinner if so."

"That's not the same. Don't cut in." A strange sound came from the car and I looked back alert. It was the police car waggling. A policeman watching on the side looked in through the window and waved at me, meaning nothing special.

"In the photo of the skeleton, I saw the buried skeleton was lying on the back, her arms folded on her chest. This is a posture placed on purpose, very peaceful and respectful."

"Oh my god! Why didn't I think of that ..."

"And Zhou Hongruo has said that Hao Jianbo cried his heart out in the last question."

"You think that's abnormal?"

"The families of the missing will naturally avoid the idea that the missing family member may be killed. So if Hao Jianbo was really crying like that, it's a little suspicious."

"But only from these two points, although we have a suspicion about his knowing of Wang Xianping's murderer, maybe catching a sight of him, it's still way more farfetched."

"It's more than farfetched. I'm not sure either. I don't think Hao Jianbo was the suspect since he's got problems with motives and time, but he does have enough reason to cover the fact of his wife's death. Unless Wang Xianping died of accident, it is possible that Hao Jianbo did catch a sight of the murderer." Speaking of this, Bin joked, "And I strongly advise you to find a lawyer to lecture you guys on civil law basics."

"Ha! Then I get your point. But don't ever play this again. You cost me two whole days for that! Running around for two days! How tired it is!"

"I've told you that's not a certain direction. If I tell you without sound evidence, that's misdirection. Your way was right. It's just because it happened a long time ago and was short of evidence. I told Yang to check. That was out of pure guess. It's lucky he can find something. But this kind of lucky try will never replace your investigation."

"Oh, come on, man. Anyway, I owe you a thank you. Dinner's on me. Wait for me tonight."

"Xincheng, don't count your chickens before they hatch. This is just a beginning."

"I know. I'll work on that later. There must be some way to go."

"Oh, and pay attention. Theoretically, this is a 'mission impossible'."

Right at this time, the door of the car opened. I didn't say much before I hanged up the phone and walked toward Cao Fa. "How's that?"

Cao Fa didn't seem to be happy. He frowned tight and threw me several pieces of paper. "His confession."

I glanced into the car. With a face now turned into the moon surface after a rain, he was curling on the back seat and breathing heavily.

"It's him?"

"Sure as hell."

3

I didn't know where Bin go for dinner that night. Because I missed the appointment.

Catching Su Zhen was the first step of our long journey. And how we can find enough evidence to convict him was a Himalaya right in front of us to climb over.

Getting back to the division, Bai praised me for my accomplishments and pointed out the most important problem -- evidence. "We cannot convict him only with an oral confession. Now we can only detain him for 12 hours. If we cannot find the evidence to convict him guilty before six o'clock in the morning, he'll have to go."

Report from the medical examination center: Apart from the wound on the skull which matches the suspect's confession, no other evidence found.

Report from the Eastern Team: After interviewing, no witnesses found. Employees from Bei'an Paper Plant didn't provide any useful leads.

Report from the Western Team: After interviewing, no witnesses found.

Report from Zhou Hongruo: Since 1999 when Hao Jianbo reported the missing case, no blood, weapon or footprint found on the scene, and no witnesses.

Report from Cao Fa and Zhang Qi on the scene: Su Zhen did want to do something when he followed Wang Xianping on December 5th 1999. After their fighting, Wang fell down, the back of her head hitting a rock, which directly resulted her death. Su Zhen didn't deny the above fact, but since many years have passed, and the environment around Banjing Road changed a lot, the first scene could not be identified.

Until one o'clock in the morning, apart from Su Zhen's confession, we didn't get any other evidence.

With no other choice, I dialed Hao Jianbo's phone once again, taking it as my last resort.

To my surprise, he answered the phone. Although it was five o'clock in the morning in Auckland, his voice sounded sober.

"We've got Su Zhen. He confessed. But without enough evidence, we cannot convict him."

A sad sigh came from the other side of the phone.

"Your testimony is much needed. I hope you can identify him face to face."

Hao sighed again, paused quite a while, and answered as if feeling discouraged. "Sorry, but I can't ..."

That was totally unexpected. Holding my temper, I try to persuade him. "Hao Jianbo, I know you have concerns. Su Zhen has already confessed that when he pushed Wang Xianping down, you were just there. Although it was dark that night, he still recognized you as her husband. So he ran as soon as possible. ... It was you who buried the body."

"Your action ... was difficult to classify. But I believe that you had no other choice at that time. I can assure you, with my heart and soul, even my life, that as long as you can identify him, I'll do my best to let you walk away without any hurt."

"All you have to do is to identify. We can take the suspect to the airport. You identify him after you get off and fly back right away."

"Please. Help me on this one. Please..."

...

"Sorry."

The phone was hung up.

I stood there out of depression. And when I dialed back again, the phone was powered off.

I threw the phone onto the ground. It smashed into pieces.

Only four hours left.

It was not until I drove away for some distance did I realize that I left the sim card in the smashed cellphone. So I had to drive back. The commute cost me almost an hour and when I arrived at Shijicheng Community in Banjing Road West, it was already three o'clock in the morning.

I drove around the neighborhood for such a long time and finally found my target — a red Buick that was waiting for some illegal ride-hailing business.

That was him.

Seeing a police car stopping in front of him, the man in the car was astonished first, and when he saw me, he got off the car immediately, clearly ingratiating and nervous.

"Go back to sit." I waved at him with a poker face, came across the front of the car, pulled the door open to sit on the front seat.

"What brings you here! Why not telling me first so that I can bring you something to have fun." While he was speaking, a Zhongnanhai[1] was heaved to me.

I didn't take his cigarette, but took one of my own. The car gave off an odor of spoiled food. The mixed smell of leather that hasn't been washed for a long time and men who hasn't taken a shower for ages almost suffocated me. "Tiger, when did I ever take a single bit of your things. Save your time!"

"Come on. We are buddies, right?" Tiger was flexible and lighted up for me quickly. "What do you want me to do this time?"

"Did you take your phone?"

"Of course." He took out his phone. A black one, an old cheap copy. "Take it as you wish."

I didn't have time to complain about the type and brand of the phone. "Take our the sim card. I'll pay for that. How much?" I took out my wallet.

"Hey! What are you talking about! Can I take your money? Of course no! This is not some expensive brand. You can just take it. If you want more, I'll bring new some new ones the other day ..."

I took out 200 yuan and gave it to him. "I give you 200. Take out your sim card."

"All right, all right." Seeing that I was not in the right mood, he didn't stick to his point.

"How's everything going here? Anybody causing trouble?"

"Of course! Nothing to bother you with. You know, we are doing the service business right now. Considerate service, fair price, and definitely no cheating." While he was talking, he took out a pile of paper and showed them to me. "See, invoices and everything. And the passengers are all regular ones in the neighborhood. As long as I've got a complaint about my man, I will take them to apologize face to face. Refund and all."

"But ..." I fumbled for the switch of the window and asked, "Why did I hear that there was a car driver beating one of the customers around this neighborhood?"

---

1 Zhongnanhai, a cigarette brand in China, is one of the most expensive brands and usually used as a gift.

"Ah, that. I knew that case." Tiger looked too innocent to have be staying behind bars for seven years. "Those were not our men around Sijiqing neighborhood. They are some farmers from remote suburbs. Dirty mind, dirty hand. They didn't follow our rules. But they were all caught by Director Zhou from Shuguang Police Station last month ..."

"Stolen bicycles around Jinyuan Hotel, right? Did you play a part in that?"

"Of course not! I won't do things like that. You know, the ride-hailing is what I live on now. Although it's illegal, it's not guilty. I won't commit crimes any longer ..." He paused a little bit, and gave me an expression of enlightenment. "Look at you! All those asking around the bush. What do you want? I'm at your service."

I shot him a sideways glance. "Those little buddies of yours, anyone registered permanent residence in the neighborhood?"

"Yeah ... Yes."

"Find me two. More than 28 years old, no criminal records. They have to be absolutely reliable."

"No problem. What do you want them for?"

I stared back at him with a cold face.

"Right, right. Then ... when do you need them?"

"Now."

"What?" Tiger was clearly unexpected. "But ... so early in the morning..."

"Bring them to me within one hour. I'm waiting for you in the car." I put out my cigarette, and got off the car. Then, I bent down and looked in through the window. "You know my rules. Play it well."

When I rushed into Bai's office with the case files, there were less than 15 minutes left toward time limit.

"Where did you go?" Bai was sitting behind the desk and didn't even waste an effort to glance. "Where did you run to to fine the evidence? We cannot detain him longer. If there's no evidence, let him go now."

"Here's the evidence." I lowered my head and gave the files to him.

Know not whether he can be cheated this time.

Several reports were at his hands while he went through the files in a casual manner. The phone rang. He picked it up, eyebrows frown and answered with a sigh after a while. "Well, I don't need your house. Look at your watch. Is it good time to sell houses? ..." What a perfect timing! When I was grateful about the perfect distraction, Bai cast a upward gaze, staring straight at me through his presbyopic glasses and asked, "Two testimonies?

What the hell! You dig them out after so many years? ... What did Zhou Hongruo do at that time? Where did these witnesses come from?"

I stood as straight as possible and pretended to be confident enough. "I've got some informants around Sijiqing area. Words on the street bring back answers." I'm not cheating. They were really informants.

Bai took off his glasses, massaging his right eye with a hand, his left eye still staring at me. At last, he looked at his watch, heaved a sigh and closed the file. "Are you sure?"

I lowered my voice and answered unhesitatingly, "Yes. The witness don't have criminal records and they can testify on court any time."

"I'm not asking this." Bai was looking at me, seriously. The light in the room seemed to be darkened a little. And then, he asked again, "I'm asking you whether you are sure about Su Zhen's guilt."

He knew.

"Of course. I can guarantee it with my life."

"Right." Bai put on his glasses again and tossed me back the files. "A child died in Xiaoyue River. An unknown body discovered around Hangtian Bridge. A robbing gang appeared around Qinglong Bridge. ... There are a lot of cases to be done. Go send the files to the Interrogation. Get them something to do."

The next noon, I went to meet Bin in Renmin University, hoping that I can invite the couple for lunch to compensate my last failing to keep the appointment. But when I arrived, it was already 12 o'clock. I stepped in the house and found their lunch on the table, turning an invitation to a pure free meal.

During lunch, Bin and Yichen were discussing about their journey plan after the Spring Festival and said several times that Xuejing and I had to join them. I was a little agitated, craving to talk about the case but daring not to. Bin was too sensitive. I wasn't aware of his thoughts and also uncertain whether I should keep something to myself.

"Well, I was working on a homicide case happened in Xiaoyue River area. Do you ..." I tried to find something to say, but paused half way. The victim was a girl. With Yichen sitting around us, it wasn't appropriate to say something like this.

But Bin was not indifferent as usual. He put down the chopsticks and asked, "Xiaoyue River? The place you arrange the hunt last time?"

"More or less. It was to the east side of Zhichun Road, the east to west one."

His left eye flipped seemingly. "Homicide case?"

He was asking more today. What happened to him? I chose my words carefully and answered, "Yes. The victim is a middle school girl."

He nodded a little and massaged his nose slightly to prevent himself from sneezing. He had nonallergic rhinitis. It was a habit for him to do that to stop sneezing.

A precious chance to drag him in, I asked discreetly, "Would you like to join me on this one? Of course, if you've got time for that ..."

"All right."

That was totally unexpected. Before I could say "thank you" to make the deal, Xuejing called me. "Having lunch?"

"Yeah. I'm with Bin. We're having lunch together."

"Did you talk to him about Su Zhen's case?"

"What?" I cringed a little in my heart and then noticed Bin was glancing at me now and then.

"Nothing. Meet me in the north yard after lunch. I've got something to talk to you."

I didn't drive the car of the bureau, so I didn't park inside the yard, but turned to the parking lot to the east of the yard and walked out. When approaching the gate, I suddenly saw Yang Yanpeng's car was parking by the road. I walked around and saw Xuejing sitting in the front seat, talking and laughing with him.

I felt my blood was flooding into my head.

Xuejing saw me and got off the car just as usual. But Yang was a little embarrassed, just sticking his head out and saying hi to me.

Xuejing stuck several pieces of paper in my hand and joked, "Oh my god! Love affair discovered."

I was too angry to say a word. But after I lowered my head to see what she gave me, I was shocked to the ground. That was the two testimonies of Su Zhen's case.

Xuejing put her hands on mine and asked gently, "Cheng, what are you doing?"

It was too difficult to lie in front of my own wife. I had no other choice but to ask back, coldly, "What? Counteract my efforts?"

"That depends on what you are referring to." The other hand of hers was also holding my arms. "If you are referring to the reason why Yang was here, it's because he's coming for the case number of a fraud case. If you are asking what I've given to you, well, that's false evidence. Cheng, the case hasn't been sent up yet, it's still OK to pull it back and cancel all charges."

Lowering my head, I breathed heavily several times.

"How did you know?" It was more than a redirection of the subject rather than a reception of the truth.

"Like I said last time, it's because I'm you wife." Xuejing's smile became more relaxed. "Regardless of the question of justice, do you think it's worthy to do this just to convict a suspect? Not only me, Yang also thinks you are really taking a risk this time ..."

"Well, impulsive decisions I made ..." I tried to smile regretfully, "So, the evidence list ..."

"What?"

"There are still two testimonies on the evidence list. Did you take that out?"

"Oh my god! I forgot about that." Her hands clenched a bit on my arms. "I'm taking that out! Come with me."

I put on the expression of depression and complaint on purpose. "Hey, are you saying coming to remove the files in the office taking me with you?"

Xuejing paused and realized her mistake. "Oh yes. I forgot. You have to avoid the suspicion. Wait here for a minute."

What? She can see through my "evidence"? I won't believe a word.

Seeing that she stepped into the gate, I folded the two testimonies and put them quickly in my pocket. And then, I pulled out my nightstick and walked directly to Yang Yanpeng's car. He was so scared that he pulled up the window hurriedly, let the clutch in and wanted to start the car. But before the engine started, my nightstick had fallen down. The side mirror flied out.

I pulled the door but it didn't open. The locked door didn't stop me. I kicked right at the window. Glasses with film cracked into a net but didn't broke. I gave it another kick and the whole window collapsed. Yang Yanpeng moved to the front passenger seat quickly, pushed the door open to rush out. I went across the front, stopped him just in time and threw the nightstick onto his head...

I was really enraged at that time. That stroke nearly cost his life.

He responded quick and avoided much of my stroke, which saved me from convicting the felony of intentional injury. The nightstick hit the clutch, making a big "bang". The clutch and a pair of glasses fell on the ground. And then, Yang Yanpeng cried loud, two fingers of his right hand were injured badly. I stepped into the car, pulled his hair and dragged him out. With one hand clutching his neck, I stepped forward to trip him over onto the ground, giving his stomach several strong kicks.

The armed police at the gate held the gun with both hands, staring at me in a frightened and suspicious look. I turned at him and gave him an almost ferocious smile. "You know, we field agents are under a lot of pressure. A lot things cannot be done when in uniform. Have to indulge myself a bit when in plain clothes. Well, I don' t have much choice ..."

Bai was really outraged when stepping into the room. Before I could stand up from the chair, he kicked me strongly right on the chest. I was cuffed from the back and lost my balance, directly falling down on the ground.

"You son of bitch! Look what you've done!" Bai seemed to realize that Xuejing was still there. It was not appropriate to beat me like this in front of her. So he shouted out at me. "Are you the only fighter in Haidian bureau? One after another. At the gate of the north yard right on the street! What are you doing there! You wanna be a felon? That's your dream job? Go there! Haidian Bureau is too small for you! I don't want you either! Don't stay here to lose my face! Get out!"

Xuejing pulled me up. Although I was still in a mood, but I didn't shout back.

Director Liao of the Interrogation Office, once Bai's men, tried to mediate between us. "Shall we take off his cuff? With you sitting here, he won't dare to do anything ... Look at you! Those who come to pull you out are all my men. What did you do? You didn't listen to anyone, and even fight with them! It's lucky that the victim is Ms. Pan's classmate, and he even said that he hurt himself. ... If it's not your wife, you would be detained now! Bai, take him back. Let him know his mistake. With such strength and delicate techniques, it's a waste to not use it properly. ... Ah, and the medical fee. Let him pay all the medical fee. ..."

I didn't say a word, just lowering my head and standing there, totally aware of my mistake. Xuejing was pleading all the time, and Director Liao was mediating in the middle. Under such circumstances, Bai was like a fighter who could not find his rival in the boxing ring, infuriated. He stared at me for as long as five minutes, breathing heavily, and then seemed to calm down a little. "Go to the hospital. Apologize. Pay all medical fee of everybody ..."

That was a must. And then what? Put up an announcement to criticize my behavior? Suspension and review? Or ...

"Since we've worked together for so many years, I won't embarrass you more. Tomorrow morning, I want your resign application on my desk. Hand over all your cases to Liu Qiang tomorrow afternoon, and then leave."

We didn't thought Bai would directly resign me. Xuejing and I was too terrified to say a word. Director Liao was about to try to persuade him, but Bai won't let him talk. He said in a serious voice, "Don't think you'll get pass as long as the victim let you go. A police attacks a civilian in broad daylight. Witnesses are everywhere! What you've cost is the reputation of all policemen! Yes! You've taken criminals, a lot of them. Does that make you think you're so good? But have you thought that taking in criminals is your job! It is what you have to do! Not some asset used to brag! Look at what you've done! Are there any differences with those bullies? ..."

His voice lowered and lowered at the last sentences. I was sweating and knew not what to do, even didn't realize a figure standing by the door until Xuejing gave me a slight poke in the ribs.

It was Director of the Penal Code Research Center of Renmin University, Deputy Director of China Prison Association, Deputy Chief Prosecutor of Huairou District People's Procuratorate, member of the national committee of CPPCC, Bin's father and Bai's comrade in arms, Professor Han Songge.

4

After listening to my absurd "explanation" and "apologize", Yang Yanpeng sat straight slowly on the bed and said, "It is not talking to your wife that cost my half of my life, right? It's just that you want to vent your anger somewhere, and I was the wrong person in the wrong place."

I kind of agreed with him.

"If it's for your wife, that's easy. I will keep distance from your wife from now." He stuck out one hand to reach an orange on the nightstand with difficulty. "If you think it was I who interrupt your case, then I was deeply wronged. You should go to Han Bin and Hao Jianbo."

I didn't understand him. I took the orange, tossing up and down with one hand. "Why?"

Yang Yanpeng took back his hand, like a kid whose snacks were robbed. "Han told me to leave some information behind, afraid of disturbing your case. In March this year, Christie's Auctions & Private Sales sold an antique vase worth 6 million euros. After deducting the commission, the agency transferred the rest of the money, which is more than 400 million euros, into a bank account in New Zealand. The owner of the account was named Terry Sinner. Two months later, this Sinner married a 26-year-old white girl."

I looked at the orange in my hand and suddenly got his meaning. "Is that..."

"The cellphone number I gave you belongs to Terry Sinner."

"Where did he get this antique vase?"

"I don't know. But it's not hard to guess."

Of course. It was not hard to guess.

It was possible that Hao found that antique in Wang's house, maybe more than one. The sudden fortune completely liberate him. After he fulfilled his aspiration and arranged the transplant of Hao Meng, he chose to live in a new environment, started a new marriage and new life. He let go of the murderer he has been chasing for years and at the same time, left his first wife in that dark, humid and dirty pit.

I said nothing, but peeled that orange and gave it to Yang.

"Justice cannot always prevail in every corner of the world. You've worked for a long time in interrogation and investigation. If you think Su Zhen is the murderer, you must have your own thoughts. But in case ..., per one million ..., per one trillion, that he is not the murderer. What would you do?"

I uttered a cold and short laugh from my nose. "That's easy. I pay him my life."

"Your life's not enough." I didn't know it was because the sour orange or the wound in his mouth, Yang Yangpeng's look seemed to be a little painful. But he continued. "No one can really walk in others' shoes. It's a law-based society now. You cannot do the things beyond you reach."

"I'm a police. My reach is to catch bad guys. If I let a murderer go in public, that's a breach of duty."

"Well, that really sounds like Robin Hood." He put the rest of the oranges on the nightstand and mumbled with one hand on his cheek. "When I was in the Ministry of State Security, I've worked a case — well, the details are confidential — but anyway, I knew the suspect is him. I knew it. I really knew. Although there was not enough evidence, I did let justice prevail, well, with a certain measures. But after two years, the real culprit was caught. That was a total miscarriage of justice. In the past two years, his mother died of illness. His wife eloped, taking their kids. I was counting on my own experience too much at that time, just like you today. I depended to much on my hunch. But then what? I lost my job due to making false evidence and compensated a big amount of money. But whatever I do, I cannot pay back his suffering."

I didn't feel good at all to have the same experience with him. I shook my head and said, "Do you mean you are the lesson I should learn from? Then I have to thank you for interrupting my case, and not letting Su Zhen suffer from a miscarriage of justice. And thank you for saving me from breaking the law, right?"

Yang Yanpeng frowned out of astonishment, and smiled bitterly. "So you think it was I who told Xuejing the false evidence. ... Hell no. When she was talking with me, she's already figured out that problem of the evidence. I think, if she's not getting smarter after marrying you, she's got some instructors. I'm not the one to take your gratitude."

Driving out from the exit on the 4th Ring Road, I finally stared to talk. "Thank you for what you've done."

Holding a cigarette at hand, Bin was looking out through the window. "What's that for?"

"If it's not your father, I probably have lost my job." I said, my fingers knocking randomly at the steering wheel. "It's not my luck that brings him right in time."

"Your wife called me. Thank your wife if you want to." Bin didn't accept my gratitude. "There's no use to thank me."

With Bin's father speaking good of me, I saved my job, but was relieved of the position as the captain, my criticism announcement circulated around the bureau, and myself under suspension. At the beginning of "creating" the evidence, I never dreamed of ending up like this.

"Letting Bai take back his words, he's really powerful. What did it cost him? I don't want to get him into any trouble."

Bin didn't say anything, an insouciant smile appearing on his face.

With several cases not getting desired results, Bai was still in his position. Bin's father must have paid something, some exchange of equal values in a certain level.

"A new leader came to the political department. Rumors say that's the one competing for the head of investigation with Bai. Do you know who's that?" I talked about this on purpose, hoping Bin can verify my information.

He seemed to be fed up with this topic, shrugging and turning away.

"That's Zhou Hongruo from Shuguang Police Station." I pulled over the car and said, "Come on. Go meet Hao Meng with me."

Bin was surely not willing to go with me. "You are almost sacked due to this case. Watch out."

"Su Zhen was released and I cannot reach Hao Jianbo. I have promised Hao Meng that I'll take in the murderer. Although ... I have to give her an answer." I patted Bin on the shoulder. "Do you want me to go back my words?"

The moment I met Hao Meng, I suddenly realized that I really didn't have much to tell her about this case.

How I get the evidence, I couldn't tell her. Neither could I tell her the current situation of Hao Jianbo. All the process related to case solving couldn't be released. And at last, all I could tell her was that we policeman was good enough to take down the murderer but had to let him go due to lack of evidence.

Unfortunately, the grandparents were not at home.

After I called up all my courage to tell Hao Meng this helpless result, I couldn't even say a "sorry" in front of her crying face.

It was just like what Yang Yanpeng had said — No one can walk in others' shoes.

Once again, I turned to Bin naturally. And then I found out that he was staring at Hao Meng once again.

The last time when we were here, he was staring at her with the same expression.

Hao Meng seemed to be uneasy to be gazed like this. She lowered her crying and controlled herself not looking at the place where Bin was, sitting in a very uncomfortable posture.

Probably sensing my silence, Bin turned to me. In her eyes, there seemed to be Hao Men's crying image left, covered in a vast and condescending coldness and ... what was that? A kind of interest?

Just like a child crouching in front of a tree watching the ants running in a line before a storm, innocent and cruel.

Then I looked again at those crying eyes. In a moment, I saw something inharmonious.

I didn't know when Hao Meng stopped crying. She lifted her head, but was afraid of lifting her eyes, tears running down from her cheek, leaving winding traces. The traces drew something mature on her plain face, something sophisticated and cunning not coordinated with her age.

At the same time, Bin lowered his head and smiled. Numerous vague questions were like fragrance and shadows, pervading the entire room. An absurd idea suddenly appeared in my mind. My face was wincing out of control. Something was on the lip of my tongue, but I couldn't say a word.

"Theoretically, this is a 'mission impossible'."

The so-call "impossible" came from Hao Meng's testimony, testifying that Hao Jianbo didn't have any time to bury the body.

Unless ... unless an experienced hand like Zhou Ruohong had made a mistake, which means in the evening of December 5th 1999, from half past six to half past nine, Hao Jianbo didn't go back home.

I was astonished. I looked, speechlessly, at that young face which defeated all policemen that questioned her seven years ago.

Everyone has the desire to live on, no matter what age she is. But how old was Hao Meng that year?

My false evidence was completely dwarfed compared with hers.

Bin had already knew but he didn't say anything. I looked at him, desperately, as if seeing a bored kid heaving a kaleidoscope with different kinds of dark sides of humanity, looking down in a cold and lazy manner, and trying to get some fun from those capricious ugly patterns.

All of a sudden, a rush of indescribable sadness welled up inside me.

Chapter III
Ghost in the Closet

1

In the three months I was on suspension being a volunteer with no wages or badges. It was directly because the reassignment by Bai. I was demoted as a detective and Cao Fa was promoted to be the vice-captain. The vice-captain who authorized Cao Fa's gun in the hunt applied for a reassignment, but the boss didn't send anyone else to take his position. He only asked Liu Qiang to lead the Eastern Team for the moment.

In private, many of my colleagues, including Liu Qiang, all said to me, "Don't worry. Bai intends to leave the team with you. If you haven't been involved in the fighting, you'll well be promoted as the vice-commander, being the boss of the Eastern Team."

It sounded comforting but I knew well myself that, as a policeman with ill reputation, it was completely impossible for me to be promoted directly from a detective to a vice-commander.

But Bai's arrangement was certainly not going smooth. Liu Qiang was competent for the job, but no one could cover two shares of work simultaneously. Those tasks have clearly overwhelmed him, making his blood pressure surging high but the close rate dropping continuously.

In less than two weeks, Liu Qiang asked me out for dinner. He complained a lot and then held my shoulder. "Come on. You got to help me. The people once worked with you, especially, didn't even listen a word of Cao Fa. ... If it goes on like this, we'll be down in the end at the annual review, let alone the monthly and seasonal ones. How embarrassing!"

I was completely idle those days and agreed to his proposal at once. But my post hasn't been resumed, I could only see to the work of street raids. You know, the work of criminal investigation includes not only catching murderers. Theft, robbery, organized crime and drug dealing cases occupies most of our daily work.

After I came back, my team was naturally happy, and even Cao Fao welcomed me as it was him, not me, who was the one to be demoted, which actually surprised me. It was said that someone sneaked on my return to Bai in private, but Bai didn't care much.

In order not to let my colleagues and the boss down, I took the team to sweep away bad guys within the district day and night, either staking out in the green belt or searching among the lanes in dark nights. One of the robbers asked me in tears, after taken in, "Officer, are there any catch-criminal movements lately?"

As for the cases I couldn't take part in, they all failed. The Wang Xianping case stayed as a cold case; the suspects of the rape case in Changxin Building has never been found; the homicide case in Xiaoyue River hasn't been solved and the body found near Hangtian Bridge was identified non-homicidal. More astoundingly, a doctor was cut throat in asleep at Zhongguancun Hospital at the end of November; and in the middle of December, a prostitute called Fang Wanlin was found dead halfway when she was going through Zhichunli Community Park at midnight. After assessment and comparison, it was suspected that there was a serial killer in the district and there was a saying that the City Bureau were paying attention to it.

A few days after the New Year's Day, Bai called me to the office, which indirectly verified the saying.

"Happy New Year, boss. You asking for me?" I was a little bit agitated when summoned into the office all of a sudden.

Bai pointed to the sofa. "More diligent under suspension than in office? That's masochism, isn't it."

Although that was not that pleased to ears, but a smack was actually a good sign.

"Do you know none of the murder cases was solved in the last season?"

"Yes."

"The local stations were complaining about no one to be taken behind bars. Don't mind the street orders, leave them to the station."

"I got it."

Bai picked up his buzzing phone and was annoyed. "I'll buy it if it's 1000 yuan per square meter. And why should I buy a sea view house in Qingdao when I live in Beijing! That's nonsense!" He tossed his phone on the table and said to me, "Go find Liu Qiang for your badge and gears. Look out those murder cases first."

"Yes, sir!" I tried my best to control my thrill, though I couldn't quite control it. "Boss, which one should I start with?"

"The City Bureau thinks it might be involving some serial killers. Their consultant will come here at one o'clock in the afternoon. You go and see him. You two can talk about the case and share some opinions." He paused a little bit and a slight anger crossed his face. "The case in Xiaoyue River, please let justice prevail."

"Sure. I will see to them all."

Upon my leaving, Bai stopped me. "And this time, keep you temper."

Rubbing the back of my head, I answered, "Well, I can't guarantee that."

And you need people like me, do you?

Bai glanced me from the edge of his eyes, pushed his glasses up a little bit and said, "Get out, you."

"You'd better find out who you are facing with." Dr. Yuan Shi leaned forward, his hands putting on the edge of the conference table, supporting his tall and slender body. His face was handsome but cold, eyes directly looking at my fact, shining. "This is a serial killer with distinct dissociative identity disorder. He behaves between organizational and non-organizational criminals and owns a variety of characters. He is both a field type and an invasion type; both a prowler and a predator."

He was wearing a luxurious slim fit suit and a shirt of famous brand with famous Logo whose collar stretches out the collar of the suit. His red-and-black tie was loosely tightened, with the silver dolphin shaped tie clasp decorated clipped at the end of the tie, on which the two sapphires decorated were humbled by the diamonds decorated on his watch. As soon as he stepped into the conference room, they were shining in front of my eyes and humbled me to the greatest extent.

Fortunately, as the current leader of the workshop, I could understand his words. And he was here so early that I didn't finish reading the case files. Compared with arguing with him, trying to take in what he said seemed to be more efficient. "What's your opinion?" I asked in a very polite manner.

Yuan Shi lowered his head and wondered for a while, and then he looked up, seeming making up his mind. "Put them together. The rape and murder case in Changxin Building with a female victim Chi Shanshan, the homicide case in Zhongguancun Hospital Community with a male victim

Song Dechuan and the one in Zhichunli Community Park with a female victim Fang Wanlin are out of the same person."

"Is this ... how the City Bureau think about them?" While I was reading the case files, I said, "The same DNA has been found in the crime scenes of Changxin Building and Zhichunli Community Park. They must be committed by the same person. But the one happened in Zhongguancun Hospital Community ..."

"So you think it's their gender cause the difference, don't you?"

Song Dechuan, a 38-year-old surgeon, has been divorced for many years and lived alone. At one o'clock to half past one on December 16th last year, someone picked his door open with a iron wire, came into his bedroom and cut open his throat with a knife — neat and tidy. There was no weapon found near the crime scene, neither fingerprints nor footprints, nor any witnesses. There were no defensive wounds found on the body and the surveillance cameras from the gate and nearby streets didn't catch any pictures of any suspects ... In a word, besides a body, nothing was left by the murderer.

"And the point is, from only wound on Song Dechuan's body, the murderer should be right-handed." I pulled out the autopsy report from the medical examination center and put it on the table. "But the one who murdered the two women is left-handed."

"Which is just interesting ..." A slight smile seemed to appear on Yuan Shi's face.

Someone lost their lives and he was enjoying. That was what I prefer to see. Trying my best to hold my temper, I asked, humbly, "I haven't got time to go through the files. Are there any similarities you found among them?"

"Do you know what a criminal signature is?"

"Of course. But the murderer doesn't have a typical MO, or I didn't find any after comparing these three case. If it's not the same DNA found, I can barely say they were done by the same person."

Yuan Shi asked in surprise. "What's your name?"

"Zhao Xincheng." Actually, we have been introduced to each other when we first met. It seemed he didn't take it seriously.

He stared at me for a little while and said, "There is a team studying Criminal Psychology under Professor Han Songge's instruction, and I heard the one in charge is a policeman named Zhao ..."

I uttered a short laugh as a confession.

"Ah, that's simple." He laughed in an unpleasant way, his tidy white teeth flashing now and then, and the fragrance of his perfume and mouthwash made me sick. "You're not saying that you didn't notice any signature in these serial cases, are you?"

I sneaked a glance at my watch and said, "No, I didn't."

Vasyl Olexandrovych Sukhomlynsky, educationalist from the former Soviet Union, once said, "Observation is where wisdom comes from." He paused a little and continued as I didn't respond. "If we look closer to these three cases, we can easily find out that all three victims are all left-handed."

I was confused. "Oh ... so what? Does that mean there's a serial killer?"

Yuan Shi was a little disappointed towards my response. "The suspect chose a certain group of people to commit his crime, which is worthy of our attention. May I mind you that there's only 9% of left-handed people among all people in the world? This is a rather narrow range. And what's the probability of three left-handers dying consecutively in Haidian District?"

"So ... Does that mean we should monitor all left-handers in Haidian District?" I stroked the stubble on my chin and found Jiang Lan was looking at him, her eyes full of admiration and worship.

"Yes. All left-handers are potential victims and possible suspects." Yuan Shi turned around to look at me, the fragrance of his mouthwash puffing out. "The suspect is male, 20 to 35 years old, single or divorced. He has a domicile, left-handed and is good at using his right hand as well. He is clearly smarter than ordinary people, and well educated. His job is skill-oriented, may be working as a freelancer such as a journalist or a writer with a good financial condition. He likes avant-garde clothes such as leather ones. He has some friends, but doesn't get along well with his family. When he was a boy, his parents didn't teach him well but he has a Oedipus complex to some extent. He suffers sexual dysfunction out of psychological reasons ... and there may be other aspects that I'm not sure of now. If there's another case, I can give a more comprehensive analysis of his psychological features."

And then, he closed his laptop and started to collect. "I have to remind you that the cooling-off period[1] of the criminal is about to end. You'd better hurry up. His next goal must be a left-handed female. Good luck!"

"Please wait." I stood up to stop him. "Dr. Yuan, I'm not questioning your opinion. But just with our evidence in hand, do you think it's a little

---

1 A cooling-off period refers to the temporal separation between the different murders of a serial killer. Theoretically, it is a symbol to differentiate a serial killer from a ordinary murderer. Serial killers tend to need sometime to cool himself down and rest after the crime pushed his emotion high to a certain point. He uses that period to taste and enjoy the past experience for a second time. And some of the serial killers will use the period to assess and evaluate their last crime, maybe several crimes in the past and plan for the next crime based on his experiences and lessons learned from them.

bit hasty to put these cases together? I think ... there are many differences among Chi's case, Fang's case and Song's case. We can't exclude the possibility of two murderers."

Yuan Shi picked up his suitcase and looked at me, as if he was trying to lower his IQ so that I can understand him more easily. "It's true that there are a thousand Hamlets in a thousand people's eyes, but only Shakespeare knows the prince best."

Gazing at his back out of my sight, I murmured to Jiang, "There's no need to take the last sentence down."

"What? Ah ..., so ..." Jiang Lan flipped over the record book. "So what's his meaning by the last sentence?"

"No matter Hamlet, or King Claudius, or Polonius, Ophelia, or Horatio, they are all fictional characters of the writer. They do what the write tells them to do." I didn't know it's my emotion or the lunch I had at noon, but I felt a bit of odd in my stomach. "Dr. Yuan simply means that for the criminals, he is God."

2

"We have examined the body again. There's not any difference." He Jingcheng gave me the autopsy report and said, "The first report is enough."

I. Autopsy Report

[2006] No. 79 from BEIJING medical examination center

Introduction
Entrusting Party: Northern Team of the Criminal Investigation Division, Haidian Branch, Beijing Police
Client: Qiao Dong
Time: October 24th, 2006
Brief: Fan Jiajia, female, was found dead on the steps 400m away in the east along Xiaoyue River, Hauyuanlu Road section in Haidian District at around 18 o'clock on October 24th, 2006. She was 13 years old and was from Beijing. The victim was reported missing on October 20th, 2006 and the case was accepted and heard by Huayuanlu Station. The case registration report was attached in Appendix I.

There were several sticky notes at the end of the page. The first one reads: The acceptance time was 24 hours after reporting time, which meas the case was accepted on 21st.

He Jingcheng was waiting for his noodles. He explained, "It was lucky that the body was found face down. It was not soaked in the water and saved in one piece. So that must be the second scene. From the position it was dumped, the suspect may have it dumped at night. He, or she didn't watch out or there was no moonlight; anyway the body was thrown on the steps to the river. A waste of time for the suspect to take it a long way to Xiaoyue River."

II. Examination

The body was examined by He Jingcheng, associate chief physician in the medical examination center of Haidian Branch, Beijing Police on October 24th, 2006 in Shuangyushu Office. The body was examined according to "Public Safety Industry Standard of the People's Republic of China (Medical Examination)". The results are as follows:

i. Report from observing the surface

The dead was wearing a red-and-yellow sweater and a white long sleeve tee inside. She didn't wear anything down below and was lying on her back on the table. She was 158cm tall, and was well-developed. Purplish red postmortem lividity can be noticed on her skin on the back that was not compressed, but the color faded way upon press. Rigor mortis has decreased.

Face: A slight subcutaneous hematomas and swell can be seen on the face. Her hair was black, 40cm long. Her corneas were cloudy to a medium degree. Her pupils were equally large with a diameter of 0.5cm. Dots and patches of hemorrhage can be seen on her palpebral conjunctiva in both eyes. Tips of blood found on the oral mucosa. Her teeth were well, and her tough stretched 1cm out of her teeth. Excretion with blood can be found inside her mouth and nose. Patches of subcutaneous hematomas can be seen on her forehead and both eyebrows. A bruise of 1m^2 was found on the bridge of her nose.

There was another sticky note that reads: Less then four days from heist to murder? A kidnapping? But no ransom.

"From the decrease of the rigor mortis and the condition of the corneas, she was died thirty hours ago, which means she died on the day of 23rd. The examination report of the mouth and nose can also prove that. The others wounds on the face may be caused during the dump from the top."

Neck: On the upper left of the cornua cartilaginis thyroideae, there was a 1.5*0.5cm subcutaneous hematomas with slight skin exfoliation; another 0.5*0.5cm suborbicular skin exfoliation can be noticed above the sternoclavicular joint; another 1*0.4cm subcutaneous hematomas with slight skin exfoliation can be found around the sternocleidomastoid of the flat cornua cartilaginis thyroideae on the right neck.

And also, a long mark was noticed on the front of the neck where the the pomum adami is, 2cm wide and 0.5cm deep. The mark was pale and stretched toward both way to the back, and closed at the back of the neck. The widest place of the mark was 3cm under the left year. In the mark, blisters with blood, subcutaneous hematomas and skin exfoliation can be noticed.

Chest and abdomen: No damage.

Back and hanch: No damage.

Limbs: No damage.

The sticky note reads: Painful process since she was strangled long enough to lose her conscious.

"It's apparent that she was strangled to death. The suspect first used his hands and then a rope. The direction of the mark indicates that the murderer may be right-handed and was probably attacking from her back."

Vulva: Swollen labia. Slight blood found on the external urethral orifice. Her hymen showed an old rupture and seminal fluid was found inside her vagina.

The note on the sticky note was simple: Murder due to sexual assault?

"Children today ... She's only 13 years old. She had made love with the murderer of someone else voluntarily 48 hours before her death. It may not even be a seduce. The seminal fluid left inside her vagina was too old to run a DNA test on. Besides, there were many dry marks of urine around the vuvla, the inside part of the thigh, the abdomen and haunch, possibly resulted from urinary incontinence, but the real cause was nowhere to be found. Violent sexual assault, bladder sphincter malfunction before death or orgasm can all lead to that, or only because she drank to much water."

ii. Report from the medical examination

Head: No blood under head skin. No fracture on the skull. No damage or blood on meninx. No blood or damage on brain tissues.

Neck: Two intramuscular hematomas were noticed in the middle of the right sternocleidomastoid, 1.5*0.5cm and 0.5*0.5cm respectively. A 2*1cm intramuscular hematoma can be noticed on upper musculi ossis hyoidei on both sis. A 1.5*1cm soft tissue hemorrhage was noticed under the right thyroid membrane and around the right thyrohyoid. Tips of blood can be noticed under the mucous membrane inside the ventriculus laryngis. The trachea was in the middle, unblocked and unobstructed. The artery and vein were not damaged. The hyoid bone and the thyroid were not damaged.

Chest: No hemorrhage noticed in the chest. Tips and patches of blood were noticed on the surface and between lobes of both lungs. Spreads of hemorrhage were noticed on the epicardium. Nothing special on the pericardium, as well as other parts of the heart.

Abdomen: All organs were on their usual place. There were around 400 contents inside the stomach, in which contents like meat and nuts can be distinguished. No special aroma. There was a 5cm hemorrhage under the chorion towards the end of the ileum.

iii. Results of toxic test.

Please refer to the toxic report (Appendix II)

The sticky note reads: No anaesthetic reported from the toxic report. Violent heist? Doesn't seem to be.

"The wounds inside her body match the features of strangle to death. According to the leftovers in her stomach and her missing time, the murderer did provide her with good food. And also, there's no defensive wounds on the body."

III. Discussion

After the observation of the surface and medical examination of the body, we have found that there were patches of subcutaneous hematomas the forehead and both eyebrows, a bruise on the nose bridge, dots and patches of hemorrhage on the palpebral conjunctiva in both eyes, several subcutaneous hematomas with slight skin exfoliation in the front of the neck, 2cm strangled mark on the neck, dots and patches of hemorrhage on muscle groups and tissues in the front of the neck, dots and patches of hemorrhage spread on both lungs and between lobes, and spreads of hemorrhage noticed on the epicardium. Based on the results of medical examination and taking investigation and back research into account, we believe that the victim was wounded due to strangulation. She was died of mechanical asphyxia due to strangulation with a rope.

IV. Conclusion

Fan Jiajia was died of mechanical asphyxia.

The sticky note in the end was clearly for me: That's interesting. Tell Bin to come.

"That's all. The kid went down to fetch the newspapers at 7 o'clock in the afternoon on 20th, and didn't came back since then. Both her parents worked in Beihang Attached High School. I cannot remember their names. She was a Grade 7 student in Beihang Attached High School. She was a very lovely girl, good grades, with many friends at school, doing volunteer jobs and willing to help others. Quite a good girl. Her family was not rich, but happy. There's nothing special from the information provided by her school, but they specifically pointed out that she didn't have a boyfriend. So there's a lot of difficulties waiting for us if we are to find that sex partner who could be charged with fornication with an underage girl." He Jingcheng poured all he knew about the case and then focused on his noodles. "Of course, if we can find that one, it's not long before we solved the case. Oh, pass me the vinegar."

"A family case." I said while I was thinking about whether to eat my noodles first or talk about the case.

He was very cooperative. "Why do you say so?"

"I don't know." I decided to have my noddles first before they turned into a bundle. So I flipped the report to the last page and pointed to the sticky note and said, "You said tell Bin to come. Now he's here. Why not ask him?"

Bin was a real gentleman with good manners. Even if he was siting in Haiwanju, a Beijing style restaurant selling noodles with brown sauce, he treated the noodles in front of him as some French cuisine. He was holding one chopstick with each of his hands and selecting the toppings to stir and mix with his noodles. Hearing that I mentioned him, he glanced at He Jingcheng first, and then lowered his head to continue with his noodles. "Confucius once said, 'Don't talk while eating as you do not talk while sleeping.' Don't you know that?"

"If the suspect spare a lot of effort in strangling a 13-year-old girl, using a rope after hands failed, the one must be not strong enough." He Jingcheng tasted his noodles and added some vinegar. "It's likely to be a female or someone old. A kid may also be possible theoretically. But normally, children cannot plan a scheme as complex as this. So children can be excluded first."

"If the murderer didn't have any affection with Fan Jiajia, he wouldn't do it from the back. Attacking from the back means he wasn't able to face the kid. And also, the victim didn't struggle ..." Taking the chance of their talking, I gulped half of noodles in. "However, the body was found half naked. If the murderer really were her family, normally she wouldn't be treated like this. This is where it cannot be explained, or to say, contradicted itself."

He Jingcheng was still putting vinegar into his noodles, making me start to wonder whether there's any problem about his tasting system. "Maybe the murderer took the victim's pants as the noose, or maybe there's something that will reveal the murderer on the pants, or if the murderer changed pants for the victim, it would blow him off ... these are all possible. But what I think really strange is that Fan Jiajia was not thrown into the river. I have several assumptions. First, the murderer didn't intend to throw her into the river and it was a total gild of lily for the murder to take her to the river bank and dump her. Second, the murderer has poor eyesight. He, or she, didn't see clearly enough in a dark night. And third, the murderer has poor hearing. He, or she, cannot distinguish the difference of a person falling into the river and a person falling on the ground. Fourth, the murder has good eyesight and hearing, but he isn't able to walk. He or she cannot get down the steps. And fifth, there's someone coming near when the murderer was dumping the body. So he or she just throw it down and run away ..."

"So, the murder was either poor in eyesight or hearing, or cannot walk properly."

"Someone old may be possible."

"Or a female."

"In the cases that a female murdered a female, the murder was usually caused by anger. But I have examined the body carefully. There's so sign showing that the victim was beaten or ill-treated. One point for male."

"That leads us to the old and the disabled."

"Old male families."

"Agreed. So the murderer knows when she would get downstairs and can take her to leave without anyone's notice. No binding, no violent heist, no defensive wounds. She was not reacting to the heist at all. Oh, look out your vinegar. Is it sour enough?"

"There are no marks due to violent sexual assault, which means she was doing that voluntarily. ... This person must be someone who she trust. This kind of trust, may be sexual relationship, was no way a recent one. It can even make her ignore her parents."

"That means the murderer's family status was higher than her parents."

"Her grandfather on her father's side?"

"Or on her mother's side." Apparently, I took more advantageous of my eating speed during the discussion. While Jingcheng was still struggle with his noodles, I was already sitting there, holding a cup of tea and asking Bin, "What do you think?"

Bin took a chopstick of boiled cow's stomach with coriander in sesame sauce and put it in his mouth. "Why dump it in Xiaoyue River?" Bin sighed.

Back then, I thought, I really thought, he was really pointing out something questionable in the case.

"A criminal police and a medical examiner were sitting here talking about the case. You are both experienced hands. You've talked about all possibilities, and you've searched all places you can search." Bin put down his chopsticks, wiped his mouth with a napkin and then started to massage the bridge of his nose. "Now you're talking on end in front of me. What for?"

"For your promise." I held a cup filled with tea and saw through it, and suddenly found that the world became softer behind this cup of amber fluid. "You've promised that you'll help me on this one. I still kept that in mind. Come on, bro! I'll set a prize. The one who find out the murderer first will get my precious 30 years Glenfiddich."

"Liquor is not attractive to me. And that sounds like I owe you something."

I smiled to him through the cup of tea, the smile seeming to be a little fake.

"We've finished the background research of the two main suspects, which leads to the problem." I put down the cup, complaining in my heart why Bin's eyesight can directly pass through the cup. "Fan Chengguo, Fan Jiajia's grandfather on her father's side, 79 years old, was a retired worker of Beijing Chemistry Industry Group, II. His wife died several years ago and he now lives on his own in No. 102, Building 6, Beihang Community, which is to the bank of Xiaoyue River, just a street away. He is right handed, and is in good condition although he suffered from diabetes and mild liver cirrhosis for many years and developed a little bit Parkinson. Her grandfather on her mother's side, Zhang Mingkun, 76 years old, was a retired teacher. It's said that he has been a teacher in he poor and underdeveloped frontier areas for half of his life. His wife was also dead, and he is now living on his own in No. 911 Building 1 Dayuan East Community. Xiaoyue River is to the east of the community, only a street away. He is also right-handed and is able to live alone although he has developed several diseases and suffered from heart problems. They didn't have clear alibis when the case happened, and they were both close with the victim —of course not intimate enough to be unnatural. There's no surveillance camera in both of their communities. No witnesses, no testimonies, and no traces left behind. Naturally, neither of them admits they have assaulted or murdered their granddaughter.

Bin finally got interested. "Who has the victim once lived with before?"

"I've also taken that into consideration and have checked it out. Fan's parents have to work during the day. So the kid has to stay with her grandfather during winter and summer vocation — this one or that one. According to her parents, she didn't have preferences between them."

"Then who cares about her more?"

"Equally."

"Who has records of sexual assault or other criminal records?"

I drank up all my cup of tea. "Well, clean as the cup. Nothing at all."

"Comments from neighbors?"

"Good and bad, but more on the good ones."

"Marriage?"

"Not happy, but they were loyal to the family. No affairs."

"Childhood?"

"Well, I cannot dig out stories as far as before liberation."

"Then let's talk about something close. How about their sexual ability?"

"How ... can I know about that?"

He Jingcheng has just finished his noodles and cut in, "Well, theoretically, men are likely to have normal sexual capacity until they die. Diabetes or heart diseases won't affect that."

"Then I can only tell them to watch some porns with their pants off so that I can observe their reactions, or to observe who reacts more when watching a porn with a girl as the main star. Come on, man! Is there anything practical?"

Bin held a unlighted cigarette in his left hand and played with a silver older lighter in his right hand, with some lizards or crocodiles carved in the front and several lines of words that I could not understand at the back, in which four characters caught my eye — NAGA. He stayed silent for a while and suddenly asked me, "You questioned them in person?"

"Ah ... yes."

Bin's smile was a little weird. "Then who do you think is the killer?"

The confirmation of suspects must be well-established. Fan Chengguo and Zhang Mingkun were both likely to be the murderer, but I must have proof for that. "What I think doesn't matter. What matters is the proof."

But he didn't let me go. "After all these years, you got to have some hunch for a case."

"My hunch tells me that you are the murderer!" I took his cigarette and put it in my mouth, fumbling around to find my lighter and murmuring. "If I can find any evidence, you'll be the first one I'd like to take in! Only if you help me to point out the one who killed Fan Jiajia will I consider to let you out. Or I must want more! Clues are not enough! I want evidence! In case that someone come out to scold on moral high ground."

Bin was sitting there, squinting, seemly to repeat the phrase "moral high ground" silently. He poured a cup of tea for himself and lighted the cigarette while I was fumbling with my lighter. "There's a large urine mark on Fan Jianjia. It's not possible she had done it herself. ... Those two old men, who has prostate diseases?"

I paused a little, and swallowed all the smoke down through my throat.

"Well, I do read about the medical history of them both." He leaned back a little bit and asked me, "Xincheng, I don't drink. Can your Glenfiddich be exchanged into cash?"

3

Since I stepped in, Bin and Zhang Beitong was talking by the bar counter with several pieces of paper being pushed back and forth. Earnest and passionate, they seemed to be checking their business accounts. He Jingcheng seemed cannot understand why I looked so seriously while resting leisurely on the couch, so he asked, "What are you thinking about?"

I answered with my eyes gazing at the bar counter. "Well, I was thinking that it's lucky that he didn't choose to commit a crime."

"Ha!" He Jingcheng stirred his coffee with a tea spoon. "I'm always saying that he is dangerous."

"What do you mean?" I turned to him as if I was alerted. "Do you think Bin is likely to commit a crime?"

"Well, I don't know. But you know, he's a lawyer. Doing things under the table is normal to people like him." He tasted a little bit about his coffee, but his eyes were gazing straight at me. " And for real criminals, he is a real dangerous person. Oh, have you contacted the division office yet?"

Every time I was gazed by He Jingcheng, I would feel a little bit uncomfortable. It was not about his strong figure, or his athletic height, but his face, square with dignity. To tell the truth, He has got a real handsome face. His eyes, eyebrows, nose and mouth were all perfect and the black frame of his glasses made his face real clear and tidy from afar. The perfect dignity and solemnity of him would attract most ladies, but would also press his colleagues and friends a lot. I would always feel to be an errand boy in front him, a junior. Bin and him were classmates. They were both gentle and kind, but in a totally different way. In a word, coming from the family of a senior official, He Jingcheng would sometimes act like a person with a real position, and the friends of him, including Bin, had no choice but to play his followers.

"Zhang Mingkun was already under supervision. But there's no point questioning him now. They will start a more comprehensive research tomorrow. Money is not possible, just that bottle of wine. Take it or nothing."

"The case hasn't been solved. And maybe this one comes out like Su Zhen's case. Suspect, yes; evidence, no." He laughed a little. "If you really want to donate it, give it to the cafe. We've come here for free for a long time. It can be served as some gratitude."

"Yeah, my wine for your gratitude. How nice. I should think out giving it out after Zhang Mingkun being arrested."

"You don't have to worry about that." A slight smile appeared on He's face, not to me, not to anyone else. "If he really committed that crime, he's a dead man."

I've never seen him like this. "Such a strong confidence. Are you sure?"

"Even Oskar Schindler comes with a Noah's Ark, he wouldn't be saved." He lifted his cup again, that smile again appearing in his eyes, somewhat strange and ambiguous, but not to me either. "Yes. I'm pretty sure."

"Tong's asking you whether you want to come and play bridge?" Bin came to my side, holing a cup of brownish black liquid in his hand. I didn't notice his coming and was startled a lot, nearly dropping my cigarette into He's Con Panna.

Bin seemed happy toady and had a bit of drink. I knew what he was holding was a cup of bourbon infused coffee. He was not a drinker at all. But whenever he wanted to have a taste, that would be his only choice.

I gave it a taste the first time I saw him drinking it. It was bitter and spicy. I couldn't understand why he wanted to drink something like this. Bin said, "It's because a troubadour in New York likes it, so I want to try some."

"But it's not even drinkable."

"But it's said that the coffee and alcohol can counteract each other and neutralize the effect."

"Who said that?"

"The write who created that poet."

"Wait. Your mean that you'd like to try it just because a god-knows-who in some god-knows-what story likes it?

"I don't drink often. So every time I want to try, I didn't remember its taste."

"That's ... strange. This is you only choice. There must be some reason behind."

"Then join me."

"Well, does it make him a Shakespeare at last?"

"No. He is s private detective, but he was a police before that."

"Right. Whatever ... You can just tell me what this thing makes him at last?"

"Well. He cut out drinking at last."

...

Later on, Bin did invited me several times to join him, so the liquid in his glass gave me a more or less mixed feeling. I stopped him from playing on and dragged him to stay with us. The Xiaoyue case has got some leads, and the serial murder one to which the City Bureau paid great attention had to be pushed forward. Since he was in good mood and He Jingcheng was around, this was a good chance to drag him in. So I asked him to sit down and introduced these two cases.

I didn't talk about Song Dechuan's case and Dr. Yuan's profile. On one hand, I was a little reluctant in putting these cases together hurriedly; on the other, as a expert in profiling, Bin respected the profiles from the Bureau a lot — maybe too much. If I told him the consultant from the City Bureau has already made a profile, he wouldn't say a word about his own thoughts and would advise me to "follow the lead of the expert."

On December 17th last year, Miss Fang Wanlin, a so-called representative of public relations[1] from some karaoke bar was killed in a park in Zhichunlun Community at around three o'clock in the morning. Her throat was cut and the blood spurted out left an arc of nearly 120 degrees in front of her. The body was naked on the top with only a bra left. But she was not sexually assaulted.

Fang Wanlin, from a city in the north of China, came into the industry when she was 19 years old. She struggled a lot when she was assaulted. There were so many wounds caused by strike and knife. Her leather coat

---

1 Not a real representative of public relations. These are a group of girls who worked in a bar to drink and flirt with the guests, usually with sex service.

and the shirt inside were stripped into pieces. Thanks to these defensive wounds and marks, the police tried to get some skin flakes in her nails. After running a DNA test, the murderer was the same one with that who murdered Chi Shanshan in Changxin Building.

He Jingcheng also pointed out that the wound of Fang Wanlin shows that murder weapon is a clasp-knife with distinctive features — about 1cm blade on the tip and the rest serrated. The first half of the knife was no more than 10cm long, narrow in the front with a little bit of arc. The whole knife was no more than 22cm, and may be able to be self-locked. Since there's no mark left in the wound, it was reasonable to believe that the knife was made of high-carbon steel. ... All in all, it was a real good knife.

Hearing this, Bin asked Zhang Beitong to come and introduced, "See? We've got an expert in knifes here. He is even better than the guys in dangerous goods."

Dangerous Good Management Team is a group of police who confiscates and manages guns, knifes and explosives. They know no more than the standards of controlled tools and sales channels. In terms of knives themselves, lovers for knives may have much to say. I hurried to call the waiter and asked for a cigar. "Put it on my bill. Pay in cash."

Zhang Beitong waved a little his half Partagas Lusitanias at me as a sign of saying no to my attempt of spending 88RMB to buy him a cigar only worth less than 30RMB. "No knife can cut without being worn. It's just a problem of degree. This one is only a folding knife. It's just impossible to not leave a trace. The one you talked about should be a serrated one. It's like a saw, suitable for cutting meat, maybe good for person."

"Is the murderer likely to be an expert on using knives?"

"It's hard to tell. Maybe he learned from a master, or He himself possibly, or maybe he is a member of knife club, or maybe he is a retired soldier or police. It's possible that he used this knife to have a manicure frequently. It's also possible that he's just lucky to not leave a trace in the wounds. Who knows? It depends on the material of the knife, the things he cut and his own technique." Zhang Beitong took some puffs, the sweet amour of the cigar drifting around us. "In the case of attacking from a very short distance, even an expert can only have a relative idea about the position. There's no time for him to pay attention to the blade."

"Even if he's really good at it?"

"Yes. It just take minutes, even seconds, to stab a person or to be stabbed. When the knife gets close, a judgement must be made: stab or stroke? Step aside to avoid the attack or fight back? If you wait for the knife go into the muscles, no matter who you are, even Bruce Lee has no chance to win the fight! Like I said, if it's really urgent, no one would care about the knife. The fact that there's no trace of the weapon doesn't mean that the murderer is some expert on using knives. It's more about luck."

"How about the material? If it's high-carbon steel?"

"Since there's no fragments found, I cannot draw concrete conclusions. But in terms of its toughness, I'd like to say it's a low-carbon one."

"Why? Is that the more carbon there is in the steel, the better the steel is?"

"Well, rigidity and toughness are two factors of steel, but they are two contradicting and uniting sides of one coin. Knives of high-carbon steel are sharp and hard, but they are easy to break; the ones of low-carbon steel are more likely to be a folding knife, for example, a Butterfly or Spider."

Where did these two insects come from? Ah, they seemed to be some brand names.

"It's lucky for you. This kind of serrated knife between half serrated to whole serrated could be a Spider from Sipaiderke, or a Dragon from Cold Steel. But the latter is rarely seen on the market. It's too showy, not convenient to take so less people would like to use it. And the blade of a large Dragon should be longer than this ... This should be a Spider, or at least, a good fake of Spider."

Awesome! An expert is an expert! "So, how about the model number?"

"C07, C08, C11, C12, C21, C23, C24, C36, C51 ... They are all possible. Is there a big angel inside the tip? Yes? Then that's C08, C12 or C21. The blade of C12 is so thin that it's easy to break and difficult to sharpen. C21 ... Well, if you ask me, I think C08, Spyderco Harpy, is the most suitable one. And it is easy to use. That cannibal doctor in *The Silence of the Lambs*, he likes to use this knife. V10 is a whole steel one, and BK has a black plastic handle ... Anyway, no matter which one under this model, with scores of serration on the blade, it is a real good one."

"Is the sales channel available?"

"You can get one for around 1000RMB from almost anywhere. A good fake is even cheaper. Well, the advantage of online shopping is that you'll always find ways to get something that couldn't be sold on the market except for adult products. Some large online knife shops may be a good choice to start, or you can find some hacker to sneak and check the sales records of Sipaiderke. He can't just go to a vendor abroad and buy a knife there, right? Well, if he really did that, there's a lot of effort to make ..."

Somehow the way Zhang Beitong talks, his one hand waving with a cigar, reminded me of the mafia boss I met when I was a green hand — only that he was waving a hand with joint which can be recognized just by a sniff. He was wearing a black strip suit and a pair of sunglasses with square frame on his nose, sitting behind a desk in the largest shop of the Auto Parts Plaza and asking his errand boys to charge some protection fees or make some forced sales.

It was not until the other salesperson able to put up with him did they start to ask help from the police. When I came to arrest him with two senior officers, he was just sitting there, talking and bragging with the joint. I didn't remember his talk much, maybe something like "who are the cops" or "I'm not afraid".

When I rushed in, his only errand boy came out to protect him. Yes, only one. The others were all running and escaping after I gave him a blow and broke two of his ribs with a cuff in my hand. The boss, who looks like a blind then, took a paper knife from the desk and rushed at me over his only follower. My jacket boot make of cowhide with thick soled steel palm kicked him on the hand, making the paper knife broken into halves. The sharp blade reached his hand and cut his right thumb off.

Obviously, he didn't know knives as well as Zhang Beitong.

It was said that there were other bosses over this one and the five people and three knives waiting for me at the gate of Chaoyang Park were their pay back. I was at my twenties by then. A nightstick in my hand resulted in one minor injury and one serious, and two slight ones as well. But I was also hurt on my left arm. The one running away took all three knives, making the whole case a little bit ambiguous. Afterwards, therefore, it was rumored that the reason I was end up with reassigning to the Interrogation was a complete set up, and also that I was reassigned out of the boss's kindness, preventing me from being hurt by those desperadoes. Anyway, I had to give my gratitude to that reassignment, otherwise I wouldn't have had the chance to meet Xuejing and have a family.

A year later after I've been working in the Interrogation, I got a case about illegal selling of controlled knives. The suspect was strong and tough, and handsome as well. His pony tail and beard endowed him with something like a samurai in Japan. That man was Zhang Beitong. When I was questioning him, I found this man a frank and decent person. Of course, the handsome face of him wouldn't deprived me of my faith to the law system until the next day, I saw a man in black was having tea with my boss in his office ...

And through my boss, I knew he was the lawyer who came to bail Zhang Beitong out. That was Bin.

And after that, Bin and I became close friends. His father treated my as his own son and helped me to resign my job. We worked out the workshop together, and then the cafe ... And now, the former interrogator, suspect, lawyer and his classmate, the medical examiner could sat and played bridge together.

Although Zhang Beitong's lead was no better than searching a needle in a haystack, it was good enough to cheer me up to have a direction to search for the weapon. However back then, what I didn't know was that while we were sitting in the sofa in Fingerprint, chatting about the color, shape, model and price about a folding knife, and consuming several cigars, coffee, wine and dessert, the murderer was enjoying the convenience and thrill that the weapon brought to him.

Otherwise, I wouldn't laugh at all.

The next day. January 30th, Saturday.

In the afternoon, Zhang Yan took a bus and arrived at Zizhu Bridge. She was from Chongqing and worked in a small hair salon to the northeast of the bridge. She walked there, opened the door and a scary scene came into her sight. Xu Chunnan, her fellow townswoman, was tied onto a clothesline pole in the middle of the hallway. The body was nearly naked, and was described by Cao Fa, the first to arrive on the scene, in a self-styled humorous tone as "a pole dancing roasted suckling pig".

The victim was in her underwear. Her arms and legs were tied together to the pole with a electric wire from behind. Her limbs were embracing the pole in a reverse way, her head down and her face facing the door. The clothesline pole belonged to the salon and was used by the murderer. It was poked to a pot originally for a evergreen and the upper end was tied to the ceiling lamp.

I was among the second group who arrived at the scene. Before I stepped my foot on the salon, I saw Jiang Lan, who was on her first crime scene, running out from inside, weeping and vomiting. Cao Fa was after her with a bottle of water in hand, and filled me in with the body in a face that I want to beat on.

He Jingcheng stood by the door, with blood on his gloves. But he was one of the few who still got lunch saved in stomach. "Waiting for you ONLY. Come on and take a quick look. We are going to take the body."

A guy from the technical team gave me gloves and shoe covers at the door and asked if I wanted a mask. From the dull pupils of Xu Chunnan's body, which was just meters away from me, I saw a silhouette hooded by horror while I was adjusting myself to the stink from the inside. I wasn't able to accept it, and refused his proposal.

"We didn't touch anything except this one." Liu Qiang came out of the room and passed me an evidence bag. "The murderer cut her tongue and stuffed this in."

I glanced at the bag as if afraid of being burned. It was a train ticket. Another glance. It was Express T9 on January 13th, leaving at two o'clock in the afternoon from Beijing to Chongqing.

Ah, right. It was only five days before the Spring Festival.

If she didn't end up here, she should be in a crowded carriage with her big luggage, holing her savings in her inner pocket and waiting to get home. She could have been talking with passengers alongside about what she had done here in Beijing, or thinking about how to explain her past year to her family. But now, she was hanging right in front of me, head down to the ground. Even if we could free her right away, put her down and send her to the station, the train was long gone.

She couldn't have made it. She couldn't have come home.

"The victim was dead between 12 o'clock to 1 o'clock at night. She was probably died of excessive loss of blood, or choked because of the blood from the cut at the base of the tongue splitting into the windpipe and lungs. Maybe the reason the murderer put her upside down was to let the blood out, or maybe he just want to admire the posture." He Jingcheng was talking slowly, probably finding some words that wouldn't show any respect to her. "She was tortured for a while before death, maybe an hour or two. I didn't know ... But she has got four fingers broken, and her left wrist and right leg as well. Her clavicle was broken inside and the phalanx was injured much more badly. There were 61 visible cuts and the fatal one was on her throat. That is this horizontal one of almost 10cm, wound edge everted which is lucky, well, I mean, which means she's already been bleeding to death before."

I gave the evidence bag back to Liu Qiang and circled around to the back of the body to check, or at least, to avoid her eyes.

"There are too many wounds. You can wait for the autopsy report later on." He Jingcheng looked at the ceiling first, and then out of the window. "It is estimated that the suspect knocked in at about ten or eleven o'clock, beat her down, tied her up and cut her tongue. He raped, sodomized her or poked in with some other things. Most of the wounds were left during the rape, or at least while she was alive. The suspect seemed to enjoy the process of raping and hurting together. Before he was leaving, he took a shower with the bath in the inner room, may changed his clothes. We can find fingerprints, footprints, hair and seminal fluid on the scene, together 61 wounds resulted from Spyderco Harpy. If Mr. Zhang was right, it was that serrated knife he mentioned last night that leave her with all the wounds.

I left my eyes roaming around her body, scanning the 61 wounds all over her. Some were like crevices, some tooth marks, others the crack of a ripe watermelon. ... 61 wounds, 61 bloody mouths. They were laughing silently to the surrounding world in a evil and sick way on the cold dead body of Xu Chunnan.

I felt a little hard to breathe. "What the fuck ..."

"Freud once said that everyone's got a storage to store some sort of invasion energy, whose total volume was fixed but has to be released in some way at some time to make the person less offensive." Well, statement like this made me knew who's coming in no time. Dr. Yuan continued, "Unfortunately, she was the carrier of the invasion energy of some people this time. And if we couldn't catch that guy with Oedipus complex quick enough, there would be more ..."

Yuan Shi circled around to the face of the body and squatted down to gaze at it. "The murderer showed great power of control while he was releasing his temper — a marvellous power of control actually. He enjoys this kind of power, a power to manage life and death. The train ticket is his show of sympathy, only mockingly. The way of putting it in her mouth shows his value towards life — the unity of life and death — he wants the woman to die in hope. In his view, every living day is no other than a pace towards death. Nothing more, nothing less." He leaned forward, a sliver necklace slipping out from his collar. I remembered that Bin's got a similar one. Are the guys studying criminal psychology in favor of necklaces?

But I wasn't interested in the value of the murder at all. "You mean Oedipus complex?"

"Quite possible. According to ViCAP, Violent Criminal Apprehension Program, up to 71% serial killers who commit sexual crimes have Oedipus complex. For example Edmund Emil Kemper, the man who killed 11 people, he attributed all his crimes to his mother, and cut his mother's head and sodomize her body. And the other victims killed by him were just like Xu Chunnan's ..." Although he had gloves on his hands, he still drew a light blue napkin from his coat pocket. Touching the ghastly white face of the body on the other side of the napkin. He continued, "She's only the carrier of the invasion energy. This case is quite typical. Have your workshop studied something like this?"

I noticed that his necklace is a twisted circle with a pendant carved with "MS" down below, which probably means Moebius Strip, or may be a gift from a condom called Mirror Sex. A fragrance drifted out from him. The odor, mingled with the smell of blood, urine, sweat and fresh human flesh, made me finally feel sick.

He Jingcheng stepped forward to pull him aside, said with a decisive tone. "She were hanging here for more than ten hours. It's time to get her down. Guan, come and help."

Yuan Shi smiled generously and said nothing. He stood up and turned to me. "How's your interviewing going?"

Liu Qiang looked at me, clearly telling me to give a proper answer. But I've already bored with him and just said, "It's still going."

"Well, you'd better hurry up ... And I don't know if you've noticed, but she's also left-handed." He stretched his hand finger by finger and took off the gloves. "The cooling-off period gets shorter and shorter. I didn't want to kick the ball every time, but his next victim must be a left-handed male."

Cao Fa came in right in time, smelling like a cigarette in a ditch. "Hey Dr. Yuan. Thank you so much for coming! Would you like to have some water? It's so nice of you to come and help us."

Yuan Shi threw the gloves outside the door in the dustbin, his eyes still on the body. "Well, there were so many cases in our hands. I cannot come to help every time you call. You see, can you tell that Professor Han come back to help? As far as I know, he's good in all the experts here. And Dr. He, you might pay more attention to the knots the murderer tied ..."

"Your advice is very much appreciated. You know what? The last kidnap case? The suspect was exactly the same as you described." Ca Fa continued his flattering, but didn't get any feedback. He turned to me and Liu Qiang, "Zhao... Commander Liu, Team Two's interview has got us something. This place hasn't been registered. It's illegal. And it's said that Zhang Yan and the victim were all prostitutes and this time, they just ran into someone who didn't want to pay. Maybe that's the murderer. Well, it sounds harsh, but what I mean is ..."

In face, neither Liu Qiang nor me gave him any feedback, only He Jingcheng yelled him to go away while they were moving the body out.

"Well, it's nothing." I said to Cao Fa, but looked at the expert from the City Bureau. "She's not able to talk back anyway, is she?"

Bin once told me long ago that what a serial killer needs most was luck.

"No matter how well he plans, luck would always cost him everything."

Unfortunately, we happened to meet one with perfect luck. His plans were not flawless at all, but his luck surely was.

The marks left on the scene showed that the murderer has killed at least three people. Or exactly, three young left-handed young ladies. But no one has even seen him, not even his back, let alone his face.

And more unfortunately, Bin has no interest in this case at all. His reason was simple. "I don't have a left-handed in my family." No potential suspects, nor potential victim.

Bin wasn't a cruel man, nor was he a person who only focused on himself. He might have many concerns, including his influence on me, the relationship between him and his father, and the possible contradiction between his profile and the Dr. Yuan's. But if you ask me, I'd say his laziness was the primary reason.

And the most unfortunate was that Xu Chunnan, who died in a most miserable way, might be just like Chi and Fang, being the victim of a cold case. We've got fingerprints, footprints, DNA and the murder weapon, but there's no one for us to interview and investigate. It seemed that the lord didn't mean to let any criminal convicted and serve their time, or the fact that law is enacted was a violence to His almighty power. Anyway, there must be one thing missing, either evidence or the suspect,

The more I started to deal with actual cases, the more urgent did I feel to have a proper position. I was only a detective. Working in the Eastern Team for such a long time, I didn't came across big difficulties in asking my former team member to do something. But whenever I needed people from other team, I had to ask Commander Liu to negotiate for me. Even for a communication line, I had to ask the current captain to apply it for me, let alone hastening the technical team.

Obviously, I can't have Liu Qiang with me all day long for my own convenience. So, I went to Bai to apply for a proper position for all the jobs.

I thought that he was going to give me a temperate position or some promises like "If you solve this case, I'll make you a caption" since we've worked together for so many years and he was once my master. But Bai was like a man who had just eaten a hedgehog for lunch, talking in an acerbic tone. "What? All the boys are working hard here. What makes you deserve a promotion? Even if I promise you that, the bureau won't grant it. Go on with your work!"

As I was about to leave, Bai stopped me and asked me about the progress of the case, which was quite rare. "How about that dead kid in Xiaoyue Rive?"

I told him we've found the murderer, but without any evidence, we wouldn't dare to move.

"How about the others?"

Well, this one was quite the opposite. We've got so many evidences, but no suspects.

Jiang and I have been working for several late nights to search for the missing records of recent years. However, we didn't found many left-handed there, nor in the victims of the cases that have been solved in recent years. So, first of all, this one was probably a "green hand". but if his luck continued, he may well became a "rising star". And second, the victims of the serial cases were all left-handed, whose probability was almost the same as the lucky draw. Although there were male victims and female victims, we could not exclude the fact that Dr. Yuan has proposed: the murderer didn't mind the gender of the victim. He killed them all.

"And also, that robbing gang was arrested last night, and they even had someone riding an electromobile! You'll have the report this afternoon." Suddenly, I wanted to try my luck once again. "Well, if the bureau agrees my promotion, would you let me?"

It seemed my words surprised my Bai. He didn't lift his head to look at me, but his attention was clearly not on the files. "Go and ask Zhou Hongruo? Is that your idea?"

Although I did meet with Zhou Hongruo once, but she was the future Deputy Director. Would she be easily persuaded by my words? I didn't know. But I still answered, "Well, I don't what to embarrass you. I 'll go and ask her. If not, it's better to put me back on street raids. At least more efficient than solving these ones."

Bai didn't respond. He just waved at me, which was a silent agreement.

I didn't go to find Zhou Hongruo after a long time. It was not because I believed my luck was better than that serial killer who hated left-handed so much. Maybe deep in my heart, I hoped Zhou Hongruo would refused me in no time, giving me a chance to walk away from these cases.

Being a criminal policeman for so many years, it was the first time that I began to get bored with my job. Being a policeman meant I cannot just beat Su Zhen to half death, or just castrated Zhang Mingkun, which would be fun if I can. This was what made my job harder. Laws and regulations were fetters. They wouldn't let you do what you want, even if you were Monkey King. At least I couldn't since every time I tried to do things out of the book, I would find myself surrounded by several Tang Monks murmuring about dos and don'ts.

Compared with that, keeping street orders was as simple as snapping fingers.

I often talked with Xuejing about my cases before sleeping, and describing or imagining details of the case in my head. Fan Jiajia was helpless as she was seduced and raped ever since she was six years old; Wang Xianping looked extremely panic when she saw Su Zhen's ferocious face in strong wind; Chi Shanshan disappeared in the dark staircase with her silver earrings; Fang Wanlin crossed the park in her leather pants, her hips swinging ... And at last, I would remember the silhouette in Xu Chunnan's pupils. It was me, but not me. I saw myself drinking a cup of coffee, a train ticket with blood on it floating on the surface ... I was startled to wake up at dawn, or woken up by Xuejing. But I was not drenched in sweat, not like someone waking from a nightmare, only a sense of empty and horror brought by falling stall hovering around me.

And the most importantly, in the morning on Spring Festival eve, I paid a visit to Zhou Hongruo to wish her a happy Chinese New Year and asked her by the way. To my surprise, she didn't even ask me any questions before saying yes. It was on my way back to the division did I realize that I was a complete tool in the whole case. Zhou Hongruo and Bai Yinshang were only using me to sound out. Zou's promotion of me was just a move to show some kindness before climbing onto a higher position, and a public rival show to Bai. But what did it concern me? I was only a tool, a gun. Only if I was pointing at the bad guy, it didn't matter to me who's holding it.

He Jingcheng came to find me at noon, asking me about the arrangements of the workshop party. We sat by the desk, holding the calender and the duty schedule, checking, and finally finding that only the second and the forth day of the new year could be spared.

"Well, if you have to visit your uncle on the forth, then the second is also fine. I'll ask Mr. Zhang to help arrange the place and the members ... can come whoever have time." He Jingcheng took out his phone to text messages. "Ah, and there's another thing. Bin said to tell him the time when we've settled. He's coming."

That was abnormal. Bin would always put his families first. "Is he coming to give out red packets?"

He Jingcheng hesitated a bit and said, "Well, he's still thinking about the Xiaoyue River case. You can talk with him on the party."

After such a long time? Interesting.

"Zhang Mingkun doesn't tell, and there's not enough evidence. There's not much I can do." I thought of his words when Xu Chunnan got killed and asked, "Hey, you've said once that if Zhang Mingkun were the murderer, and then what?"

"What?" He gave me a glance and continued typing the keyboard. I didn't respond, but he seemed to remember what he had said. "Ah, I've said that he's a dead man."

"What does that mean."

114

"It means that Bin will help you find a way to let him tell."

I was more curious. "Why was he so interested in this one?"

"Because the murderer chose a wrong place to throw the body away. Xiaoyue River was Bin's sanctuary."

He and Bin were classmates at college. He probably knew a lot about his past. "Don't tell me Bin was baptized by the water in Xiaoyue River."

"Well, more or less. He began his first love there."

I started my imagination again. "Is that the place he made his first love?"

He frowned a little bit towards my imagination. "I didn't know the details. But he has attached much importance to that place. That's for sure. Before Yichen came, he would go there alone whenever he has time to spare, standing still like a ghost."

I tried to sketch Bin's figure standing by the river, but the picture was soon covered by numerous falling train tickets.

"So? Whoever doing bad things there should be haunted by a ghost?"

"I was thinking that Yichen can save him from the past. But from his reaction in this case, it didn't work out. Well, this Zhang Mingkun hasn't made a good choice..."

"Why dump the body in Xiaoyue River?"

What did Bin look like when he made that comment? Probably cruel and indifferent ... Did he ever sound to be sad or angry? No. Nothing special. But it was not something he would say, not in that tone.

The tone in that comment, I must have heard about it, more than once.

4

It was a good day.

Compared with an azure and clear sky, I liked this one more. Lots of clouds, without layers, cut the sky into patches of blue color. There was wind so the clouds were moving, making the sun in and out now and then. It was confusing enough to let people wonder whether the cloud was moving or the sun was sinking.

"The clouds are a bit low. Maybe it's going to snow." Bing came to the window. I smelled smoke.

He was wearing a white shirt with brown dots, and a dark blue sweater vest, making him brighter than ever. It was rare to see him in a color bright like this. He was always in dark colors, which, according to his own explanation, was because he took after his father and was dark in complexion. Dark color could make him look better.

Actually he was not unsightly to look at in colors like this, but more clean and bright. In fact, I couldn't even recall a day that he looked unclean. There was no stubble on his face, no hair sticking out from his nose, nor dirty nails, scurf or dirty shirts or collars with sweat stains... Cao Fa was a real scuzz compared with him."

He passed me a cup of grapefruit tea. "What's wrong with you lately? Xuejing worried a lot."

I turned around. Everyone was having fun in the cafe, only Xuejing casting a glance to us. "These people see you as a precious panda these days. Why not go and have gun with them."

Bin put a glass ash tray on the windowsill. "Xuejing said you haven't been well these days. What's wrong? Work? Or cases?"

Well, it was the goddam train ticket.

"Not one of the cases solved these days." I gave a hard blow to the cup. "Cai Ying's dead. Su Zhen had gone. Du Yang was guilty but he's not our guy. Zhang Mingkun just doesn't tell, and that psychopath who kill women ... None of them has been taken in. They can also enjoy this festival, watching CCTV New Year's Gala, having dumplings as their dinner and all ... They've taken others' lives! But they can still enjoy their life."

Bin gave a slight massage on his nose, but I could still tell that he's laughing.

"It's true that I'm not a graduate from college and new to work, nor am I some pioneer or executor who wants to protect the law. But once I thought of them, these people who can avoid the punishment form the law, I'm pissed off! Totally and literally pissed off!"

He took my cup and took a small sip, seemingly to prove the tea was not hot, and gave it back to me. "No one could run away from punishment. If there's none from the outside, there's surely some from the inside. Why are you torturing yourself?"

I took a big drink and mopped my mouth with the back of my hand. "Yes! You're right! Everybody has to pay their debts and it's not my business to care about. Justice will eventually prevail and before that, we could just take it easy, enjoy our lives, maybe having some coffee, talking, laughing and playing bridge ... just like what we did on the night Xu Chunnan died!"

Bin always chose to be silent when I lost my temper. I knew all the rules, and he wouldn't waste his effort to comfort me. But today, I hoped he would say something, anything to continue the conversation.

He didn't let me down. He asked back, "Do you believe the butterfly effect?"

"What?"

116

"The butterfly effect. It means that when a butterfly flutters her wings in Beijing, in America..."

"The World Trade Center is hit by a plane, right? Yes, I do!"

Bin was looking outside the window, but there was no plane.

"Yes. I believe it. If there were to be someone ripped its wings, maybe less people would die at 9·11, or the one hijacked the plane were Ladin himself, or nothing would happen at all. Who knows?!" I was getting more agitated.

Bin turned around to lean on the windowsill, gazing me for a while, and said, "Well, the so-called butterfly effect would only affect details, never the trend. No matter what happened, Xue Chunnan cannot avoid her fate. You were playing cards that night, she was stabbed 61 wounds; you were working, there maybe 60 wounds, or 59 wounds, and of course, there also might be 610 wounds, or she's not to be stabbed, but another woman ... After all, that is a serial killer. He wants to kill and he is going to do it. You can't stop it."

"But he has no right to kill. Nor anyone else. Xu Chunnan was not supposed to die, even if she's a whore."

Bin's finger was tapping on the window, making a small sound. "Several days ago, a female politician in Pakistan was shot. She was at a ball and someone just came out and gave her two shots, and then the explosives were detonated.

"Err ... I have to admit that as a woman, being a whore is as dangerous as being a politician, but ..."

"There were thousands of people on the scene. Not only the target and the killer died."

I shook my head but couldn't deny his opinion. "No matter who you are ..."

"No matter who you are." Bin lighted his cigarette up and exhaled the smoke full of nicotine. "No one can stop people hurting people."

Bin, I don't like you like this. I don't like you to be cold — cold after understanding and tolerance.

"I haven't told you anything about the case. Why are you so clear?"

"It was me. I told him. I'm the one to blame." He Jingcheng was siting not far from us, eating something in his plate. I didn't thought that he's got such good hearing, nor did I know why I can ask such a strange question.

Bin patted me on the shoulder and we moved near He together. "Well, it seems that I don't need an alibi. On the night Xu Chunnan was killed, I was playing bridge with my partner, my classmate and you, Mr. Zhao, who is questioning me now. Dr. He, can you testify for me?"

I noticed that He would first cut a Y on the omelet when he ate the omelet rice. The Y was neat and clean.

Bin blinked. "Well, does that mean I misremembered the case and He wasn't there that night, right?"

"You two," He wiped his knife clean, pointed at me and said, "Still have time for these bullshits? There's a case waiting for us!"

Feeling Bin was going to talk, I took over hurriedly. "So far, the serial killer who has three women killed was the most important. Chi Shanshan died in Chang Xin Building in October last year, Fang Wanlin died in Zhichunli Community Park in December and Xu Chunnan several days ago ... Well, you haven't seen the autopsy report, have you? He, come and tell him where you found the tongue of the body in medical examination."

Holding a spoon at hand, He looked a little sick. "Didn't you see I'm having my dinner?"

"This is a Jack the Ripper." Bin seemed to have no interest in the details, so I let He Jingcheng continue with his meal. "At least with the same behavioral pattern. Nichols[1] may be the target, either tailed or randomly selected, and Tabram[2] should be OK if you say so. But Kelly[3] was killed in her house, just like Chi Shanshan and Xu Chunnan. He goes from a certain area he's familiar with to invading the victim's home. It's just like Jack, right?"

"Well, if you put it like this, they commit the crime in a similar way. Nichols's abdomen was partly ripped open by a deep, jagged wound, causing her bowels to protrude and Kelly was completely out of shape; there were four wounds on Chi Shanshan, but 61 on Xu Chunnan, almost like The Black Dahlia[4]." He cut in, but didn't stop eating. "The murderer was getting more familiar with the weapon, and more cruel as well. Jack was OK. He is a typical model."

"Yes, quite typical. Many serial perpetrators of rape are like that." I took out a cigarette and put the case on the table. "So I don't think he

---

1 Mary Ann Nichols, female, was killed on August 31st 1888 in Buck's Row. Some people believe she was the first one that Jack the Ripper killed.

2 Martha Tabram, female, was killed on a staircase landing in George Yard, Whitechapel, on August 7th 1888. Some people believe she was the first one that Jack the Ripper killed.

3 Mary Jane Kelly, female, was discovered lying on the bed in the single room where she lived at 13 Miller's Court, off Dorset Street, Spitalfields, at 10:45 a.m. on November 9th 1888. Her face had been "hacked beyond all recognition", with her throat severed down to the spine, and the abdomen almost emptied of its organs. She was the fifth victim of the Whitechapel case and the last one.

4 Elizabeth Ann Short, female, was an American woman who was found murdered in the Leimert Park neighborhood of Los Angeles, California on January 15th 1947. She was probably murdered on January 14th. The body was bisected at the waist and badly damaged. Since she liked to wear black so the case was nicknamed as "Black Dahlia". Her murder is frequently cited as one of the most famous unsolved murders in American history.

is copycatting some Jack, John, Daniel or Tom, or anyone else. He just learned from them. You've used a term when you translate *Classification of Crimes and Offences*. What was that?"

Bin's lips didn't even move at all while he was talking. "The dynamic progress of criminal behaviour."

"Yes. Dynamic progress. He learned from the past. Well, what if I were to learn that hard in my twenties. It's strange that he had left so many traces in different scenes but was not seen by anyone, any surveillance camera or other cameras. Now all we know is that he is a left-handed man over 1.8m and likes to use a folding knife called Spider or similar to Spider. That's all. And someone even tell us to search and monitor all left-hands in Haidian District! That's hundreds of thousands of people! It may be much easier that He jingcheng finds a bone from the omelet rice!"

"That's because he doesn't have a criminal record so it's unable to get any information from the Internet. He cannot reveal himself even if he wanted to." He Jingcheng cut the omelet completely open and continue with his rice. "That's not enough to say he's not cautious or he's insane. He's been improving his criminal technique, being more confident, and more calm."

Bin looked around, and nodded until we finished our discussion. "What you've said just now, the angels you've pointed out, are they practical?"

"What?"

"Will the fact that the murderer has similar MO with Jack, or Holmes, or Chikatilo, Ridgway or Dahmer[1] help you in finding him? I've seen several cases with serial killers, but none of them got the same suspect."

Fuck! We've all violated the primary principle of criminal profiling. We were too academical!

"And also, the psychopath who committed crime in Whitechapel a hundred years ago was not going from a area he's familiar with to the area the victim's familiar with. He's just like the one you're looking for. They are all typical, simple serial killer who commit crimes within their own areas. It's just the place they invade is somewhere they can feel psychologically safe. There's someone who never committed crimes outside the Whitechapel area, and there's also someone only commits crimes with Haidian District. Why? Because they live there." Bin put his thumb and index finger on his chin. "It's probably because I'm lack of patience, but I've listened to your discussion long enough. Let me ask you,

---

1 Henry Howard Holmes, Andrei Romanovich Chikatilo, Gary Leon Ridgway and Jeffrey Lionel Dahmer are all famous serial killers in criminal history.

have you noticed anything special about the location of the crime scene?"

Somewhere he felt psychologically safe!

"You are now 'playing' with the case. Of course, all those scholars and researchers do the same job. But you — " Bin lifted his eyebrows to me. "You are a policeman. You need to solve the case, not to play with it. Goddammit! What would they learn from you in the workshop? It's just beyond my imagination."

I had my two hands raised to surrender. "I've let you down and I'm sorry about that. This son of bitch committed these three crimes in the place he's familiar with. I should have noticed that long ago. Well, it we put it like this, these three places should be where he worked, lived and regularly visited. We should interview more people around them and look for a strong, tall and left-handed man ..."

Bin cut in once more. He put his left index finger in the grapefruit tea and wrote an "idiot" on the table. And then, he switched his watch onto his right wrist and said, "Does that men I'm left-handed?"

Well, I got his idea immediately. He could impersonate a left hand, so could the murderer a right hand. This was not difficult to do.

I turned to He. He was still struggling with his food, but with a slower speed. Clearly, he wouldn't want to be by my side under Bin's comment.

"Then ... what other directions do we have ..."

"Three women dead. Did you know about them?"

"We've done some background research. But the latter two were both whores ... er ... working in sexual industry. So it's hard to ...

"No. That's not what I'm talking about." Bin lowered hid head and heaved a sigh. "A white-collar worker, a whore, and a so-called hairdresser. Up until now, I've only heard three names out of your mouth. You wouldn't talk about them like what you've done to introduce your girlfriend or sisters. If you can't know more about them than the murderer, you've have to count on your luck on solving the case."

I sat still with my mouth open, lighting up the cigarette unconsciously. He put down his knife and spoon and exhaled deeply. "I'm stuffed. And there's no bones."

"Fan Jiajia's case is not in our hands." Bin finally asked me about that case that night. I told him all that I know. "The suspect was too old, and doesn't tell. We didn't have any evidence and cannot force him. So ... Well, boss told us to pay more attention on that serial killer. That case, we can take it easy. Maybe some new evidence will turn out in the future, maybe not. Who knows."

Bin listened to my explanation attentively and silently. There was no disappointment on his face.

"I'm sorry. He told me about your story. I was going to clean the riverside for you. I'm really sorry about that."

He frowned a bit, a lighter turning upside down between his fingers, as if asking: What did he tell you?

I shrugged — He told me everything.

Bin lowered his head, his mind seeming a little bit wandering. "What kind of evidence do you need to convict the suspect?"

"Well, the most practical one till now was the confession of that old crap." And of course, after our effort, we knew that's also the most impractical.

"As long as he made a confession, described what he had done, identify the scene and gave out his weapon. With all that plus the forensic evidence, we can convict him"

Xuejing had a night shift so she left before the party's over. Later on, the others also left consequently. There was only Bin, Yichen and I. Bin waved to the counter and told Yichen to help Mr. Zhang to collect things and tidy the place.

"If there's a way to let him confess. Can you take him down?"

"Well, that will be the most welcome."

Bin looked up at me, and then lowered his head again. "You're not on duty today, aren't you? Did you bring your cuffs with you?"

He would come to help! I was much more delighted. "I've got them in the car. Can you make him confess?"

"No, I can't." It seemed that he wanted to make a joke, but changed his idea. "I can only disable his psychological defense. Take you record book and cuffs, officer. You'll be the one to make him confess."

"Criminal psychology! That's the fucking criminal psychology!"

Bin looked at him from his side mirror while driving. "What?"

I noticed Yichen's hand was on Bin's hand on the gear lever, then I recalled that Bin didn't like others speaking rudely in front of his "sister".

"Sorry about that." I leaned forward. "I was thinking that why criminal psychology was nothing in my hand, but everything in yours. No. That's not right. You must have hidden something from your bro, haven't you?"

"I'm only going to ask him some questions. The results are difficult to tell."

"That's why you don't want me to call the office? Come on! Don't be shy! What's your secret? Come on and tell me."

"Well, secrets are always carved in some mysterious caves and castles. I don't have any." Bin put his left hand on the steering wheel, but his mind seemed to be on the other one. "Psychological tactics cannot be used in arresting others. They can only be used to break the old psychological fortress or build new communication channel. Or we can say it's a wand, and works on those who are evil."

"Wow! Come on Harry Potter! But why do I feel it's also effective to me?"

Bin and Yichen laughed together.

But I felt they may laugh for different reasons. So I asked, "Why laughing?"

"That's because you've got evil in your heart." Bin touched gently on Yichen's head, looking at me through the mirror. "But living in a era like this, who doesn't?"

It was not my illusion. The corner of his left eye was twitching unnaturally. I had a vague feeling that something was wrong. As his close friend, I knew him very much. He has never showed any unconscious expressions or gestures before.

I looked into him from the back. "How would you gonna ask him?"

"Eysenck Personality Questionnaire or Rorschach Test." Not surprisingly, he replied half-jokingly. "Or the Minnesota Multiphasic Personality Inventory. I don't know, but I can try."

His breathing was steady, he spoke at a normal pace, and he made no small movements.

"I'm serious. What are you going to ask him?"

"I haven't seen him yet. How can I know?"

"It looks as if it's going to snow. ... Well, let's pull over here. It's across the road." I looked outside the winder and recalled what he said: Why dump the body in Xiaoyue River?

I imitated his tone, as if recalling this familiarity. "Why dump the body in Xiaoyue River?"

"What?" Bin was telling Yichen to lock the door and wait for us in the car, probably not catching me clearly, or not expecting something like this from my mouth.

He didn't say anything after we left the car. We walked side by side to the overpass in the east, but I got my hunch stirring in my head.

It was near midnight. Bin left Yichen alone in the car only to help me to catch some bad guy. Why? He has always avoid being involved in cases. It was the first time that he was so attentive.

It started to rain when we stepped onto the overpass. At first I thought it was fog, and then I noticed it was snow, or something between a fogdrop and a snowflake.

"What would you do? What psychological tactic? I'm telling you that old crap was a real fox. I've questioned him several times, and each time I found myself more at a loss. Don't play mysterious. Share with me."

"It's snowing." Bin held up his hand, his palms up, the corner of his eye twitching again. "The second day of the new year... Well, today is Major Cold[1]. It is really cold today."

I stopped at the west of the overpass our of surprise.

It was not because he didn't answer my question, nor because I suddenly got my logic back, or there were snowflakes falling into my collar, which startled me up. I didn't know the reason, or maybe it was because all of these reasons came together to make me feel something strange. It was like I had a stranger standing by my side, or I a familiar friend standing afar.

Watching his back, I almost blurted out without thinking. "Stop there!"

Bin did stop there.

"You want to kill Zhang Mingkun, don't you?"

"Yes. I wanted to kill O.J. Simpson, Alan Dershowitz and Johnnie Cochran as well. I wanted to shoot the referee and the whole German team when Argentina was knocked out of the World Cup last year. Yes, that's true. If he were to be the criminal, I hoped him to die." He turned around, looking really relaxed, as if there's no need to be secretive about such matters. "Don't you want him to die, Xincheng?"

I ...

I looked up. Numerous gray flakes were falling down from the dark sky. Thin ice crystals fell onto my face and were immediately evaporated by the heat of my body, turning into water and then ice again by the cold wind. A scene from *Schindler's List* came into my mind out of no reason: Day and night the incinerators in the concentration camps devoured the bodies of the Jews, the ashes of their flesh and soul scattering on every corner of the neighboring town.

If Zhang Mingkun had really thrown his granddaughter into Xiaoyue River, what would Fan Jiajia be like now? In the setting winter sun, the water from the river would go into the sky, and then fell on the cheeks of passersby, leaving marks like tears and telling people the cold fact that she's already dead.

Quite similar. I could even smell the odor from that little hair salon in the air.

Yes, I did. I hope every criminal gets what they deserve.

---

1 The traditional East Asian calendars divide a year into 24 solar terms. Major Cold, or Dahan in Chinese, is the 24th solar term. It is believed that day is the coldest day of the whole year.

"You really want to kill him..."

"Not so much that I could commit a crime right in front of a criminal police." Bin smiled a bit, without any hint of defiance, seduction or coaxing. "I'm just coming to help you get his confession."

"So what do you want do say to him?"

"Ask him about his first masturbation or curse a spell. Anything that can make him confess. Where's the building? ... Ah, this is Building No.1, right?" He pointed to a building on the east side of the overpass facing the street. "Room 611 should the first window on the sixth floor, but the one from the left or the right? Well the room is dark. Has he gone to bed?"

I let out a white breath, blowing the snowflakes everywhere. "It's better that you stay here. Tell me your spell. I'll be Harry Potter this time."

Bin's smile disappeared for a second. "Do you really worry that I would take out a knife to cut him in pieces?"

"You won't. You are not stupid as that. I don't believe you'll actually kill, but even if you will, you won't do it in a wrong place at a wrong time and with such clumsy moves."

"Killing is killing. The result is the most priority. There's no good kill or bad kill." He looked at me with a naughty smile. "But that's a complement, isn't it?"

So hard to tell ...

"Anyway, you stay here. Tell me what to ask him and I'll do it. It's nice if I can get an answer; if not I'll also accept as it is." I chose to believe my hunch. I said it in a firm way, without any room for meditation.

The snow was getting harder, landing on Bin's head and coat, covering it with silver frost. Bin put his hands in his pocket. Although there was a slight smile on his face, I still knew my distrust had offended him a lot.

"It's up to you. But ..." He talked to me gently, but his eyes became cold and cruel. "If I really want to kill him, you cannot even stop me."

I walked pretty slow. The floor was wet and I was in a doubt. I pondered and pondered, feeling strange about Bin's statement.

"Special sexual orientations didn't occur all of a sudden. They all have a process. You don't have to ask whether Zhang Mingkun had done anything to Fan Jiajia. You don't even have to tell him that you're coming because of his granddaughter's case."

"Right. I just come to pay a visit to wish him a happy Chinese New Year, am I? At midnight at his door. "

"Well, you can just pick any excuse. For example, tell him the statutory time limitation of criminal cases. The statutory time imitation of death penalty and life imprisonment is twenty years. But for the ones have to be prosecuted after twenty years, they can be prosecuted after the case is verified by the the Supreme People's Procuratorate. And statutory rape is a felony that can be sentenced for over ten years, life imprisonment and death penalty."

"You're really familiar with your business. Then what?"

"You can tell him that the police is questioning Fan Jiajia's parents and his daughter just spilled the beans, telling the police about the things he had done decades ago. And his son-in-law were so angry that wanted to come and beat him to death. The police controlled him for now so you're coming to verify with him. You can work out the details yourself. Anyway, you have to make him feel that if he wants to live longer, prison is the better choice."

"Wait. You mean you want me to con him with his raping of his own daughter and forced him to admit that he killed his granddaughter? Is that gonna work?"

"Don't worry. As long as you tell him these and add some details, I'm sure you'll get something from him."

"But what if he hadn't done that with his daughter? That's the big premise of our bluffing."

"He must have done it. Believe me. He must have."

The more I thought about that, the more I felt unsure about his saying. I turned around, and saw Bin walking down from the stairs, calling someone on the phone.

For now, the first thing to do should be discussing more details about this little trick , but I felt like I should trust Bin more. After all, from what I've experienced, he had never failed in things like this.

But that kind of uneasy feeling was still lingering on me. I tried to tidy my thoughts up while walking, hoping to find out what I was worrying about. Was that the place being on the juncture of Haidian and Xicheng? That would be no big problem. How about Zhang Mingkun not even listening to me? Well, I was confident that I could control the situation. The worst would be getting nothing from him. But that was no big deal. ... I suddenly realized that I was lingering around, looking back to Bin subconsciously, again and again.

Bin seemed to hang up the phone, but rang another set of numbers again.

Wait! Who was he calling at such a time at night.

And his special attention to the case, the twitching left eye corner, his public aversion to the suspect, his sayings that didn't make any sense, and ...

"Why dump the body in Xiaoyue River?"

Standing in snow and chill, his tone was so familiar to me.

It was when I was first reassigned to the Interrogation Office. I had to sit in on court for criminal cases in order to know their basic procedures. All judges, no matter male or female, would sit behind the table and talk like this — the same tone with Bin.

The only difference was that if Bin wanted to give a verdict of guilty, he wouldn't have to, and didn't need to obey any form of legal regulations, even Zhang Mingkun ... No. Zhang Mingkun couldn't have raped his own daughter. Never!

I was really blocked by habitual thinking, or rather by my habitual trust and dependence to Bin. If Zhang Mingkun's daughter had been sexually assaulted by her own father, how could she send her daughter to live with him? No mother would ever do something like that!

I looked at Bin, clouds lowering in the snowstorm pressing me out of my breath.

Bin was still making the phone call by his car. He could saw me walking back with anger. I wiped my eyebrows off the snow with great strength, several questions echoing in my confusing mind: Why were you lying to me? What was the lie for? Were you really happy to see me running around like an idiot?

I tried to calm down. Even from a long distance I could still see his face. He was laughing. It was not some imagination after my shame and anger. He was laughing, behind the white snow fog, vague but clear. He was indeed laughing.

The closer I reached the east end of the overpass, the clearer I could see his expression. Yes, he was laughing, not with his mouth but with his eyes. Those eyes expressed his thought completely — he can challenge us all and he can win the game. The activities in my head, though short, still slowed me down: No, Bin was not like that. He wouldn't show his evil enjoyment in such a naked way, especially when it was obtained by lying to his friend. ... No, as far as I know, he was nobler than that.

He was not looking at me.

I stopped and turned around like a shuttle runner. Behind me, the light in Room 611, Building 1, Tayuan East Street Community, which is the light in the first window on the sixth floor from the north of the apartment building, was opened.

Oh my God!

"Hey!" I shouted at him and ran to his place. Something's gonna happen. Bin made some effort to send me away and called the suspect that he "hoped" to die. It was sure that something's gonna happen!

Bin didn't respond. He walked around the car and opened the door of the front passenger seat to call Yichen out. And at the same time, I felt a slight strange noise somewhere behind me.

Before I turned around, I guessed what I would see. The light in Room 611 was open, and the window as well. Zhang Mingkun, short and thin, was standing by the window in his sleepwear, with one hand holding the handset and the other the telephone. He looked small but was eye-catching in a black and white world. I could feel his tremble even standing down below.

And I was finally sure about my anticipation. Bin wanted him to die.

After that, I made a fatal mistake unconsciously or subconsciously. I ran back, to the direction of Building 1, Tayuan East Street Community, which made me a helper to the following case. During my running less than tens of meters, Zhang Mingkun jumped from the window of Room 611, in a speed quite discordant with the surroundings, like a broken kite.

Maybe I haven't expected the accident, or maybe I knew what would happen the first step I made, or maybe I just didn't want to face the reality alone, or maybe I didn't want to be constrained by any rules or regulations ... Or maybe I chose to believe. I believed that, at that moment, what floating down from the sky was the tears of that poor girl.

Or maybe, I had the same idea with Bin. I hoped him to die.

From the stiffness when I turned around and my numb feet, I knew I must have stood there for a very long time. I didn't know the exact time because up until I turned around, I still felt dark, cold and empty, just like this night.

Bin has already walked to somewhere close to me, hands in his pockets. He asked, "Shall I call 120[1] or 110[2]?"

He talked calmly as usual, without a slice of sneer, complacent, excitement, compunction, worry or fear... He was just like what he looked like when he was holding a cup of bourbon infused coffee. Nothing, nothing indicated his thoughts just now. He was just like others, like us all.

I frowned a little and walked slowly to him, reaching my left hand to his right wrist. "Well, He Jingcheng was right ..."

"What?"

While he was waiting for me to continue, I've reached my right hand to cut on his left elbow and my left hand was breaking his left wrist to

---

1 For emergency medical services.

2 For the police.

the opposite direction. Pressing his neck through his back, I reached out both arms to pull him near me and tried to trip him with my left leg. But it didn't work out. He turned around and tripped me instead with his left leg. And then he lowered his back and threw me out. He didn't use much effort and even pulled me back a little maybe afraid of me falling down.

At that moment, I learned at least two things: First, no matter out of disappointment or guilt, I was really angry at that exact moment; and second, Bin knew how to release from holds.

"That's good, Mr. Han!" I kept my balance with one of my elbows supporting me on the cold rails, and the other hand reached out to snatch his hand that was reached out to pull me back. "Let's have a try!"

Bin moved his arms to get rid of me and stepped back a little. "Yichen can see us in the car. Do you really want to have a try with her present?"

Well, when he talked about this, I didn't have anything to do.

Every friend of Bin knew that he loved his little girlfriend very much. He was mild and gentle at all times, expect for us talking about something dirty or vulgar in front of his girlfriend. He would even turn his face over just because we spoke rudely with her present, let alone I should want to fight with him. Although I didn't get any advantage by knocking him cold, I was still confident in taking him down. Well, I was just unwilling to break up with my best friend due to a sudden wrath.

I stepped towards him, hands in fist, and asked, "Were you calling Zhang Mingkun just now?"

Bin took a look at the window with lights on. "Shall me go and see the falling guy? May be we can still ..."

"Answer my question! Did you just give Zhang Mingkun a call?" I lifted my hand to take his collar, but held my move halfway. "Don't redirect! I can pull your record from the cellphone company. Don't you try to trick me again!?"

It seemed that he didn't understand why I was asking this. But he still answered, "Yes. Why?"

"How did you get his number?"

"The case file ..."

"Bullshit! You didn't even read the file! You've only read the autopsy report. His phone number is not there."

Bin put one arm on my shoulder, his voice lowering down. "Do you think you are the only police I know?"

He pressed me a little with his hand, but not with much effort. However, it was enough to relax my stiffness. I began to feel disappointment welling up in my heart. "You've killed him ..."

Bin shook his head slightly. "I didn't. I just called him. The gravity killed him."

I pushed away his hand. "It isn't funny. What did you say, Bin? You forced him into suicide?"

"I just told him that Officer Zhang Xincheng was coming to question him, sort of a notice in advance." He stepped back and put his hands back in his pockets. "As for the reason why he wanted to see you so much that he even chose to be closer to you by free fall, I had no clue."

"Gravity and free fall ... Ha!" I leaned on the railing and heaved a long breath, snowflakes wafting violently in front of me. "You don't have to pretend to be kept out of the affair. I know you're proud. Right? You're good! So good! You can not only help the police find criminals, but also control the criminals and tell them when to die! And you do it before a policeman, a friend, a buddy! Yes, you're right. If you wanted him to die, I cannot stop you. You're so good! Are you satisfied?"

"Aren't you satisfied with this result? I gave you a criminal back and let's call it even." Bin strolled to my side and blew away the snow on the railing and said, "Well, do you really didn't want to check on him? Just in case he's lucky enough to stay alive?"

"You don't have the right. You can't decide his death." I stared at him. "You can come out an idea to let Su Zhen go, but killed Zhang Mingkun yourself. Is it fun to do something like this? Is it?"

"The case in Banjing Road? That was to give you a hand."

"Give me a hand? A hand to pull me down from a future vice-Commander to suspension? I have to thank you for that!"

Bin sneered. "Finding two yobs to testify on the court? What if they do something dirty in the future? Will you save them out? Well, saving or not can both lead you trouble. Did you waste all your time in the Interrogation Office? If you want to do it, then do it clean."

I answered him angrily. "Don't say it like we are on the same boat. Whatever I did, I didn't plan to kill someone who hasn't been proved guilty by the court."

"Making phone calls doesn't break any laws."

"Inducing a suspect to commit suicide and tricking a policeman. Is this what gives you your confidence?"

It seemed that Bin wanted to end this argumentation as soon as possible. So he replied, "So what? Arrest me? Beat me? Or just break off with me?"

I couldn't give an answer. He was right. I couldn't do anything to him."

"You ... Since you are capable of forcing him into suicide by a phone call, why can't you just do it by the book and take his confession? And we didn't even have any evidence to confirm him to be the murderer. Nothing, nothing could directly serve as an evidence that he was the one who killed his granddaughter! OK. Even if he really did that, with his death, we could knew anything behind the story. Maybe Fan Jiajia wasn't the only one. Maybe there are other victims. You didn't know ..."

"It's him."

"You don't know! The current evidence, research, logical theories, forensic results or even your fucking psychological analysis or criminal profiling couldn't prove that's him! You don't know it was him! You don't!"

"Yes, I do."

"You fucking do not! What's the point of confirmation after you've killed him? There's not any chance to prove it! If it's not him, I mean, if, for the slightest possibility that it's not him, you've just killed an innocent old man! There's not a slight difference between you and those murderers. None!"

"I told you, it's him." Bin put his hands carefully on the clean railing, as if afraid of being burned. "And you know that too since you've questioned him so many times. Yes, you know."

"How can I know ..."

He didn't even turn to look at me before cutting in. "You don't know? Are you sure?"

"You probably think that I had a certain ... feeling, like hate, to all criminals who commit their crimes around Xiaoyue River, so I played some tricks to force him into suicide." He looked up and heaved a sigh. "I cannot blame He Jingcheng for that, but I'll repeat for the last time: It's none of my business. Yes, no one would ever like the suspect who raped and killed a little girl, but I didn't have to make my own hands dirty just because someone threw a body around Xiaoyue River. I didn't have to."

The wind started to blow. I fastened my collar to prevent the snowflakes from falling through my collar. But Bin didn't move.

I turned around to look at him.

But he was not here.

What I came in sight of was that Han Bin standing in a daze by Xiaoyue River. No matter in a sunny spring afternoon, a storming summer morning, a chilly and windy autumn night, or a cold winter day, he was standing there, in black, like a cicada lying quietly on a tree. The river flowing through and boy turning man, he was still there, unable to leave the lonesome and desolate maze. Well, I'd say, the scenery on the other side of the river must be gorgeous.

Although I didn't know well of his past, I was with him now, which is enough. After all, no one could hide perfectly from others.

Not even Bin.

"I was very disappointed on a case I dealt with last year." Unexpectedly, he returned to the overpass before I did. "The client is a state-owned facility and was sued by some company because of defaults on a payment. Well, the case is complicated, but in a nutshell, the IOU was forged, but the stamp of that state-owned facility was real after authentication. I told the leader of the client that unless we can find some "special approach" to change the authentication, there's nothing I can do about the case."

I didn't get his meaning so I let him do the talk.

"The leader, well, was talking with all his dignity about acting by law. He told me that pulling connections was not right, and they couldn't do anything to damage their image, well, quite different from what he looks when he was talking about the loss of state assets."

I was still not clear about his point but I knew his next move. "It seemed that you were the one who went to find the "special approach" to re-authenticate the stamp and helped them win the case, right?"

"Exactly."

"And then what? Save the loss of state assets? Quite good. What's your point here?"

Bin also tightened his collar as if he was suddenly aware of the strong wind. "Later on, the company refused to accept the verdict. They appealed and accused us of tampering with the authentication conclusion and colluding with the authentication guys and the judicial officers of the first instance. And then, after talking with both parties, the intermediate court sent a letter to the Justice Bureau and the Lawyer's Association. I was immediately suspended from practice until the hearing was over. On the hearing, that leader testified himself that I was the one who had once seduced him into illegal approaches, which, of course, were sternly refused."

"So what? Did you want that leader die too? And call him at midnight sometime later?" Although I chose to tease, I could get his point this time.

"Want him die? No, I can understand him."

"What?"

"A lot of people are like this. If they can get what they want, they didn't even care about how. But, they have to fake the fact that they were getting it through a right and dignified way. If someone else helped them to the goal, it is possible that they would come out and scold the person who had done the dirty work for them, not only for protecting, well in your words, their moral purity, but also annoyed at exposing their most evil self to the world." Bin smiled at me, mockingly, his gaze penetrating straightly through the snowstorm to my eyes. "You know, every family's got a skeleton in their closest. If it is taken to the public for show, you had no other choice but to deny it. Xincheng, I mean, Officer Zhao Xincheng, do you think it's me who collect the skeleton in the closest?"

I said to myself, all in a hurry, that he was using some sort of psychological strategy, something like hypnosis to try to break down my moral defenses. "Don't speak with such insinuations!" I raised my voice to show my toughness. "I don't want Zhang Mingkun to die. I've said that we didn't know whether he's the real criminal or not. Even if he is, his end is not for us to decide!"

"Don't ... talk like this, Xincheng." Bin took a cigarette and lighted it up with that silver lighter. Along with the click, he said, "Your talking like this would make me question your moral character. You know, decent men don't tell lies."

"Bin ... Oh, no. It's silver-tongued orator, professional lawyer, Mr. Han Bin. I'm telling you, the closest and the skeleton are both yours. I cannot afford such things."

"Oh yes?" Bin took a smoke and passed the cigarette to me. "Well, if so, then I've asked you several times whether you'd like to see whether he's still alive for the past dozens of minutes. But you didn't call 120, or gave him a check, but instead, you stood right here, fighting, babbling and complaining about god-knows-what. I was just wondering that even if he didn't die from the fall, he would now freeze to death."

My hand, which was going to take the cigarette, stopped immediately.

"Are you sure you didn't want him to die?"

On our way back, I didn't say anything, just smoking heavily. I couldn't find anything to say. Bin, instead, advised me not to get into any trouble when I just resumed my post. It was sure that someone would see the body and call the police. If the police found out that the last call Zhang Mingkun made was to him, he had his own way to deal with it and wouldn't get me into any trouble.

Too ashamed to nod as an agreement, I kept asking him, "What did you say to him in the phone? You can just talk him to death?"

For my embarrassment, Bin smiled gently. Seemingly afraid of adding to my guilt, he answered, "Why bother to ask? You wouldn't want to know. Trust me, you wouldn't want to know."

I was probably suffering from Stockholm Syndrome[1].

Upon we were approaching the car, I asked him, "If Zhang Mingkun would make Fan Jiajia his long-time possession by seducing and raping, why would he take the risk to kill her this time?"

"No idea. There are so many possibilities." Bin didn't turn around to look at me. He just answered, "Maybe because the kid didn't want to do it this time, or he mistakenly chose some strange postures and led to this accidental consequence ... But anyway, it won't be that kid who strangled herself, right?"

His answer was perfect, so I could only choose to ask some other farfetched questions. "Even if Zhang Mingkun was the murderer, the victim still had the experience of staying with both her grandfathers. Will her grandfather, I mean, her father's father, Fan Chengguo, had once been ..."

"Right ..." Bin suddenly stopped, making me almost bumping into him. "Although it's a really small probability, your idea still makes some sense. I didn't think about that before ..."

And then, he turned around, took the cigarette in my fingers. He took a deep smoke and then gave me an upward gaze with his clean and dark eyes.

"Well, in your opinion, do I need to give Fan Chengguo a call?"

He was saying this in a way an ordinary citizen coming to the police for help, a professional and responsible lawyer asking for his client's opinion, an intimate friend requesting his best friend's advice — simple and sincere

I could not help but feel a cold shiver running through me.

What a cold day.

---

1 Stockholm syndrome is a condition in which hostages develop a psychological bond with their captors during captivity. It results in the captive begins to identify closely with his or her captors, even trust, depend on or help the captors.

Chapter IV

The Spider

1

"One side of your shoulder shrugs, your pupils are getting larger and the corner of your mouth is coming down." Yuan Shi was turning a pen between his fingers. "Miss, lying to my face is not sensible at all."

I sneaked to Jiang Lan and asked by her ears with a low voice, "What's the matter? What brings him here?"

"He was coming to profile for another case and heard that we've got a witness here of the Xu Chunnan case, so he asked to question her himself. I didn't know in advance." Jiang put her voice so low that I was almost guessing from her lips' move. "It seems that Dr. Yuan is very interested in the case. And, he has already seen through Zhang Yan is telling a lie with just a few questions."

I saw Zhang Yan, Xu Chunnan's former "colleague", sitting on a chair in the corner of the meeting room, staring down the cuffs on her wrist, ill at ease.

"Brilliant! Look at her! If he didn't came to question her, our whole team would be tricked." I nodded with a big move. "But she's just a witness. Is that necessary to put on cuffs? It's a violation of human rights."

Jiang Lan was giving a complete silent answer this time. I looked at her mouth but can only tell some words like "the City Burau", "expert" and "safety concerns".

But Yuan Shi still noticed our moves behind him. He turned around slowly and smiled at me friendly. "Hello, Officer Zhao."

I took a step and held my hand out. "Hello! Sorry, Dr. Yuan. Am I disturbing you? The boss told me to ..."

Yuan Shi didn't move. He just stretched one of his hands to the back and touched my hand, so fast that as if I were some HIV carrier. "Well, let's talk outside."

I followed him to the passage and he asked before I could say anything. "Are you sent to get her confession?"

"Yes." I squeezed some forced smile. "What do you think?"

"A sophisticated prostitute. But I can let her tell." Yuan Shi gave me an alert look, his arms folding around his chest. "Don't worry. I'm sure I can get her tell by today." he said in a deep voice.

I clapped my hand and said, "Perfect! Well... Director Bai was asking for you about the serial cases. He would like to invite you to his office and have a little talk. I saw that Jiang didn't do the background check, which is a required procedure. I wouldn't want you to waste your time on this, so how about Jiang and I doing the background check while you are discussing with Bai so that when you come back, you can continue with your question."

Yuan Shi looked down at my smile, agreeing with my proposal with a "yes" uttered from his nose. He came back to put the pen back in his pocket and, seemingly thought of something, asked, "Well, Officer Zhao. I've heard that the former leader of the workshop you've set up in studying criminal psychology is the son of Han Songge, is that?

My body tightened a bit at his words. "Err ... Yes. What's the matter?"

"Well, like father like son." He paused a bit and then continued, "Some student showed me a paper on the Internet about the combined application of inductive statistics and behavioral deduction in criminal profiling. It was not perfect written, but a readable one. It seemed that the writer was the former leader of a Fingerprint workshop ..."

"Well, that one. Yes, I know about that." I looked down and laughed. "That was not his work. It was a shoddy one by some kids from the workshop after reading several foreign works. They just put his name on it. Please don't take it seriously."

Yuan Shi nodded, thoughtfully. "Well, I see. So ... you know him well, the son of Han Songge?"

"Not very much."

"How's his professional skills? I've heard some stories on the Internet, saying that the detection rate of the case involved his efforts is quite astounding. In a case, it only took him several hours to identify the suspect..."

I knew the case he was talking about. It was case happened 8 years ago. The No. 1 beauty detective spent almost three hours to collect all clues, profile the suspect and ask us to interview all around. Bin popped out in the last five minutes... And afterwards, he and I both felt that a psycho may have it solved in less than one minute.

"Well ... After all, he is the son of Han Songge." I walked him outside, looking around for several seconds, and pretended to talk in hesitation. "Things get mysterious on the Internet. He was ... good, but ... what I want to say is ... well, if he is really as good as his father, will I have the chance to be the leader?"

Yuan Shi blinked and smiled understandingly. "Then we have to share more in the future. Criminal psychology is still new in China, with less people paying attention to it, and even lesser fund. Since we are both working in this field, it's better for both of us to have more discussions."

He was all smiles when he said this. I flattered to sent him away and returned to the office.

I didn't have much time so I'd have to hurry.

"Zhang Yan, it's not the first time so I will come straight to the point." I pulled a chair near her and sat on it. "According to the information we've acquired, you and Xu Chunnan were on duty every other day. So that would be 365 days per year and 730 days for two years ... You've worked like this for many years, but it was only on the day she was killed that you changed the schedule. You were suppose to be on duty that day, weren't you?"

Zhang Yan was no more than 21 years old, but was already corrupted by her job with wrinkles creeping on her forehead. Her face, plus the little embellishment provided by some cheap makeups, told me why they can only "work" in dim light.

She nodded.

"Listen, I don't have the slightest interest on what you do, none at all." I parted my hands left and right as if I were opening the door. "As long as I didn't see you making love with some old crap, with notes dangling from your lips, I wouldn't care about what you do and how you do it. The only thing I care about now is that your friend has died for you. She had 61 wounds on her body! That is sixty-one! Do you know the feeling to have been stabbed in every hole in your body and then been cut 61 times with a serrated knife? Do you know that?

I hated to see women cry. It made me annoyed. Even if it was a woman like Zhang Yan — no matter what she did to make a living, she is a human in my eye.

I took out a photo and put it before her eyes. It was effective. She stopped crying because of fear.

"There was an Officer Cao asking you about the schedule and you said Xu Chunnan had asked for it. He told me you were lying, and the expert questioned you just now told me the same. No, I don't want any explanations. I know you are not the one who made the schedule and you have to lie to cover for whoever made it. — No records!" I stopped Jiang from taking that down and continued. "Who's that? Give me a name! An address! Who's your boss? Is he or she making this schedule?"

Zhang Yan started to cry again. "Oh ... I can't ... I just cannot ... Please officer, I couldn't ..."

Well, if she was to act like this, I would get her confession in less than 15 minutes, or I would just jump into the Xiaoyue River. But, the only problem was, I probably didn't have that 15 minutes, and I didn't know how to swim.

So, I turned around to Jiang Lan and said, "Give me the keys, and the record book too. What's that book under it? Let me see ...Oh, give me the book, then, not the record book. Now, you, out. Close the door. I told you to get out!"

The direct consequence of driving Jiang Lan away was that there was less time left for me. I glanced at the big book in my hand: *An Omnibus of Test Papers on National Judicial Examination*. She wanted to take the national judicial exam? Quite an aspirant.

After opening the cuffs, I twisted her arms to the back of the chair and cuffed again before she could even knead her wrist. And then, I pull her out a bit, and sat opposite her nearly face to face. I said quickly in a low voice. "I know you were living a difficult life, always on the way to practice your flexibility and listen to complains. Well, everyone's under pressure in such a world. So do us. Frankly, I'm even delighted to have people like you to listen to my complaints. That would be a way to relax."

I knew she was staring at me, nervously. So I acted as someone who couldn't really focus, with my hands massaging the cover of that book deliberately. "You know, I've been working as a policeman for decades and was about to be promoted last year. But a fight cost me all my career life. I beat a crap at the gate of the holding cell and err ... a few of my colleagues coming to stop me. Well, I didn't intend to beat them, but, you know, I couldn't really control back then. And my career was ruined. My entire career! Fuck!"

She took both of her legs back and crossed them together, very tight.

"But I don't regret it! Just because what he did, we have to let a murderer walk away freely! He killed a woman! A mother!" I sniffled a bit and continued. "Well, people like you are called 'poule' in French, and 'prostitute' or 'whore' in English. But no matter what, we are all human. Both you and Xu Chunnan, and the one killed by that run-away murderer, you are all human. — So I hate him! I hate him because he deprived others of the chance to live! Do you understand? I hate murderers! Murderers are not human beings! They are animals! Beasts! They cannot be forgiven!"

Zhang Yan twisted constrainedly on the chair, her lower abdomen having a twitch as if she wanted to pee.

"Yeah, I know it's wrong to fight. That's my problem." I flipped the book, making big sounds. "When I was young, I was taught that knowledge is power. I don't believe it, didn't study hard so eventually, I failed in my college entrance exam and didn't go to a good college. Although I was fortunate enough to end up as a policeman, but, you see, I'm still who I was." I heaved a sigh and lifted my eyes, standing the book up on my knees so that she could get an idea of its volume. "Now, tell me who that person is and where he or she lives, or you will immediately feel the power of knowledge, starting from this book."

As I was speaking, I opened the book to let her feel the power in advance and then said, "I can promise you that no matter what you will end up with, detention or reform through labour, you will be accompanied by a pair of breasts, necrotic in purple. I know you're less than 21 years old and there's a long way before you. But, that pair of necrotic breasts will keep you company for the entire life. And all those sufferings come from your cover up of a murderer, who may not only kill your friend, but also so many other people! Now tell me! Who's that person!"

I opened her cuffs and put the book on the conference table in front of her. Tapping on the cover of the book, I said, "Listen to your teacher more. Knowledge is power. Buy a book sometime and you won't be doing this ..."

"Bravo, Bra——vo——"

I had to admit that when I saw Yuan Shi standing at the door as I turned around, I was a bit surprised.

I sorted out my expression and walked to him with a smile. "Ah, Dr. Yuan. You've been back so quickly ..."

"Yeah, I didn't even go. Or I should say, luckily, I didn't go." Yuan Shi clapped his hands with a cold smile on his face. "Or I would miss such a wonderful lie, which, I mean, is your interrogation just now."

"Well, that was a normal enquiry. She is a witness so I want to ask her a few questions, just for your convenience ..."

Yuan Shi didn't buy my story. "If we assume someone is lying, what we normally do was to believe him first because the more we believe him, the more confident he will be, and he'll tend to tell more lies. And eventually, he will let the cat out of the bag ．

I also put away my fake smile. "Is this said by a Hegel?"

"No, it was by Schopenhauer." He looked into my eyes. "A deadly foe of Hegel."

"I don't understand ..."

Yuan Shi put his arm around my neck with a big smile and pulled me outside with a smile, but what he said was quite the opposite to his expression. "After all, I'm the one who came here to support on the City Bureau's behalf. You want to play me? You stupid Jerk ... But, I have to say, Officer Zhao. Do you really think I am the same kind of person with you?"

I answered by with the same expression and tone. "Well, look at you! I just want to help you with the dirty work. You're way beyond that, but someone has to do the dirty work."

"Just not in the right way ..."

"Well, like what I said, it's dirty work. Do you suppose the man who cleans the toilet wears perfume like you? That's too compelling." I said with great resent.

"Zhao Xincheng! I won't be serious with the man who cleans ... with you." Yuan Shi finally spoke from his heart. "But if you want to keep your uniform, don't ever try to play me."

I immediately patted on my chest. "Oh my goodness. You scared me. That's really scaring ... Should I have known you hated being dominated, or liked to pursue sovereignty, I wouldn't play such a joke on your, would I?"

"I don't have Oedipus complex. Don't trick me on the Freud theory. I know what you mean..."

"No. You understand me wrong. What I mean is ... well, to be frank," I just couldn't control my tongue before running away. I patted on his shoulder and said, "I just see you as my own son."

"Not a Pang Xin fitting your description." Jiang Lan was looking at the screen, the mouse making a clicking sound. "Either too old ... or too young. Or a Beijinger. None of them fits your description. Cheng, are you sure what Zhang Yan told you is the truth?"

Staring at the screen, I frowned. "None? No way."

"You don't know her address?"

"Zhang Yan couldn't tell. She came to the hair salon to meet them and collect money. She just know the name and age vaguely."

"Go and ask her for another time?" Jiang asked with a wicked smile.

"What? You knew that Dr. Yuan is with her now!" I tapped on the computer. "Print the addresses of these four "Pang Xin". Where is our men?"

"They went to work on a cross-province heist. And when Dr. Yuan got back to the City Bureau, you're doomed." Jiang Lan made a gesture of decapitation. "But these four were not even like Zhang Yan's description."

"It's good that they were all women." I pulled the address list from the printer and kicked out Yuan Shi out of my head. "I didn't mind to interview around, just taking it as the entertainment before my decapitation."

At around dusk, I saw her at the door of a yard located at the west side of Xuegezhuang North Bridge.

According to Zhang Yan's description, their procuress Pang Xin should be a woman of thirty years old, which fits who I saw, but the register information told me that the woman standing in front of me was already 44 years old.

No matter from her appearance or her figure, or in her eyes or voice, there was no marks of time could be found.

But my instinct told me, at my first sight of her, that this women, who got rid of the influence of the time, was Pang Xin herself.

After seeing my ID, she stepped back politely to let me in. "Is this for Chunnan? Please come in."

The first two Pang Xins wasted me a whole afternoon, causing me extremely sour in by right calf. It was not because the walking, but some "gift" left by my college coach. As I stepped into the yard, I found myself in a botany, which suddenly pleased me in some way.

The yard was really big, with various kinds of plants and flowers growing well-arranged. Several paths were arranged between them and the house located at the end. While taking me to the one right in the opposite, she picked a little shovel from the garden, knocked it a bit to let the earth fall. "I'm sorry. I was busy with these stuff just now. Quite a mess."

Up until then did I notice that she was wearing oversleeves on both her arms and there were mud on the hands and jeans. It seems that she was working in the garden before I came.

"It doesn't matter. And ... It's quite pleasant to see. I've never seen so many flowers in winter. I thought only wintersweet would bloom in winter." I pointed at a patch of blue flower. "Is this some sort of Blue Enchantress?"

Pang Xin lifted her eyes a bit to the direction I pointed at. "Oh, that's a kind of chrysanthemum. That Blue Enchantress you were talking about is a kind of rose. They looked quite differently."

"Ah? Oh my! Are there blue chrysanthemums?"

"Of course!" She turned her head a bit, gesturing me to the back. "And those white, purple and pink ones, they are all from the same kind of this blue one. Ah, I'm sorry. That white one with round leaves is primrose. I transplanted it in last week. It's rare to see such a hardy primrose, though."

I was totally enchanted.

Pang Xin was introducing the flowers slowly and steadily: The bright ones on the west side were camellia; those yellow ones on the tree in front of the northern room were calycanthus, and the yellow ones on the trees to our right-hand side were wintersweet. Though they seemed to be in the same color, the latter ones got purple grain on the petals, which made it simple to separate them from each other.

As she was talking, she smiled slightly, seemingly to be a little awkward. "Look at me. Talking to myself like this. I'm sorry. I almost forgot you've come to ask about the case."

"That's all right." Although it was a little weird to listen to a procuress talking about gardening, it was still a good chance to observe this distinctive hooker. "Don't worry. You see, I came alone. It's just an informal interview."

Pang Xin had a really fine figure regardless of the fact of being too slim. There was a curve from her chin to her neck, a somehow attracting one. Her skin was pale, almost transparent to show the vines under the skin. Her eyelashes were long, but few; Black shoulder-length hair fell neatly over the shoulders, with a few sliver in between. Considering that she didn't wear any gold, silver or jade decorations, she may have been retreated from her career since clients wouldn't like those with silver hairs. And no makeups, no hair color and no colored nails were not something that a hooker would do.

The sight of her reminded me of Tong.

Tong was the No. 1 backbone of the workshop and was considered as the most beautiful girl in the field. She was several years younger than me, and was Bin's most proud student. There was a mysterious and secret connection between her and Bin. It was probably like Bin was still thinking about whether to take a smoke and Tong has gone to take a lighter. I still remembered the first time I met her, she was standing behind him on the left, semi-invisible, like a good wife.

But it seemed that Bin was not as close with her as what we though of. In fact, since Yichen appeared in Bin's life, Tong chose to leave, or Bin chose to leave her. When Bin announced his retirement, we all thought Tong would be the one to replace him. All men in the workshop became so excited, taking it a good chance to flirt with the beauty.

Bin's chose was beyond everyone's comprehension, and Tong just disappeared. From what I could recall, she had never showed up ever since

I took office together with He Jingcheng, not for once. She disappeared so completely that everyone seemed to forgot her ever existence.

Until today, I happened to meet a former hooker pleased to the eye.

"Look at me! I just let you stand outside in such a cold day. How stupid I was." Pang Xin lowered her hands and dusted them, as if afraid of the dust from her hands would hurt her flowers. "Come on in."

The room was warm. I didn't see any stoves so maybe she's got heating system. There was a set of sofa and tea table in the middle of the room, under which an off-white round carpet was placed. In the west of the room, there was a desk. I could see stationery and magazines, but no computers. In the southeast corner, there was a closet with glass doors, in which there was an old record player. Apart from these, the room was filled pots with flowers and plants. Well, this seemed to be her living room.

"It doesn't matter. There's no need to change shoes. Please have a seat." She bent down to move some pots away, making my way to the sofa wide enough to pass through. "Really, it doesn't matter. Just come on in. Vacuums are quite helpful"

I didn't know whether it was because of her hospitality or the entire coziness of the room. Although I kept saying yes, I still only put half of my hips on the sofa, tilting to one side, which means in this way, I didn't have to step on the clean carpet.

Pang Xin was standing by the door, a little bit nervous, with her hands gripped in front her chest. "Well ... it was my first time to be questioned by a policeman. Do I ... do I need to find a lawyer or someone to accompany me?"

She didn't seem to act and I simply didn't know what to say. "It's not as serious as that. Like I said, it's an informal interview. I just want you to answer some questions. You see, the bureau even doesn't know my coming. If nothing goes wrong, today's conversation won't be recorded."

"You won't take me away? If I'm not here, I have to find someone to look after my flowers ..."

Actually, she was suspected of organizing prostitution, but for now, there was no direct evidence to accuse of Xu Chunnan and Zhang Yan were prostitutes. So I could just avoid this sensitive subject, at least for now, to help calm her down and let me continue my questioning.

"No. You can go on with your flowers and plants, as long as you can answer my questions honestly."

But I didn't expected that the answer was just as simple as this.

"It was Chunnan herself who requested for the shift. She told me that she wanted to have a day off after the Spring Festival — probably wanted to stay with her boyfriend more." She seemed gloomy, her face being much more pale, only her eyes blinking with red round marks.

"She had a boyfriend?"

"She said she did."

"For how long?"

"May be a year? I didn't know whether they were still seeing each other back then."

"Who's her boyfriend?"

"I didn't know. She hadn't told me."

"Have you seen him?"

"No."

"You haven't asked about where he comes from or what he does for a living?"

"No, I haven't. I don't ask much about their private life."

I started to push her in spite of myself. "Apart from collecting money, you cared nothing? Even if they were just your ..."

Tears running silently down from her eyes stopped me. She wasn't really weeping, or in other words, she didn't even realized her tears were bursting out like a broken bead curtain.

But I didn't intend to act chivalry. "Are you sad about Xu Chunnan's death?"

Her voice was so vague that it seemed to come from the other side of the world. "I don't know."

"Then what are the tears for?"

"I've no idea myself." She seemed to be embarrassed, covering her face with one hand, and reaching for the napkin on the tea table with another. "I'm sorry. I ... just lost control of myself." Maybe realizing there was mud on her hand, she stood up hurriedly. "Excuse me."

I was also at a loss as to how to proceed.

She came back after a short while, neat and tidy this time, and kept apologizing. "I'm so sorry. I ... I even forget to make you some tea."

I waved to say no but stopped half way, without saying it out.

She floated through the flowers and took a glass tea set from the bottom of the closet. "Ah... where do I put my tea? Please, wait for a minute." She then ran out to find tea leaves, heated water with electric kettle and conjured a small alcohol boiler and a lily-shaped cradle somewhere from the room... I saw her running back and forth like a white deer. And in less than 15 minutes, a pot of flower tea was boiling some fragrance in the alcohol boiler on the cradle.

"The water is boiling, but it's better to have it boiling for a little longer."

Pang Xin put a glass tea cup in front of me and a mat under it. "Well, it's not really better, but I'd like it to be boiling for a little longer. Have you tasted yerba mate?"

"No...no."

"Then I have to surprise you. Tell me if you don't like it." She poured me a cup. "Want to taste it now? The longer it is boiled, the bitterer it is. Oh, take it easy. It's a little hot."

I took a sip and frowned immediately.

"Really bitter? Do you want some sugar?"

I took another sip in her expecting eyes. "No, no. ... But, are you sure it's not Kuding tea?"

"It's a specialty from Argentina." She coughed a little with her head tiled, hands on her mouth. "Hollies are bitter. I'd better give you some honey or grenadine syrup."

"No. Don't bother."

"It doesn't matter. I'll be right back." She floated out and then in, taking two glass jars with her, a red one and a yellow one. "Honey? Or ..."

"Honey is good. I'll help myself."

When I stirred my tea, she added some hot tea inside. "Cold tea is not helpful to melt the honey."

I saw her putting the tea pot on the shelf and asked, "You won't have some?"

"I like bitter ones, so I'll wait."

Honey neutralized some of the bitterness, but it was still unpleasant to my taste. I couldn't but praising, "Yeah, you're really good."

"Just used to it." She too the electric kettle and added some more water. "Thank you."

"What?"

"You see, I was quite emotional. It's very considerate that you didn't force me to answer more questions. Stuff at hand can get me over those emotions, which, well, makes me less sad." When she was taking, she seemed to be used to put her hands crossed in front of her chest, like a believer in confession. "I really don't know what I'm sad about. Zhang Yan told one of the sisters here, who told me that Chunnan was, Chunnan looked ... terrible."

I sipped my tea silently, praying that she wouldn't get emotional again.

"When I first heard about the news, I started to think that if it was I who killed Chunnan. I shouldn't have agreed to her proposal of the shift. I should have ..." Pang Xin looked up in a helpless gaze. "But if I didn't agree to her proposal, then its should be Yan on duty that day, which means

... Well, Yan would be the one. So whatever I do, I would be a helper in killing one of them, wouldn't I?"

It was just like what Bin said —

"After all, that is a serial killer. He wants to kill and he is going to do it. You can't stop it."

But I couldn't bear to tell her truth: Yes. Nothing can stop people from hurting each other.

In our conversation, I've learned that Pang Xin was from Xiang Tan, Hunan province, the place were Chairman Mao comes from, and she said that her home was not far from where Chairman Mao used to live. Her parents died when she was young and she only had primary education. When she was 14 years old, she came to Beijing and finally started to engage in several kinds of "service industry". About four years ago, she bought this little yard and invested in several small hair salons. Xu Chunnan and Zhang Yan worked in one of them.

I asked her a sensitive question cautiously. "Are you really hiring them to cut people's hair?"

"Well, they can do anything there. I only want the rent, and one forth of their income. I won't pretend that I don't know what they were doing there. After all, I was one of them in the past. For businessman, money from women and kids is the most easy to make; but for women, it is much easier to make money from man."

Actually, I would rather she was not so frank.

"What if they lie?"

"Will they? Maybe ... but I didn't think of that."

Zhang Yan was right. Pang Xin was a kind, even simple "boss". The reason she didn't want to give Pang Xin away in the beginning was not out of "fear", but out of "gratitude".

"Right. I can see from your life now that they didn't lie to you about their income." I pointed at her wrist watch. "Nice one. Quite expensive, right?"

She shook her head with a smile and added me some tea. "Quite an expensive one, if it were true."

I noticed her blame and added, "It depends on who's wearing it. If it's on my wrist, it's a fake one even if it was real."

I'd better shift the subject. I took the tea pot she had just put down and filled her glass. "It's getting bitterer if you cook it any longer."

"Ah, I forgot that. Thank you." She tilted politely and took a sip. And then, she suddenly stood up. "Look at me! I haven't changed at all. All this dusts and ashes, and even make you the tea! I'm so sorry. I'll get changed first and make another pot. Leave it there, leave it there. Just give me one more minute ..." In spite of my repeated assurances that it was all right, she still took the teapot out of the stove and asked me to wait for a new pot after she changed her clothes. "Just a minute."

When she went out to change clothes, I took me cigarette out and put it back after a second thought. A gentleman should be able to think even without cigarettes.

For now, it seemed that she didn't have much connections to Xu Chuannan's case.

I couldn't deny that Pang Xin had left me a good impression with her behaviour and hospitality. And from my observation, she didn't lie during my interview excluding any subjective factors. She was single for the moment since I didn't see any men clothes or necessities in her room. She didn't live with any women either as she were wearing a pair of flatties and there was only one pair of slippers on the shoe shelf. Her parents die when she was young and she didn't have any close relatives — there was no photos on the wall or on the table. She was mild and docile — a potential killer may keep a pet at home, but not usually plants, let alone a garden. Her financial condition was good — well, a person without money couldn't be able to afford such a garden. She didn't have much education, which accorded with her background and explained the absence of books and computers, but her taste was good — her record player, the bitter tea from Pampas Steppe and that watch which made me really curious.

The two years I've spent in the Social Order Crops has seen my experiences of retrieving personal belongings. Therefore, besides that little black cross, the neatness of the glass, the material of the watch strap, the shape of the needle and the joint of the crown ... they all told me that it was a Vacheron Constantin — Malte, and it was a real one.

However, compared with living in a garden and listening to records while drinking bitter tea, it was normal for a former prostitute with several illegal businesses to have a watch worth billions of RMB.

So in a nutshell, Pang Xin wasn't qualified to be a suspect. First of all, she doesn't have motives and I could not find any propensity to violence in her behaviour. She didn't have to kill for money and Xu Chunnan has got no money for her. Even if it was a revenge on their lying, she was not silly enough to do it in her own place. And second, there was no psycho around her, so she didn't have to and wasn't likely to be an accomplice of certain violent sexual assault. Third, she was such a delicate women, slim and thin. She didn't have the physical condition to commit the crime. And last, she wore her wrist watch on her left hand and poured with her right hand. She didn't have any visible disabilities or flaws on the left side of her body, so if Dr. Yuan's left-hand theory was working, she wasn't capable of committing the crime.

I relaxed a bit after I excluded her suspicion and then started to worry again. The lead was a dean end. Oh my god!

Since there was nothing more to ask, it was naturally not proper for me to stay in the house of a single woman. I stood up and prepared to say goodbye to Pang Xin when she came back. My eyes were too heavy, probably because I watched a movie and stayed up late last night. Anyway, there was no need to interview the last "Pang Xin". I was too tired, hungry and sleepy. I just wanted to come home and have some noodle soup with eggs and tomatoes Xuejing made, and then slept until tomorrow morning.

Pushing the door open, I walked into the yard. Maybe it was because the fresh air outside, my leg didn't hurt anymore. Taking several deep breaths and moving my numb arms, I started to wander in the yard, and was disappointed to find flowers in winter were not fragrant at all. I strolled here and there, and suddenly stopped when I saw Pang Xin at the window of a house pained brownish red in the west of the yard. She was like Flora, gentle and placid, but was naked from her head to her toe.

There was a boy called Hamlet who was once puzzled about "To be, or not to be". Now my question was: To be here, or not to be here after I saw a naked woman?

When Pang Xin turned around and found me, she was quite calm.

Her bedroom was small, crowded but tidy. I found that her bed sheets, pillow covers, wall paper, wardrobe, dresser and two little beanbags were all warm-toned, very different from all the green and emerald in her yard and living room. Hearing the sound of me opening the door, she turned around — not only her head, but her entire body, presenting all in front of my eyes without any cover.

There was no indignation or fear, nor embarrassment or shyness. I enjoyed the beautiful and attracting nude and she looked back, as if we were painters and models making silent intercourse with our souls.

I didn't expect that it was she who first apologized. "Sorry to keep you waiting. I would always hesitate in choosing clothes. It took me a century to decide and I even forgot about your presence."

Then, she put on a black dress slowly to cover her body, and then a white shirt, lowering her head to deal with the buttons.

"No.. there's nothing to feel sorry for. I've finished my questions and was about to leave." I pretended to notice my impoliteness just now and looked somewhere else while I was speaking. "Well, I was strolling in the yard and bumped in here accidentally."

"Do the flowers smell good?"

"What?"

"The flowers outside."

"Oh, yes. It's really good to live here."

"But burdensome to tidy things up."

"Quite true ..."

Well, we deliberately avoided to discuss the scene half a minute ago.

And I've noticed a little secret in my glance: There were at least twenty photos on the walls of the bedroom, on which there was Pang Xin, each with a different man,

She was never former prostitute.

Having finished fussing with her buttons, Pang Xin lifted her head, looking around following my lead, and then lowered her head again. "Very nasty, isn't it?"

My heart hurt a bit. "The salons you invested, they are not profitable at all, right?"

"Yes."

"So you've been working to support those girls?"

"If seeing different men is a job, yes. And they are all married men. Well, they seemed to call someone like me 'professional mistress', or something like that. Anyway, not some good ones. "

"You mustn't understand me wrong. I mean ..." I walked back and forth, my mind completely frozen. "I just didn't think about ... I mean, I thought that you were ..."

"That I was away from this career and turned to be someone behind the curtains, right?" She shook her head, a little helpless. "Sad, right? Life is hard."

Once again, I looked over the photos on the wall, standing in a daze.

She walked by my side. "What's wrong?"

That was the reason ...

"No. I was just ... reminded of several late nights spent with a young girl." I answered. A sudden phone call startled me up from my unconscious murmur. "Excuse me."

It was Bin.

"Aha! I thought you won't call me until the end of my life. My voice? Nothing. It's just I'm a bit tired. ... Yeah, I was out on the Xu Chunnan

148

case. Almost over. ... OK. When? No problem .... Oh, by the way, I just thought of that murderer using that Spider. Is Beitong talking about a C08 and with two different types? One is called V10, a whole steel one and the other is ... whatsoever ... with a black plastic handle. Yes. Now I'm pretty sure that the murderer is using a Spider folding knife with a black plastic handle. ... I'll explain to you later. You call the division at once and that should help them narrow down the scope. Remember, it is a Spider with a black handle. ... Yes, all right. I will stay on the line and keep me updated ..."

Not until I hanged up the phone did I discover that Pang Xin was standing really close, and she was looking at me. "Your colleague?" she asked.

"Not ... really, but almost." I rubbed my eyes. "Why are you keeping these photos on the wall? Will you feel a little uncomfortable?"

"Uncomfortable? I don't know ... Maybe it's good to con myself."

"Con yourself?"

"Yeah. I was always hoping that my body wasn't the only thing they want when they were with me." Since we were really close, I could see the capillaries on her cheek shivering under her skin. "Maybe they liked me, or even loved me. Maybe just a little ... There must be a little."

"Then, what do you think of them? Do you love them?"

"I don't know."

"What?"

"I don't know ..."

Shit! Why was she crying again!

"Am I only a mistress depending on them to live? I don't know. ... In fact, they were good people. And they were good to me, too. They liked me ..."

Yes. I could feel her loneliness.

"Of course ... Of course ... I thought ..." I wanted to say something, but my tongue wasn't helpful at all.

Suddenly, Pang Xin fell into my arms like fallen leaves. She was crying. "I really don't know. I don't know whether there's someone, anyone, who ever liked me. I've never felt ..."

The world was upside down.

Her body was just like what I thought, warm and slim, gentle and soft. I didn't know why, but I stretched my arms to embrace her out of great sympathy. After a while — I couldn't remember how long or how short it was — I pushed her out a little with great regret.

In my vague memory, what I did last was to swing my right fist on her with all my strength.

2

"ACheng, did you really break in without any hesitation when you saw a naked woman?"

I woke up and found myself in the hospital. I drank some water, feeling the dizziness in my head and listened to Jiang chirping like a bird. "Are you simply counting on your luck?"

"An experienced policeman has to be sensitive like this. And please don't exaggerate. I didn't 'break in', I just pushed in, with my hand."

"But why did Mr. Han called to say something's happened to you and you need immediate backup? Did you find a chance to contact him?"

No. It was he called me. Bin was absolutely my saviour, who called me at the very moment I needed him.

"Aha! I thought you won't call me until the end of my life." — Absolutely bullshit! Xuejing and I had dinner and watched a move with him and Yichen last night. He must know something was wrong when I started to talk like this.

"I was out on the Xu Chunnan case. Almost over." — This was telling him that I was with a woman named Pang Xin. You don't know him? Go ask Jiang Lan. Remember to check the address list!

"You call the division at once and that should help them narrow down the scope." — A policeman asked a lawyer to report a case? What the hell? Man, if you don't get my point until now, I would die in no time.

"I will stay on the line and keep me updated ..." — I cannot tell you the address. But you can get my phone located, right?"

But the key factor was that it must him who was calling, no one else would do the trick.

"Now I'm pretty sure that the murderer is using a Spider folding knife with a black plastic handle."

"Remember, it is a Spider with a black handle."

A black spider.

Black Widow Spider, or Black Widow, is a notorious kind of spider identified by its black body with a red back. They can be distinguished by an hourglass-shaped marking on the abdomen. The bite of the black widow often produces fever, muscle pain, nausea, and mild paralysis of the diaphragm, which leads to difficult breathing , even death. And also, black widow are quite distinctive because they eat their own kind. The male is often killed and eaten by the female after mating in order to guarantee the reproduction and, of course, even if the female reproduces her child, she will eat her own babies in order to survive.

Being poisonous and cannibalistic, black widow is also used to name a certain kind of serial killers in western criminology field. They refer to female killers who take their husbands, relatives and lovers to be their primary victims.

In conclusion, what I told Bin through the phone call was a very obscure message, so obscure that anyone except him would be in a puzzle, but very simple at the same time, which I was sure that he could get my point the first time he got the message —

The Black Widow.

"You are being so senseless. Push in every door with naked woman. So urgent? Ah?" The next morning when I met Bai, he was in that botany of Pang Xin, managing a team to do some digging work. "We've got a dog from the City Bureau to help. It's more useful than you at the moment. Go back and have some rest."

"How's that Pang Xin?"

"That punch of yours directly sent her into hospital. The back of her head hit the dresser. It depends on her luck to be still alive." It seemed that something occurred to him and he stopped me from leaving. "When did you start to pay attention to the issue of missing persons?"

Because —

"I was just ... reminded of several late nights spent with a young girl."

In order to investigate the Xu Chunnan case, Jiang and I spend a lot of late nights to read the files about missing persons. Although nothing was found, those faces of the missing ones were still in my mind. So I recognized them the minute I stepped into Pang Xin's bedroom.

A room of wraiths. They were staring at me, silently.

So the botany in front of my eyes made me sick more or less. "How many did you find?"

"Seven were dug out, in which five of them were sent away. And God knows how many were waiting for us down there. You didn't catch the serial killer, but get me another big fish." Bai stood in the yard, holding a cigarette in one of this hand and sucking in the smoke heavily into his lung, watching little red flags planted everywhere. "This fucking dog has a really good nose." he said.

"The current number is fourteen. I don't have enough room, so the City Bureau took some, which means the total number must exceed fourteen." He Jingcheng took off his gloves, rubbing his red eyes due to late nights and said, "Slanders cluster round a widow's door, but this one got more dead men in her backyard."

There was no light in the entrance of the passageway in the medical examination center. The darkness alerted me, making me looking around unconsciously. "Are they all registered as missing?"

"Even if they weren't in the past, they are now. Their IDs are difficult to identify. The Acting Squad and local stations are working on that. I've identified two of them. No message from the City Bureau."

"Bai told me that there were 27 photos found in her bedroom. That's a lot. You'll be busy."

"That's all right ... I mean, I don't mind working overtime for some days. It's just with so many people dead, the City Bureau's got a lot of pressure." He said, his two hands dabbing his lab coat, "I was just happy that I don't have to see you on the table. I mean, are you even scared?"

"Well, ... to be frank, I don't have any special feeling."

"The toxicology report says that there's triazolam tested in all victims body including yours. It is the key ingredient in a knockout drug, which is top-class controlled. Don't know where she got them."

"Not a poison?"

"No, a narcotic. I've learned from the City Bureau that they've got a victim, buried less than a month, died from asphyxia after anesthesia. And all that I can find here are pretty the same. Well, if you didn't knock her down the minute you smelled danger, that would definitely on your autopsy report."

"Ha! That's because I'm smart and strong."

"Well, I'd rather say it was your crush on a naked woman that saved you." He patted me on my back, a tingle of smile creeping onto his mouth, but not into his eyes. "If you haven't seen those photos, then you're a dead man by now.

"I knew." His saying started to scare me. "And thanks to Bin's phone call."

"Yeah. You should thank him."

"It's hard to imagine that such a weak girl would be able to..."

"She's clever. She know how to play her strengths. Most victims were buried after dismemberment."

"Dismemberment?"

"Take it easy. She's not as brutal as that. The tools were found."

"A female version of the Texas Chainsaw?"

"Handsaw. Don't forget she's good at gardening."

"Are all the victims men?"

"At least one female who's already identified."

"She's not only killing men?"

"Yeah. She killed herself."

"What?"

"After comparing the marks left by craniocerebral operations on that body, we are sure that there's a Pang Xin buried in the yard. And yes, she is the one on your list."

"What the fuck!" I looked around a second time out of complete horror, "Then who is that Black Widow?"

"That's the problem." He took out a small bag of peanuts and starting eating. "Xincheng, it should be me asking you that question."

"You don't even know her. And you don't have any reason to enter the bedroom of a woman ... I mean, a serial killer. It's a women's bedroom, right? And she's changing! Hey! I'm asking you!"

Xue Jing had already asked me once when I was in hospital, and again when I get back to the office, and then at home. And now, she was at my scene and asked me again.

I asked back, "Why are you here?"

"The lead was provided by a drug leader interrogated by me. Concerning it's about whether he'll be considered helpful to the case, I'm here to wait for your outcome."

"It's 21st century. I can call your after I finished here."

"Seeing is believing." Xuejing followed me tightly. "Any other questions? No? All right. Let's get back to my questions. Who am I going to ask when there were only two people in that house and one of them is now a vegetable."

I took a glance at the van in the distance, in which Liu Qiang and half of the quad were staying, maybe laughing and enjoying this drama, and all they need was some popcorn and drinks.

"Can I talk to you later? We are in plainclothes. We don't want to alert the target."

"I don't care! I'm the one who's asking."

"Keep quiet ..."

"We are on the street. Are you afraid of someone eavesdropping on purpose? Are you gonna tell me or not!"

Well, now that I couldn't avoid her questions, at least I have to block others from hearing us. I tuned the controller secretly and the current noise was getting larger in my earphone.

"Do you have any idea how dangerous it is? Got visual on the target. ... What's wrong with you channel?"

"Yeah, I see. Two of them? Where did the information come from? ..."

I took out my phone to make a phone call and explained to her at the same time. "I was planning to knock her down before I entered. I've long been noticing that she was taking all excuses to not drink that tea, and I was getting more drowsy after drinking it. And my leg didn't even hurt when I stood up. I cannot smell properly after I entered that yard. ... Even if I want to call for backup, I have to save my life before she dismembered me. I have to find her."

"This means you knew that she is a murderer? The two of them coming. Shall I take that women?"

"You stepped out if it. — Cao Fa!" I walked to the target, holding the phone in my hand. "Did you see him? Yeah, I know. I can see you. The channel is not clear enough. The woman is yours. You can walk in to meet her. ... Certainly I did. Why do you think I'm the one who's praised every year? I can tell them at my first sight."

As I was talking to Xuejing, I put my phone back in my pocket, and gave a heavy punch to the dark and short middle-aged man walking to me. That guy was threw to the air and fell down on the ground like a sack of flour. At the same time, Cao Fa and Zhang Qi dashed out from the flank, controlled both of them before the woman behind could even shriek.

I bent down to turn over the suspect, one of my knees pushing against his waist. I took out the handcuff. "Everything's under control. — Take it easy, sweetheart. I knew what she's planning way before I enter that room."

"Are you?" Xuejing took off her earphone, eyes on her pointy high heels. She said with a weird smile, "And I'd have to tell you, smarty, there's no drug found in the tea. The drug is in the honey."

"Such a fox! ..." I lifted the suspect's sweater and pulled him up covered in his own clothes. "But all in all, now you've understand that I've got the situation under control before I entered that room, so I decided to meet with her. It has nothing to do with whether she's wearing any clothes."

"Maybe. But apparently she's got everything about you before you got her as the honey is drugged, but the grenadine syrup is clean."

"What? You mean ..."

"I was just wondering, why she knows you would take honey, not grenadine syrup?"

"Because she's a distinctive serial killer! A very rare one!" Yuan Shi was almost dancing out of excitement in the conference room. "The Black Widow type was rarely seen since the end of last century, let alone a woman who has killed dozens of people! You've discovered a perfect case

154

to study on! Of course, if you haven't beaten her into a vegetable ... Never mind. It's an emergency and you're not the one to blame."

"An identified woman, who poisoned and strangled a dozen of men to death by her beauty probably for their money, grew a garden of flowers and plants on their dead body. It's a clear case. Now I only want to know..."

Yuan Shi stopped me excitedly. "No, you don't understand. This is an almost perfect female serial killer. For now, 21 bodies have been found. Neighbors told us that she moved in three years ago, which means she would kill one person per month. She kept killing people for such a long time with a steady cooling-off period. Clearly, she's taken killing as part of her life. She kills for the sake of killing! This is a real serial killer!"

"Right. You can save that or further study, or work out an compendium of rare serial killers. I'm only saying that ..."

"She has very distinctive antisocial behaviour, even antihuman. She bought the house and the yard to guarantee her a place to commit crimes for the long run." Yuan Shi stretched his arms in an exaggerated way. "Have you thought about that whether she had killed people in order to buy the house? Or I should say, how many did she kill?

"No more than Bathory or Tossania[1]. You can do the calculation later. Oh, and interview the family or the victims by the way, you know, talking with them so that you can get what they were thinking." Frankly speaking, I was totally impatient and I didn't have the slightest intention to hide it. "Now I only want to know, is she related to the serial cases we are working on? The cases that the suspect only kill women ... or in your words, left-handed people."

Yuan Shi rubbed his beardless chin and said, "From what I can tell, no less than Belle Gunness[2]. Do you know murder swap?"

"You mean two criminals provide their targets to each other or provide alibis to each other?

"My suggestion is to look into the background of this 'Pang Xin'. She doesn't have any contact tools, but she has to make some contacts. So you may get something if you check on the public telephones within miles. And my instinct tells me that she must have reached a certain kind of "murder contract" with that killer targeting left-hands. Find the connection between them, you'll find another serial killer.

---

1 Both are notorious female serial killers in history. Elizabeth Bathory, Hungarian countess who purportedly tortured and murdered more than 300 people (more than 650 in other files) in the 16th and 17th centuries. Tossania, female serial killer from Italy, killed more than 600 people in the 17th and 18th centuries.

2 Belle Sorenson Gunness, a famous black widow from the United States, at least killed 49 people.

What the fuck! This was a complete waste of time.

The background of that "Pang Xin" has been thoroughly investigated, but nothing was found. She didn't use any of the public telephones around her house. Her water and electricity bill was prepaid on annual basis. Her ID card was a good fake, which was made of the real Pang Xin's ID card plus her photo. She didn't have any books, diaries, letters, contacts, deposit books, credit cards, policies of insurance or driving licenses ... Who is she? Nothing could tell us, nothing. Not even a clue.

"Why does she intend to kill me when she's already known I'm a cop?"

Yuan Shi smiled. "It's just like the reason you pushed into her bedroom — hard to tell. Maybe she saw the fun of challenging the state apparatus through you."

Meaningless hope was equivalent to disappointment. Dr. Yuan was very "dependable", which was probably the only thing that lived up to my expectations. I'd rather count on the development of medical technologies or her recovery from a vegetable. Upon leaving, Yuan Shi shifted his attention, once in a lifetime, from the piles of photos and files to me. "And, Officer Zhao. I've learned from Jiang that before you took actions to the suspect, you've asked for backup through a phone call with code words?"

I nodded.

"The person who talked with you, is he Han Songge's son?"

I didn't bother to nod this time.

"Interesting ..." Apparently, Yuan Shi didn't need my answer. His attention turned back to the pile of files on the table. "I want to meet with him if there's a chance."

When Bin was at Fingerprint, he was always sitting in a listless and slouching way. He talked to no one and answered no greetings. If you don't know him, you may think that he has getting high with some marijuana. When he was here, the whole cafe was getting gloomy. I once proposed that we should make a statue of his slouching posture and put it at the door. It should serve as good as Colonel Sanders outside the Kentucky Fried Chicken. Surprisingly, he even agreed with my proposal. "Right. An ideal cafe should be like this, murky and gloomy, but there's always a cup of coffee to keep you sober."

I was coming specially to thank him and to discuss with him the cases. Bin listened to me patiently and asked all of a sudden, "Do you have the habit of fiddling with your penis with your hands in your pockets?"

Although we were close to each other, his weird question really get me confused.

"I recalled that there was some statistics said that 95% of men had done that. I was one of them when I was a boy, but it wasn't commonly seen in daily life. How do they get that figure? Well, we are lucky today ..." He cast his eyes on one of the tables, "That man over there repeated the movement at least nine times since he sat down. The person sitting opposite him was probably a buyer. You may notice his gesture. He leaned back on the sofa, and stretched his arms. And he crossed his legs. Those are demonstrations of his confidence. That man touched his penis repeatedly with hands in his pocket. It is a way to inspire his manliness, and a sexual habit of his own. Well, not everyone can relieve his tension or get himself encouraged from that. No matter he is selling some products or selling himself, I hope he'll achieve it soon. After all, this is not a masturbation club."

"But things are different concerning the couple at Table Two. That boy did it twice. His expression and the really deep V neck of the girl explains well that he is adjusting his erectile penis. His jeans are tight and he's got strips on his legs. ... Oh no, he must have been sexually aroused. Look at his eyes, the flanks of his nose shivering along with his movement. ... his hands on the table unconsciously making fists ... People say that the so-called honeymoon is a month floating on the river of sex hormones. So true!"

"Yeah, your taste is really special." I was really used to this, which was something he would say before mocking at me. "What do you want to say?"

Bin seemed to be awakened all of a sudden. He sat up and said, "Is it boring to call you an idiot from the very beginning?"

"Everyone's curious about why I would push in after seeing a naked woman. You're the only one not gossiping about that. I thought you knew I was alert before I entered her bedroom."

"Alert to what? Your numbness or that expensive watch? That's enough for Xuejing." He lighted a cigarette with a lighter carrying NAGA. I noticed he lighted it carefully so that the click wouldn't disturb other guests. "It was the instinct to survive that saved you. Humans are mysterious. I advise you to go for worship sometime."

I didn't recognize that was a snake carved on the lighter in his hand until I stared at it for several seconds. "Second guessing is easy ... but the so-called 'Pang Xin' was really impeccable. I've noticed all her tones, logic, body gestures, breaths and facial expressions, even the minor ones, but there was no sign of her that showed she's lying."

"Not working out when meeting a good liar? That's why I think you need to train your observation ability more." Bin pointed at the floor. "Come here now and then to observe the guests. It's a good way to practice, providing you with some leisure time at work and saving your life at emergencies. Good choice!"

I didn't agree. "You were not there ..."

"You told me just now that she didn't have a television in her living room."

"Yes."

"And no computers."

"Yes."

"And you didn't see a telephone."

"No."

"Cellphone?"

"No. Later investigation shows that there's no communication equipment in her house."

"Then you didn't feel something is wrong?"

"Just because she didn't watch TV, or use the Internet, or didn't want to get phone calls, she is to be identified as a serial killer? Oh my god! Your analysis is even smarter that Dr. Yuan's ..."

"She secludes herself from the outside world, on purpose."

"You can say she's autistic, but she plants trees and grows flowers. Is that gonna prove her guilty?"

"No autism will let you in just like that. They won't talk to you with tears or undertake or invest in adult industry." He was playing with that lighter while he was speaking, making it rotating under his finger. "Either the whole seclusion is for another purpose, or her activities while talking with you is fake. And they contradict with each other. And of course, if it wasn't for her lovely face, I believe you should have be alerted."

"He who has mind to beat his dog will easily find his stick."

"Let's start with a simplest common sense. She's got both flowering plants and foliage plants in her yard. But they need different fertilizers. Unless she's not using fertilizers, they won't be put together. Instead, she's got all of them in one yard, and dug around in a cold windy winter day. Does that sound suspicious to you?"

"She can just get some compound fertilizer."

"Do you think an audiophile will be satisfied with a RMVB video?"

"Yeah, I know. I'm not an idiot, but I really didn't know anything about flowers. Are you satisfied?"

"You've touched her?" Bin squeezed his eyes to look at me. "Ah! You've really touched her. ... Look, you didn't mention that at all. You touched her before I called? ... Oh, seemed to be after the call. Then it should be in the bedroom. You touched her hands? Hugged her? Or ..."

"Come on! Would you please stop observing me?"

Bin was annoying sometimes. He would point out all the details I've ignored with understatement, and then mocked at me while observing my justification. And the most annoying part lied in that he wasn't doing that intentionally. He didn't want to brag, or at least, he didn't take it as bragging. It was just like I've exerted all my effort to only work out a sandwich, but a chef can make a feast by only lifting his fingers — we were just not at the same level.

He unfolded the hand with a cigarette between his fingers. "Before you got annoyed, I only want to say that no matter before or after you stepped into her bedroom, what you saw, learned and inferred are much more that what you told me."

I turned away and pulled out a cigarette, but reluctant to light it up. "Anyway, I've given you hints through the phone. You can't blame me that I didn't take any precautions about the current situation."

"If you can immediately get me your location and told me what you're facing with, or simply control her by force, nothing will happen. At least, you won't have to explain to so many people about the reason you stepped into the bedroom of that woman, who was naked."

"I just don't want to alert the snake."

"Well, since you can tell that's a poisonous one, alerting the snake is not what you have to think about, but whether to kill it or not."

"But this one looks so much like Tong."

Seeing Bin narrow his eyes, I quickly switched to another subject.

"But I'm curious about the reason of such a sweet woman doing this ... I thought that if I pretended that I didn't notice what she was doing, there's a chance that I could get her tell. I knew that I was dosed with something, but if she gets the idea that I was under control, it's possible that she would say something to a man who's going to die. You know, it such a precious chance that Dr. Yuan would be screaming about it." Putting the cigarette between my lips, I took a glance at Bin only to find that he was still staring at me. "As a criminal investigator, and a researcher on criminal psychology, curiosity is a very essential quality, right?"

"I only know 'curiosity kills the cat'." He switched the grinding wheel on the lighter and a warm light came out before my eyes. "But the only problem is, you don't have nine lives."

The "Pang Xin" case was soon completely taken over by the City Bureau, probably serving as a precious research case for Dr. Yuan. Since it wasn't

159

helpful all for me in cracking the case under my jurisdiction, I don't have much interest in paying more attention to it.

But I did get much praises from this one.

Personal Merit Class II, Group Merit Class III, Outstanding Personnel ... and the Vice-Captain promoted directly by Zhou Hongruo, director of the General Political Department. Haha! I'm back boys, I'm back!

When Director Zhou announced my promotion, she came to me and said, "Well, if you ask me, you were overqualified for a vice-captain."

I pretended to be shy, fiddling with my hair. "You flatter me. I was counting on your compliment in front of Director Bai."

"Well, I knew you can be at least a vice-commander, from the first sight I met you." Zhong Hongruo nodded at me with a smile, and continued, "But..."

But it was Bai sacked me personally. How could he resume my post to break his own decision? I know the tricks here.

If I wanted to get promoted, Bai couldn't be my leader. It was better if Zhou, who liked me for now, was in his place. But Bai wouldn't leave by himself. There must be some pressure from the City Bureau, which was probably the close rate, or the serial killer's case that hasn't been closed by now (and if there were to be new cases, the pressure from the City Bureau may be more). If we couldn't solve the case by the end of the years, someone had to stand out to take the responsibility which, under the current situation, would be ascribed totally to the director. That would lead to the dismissal of Bai (and probably the first person of the Social Order Crops, too), and the promotion of Zhou (and that depended on whether she's got good connections). And then, Zhou would repay me, and promoted me as the vice-commander.

Ratiocination completed.

I smiled back, brightly. "I'll try by best."

As a seemingly response to our tacit agreement, no serial killing cases have even happened within the district in the following four months. The whole division and I were all doing the same thing: beating all kinds of criminals in the jurisdiction, and then try to work that serial killer out.

Xuejing would be surprisingly happy about my buying her roses and platinum earrings on our wedding anniversary. He Jingcheng would be upset about him cutting a weird wound on the chest of a body out of tiredness. Jiang would pull me to coach her since she wanted to attend the Sanda competition held by Haidian Branch, and Bai's yelling was still echoing around the passageway of the office building. In Fingerprint,

Zhang Beitong would be standing behind the counter, holding a cigar in his mouth and wiping the glasses, and Yichen would always try to steal a kill when Bin's napping on the sofa ... The wind was blowing, the cloud floating, and the cicadas were chirping in broad daylight.

Well, summer has come.

Since Yuan Shi switched his attention, the names of Chi Shanshan, Fang Wanlin, Xu Chunnan, and that left-hand doctor Song Dechuan were rarely mentioned. I knew that if we let them go like this, they would be forgotten as days passed by, like all the victims of other pending cases just as what the Ebbinghaus Forgetting Curve shows. Someone died, and the earth is still spinning, and life is still going on, as if they had never existed.

Even I would often take it a good thing, that this was good for everyone. Until one day.

On that day, I've just finished tracking down a helpless lead and happen to be around near Haidian Hospital. Out of a familiar feeling, I walked in the gate in spite of myself. It was in the afternoon. The policeman on duty was napping outside the ward in the fourth floor, which even saved me from explaining.

The small ward was all white. If she were to wake up, she wouldn't like it.

Sitting by the bed, I discovered sadly that the once beautiful and gorgeous lady has eventually fallen into this earthly world. When her mind couldn't control her body, she seemed really ordinary, and old. Wrinkles crept onto her forehead and the corner of her eyes, and from that moment on, I was sure that she, or the woman I saw in that yard, would never come back.

Even if there were a chance to wake up, I thought, even if there were, she would refuse it. The punishment from the legal system was not fatal. For her, she just lost all the meaning to exist in this world.

What she wanted most, and also what she was mostly in need of, was an identity — an identity that can be approved and accepted by the mainstream society.

She killed Pang Xin, and became a "Pang Xin" herself. But she wasn't able to steal her life. A person who couldn't find her identity in the society generated strong antisocial personality. She struggled in the swirl of dilemma. She hated the normal world, but tried every means to be one of them.

In her broad yard, she lived alone, ate alone, and slept alone, and grew flowers alone, and even cried alone. Maybe when she did all these, she felt the same with that when she killed alone — lonesome and desolate, isolated from the whole world.

So, she was scared of separation.

Is hanging the victims' photos on the bedroom wall a way to emphasize your existence?

Can the fragrance of the flowers in the yard remind you of their smell?

Is killing me a way to keep me by your side, like all the others killed here?

Yuan Shi must have come here for a lot of times. I could even imagine him staring at this woman, poking around with his eyes in a complicated feeling, curious and greedy, pleased and satisfied, as if she were some baby lambs in a cage with two heads and six legs.

I should thank her actually, because she has conveyed something that Yuan Shi would never get an insight on.

She only took the one she liked as her prey, so someone like Yuan Shi, who would probably disgust her, wouldn't even got the chance to be kept in the yard.

So, what kind of person would be qualified to keep her company?

A man with similar fate, right?

3

July, 13th, 2007, Black Friday.

I, once again, arrived at the gate of Haidian Hospital. But it was not for a visit this time.

Bai's strapping figure was like a statue with bold outline in the drizzle. He spoke calmly, but I could still feel his wrath underneath.

I lowered my head, unable to speak anything.

"Three kilometers, only three kilometers. No more than one kilometer away from Huangzhuang Police Station. It's the center of the center in our jurisdiction. People depend on us to protect their safety, but can we... can we meet their expectations?

In a serene summer day, when raindrops made no sound when falling on the ground, what Bai said were really harsh and strident.

According to the witness and the surveillance footage, Peng Kang, deputy director of the Cardial Surgery Department in Haidian Hospital, rushed into the office building and then directly to his office on 3rd floor before 10 o'clock in the morning, and locked himself inside.

At about 11 o'clock, a case was reported to Huangzhuang Police Station. In one of the lanes outside the west gate of the hospital, three bodies and a fainted boy were discovered. The three victims were all unemployed.

Zhang Xin, male, 19 years old, came from Beijing. Yan Shijia, male, 18 years old, came from Baoding, Hebei province. Zhao Changxing, male, twenty years old, came from Panjin, Liaoning province. According to He Jingcheng, they were all killed with a serrated sharp weapon.

In about half an hour, a second case was reported. Peng Kang was found dead by his colleague, who came to invite him for lunch. When he was discovered, the victim was lying under the desk, his throat cut open with the same weapon. He Jingcheng told me that for now, it was estimated that Peng Kang died at about ten minutes past ten, and the other three before half past ten, which means Peng Kang was the first one who's got killed and then the three young men. .

Four people died in broad daylight. Meanwhile, the victim Peng Kang was left handed.

All manpower from the local police station, the Criminal Investigation Division and the Social Order Crops had come. Since hospital was such a special location that it couldn't be on lockdown for a long time, Cao Fa had taken a team and the searching was already finished when I got there. He Jingcheng was taking some others the move the body, and Jiang told me that the only witness, whose name was Sun Duo was on his way to be questioned accompanied by his parents after some medical treatment. ... However, I was still wondering whether there was someone missing until I came in sight of Dr. Yuan.

Seeing his tall and straight figure, I finally felt that everyone that should show up was here.

Bai was gloomy, Jiang was frightened, Cao Fa was trying to keep calm and He Jingcheng was busy with a poker-face. Yuan Shi was ... Well, it would be a slander out of prejudice if I depicted him as excited, but his easy look was seen by everyone.

Jiang's introduction was simple because it was a simple case. There were surveillance cameras everywhere in the hospital and they were shooting the whole process crystal clear. Well, if they could get even one shot of the face of that guy in black military raincoat, that would be perfect.

Peng Kang rushed into the office building at 9:56, and at 10:01, the murderer followed him in. Since it was raining that day, his black raincoat didn't arouse any special attention. He lingered about half a second in the introduction billboard on the first floor, lifted one of the test records on the desk in front of the laboratory, and then climbed to the third floor through the staircase.

Standing outside the door of Peng Kang's office, he didn't knock, nor push it open. He extracted one paper from the records and inserted it through the little crevice to see whether the door was locked. Discovering the door was locked, he took the paperclip on the records and opened the door in less than five minutes. And then, he pushed in.

He Jingcheng estimated that from the location of the body, it was possible that Peng Kang heard something outside the door and started to walked to it. At the same time, the murderer came in. He punched Peng Kang on his left abdomen first, and then on the throat with his fist or elbow. After a series of attacks, Peng Kang was pinned to a desk by the murderer and cut throat from right to left with a serrated sharp weapon. Peng Kang may have died immediately, or he may struggled for another three or fours seconds. Anyway, when he rolled down on the ground, he was already died.

The surveillance camera got the murderer in and out in less than half a minute.

This was no serial killer, but a professional assassin.

He followed the target into a public place, searched the billboard to identify his possible location. He took the staircase to avoid surveillance cameras to lower his risk of exposure. Using the test paper he lifted on the way to test whether the door was locked without the victim's notice and then picked the lock open with the paperclip on the files. His first hit was to deprive the victim of the capability to defend, and his second move was to mute him. At last, he cut his throat, neat and clean.

Oh and the murderer was wearing gloves. He was really professional, no loose ends, no traces left.

If he really was that invisible and elusive serial killer, then I was willing to throw in my sponge. He was not an ordinary murderer, and this was definitely not his first time to kill. I would even believe this was his 100th murder.

Upon leaving in a hurry, He Jingcheng reminded me. "Pay attention to the wounds, the killers were not the same one."

Yeah, I've already noticed that the murderer was right handed not only from the cuts on all the victims, but the punch he gave Peng Kang and the gesture he picked the lock.

When he was leaving, he went out through exactly the same route to 1st floor, but didn't walked out from the front door, because this would let his face exposed in the surveillance camera in the southwest and east corner of the hall. He passed through the registration and charging offices, and left the building through the door of the west wing. There was a parking lot between the main gate of the hospital and the building, in which eight surveillance cameras were applied. He probably thought it was too risky to walk out from the west wing to the south gate, so he climbed the west wall of the yard, and left successfully, or almost successfully.

Because an accident took place just at this time.

The office sent what they got from the witness back to us at the first time. Sun Duo, eleven years old, was a Grade Five student from the Peking University Elementary School. He lived in the Dahejiayuan Community to the northwestern of Haidian Hospital. He attended an extracurricular class during his summer vacation which was located in Zhichunli Elementary School. The class finished at ten o'clock in the morning, and Sun Duo was taken to a lane in the west of Haidian Hospital by Zhang Xing, Yan Shijia and Zhao Changxing. When they were about to terrify and rob him, there was a man jumping down from the wall.

And that was all. That was all that he saw.

Since Sun Duo was extremely terrified, he showed some symptom of PTSD after he woke up. He couldn't completely recall what had happened on the scene, especially after the murderer had shown up. Considering his situation, his parents were strongly against our further question on him, and the doctors also suggested us to stop questioning him since his many symptoms showed he's been suffering from temporary insanity.

Zhang Xing, Yan Shijia and Zhang Changxing were all yobs strolling around the hospital regularly. The research of their background showed that they've robbed different students for various times. The Security Department of Haidian Hospital reported that they attempted to rob a patient at the beginning of the year but failed. In early March, a case was reported to Huangzhuang Police Station by a parent and Zhao Changxing was taken in custody. But since the money he robbed was not much and the reporters didn't want to get into any trouble so they gave up testifying, he was released after several days.

If they had known that they would lost their lives for robbing a kid and ended up with death, they would definitely choose to be choir boys. But it was unfortunate that there was nothing called regret pills in the world,

After learning about all the information, we have finished the investigation of the crime scene. Now it was the time to clean our ears for Dr. Yuan's comment.

However, Yuan Shi didn't make any comments as he usually did. Instead, he put forward a proposal that sounds quite irritating. "This is a complicated case. Can I get Professor Han or his son here? Just for suggestions. What do you think, Director Bai?"

Bai turned to me to ask for my opinion silently. I didn't say anything, but present my cellphone instead — I could do nothing to this ridiculous request. If you want to say yes, then you'll have to ask him personally.

"Broad daylight, public location, four victims, and close to the Branch and police stations. Uncle Bai must be getting crazy."

Bin parked his car outside the warning line at the gate of the hospital. I asked one of our girls to accompany Yichen in the car and then shrugged to Bin. "Speaking of getting crazy? I'm one of them."

"Well, you should not be that crazy."

"Neither did Bai. It was that James Brussel who asked you here personally."

Bin didn't seem to be surprised. He just looked up into the gloomy sky and said, "Well, no wonder they say 'Steal in a windy day, not when the moon is in the sky; steal in a rainy day, not when snow is " 所以呢？ "

"So?"

"So, it is a good day to kill."

"Your father does have a certain reputation in the academic field in mainland China."

I'd rather Yuan Shi didn't say things like this. He didn't even mean to flatter by using "mainland China" and "certain reputation", and he didn't talk about Bin himself, but his father. The condescension in his talking was no less than a demonstration of him winning every Golden Raspberry Awards on criminal profiling.

Bin gave him a bland smile, cautious and respectful.

"Anubis?" Yuan didn't give up observing Bin. "The God of Death in Egyptian mythology." He held his pendant with MS carved on it between his fingers. "It seemed that we took opposite sides concerning fatalism."

I knew Yichen and Bin were wearing same silver necklaces with the pendant of a werewolf. He told me they bought them with 70 yuan in a random shop on the first floor of their office building. Does it have any connections with their living philosophies or values?

Jiang cut in just in the right time to stop all this nonsense. "We've checked all surveillance footage within the surrounding two blocks. No trace of the murderer. If he's not deliberately avoiding the surveillance cameras and IR dome cameras, he is driving or taking a taxi. Shall we check all vehicles that passed before and after the crime?"

I shook my head. "No, he's not driving. Few people would wear such kind of raincoat nowadays, especially for those who drive. They won't keep a raincoat in the car, an umbrella at most."

Finally, Yuan Shi switched his attention to business. "If he didn't want to be turned down by the driver, he wouldn't wear a raincoat. It seems that the people who ride bicycles are more willing to wear raincoats. But if the suspect is riding a bicycle in such an ancient raincoat, we can definitely catch him from the footage.

"He is afraid of exposing himself. He wears that raincoat to cover him better."

"Probably." Yuan Shi turned around to look at Bin. Seeing Bin was reading the investigation record attentively, he continued, "The point is what the suspect is hiding from? The surveillance cameras? Or Peng Kang? What do you think?"

I was about to speak when I found that he wasn't asking me.

Looking up and happening to meet Yuan Shi's eyes, Bin answered with no hesitance. "From the victim, I suppose."

It seemed Yuan Shi was holding his smile. "Whoops! Why is that?"

"I don't know."

"What?"

"My assumption."

"Your father may not be satisfied with your explanation."

I was a little annoyed. "You're not the one who raised him up."

Bin gestured me to calm down and explained, "I didn't even finish the investigation record, Doctor. You asked, I answered. If you think it's not good, then I'm sorry."

"Your hunch is good." Yuan Shi scanned from me to Bin back and forth. "The suspect, or the murderer, was not planning this murder in advance."

The location and time was not good, and he chose something on the scene to pick the lock. He even didn't know the victim's office before he got there. Bin's a gentleman, but I am not. "Dr. Yuan, would you share something that we don't know?"

"It's simple. The murderer is following Peng Kang, but somehow he exposed himself. So he decided, on the spur of the moment, to kill him."

Bai lost his patience. "Are they the same person?"

Yuan Shi answered with full confidence, "Yes." And I responded calmly, "No."

Now there were disagreements. Yuan Shi, the pro. Zhao Xincheng the con. Bai Yanshang, the judge, and Han Bin, the special guest. Jiang Lian, the recorder, and Cao Fa, Zhang Qi and seven other policemen were watching the show. Each side gave their opinions alternately.

OK. The debate began.

The pro said, "Same weapons and both left-handed victims — those three outside the hospital don't count, they're not the planned target of the murderer — this corresponds with previous serial cases."

The con answered, "Yes. But the killer for this case is not a left-hander. The wounds show that ..."

The pro cut in. "I know that the marks left by him picking that door and the traces left by his punch all show that he had done it with his right hand, but I have to point out that using his right hand doesn't mean he is a right-hander."

The con reprimanded. "You can't expect a left-hander to pick a lock with his right hand in two seconds."

The pro talked back. "We didn't know whether he's a left-hander or a right-hander. But what you said just now shows that you're sure he's a left-hander."

The con took an example. "All female victims in previous cases were killed by someone using his left hand."

The pro continued to talk back. "Why can't he kill someone with his left hand while being an right-hander? It's easier than picking a lock with his weak hand."

The con started to talk back too. "Then why can't there be two murderers? The current five murders were showing two distinctive MOs."

The pro defended. "Do you mean there's a copycat?"

The con concluded. "In my opinion, there were two serial killers, one raper focused on killing woman, and the other focused on killing men whose motive hasn't been fount out yet."

The pro asked, "Did you say two MOs?"

The con continued. "In Chi, Fang and Xu's cases, the murderer held the weapon with his left hand. He has a clear sexual attempt, and he takes random targets. He is a passionate murderer with cruel but simple means, which makes him leave so many clues that can be used for matching his identities. In Song and Peng's cases, however, the murderer is a mature and experienced one. These two cases are both home invasion. The murderer cut out their throats with weapon held by his right hand, and picked the door open with an iron wire or a paper clip. They both avoided all surveillance cameras, they chose doctors as their victims and left no fingerprints of footprints. ... This is a total violence to the Locard's Exchange Principle[1]!

---

1 Locard's Exchange Principle is an important part of forensic science investigation. According to Locard's Exchange Principle, the perpetrator of a crime will bring something into the crime scene and leave with something from it, and that both can be used as forensic evidence.

This man is a professional assassin, and a really good one."

The judge stopped the debate and answered a phone call. "Hello? Fuck! I'm the one who built your sea-view house! Why do I fucking need yours!"

The pro nitpicked. "Two serial killers with distinctive motives and MOs happened to kill five left-handers?"

The con didn't give up. "The murderer who killed Song and Peng used different weapons in the two cases. So maybe he chose a serrated knife on purpose today. So from a certain perspective, the theory of a copycat may work out."

The pro continued on trapping the con. "But if he's a professional, does it make any sense to do this? Does he have a certain desire for using serrated weapons? Or curious about that perpetrator of rape?"

The con jumped into the trap happily. "I've heard that curiosity can kill a cat. No matter he is copycat or not, he probably wants to take the chance to stir the water, making some troubles to our investigation. That's frequently seen in a case."

The judge asked, "A copycat?"

The special guest answered, "Yes. That's a kind of behavioral classification in western criminology field. It means a perpetrator who chooses to use the same or similar means to assault the victim when there's a well-known serial killer is committing some crimes. Most copycats commit their crimes to pay respect, or misdirect the investigation."

The con suddenly defended. "If there were a copycat, that would be a right-handed man no less than 30 years old. He would be middle-figured, and is familiar to the previous cases with women as victims. He would also have a good knowledge of police's searching procedures and acquires a certain counter-reconnaissance ability."

The con turned his head. "Yes, and we can narrow the scope down when more details came out."

The judge smelled something wrong. "If you say so, half of the division would be suspicious."

The con was still happy about the temporary triumph. "Including you and the Director. We can all be questioned in turn."

The pro finally said, "I didn't suspect it would be someone with the police system ..."

All the people present looked awkward, except for Bai, who was staring at me angrily, and Bin, who was passing the files to Jiang calmly. I then realized one thing: I was totally defeated.

Fuck! I was played.

"Well, the women who was beaten to a vegetable several days ago was still lying in this hospital, right?" Bin said, straight to the point. "I didn't expect that I would a part one day in a serial killer's carnival. Male, middle-figured, will be 30 years old this October, right handed, familiar to the police system, get a knowledge of the case and a certain counter-reconnaissance ability maybe ..."

Yuan Shi's purpose was never refuting me.

"I would be you primary suspect."

Victory was on his side.

4

Bin was straightly taken to the City Bureau to be questioned, and the case was reported to the Criminal Investigation Division of the City Bureau.

Bai went to visit Professor Han in a hurry after scolding me. I followed him all the way to the interrogation room in the City Bureau and, outside the explosion-proof one-way glass, I could see someone putting the respiration sensor and sphygmomanometer of the polygraph onto him.

At the same time, Yuan Shi walked in with the case file. He glanced at me, unhappily. "What are you doing here?"

I stepped forward and seized him by his tie. He almost toppled over. The two policemen in the room were probably not field agents. They were trying to talk us apart but didn't even come to pull me out.

"Do you want to stay any more?" Yuan Shi spruced himself up in a blush. "As long as I ..."

"As long as you report this and I have to leave, right? Nothing new?" I took a glance at a policeman sneaking away from the room but I didn't stop him. "I come to take him out on the division's behalf. You'll have to thank me."

"Zhao Xincheng! Don't forget you're a policeman. It's about several murders, and you'd better clear your mind!"

"You are the one who doesn't have a clear mind, Doctor."

"I don't have any personal issues with him. This is entirely for the case."

"Is Han Bin in custody, or he's already been arrested?"

"Neither. This is just a normal interrogation."

"Then you shouldn't take the one who should be questioned by our division to here. You shouldn't put him in the interrogation office, nor the fucking polygraph!"

"He agreed."

"Bullshit! What if he doesn't? Will that give you more reason to suspect him? Don't play like this. If you want to question him, that's OK. I'll take him back to Haidian Division."

"People in Haidian Division are very close to him and his father. You should be excluded."

"Then you are the one who's competing with him in the field of criminal profiling. You should also be excluded."

"Me? Competing with him?" Yuan Shi's shoulders heaved with laughter. "I don't have to degrade myself to compete with a former leader of a non-governmental community.

"You didn't even meet him in person before today. Your playing with him is just an approach to depress his father. You only follow your own way. Being an expert of the City Bureau and you still want to expel your peers how mean you are! Besides, do you know who Han Songge is?"

"Only someone fishing for fame and credit using the bureaucracy system here in mainland China."

I pointed at him with my index finger. "I'm not a rude man. But if you ever dare to say that again, do you believe I can sent you to be roommates of that "lab rat"of yours lying in Haidian Hospital?"

"And should you dare to continue like this, do you believe I can actually get you out of the system?" Yuan Shi blushed heavily. "My patience is limited!"

We stood in a stalemate for a while and I shrugged. "We both understand that Han Bin comes from a rich family. He doesn't have any financially problems. He lives a normal life both in terms of his work or his personal life, and he is gentle. He won't be any suspects. I believe the alibi would clarify his name in just a short time. Haidian Division has the ability to conduct the investigation objectively, and you can save your time here."

"I ..."

"Let me finish. I can tell you what's going on right now. Bai must have told his father and would come to take Han Bin away after his coordination with the City Bureau. Right at the time we are speaking, numerous phone calls have been made to every leader in the City Bureau and their Criminal Investigation Division, including Bin's father. But I can tell you, Bin's father will say it's Bin's duty to cooperate with the division, and the City Bureau doesn't have to have any concern and just focus on the case."

Yuan Shi's chest was still heaving, but I can tell he's starting to calm down. He was thinking.

"I can tell you what will happen next. You may discover now that this is a really big joke, but you would insist on questioning and detecting since it has already started. The process may be interrupted, by a call from leaders of the City Bureau or the captain of the Criminal Investigation Division? I don't know which, but the content would be the same. You will be asked about the reasons you did this, and introduced to Han Songge's background with a blaming tone. Finally, you'll be told to apologize and let him go the minute he is cleared of suspicion."

"But he is on suspicion."

"Yes, just like you and me. I don't want to argue on that one." I turned around to see Bin in the room, and turned back. "The last thing I want to say it, Yuan Shi, you're not good-for-nothing. You have a good theory, plenty of experiences, support from the government and the power to say a word. But you're too dogmatic, too elite, and too proud. You take yourself superior than others. I'm telling you, the moment you push open that door, you have to be prepared for the consequences."

"Thank you for your concern, but I'm immune to this kind of mechanism."

"No, I don't mean any pressure you're going to take from the outside. It's that you don't even understand you're going to face."

"Do you?"

"Of course I do."

And I have seen it in the snowy night with my own eyes.

Yuan Shi walked by my said, apparently pull me closer from the side of his enemy. "Is he, Han Songge's son, difficult to deal with?"

"One last time, let me deal with him. And I was doing this to avoid more contradictions, and also to help you."

"Don you think I'm the one who's gonna compromise?"

"You silly ..." I murmured. Then I bowed a bit, and waved at the door. "Not scared of being humiliated? Help yourself then."

Two hours later, the persistent Dr. Yuan walked out of the interrogation room, pretending to be calm, and found himself surrounded not only by me and the policemen who were in charge of recording, but also the captain of the Criminal Investigation Division of the City Bureau, leader of the Supervision Office, vice-captain of the technical team of the City Bureau, Bai Yinshang, Liu Qiang, Jiang Lan and some other people, even He Jingcheng who was just coming to join the fun. He was totally unexpected and took half a step back by a room of people.

Actually, the Haidian Division has already brought a dozens of reports. Today when Peng Kang was killed, Bin was at home with Yichen since she caught a cold. He stayed at home until Bai called him to the crime scene. He drove out, which can be verified from the surveillance camera at the gate of the community where he lived in, and the time corresponded with the time Bai called him. And a more concrete evidence was, when Song Dechuan was killed, he was out on a journey with Yichen in Guangxi province. On the day the crime took place, they stayed in one of the resident's home in Sidao town in the south of Jingxi city. There was a certificate from the local police station showed that it was verified that a couple had been paying to live in No. 27 Minzheng Rd. from December 13th to 18th, 2006. The girl is young, and they didn't get a name, but the man was no more than 40 years old, and was named Han Bin.

Be that as it might, all of us present, all of us didn't intend to help Yuan Shi out of this awkward situation, or at least stop the drama that embarrassed him a lot. People talking and laughing, even had a bet on the final result, gloating over his embarrassment and expecting a subtitle like "Next Episode" when it ended.

Gentle as he is, Bin was no coward. He could chose not to get involved, but if he put his hand on it, he would spare no effort. And he might have done it on purpose because the words he uttered were really harsh when he talked back on Dr. Yuan's comment to his father.

I even started to have sympathy for him somehow.

And then, there began the interrogation inside the system.

"I was staking out on Hailong Building at that time."

"My team members and I went to deal with that kidnapping gang. You can ask others if you don't believe me."

"I was on duty that night. The schedule is on the wall."

"Zhang Qi and I had some midnight snack before we headed to the scene, and we brought shaomai[1] back for you. Did you forget all that after having all of them?"

"I was out on a training program! They've got armed police guarding the door. Go out and kill someone? I have to climb over the entanglements for a mutton shashlik!"

"I was alone out on a case that night. No witnesses. Fuck! Do you think I want to stay in the bush for half a night?"

......

Most of the alibis were out on duty, most of the witnesses were colleagues, and most of the answers were sarcastic rhetorical questions. I was not looking for a copycat, I was serving as a garbage bin. Spending

---

1　A traditional Chinese snack with fillings inside.

two weeks listening to sarcasm and ironies, complaints and grievances, I reported to Bai with hot tears in my eyes. "The investigation's over. We are all clean. Please let me go, boss, please."

Bai didn't even give me a response, probably because he thought the result should be like his. "Go and apologize to Bin's father."

I didn't have the courage now to face Bin's father, but the apology to Bin was necessary. Of course, as friends, he could understand my situation, and I could take that he understood my situation. So the so-called apology could be left behind. The dinner at his place was a normal dinner and a chance to get his comments of Yuan Shi's profile for the suspect.

However, the speaker was not as patient as the audience. After omitting several theories in western criminology statistics, technology terms of criminal psychology and some quotes from celebrities, I concluded Yuan Shi's profile like this: There is only one murder who committed several crimes and killed eight people.

"A serial killer with dual personality and probably suffering from sexual deviation?" Bin asked with a light voice, probably afraid of waking up Yichen asleep in the bedroom.

"Not really, I mean, Yuan Shi thought it was not really. In his opinion, he believes that the murderer has dissociative identity disorder, but no sexual deviation."

"So one of the identities is left handed, and the other right handed."

"Yes. That's what he said."

"But he only kills left-handers."

"Those three yobs are not, but they were not his planned targets."

"I can understand that each identity has a strong hand, but why does he only kill left-handers?"

"That's the tricky part. Can you guess his explanation?"

"Well, in fairy tales, the gods of the sun and the moon were converted from the two eyes of Pan Gu, the ancient god. The god of the sun, Fu Xi, stays on the left and the god of the moon, Nüwa on the right, which is probably the origin of 'men on the left and women right'."

"What the fuck! You ..."

"If it is because this kind of god worship, then it would be able to explain why the murderer thinks that he has the right to brings death and makes alive since he can both use his right hands well and left hands."

"But don't forget he only kills left-handers."

"Yeah, that's bad luck for the victims. Do you know 'right live but left die?' A traditional saying from the past."

"Er... You first."

"Clothes in the Han Dynasty were different from ours today. They use different position of their collars to express different meanings. When you're alive, you right collar should be put on your left one, and opposite after you die. Now we didn't wear their clothes, and no one wears graveclothes alive. Taking left-handers as a standard for life and death can be seen as a distorted replacement. He will kill anyway, and he'll find himself an excuse."

"You've been told that?"

"What?"

"Then you've talked with Yuan Shi."

"How come!"

"Oh my! What you've just said is exactly the same with Yuan Shi. Exactly!"

"College students studying ancient Chinese history would say something similar, OK?"

"You don't agree with that, do you?"

"Does it matter? They are all assumptions anyway before catching the murderer. Assumptions can be brainstormed. No big deal."

"You agree with him? Come on! Are you feeling guilty to have dissed him to hard?"

"Even so, that means I wasn't mature enough. I'll blame myself."

"Back to business. I still think there's more than one murderer. What's your opinion?"

"I don't know the details. No opinions."

"I brought the case file with me."

"Bring them back the way you bring them in. I don't want to talk about this."

"Hey!"

"I'm not joking. You said there's a copycat, and I agree with you. Therefore I don't want to bring myself in. Cooperating with the police on questioning or interrogation is the duty of a citizen, but no one likes to frequently expose their privacy."

I heaved a sigh. "You still blame on me bringing you in."

"Xincheng, I'm not a policeman, nor a detective who's making a living on this, let alone some justice advocate who likes to digging into crimes. I'm only a lawyer, and like everyone else, I'd like to live my own life in a normal way."

"But you're Han Songge's son, and the founder of the workshop."

"Working for my father is filial piety, and the workshop was just working my hobby out. Finding some foreign cases to discuss is something to enjoy in my spare time, but walking into a crime scene is just too much for me."

Hearing this, I could only took out my last resort. "I'm coming to ask for your help."

Bin avoided my eyes. It was the first time that he really refused my request after all these years.

And it was also the first time that I didn't continue my persuasion brazen-faced. "Don't feel sorry. I'll try myself. Well, I'm leaving. You have a good night."

Bin was surprised at my response. It made me happy to see his unexpected face. When he stood up, he said in a state of panic. "I'll see you out."

It was midnight when we came down. Bin lived in a community with good landscape. The night was cool and pleasant. Street lamps were far away from each other and most of the time we were walking on the paths flanked by luxuriant shady trees. Cicadas chirping and breeze passing through the foliage, all seemed to be serene and enjoyable.

"Live your life in a normal way ... that would include a wife and children." I blinked to him. "The latter part ... How old is Yichen now? How many years to the legal marriage age?"

"That's my sister. What are you talking about?"

"It doesn't matter that you want to be a bachelor, but don't ruin her life."

"She will have her own life when she grows up."

"She won't be able to leave you." Seeing that he's worried, I thought the age gap between them was a big barrier. "You won't either."

"Actually, I agree with you. It's more possible to have two murderers."

I knew he was redirecting, but the direction was to appealing. "One of them is a perpetrator of rape, and the other a professional assassin?

"Probably."

"About that professional assassin, Peng Kang and Song Dechuan were both doctors. Although there are no other connections found between them, but there must be something behind it. In my view, I think Peng Kang probably knew the murderer. You see, he was panic and locked the door, and ..."

"He didn't call the police."

"Yes. Before the murderer broke in, he had already knew that he was in danger, but he didn't call the police. The investigation of his phone calls shows that he had made a phone call from his office, and the receiver had a phone number of 17 digits."

"An international call?"

"It's not registered. We can't fine anything about it. Yang Yanpeng said this is a kind of satellite phone. I told him to look into it. Maybe that's a point to wedge in."

"In this way, the phone call must be very important, at least more important than calling the police."

"He doesn't call the police for help, but called a eccentric number. It's either that he thought the person on the other side of the phone was more capable than the police, or he had some secrets that didn't want to be revealed to the public."

"Maybe he just didn't thought that he would followed and killed in broad daylight."

I shook my head. "Then he died of innocence. ... The murderer dashed in and out in broad daylight. Maybe the police won't make it even if the victim called. Well, just like what you've said, the rain helped him. Or he will be remembered as a wired man wearing a raincoat in a sunny day — although I don't believe Peng Kang would ever avoid this."

"People with experience of serving as an armed police or related training experience."

"Yeah. We've already worked on that, but I think the scope can be narrowed in a further way. Do you remember Shi Zhan? That retired armed police in that fake kidnapping case last autumn? He was harder to deal with than ordinary criminals, but not as hard as this one. Actually, normal armed police and soldiers won't be as good as him."

"Because four killed?"

"Because he's not killing the fifth. I don't think he is just being conscientious when letting Sun Duo go. He doesn't have any moral bottom line or professional codes to follow. It's because he just kills two kinds of persons — his target, and the potential witness. If Sun Duo is qualified to be a witness, either old enough or clear enough, he would never let him go."

When we arrived at where my car parked, Bin especially reminded me that for a criminal focused on killing women, there's no need to pay much attention to whether the victim is left-handed. That isn't an appealing body feature. So far, there isn't any serial perpetrators of rape who take this to identify their targets."

"But it is his most obvious feature for now." I opened the truck and put the case file inside. "Of course, and that Spider. By the way, you don't really believe Yuan Shi's fairy tale theory, do you?"

"I don't really care about that." Bin looked up to the crown of the trees. "It isn't something you need to pay attention either. The motive of the murderer wasn't that important. What you need to find is the clue that can help you identify the criminal."

"Yes, we do have so many clues. We've got DNA and fingerprints, and weapons, and his height and age. We know he is left handed, his target groups and his MO. We know a lot things. We just couldn't find him."

"Speaking of MOs, that day when you were arguing with Dr. Yuan on the crime scene, you've said that there are two distinctive MOs if we divide the cases according to the gender of the victims. But you can also pay a little more attention to that perpetrator of rape. He would have more than one ..."

Here, he stopped all of a sudden.

I first thought he was thinking or organizing his words, but I soon discovered that his attention was not on our conversation any more. He seemed to be puzzled, eyes looking around and blinking a lot.

He made me upset.

The so-called "instinct" may not entirely depends on the psychological sense out of physical feelings, but more on professional training and practices. And on that tranquil late night, my "instinct" reminded me, once and again, until I noticed something was not right.

The night wind passed by me, like a lingering traveller who didn't want to leave.

The one who felt upset was Bin.

Then followed the quiver. When our eyes crossed for a second time, we both saw confusion, doubt and uneasiness in each other's eyes. But whatever it was, the reason was clear — the gentle wind, a quiet companion, a tranquil night, and the only one that didn't go with the others —

The chirping of the cicadas has gone.

Chapter V

Diverged Road

1

The minute the sound came from the bush behind us, an iron hand, which almost maim me, has strangled my neck before I, who graduated from the police school and won the second place in a fighting competition, could find any time to defend, and Bin was unable to utter his warning.

At that time, I totally got the meaning of "as sudden as lightening": it was so fast that you couldn't find any chance to react.

The pain started from my neck, and sent me to another world as if there were a black whole on my back and I was sucked into it.

It was Bin who dragged me back.

As he was saving me, he stepped up to fight with the attacker. I lied prone on the front of my car, probably passed out for several seconds. When I became conscious, I looked back and saw Bin and the attacker were both on the ground. Bin was lying under the attacker, his legs locking his left hand, his both hands clasping the attacker's right hand holding a black dagger — not trying to grab it, but aiming at controlling him.

I dashed up to help, but the attacker struggled all of a sudden, his two legs pining my knee and my ankle, and tripped me over from a side. At the same time, he bounced back with the help of my weight and got himself straight up, as well as Bin. As Bin was swung out, I heard a the sound of metal falling on the ground — he should be rid of his knife.

I took a long roll and got up to hit him in a hurry. But he grabbed my fist and dragged me close him. What the fuck! I slipped aside to support my body by another feet and intended to kick him on the shank, when there was a swift wind coming from the right. Instinctively, I lowered my head and my elbow and lifted my arm in front of my face, which was pressed directly on my face by a hard swing.

He was too fast to be a human being.

After he forced me back, he didn't follow up, but turned around to deal with Bin. Vaguely, I saw two figures hitting each other with fists and elbows within a very short distance. But they were both fast, too fast.

Seemingly stepping on the clouds, I propped my self against the car, opened the front passenger seat door and reached for the lid of the storage. It didn't open for the first time. I pulled it hard and the whole lid was torn out of the storage, things inside littering all around. I knelt down to fumble on the mat and finally got a touch of the familiar plastic handle.

However, the handy weapon was not so useful as a toothpick at the moment. I waved it at his head, but missed. As if having eyes all over his body, he moved his right shoulder a little bit, clamped my nightstick with his elbow and kicked me right on my ribs. That was a hard one. I twitched under his hard attack and the nightstick was swung out.

And then, he was badly hit and fell towards me. Behind him, Bin gave him a hard blow.

The attacker stumbled a bit, which gave me a chance to grab his neck. Before I could tripped him over, he bent down to lift me up. He was too strong. I couldn't even pull my arm back and was directly thrown out.

When I got up on my feet, he was nowhere to be found.

"I've thought that there were loads of clues, just without a search range. Well, now they've come to me and I just messed up a sure thing." I said to relax myself, as well as to comfort Xuejing.

Xuejing got tears in her eyes. She wasn't in the mood to respond to my tease. "Take off your clothes and let Mr. He check your back."

I behaved like a good boy and started to undo my buttons. "Don't worry. I'm fine. People like us are bound to meet several occasions like this. I've met too many, and life will treat me well in the future."

Several of my team members come to check my situation after they've finished checking the scene, and even Cao Fa came to comfort. I was really touched, but still asked about Bin first. "How's Han Bin doing?"

"He was sent to hospital." The voice came from behind.

"His hand?"

"Yeah. The wound was along the vein on his left wrist, as long as seven or eight centimeters. And the blood vessel may be hurt. He remembered that it may have been caused when he snatched his knife." He Jingcheng patted my on the shoulder. "Put your clothes on and go get X-rayed."

"I'm fine." I put my shirt on, the shoulder aching as if it were torn off my body. "Cao, send some of our guys to protect him."

Bai, who spoke nothing from the very beginning, said, "Go and get X-rayed. Don't let Pan worry."

I didn't care about where I was anymore and enfolded Xuejing in my arms. "I'm fine, honey. I'm not the target."

Dozens of eyes looked at me simultaneously, in doubt.

"Now that the attacker's got a knife, he could just stab him from the back. Now he's still alive, which means the attacker didn't want to kill him." He Jingcheng nodded and turned to me, pointing at my neck. "Your neck was badly hurt. Are you sure he has done his with his hand?"

"I supposed so. What?"

"He's tough. Take off your shirt and give it to the technical team. Maybe they can get a DNA from it. And ... did you say it was Bin who pulled you away?"

"Yeah. I was completely out of strength when he took me."

"Well, he saved your life. You owed him this one. That was aiming at your fourth vertebra. If Han was late for half a second, you'd have to live your life on a wheelchair."

I patted on my chest. "Well, we'd have to put those who's got sharp fingers within radius."

"His plan should be to take you down first and then deal with Bin." He Jingcheng took my shirt and passed it to others. "But attacking from the back was normally aiming at the back of your head or to strangle your neck. ... This one is weird. His move was difficult to perform, but he did it well."

Not wanting Xuejing to continue hearing this, I lifted my chin to some of the police on the scene not far from us. "What are the technical guys doing there?"

"Searching the ground maybe. Want to find some hair left by the attacker."

"What about the surveillance camera there?"

Cao Fa shook his head. "Nothing found. He definitely didn't go through the gate."

I sneered. "They were all for us good civilians and the pilferers."

Bai gestured me to hurry to the hospital, but still asked, "Do you mean this one is the killer in Haidian Hospital?"

"Not sure. But in my view, if there's a man who can kill four people and disappears into nowhere, he must be our No.1 candidate." I looked at Cao Fa and said, "The way he avoided surveillance cameras is the same, isn't it?"

"Are you saying you're the tough one? This one is tougher than you."

"Tougher? He is the the most cruel one I've ever seen!" I put on the shirt Jiang passed me, the wound on my back hurting heavily. "I didn't know Han Bin was tougher than me until today. He can really fight with that guy. With both of us standing together, we can barely survive in his hands."

"You didn't see his face?"

"No. I was in complete daze after the punch. I cannot see a shit!" I lowered my eyes and tried to recall some memories. "He was male, that's for sure. Thirty to forty years old and has a middle figure. He has a wide shoulder and wears rubber shoes and a overall. Nothing more that I can recall about his clothes, only that he was wearing long sleeves. He held the weapon in his right hand. He's got a long face and no beard, which I cannot be sure of. He's a real fighter, but not the way of fighting a free combat. His speed, strength and reaction was overwhelming. He must be an expert on that business."

Bai must have thought of Shi Zhan because he asked, "A retired armed police?"

"Not many people to search from ... I've fight with Shi Zhan. Considering there were factors disadvantageous to him, I was no better than him. But this one, I don't know whether he's from the mainland or not, but he was way better than me or Shi Zhan. You'd better get some good ones when searching for him and doing the interview. Ordinary policemen cannot even approach him."

"Yeah ... and ask Bin later on or pay attention his acquaintances. He may know Bin ..."

Bai's phone was ringing. He didn't pick it up and continued to ask, "Do you know anyone that would do this to Han Bin or his father?"

Still thinking about what I have missed, I just answered, "No."

"Then why would he want to kill him?"

"Hate? Or jealous? About his cafe business running too good? Who knows. But from my point of view, the most possible reason could be ..."

I stopped for a second thought. Bai urged me, "What?"

I blinked my eyes. "He must have been sure that once Bin is involved in the investigation, he will finally be caught."

That was big.

Although Bin was a just a nobody, but his father, though retired recently, was a sure somebody. Since it was related to attacking police and several murder cases, the whole system knew about this just in few days.

Having it discussed for several days, the City Bureau announced

182

it as "Cast 0812 - A Violent Attack to Police", turning it from "a case supervised by the City Bureau" to a "special case".

The first thing Yuan Shi said to me when he saw me was, "Is there a chance that it was Han Bin who plotted all these to wash himself out of suspicion?

I asked back, "Have you ever fought with someone?"

"I am Black Belt Phase II certified by USTU."

"Wow! Such an intelligent and charming person!" I flattered him before he could talk back. "But as one of the victims, I can assure you that it was a tough fight. Nothing fake, all real.

Yuan Shi mumbled unwillingly, "Then there should be two serial killers."

"I've told you there were two very different criminals with distinct MOs."

"I've heard that the attacker was targeted at Han Bin?"

"That was from me."

"Why do you think he was targeted at Han Bin?"

"Two possibilities: First, he was the target of this attack. Then your left-hand theory won't work. Being friends for so many years, I can assure you that Han Bin is a right hand. Second, the attacker is afraid of his ability and presumes that he could solve the case. So he takes some precautions."

Dr. Yuan was clearly displeased with my speculation. "If so, why not ask Han Bin to lead the team?"

"You wish. Things like this may be nothing to us, but not to a civilian like him. He was almost freak out. Don't count on his involvement in the case any more."

"Are there any 'secret weapons' in your team besides him?"

"Yes."

"Who's that?"

"Me."

Yuan Shi put both his hands crossed in front of his face to cover his mouth, or to prevent him from mocking at me. "The way to attack you from the back should be some special skill. You can take that as a lead. The fact that the attacker abandoned the normal and simple way and specifically chose this way which needs great accuracy shows that he was very familiar with it."

"Yeah, I've noticed. I've already sent a 'secret weapon' to follow that lead."

"Are you the secret weapon?"

"Yeah, but a secret weapon should be protected."

"Ha! A weapon used to arm a 'secret weapon'?"

"FBI, KGM, or ... how about our local psychological research team?"

— That was total bullshit. The standard answer was: the Ministry of State Security.

"Actually, there's no need to search since I can tell you now that the way the attacker controlled you is called 'Tiger Bite'." Yang Yanpeng passed several pieces of paper to me. "But that's not a fighting skill. It's said it was an ancient means of interrogation."

"What's that?"

"It was once used by the guards of Kim Il-sung and Tou Samouth, as well as the Japanese Red Army when they attack the French Embassy in Holland. Anyway, all the people who know about that are the Left, or more precisely, the Left from abroad."

"That doesn't seem like a large range. Anyone to go on for a further search?"

"Well, that's the tricky part. They were overseas organizations. We cannot reach that far. And it's a modern world now. China doesn't provide asylums for these people."

"Sneaking in?"

"Sneaking in for two doctors? To such a big country? That's not practical."

"Well, it's a meaningful lead. Go on with that." I flipped through the pile of paper he gave me. "What are these?"

"St. Raison Center is the New York office of one of the institutes for infectious disease research in America. It was founded and sponsored by a medical foundation with the same name."

"And ...?" After all, it was I who ask him for help. I had to show some patience.

"The founder of the foundation was called Steven Barrett, a former U.S. Navy officer, and now he is the second largest munitions smuggler in America."

I nodded.

"Around 1999, Barrett was recruited by Lockheed Martin and became a shareholder and was assigned as the CEO of Biochemical Technology Development Department."

"And ...?"

"And then, Lordan Electronic Products Sales Group, one of the subordinates of Lockheed Martin, cooperated with Donard Consultancy and invested in several businesses in America, French, England and Finland, in which the performance of William Wales Company was the best.

"And ...?"

"And then ..."

I wasn't able to bear any more. "Yang, do you want to deliver a speech on international economics?"

"Patience, man! Patience! I spent a lot of effort on that."

"Spare the background and go straight to the point. Come on! I'm waiting!"

Yang Yanpeng pushed his glasses up and continued, "Song Dechuan and Peng Kang have both worked abroad. Before 1992, Song was working in that St. Raison Center, and at the same time, Peng was working as a secretary in the foundation."

"That's the point! All those nonsense .... Does that mean they may know each other?"

"Well, I cannot identify that ..."

"Come on and identify it!"

"Hold your fire! What's the hurry for! There's more than that."

"What?"

"The phone call from Peng Kang's office before he died, that satellite phone call, is registered under a foreign company here in Beijing, whose name is Wales Medical Device Research Group."

"What? What's that company you've just said ..."

"Yes. That's William Wales Company. It is the controlling shareholder of the foreign company."

I thought it over for a while and said, "Which means that all the information leads back to that Martin company, right?"

"Correct."

"What's that company doing for a living?"

"You didn't know? Lockheed was opened in 1913 and became famous for making airplanes in 1930s. Making planes is a high-tech industry at that time, so now it's a time-honored brand. In 1995, it was merged with Martin Marietta. And now it is the largest defense contractor in the United States, which means it is now the largest official defense contractor in the United States."

What the fuck! It was a really big case!

"Such a conspiracy! Fashionable it is!" He Jingcheng was talking while eating his favorite peanuts, not taking it seriously. "Definitely conspiracy. A big one! All these you've experienced, dude, are all preparations for this. You're the one to keep the world safe and peaceful."

"Thank you for saying that. Anything useful?"

"Got to prepare your mask and cloak. And for those companies you've been talking about, I didn't get a single clue."

"Well, it was complicated by Yang. In fact, it was just that big arm dealer merged the company Song Dechuan and Peng Kang worked for and it was also the company that Peng Kang asked for help before his death."

"Then what? Ask Bai to report it to the Director? And then the Director to the City Bureau, then to the Ministry of Public Security, and then to the Political Bureau of the Central Committee of the CPC, and then they would call the White House to ask a favor from their President to let the boss and staff of that company to show up in the interrogation office on No. 4, Shuangyushu North Road, Haidian District, Beijing to wait for your interrogation?"

Well, it sounded ridiculous. We looked at each other and didn't find any solution.

"If you ask me, I'd say you put you attention to that left-handed killer, the one who killed women. Have you searched within the group who has sexual assault records?"

"Way long ago. Nothing found."

"The background of the victims? If there's a connection between man and man, there may be some among those women."

"Chi Shanshan and the other two are just two types of person. Nothing similar and not a single connection."

"Have you retrieved any DNA on the clothes?"

"No. And the technical guys has stripped my shirt into pieces. It was worth more than 200 yuan!"

"Witness?"

"The kid went to identify the photos once again."

"And?"

"And he was almost pointing my photo to identify the killer."

"It's normal for the witness to experience a delusion or lack of memory under emergency. You didn't see the attacker's face that night."

"Anyway, that's a dead end."

"Are there any possibilities to circle a psychological safe zone?"

"You know it's Haidian district in Beijing, with almost three million people and covering a area of 426 square kilometers. Numerous companies, schools, hospitals, shops, government institutions, houses and tourist sites are all located here. But at least, I'm pretty sure that the left-handed killer lived or worked here. If anyone can tell me where he is, I can promise whatever he wants."

"Did Yuan Shi analyze any specific features this time? Any clothes of specific color? Any particular underwear? Whether he's got a hole on his nipple?"

"None! Bin has praised him as 'as good as James Brussel'. Now he's not capable at all. Nothing got from him."

"I've heard of that case. Did the criminal wear what Yuan Shi described when you caught him on the construction site?"

I picked up two peanuts and threw them into my mouth. "Yeah. But half of the people there were wearing like that. And people on other construction site. It's too normal for a migrant worker to wear something like that. If it's not the informant, how can I find him!"

"The regular play is not useful. You'd better stick on to your 'secret weapon'."

"Yang Yanpeng's really got something. But the results he took back..." I took a second thought and said, "Are you talking about Bin?"

"Or his father. It's not long since he's retired. You'd better pay him a visit before he really leave the business."

"Bai must have asked him. He probably wouldn't like to be involved in these things."

"Right. Then it should count on Bin this time."

"Actually, I was going to try myself. And it was really scary for Bin this time."

He Jingcheng bowed deep. "Well, we are not that capable at all. Go and find that master and save more lives. The cooling-off period waits for no one."

I bowed back while chewing my peanut. "We've been through so many cases together. Is this one so special as to ask Bin out specifically?"

"It's right we've solved so many ones. But this one is really tricky. It's beyond us."

I took another handful of peanuts. "Well, it's really a shame for me to ask him out this time. He'd better be good."

Sitting silently for a while, He said, "Well, it's not for us to worry. He's good well before we knew."

Down below Building No. 5 in Linyuan Community, a police car was parking there, serving as a deterrent more or less. I waved at the guys inside, and they waved back, one of them holding half of a cookie Yichen made.

Bin took me into the study and asked, "Would you like something to drink? Hot or cold?"

"The colder the better." I lied down on the sofa and asked, "How's your arm?"

"Better."

Yichen put a can of coke on the tea table and I thanked her. At the same time, I saw a plate full of cookies on the table.

Having stared at me for a while, Bin smiled. "Well, you've come a long way here this evening. What for?"

I didn't intend to hit around the bush. "I've asked Dr. Yuan and He Jingcheng for their opinion. It's just like Kissinger conducting shuttle diplomacy philosophy. Frankly speaking, I'm lobbying you here today."

"You knew what I thought. Let's talk about something else."

"It's different now." I lighted up a cigarette, "Do you know why he's coming to attack you?"

"You'll always have someone hate you if you're in my profession."

"Send an assassin to kill you just out of pure hate? Then you wither have been sleeping with the first lady of the Japanese mob or sued the Russian Mafia broken."

Bin didn't answer, looking down on the ground.

"We both know that this is the killer in Haidian Hospital. Did you know Song Dechuan or Peng Kang before?"

"Why do you ask?"

"Because either you're the target of the killer, or the obstacle he has to get rid of. From what we now know, Song and Peng may know each other."

He fiddled with his lighter as if absorbed in some thought. "Are those two victims connected?"

"They were both connected with a big arms dealer."

"Two doctors connected with a arms dealer?"

"Yeah ... We are not very clear about what's between them."

"Did you ask Yang to deal with that?"

"Yeah. Thanks to you, I didn't fire him."

Bin shook his head, smiling. "Thanks to you two living harmoniously. What do you want me to do?"

"Help me with the case."

"I refuse."

"That attacker didn't achieve his goal this time. He won't give up. If he's sure that you are the obstacle for his next case, it doesn't matter whether you take part in the case or not. Helping us to catch him is the best way you can protect yourself. Even if you don't think for your parents, you'll have to think for Yichen."

"That's fine. My parents are planning to travel abroad these days and Yichen and I will stay at home. With your men staying downstairs, we're safe enough."

"That's not even close." I sat straight and planned to continue when my phone rang. I picked it up. "Hello?"

It didn't occur to me that was the phone call from downstairs. "Zhao, we've got some situation here."

"Yeah. What's that?"

"There was a unlicensed black Audi parking in the east lane. The engine didn't run but we've watched it about 15 minutes. No one got off."

"Wait." I waved at Bin and walked to the balcony door to look downstairs. They were right. There was a car parking there. "Yeah, I see it."

"The order is to protect Han Bin, but didn't say anything about whether to question anyone suspicious. Is that ..."

"That's all right. Stay on the line and I'll go down to check." I put on my earphones and turned my phone into vibration. "Stay with Yichen and lock the door. I'll be back in a minute." I said to Bin.

After I came out of the building gate, I turned right, which is the direction opposite to that car. "Ask the Social Order and the local police station to see whether they've sent someone to protect him too."

"We've checked with them and they said no."

"The City Bureau?"

"It was the City Bureau who sent us here."

"Yeah, I know. But you'd better double check. Call Director Bai."

"Yes, sir."

Walking along the northwestern side of the building, I came across to the back of that car. The window was covered by anti-spy film so I couldn't see through the window. Not surprisingly, the back license was also removed. Even if it was that killer, did he have enough nerves to go in publicly?

Suddenly, the car shook a bit. And then, the left back door opened slightly, from which a strong and tall guy came out. I was so surprised that he could even sneak out from such a small space. And it was clear that he didn't want to be discovered by the police car in the left front corner so he chose to come out in this way.

Report came from my earphone. "Director Bai said no other precautions have been taken."

But this one was not the killer. "Someone's out. I'll follow him. You stay put. Call back up from the local police and Patrol Force. I'll talk to you later."

At the same time, I saw that big man walking to my direction along the building in the east. I knew there were no lights around the bush where I hid in. So I didn't move at all.

That guy walked all the way to the north of the building and avoided the police car carefully. I followed him in the bush to ensure that he was not outside my sight. He stopped half way, looked around, and walked back to my direction.

I lifted my nightstick from the back of my waist, waiting for the best chance. Numerous mosquitoes was buzzing around me, which was familiar to my long ago. That guy was not acute as a mosquito. I watched him walking no more than two meters in front of me, stopped and lowered his head to fiddle with his pants ...

And then there was the sound of taking a pee.

To be frank, before I went out to take him down, I was pretty sure that no matter what his purpose was, he was no good, not even professional. Perhaps to repay what the mosquitoes left on me, I put my nightstick back and sneaked to his back, taking two of his ankles with my hands and pulling backwards ...

"What the fuck!"

My plan was to pull his legs to take him down, and then press his waist with my knees. And then gave a elbow to the back of his neck. ... But he didn't act as an expert to reach out his arms paralleled to the body, palms down, but used his hand to support him on the ground. As a result, he now was holding his wrist, crying and rolling on the ground after a clear crack.

Clapping my hands and lighting up a cigarette, I started to call my men in the police car.

There was no need to cuff him. What a simple fight.

Police light, crowd, bandage, splint, pee smell and war of words.

Although he wasn't the one who was beaten, Yuan Shi still felt ashamed. "Who authorized you for this? This is violence! Asshole!"

Most of my colleagues were laughing. I was the one who showed a little sympathy. "Dr. Yuan, this is a complete misunderstanding. You'd better let us know when you send someone to protect Han Bin. Look at that ... Hey! I'm sorry about ... everything. Hey guys! Cao Fa! Don't ... laugh. Go pay a visit to that classmate of Dr. Yuan. He comes from abroad!"

"Zhao Xincheng, I've tolerated you for such a long time. It is you who court death!"

"Come one, man! Don't be like this. I apologized. Come here." I gestured him to the other side, "Come here."

"What!"

"Something to let you know. Come on!"

Leading him aside, I put on a serious face. "Yuan Shi, you've said a lot. Now it's my turn. Before I caught him, we've asked the local police, the division and the City Bureau. You said you've sent him to protect Han Bin. Let's put your real purpose aside, he removed his license plate and avoided the police. All his sneaking and stealthy movements, how could I not take him down? Besides, if he's really the attacker that night, I have to move first. Waiting for he attacking him? I'll be a dead man now."

After these words, Yuan Shi shifted away his stare, admitting my explanation was reasonable.

"Strictly speaking, as a consultant for the City Bureau, sending someone, who is a layman, to stake out without reporting to the Bureau, you are in the wrong this time. By the way, that classmate of yours, though looked like Rambo, he's really slack in these things. Is he wearing the same colorful band from USTU? He will definitely be killed in no time if he encounters that killer. You're sending your classmate to death!"

He took a long breath. "I sent him there to ..."

"To monitor Han Bin, right?" I cut in. "I knew what you're thinking. You're still unwilling to give up, right? OK. Let me ask you this. Leaving the evidence we've acquired aside, if Han Bin is really suspicious, how can he go out to commit a crime when there are several of our guys to stake out downstairs? You're just thinking about nonsense!"

"I ... I ... I was just ..." Yuan Shi didn't know what to say. "I just want to check out this daily routine."

"Because you didn't reach down to his basic line in the last lie detection?" I thought over his words and laughed knowingly. "Ah... I know. You like him."

"What? What are you talking about!"

"Don't be ashamed. That's just a delayed demonstration of youth homosexual syndrome. You're interested in Bin, just as you're interested in the serial killer. You're obsessed in everyone who is psychologically abnormal." I patted him on the shoulder. "Are you shocked by his performance when doing the lie detection? That's nothing. At least nothing to him. But he is not really psychologically abnormal. He's just better than us, or than most of us. If you want to communicate with masters, that's right. But come on, can you not follow him like an obsession?"

Yuan Shi must have wanted to say something. But he didn't. At last, he took a deep breath and smiled.

My phone was ringing. It was from Bai. "The boss called to ask. What? Let us both take a footstep back. I'll go apologize to your classmate later on, and you let it go this time."

Yuan Shi nodded a little and walked away. I picked up the phone, smilingly. "It's all right, boss. That's just a man who's not being environmental friendly. I've already ..."

Bai's voice was deep and hoarse. He talked in a slow pace, not aware of what I was talking about. "Is Yuan Shi with you?"

Something was not right. "Yes."

"And Han Bin?"

"He's here, too. He's safe."

"Come to the office at once."

"You mean ... now?"

"Call everybody and back to the office at once."

Not right. Definitely not right.

"Yes, sir. Is there another case?"

"Yeah."

"Should I tell them to go back to the office and I head to the crime scene straight away?"

"I'm asking you back to check the crime scene."

"What?"

Nothing came back from the other side of the phone. He hang up. My mind stopped for half a second and then swirled around madly.

Oh my god! Did that mean ...

2

How many people did Jack The Ripper kill?"

In the late summer of 1888, when Mary Ann Nichols faltered into Buck's Row, when Annie Chapman fell in the backyard of No. 29, Humphrey Street, Elizabeth Strider stumbled along Bernina Street, Catherine Eddowes opened her dizzy eyes to look at Mitre Square, Mary and Jane Kelly opened her house door as usual, and maybe when Martha Taibram looked back in horror in Les Saint-Georges, they, with no exception, fell into the arms of the God of Death.

And today, how many of us would still remember them?

Every time I flipped over the cases, I would complain about those long and awkward foreign names, or find something to laugh with the limited foreign language I had. And every time, Bin would remind me to show some respect. "They are lives. Lives are not symbols." he said.

But actually, I laughed at him secretly. For us policemen, be they lives or symbols, we were so used to them. We didn't take them very seriously.

So, no matter it was Chi Shanshan, Fang Wanlin, or Xu Chunnan, or Fan Jiajia, they were all the same. Whatever result might come out at last, they would become symbols and faded away from our lives. Sooner or later.

But this time, when I stood at the lane to the south of the division office, He Jingcheng, walking by my side and pulling his trolley, told me that the one in the body bag, was Jiang Lan.

At that moment, my mind stopped.

Bin was right. This is life. Lives are not symbols.

She was not a symbol. No one is a symbol.

"Experts?" Bai turned to look at Yuan Shi, and then me. "Outstanding officer?"

"..."

"A total airhead!"

"..."

"She's just 27 years old." At last, he heaved a long sigh, as if to breathe out all his grief in that breath. "Me too. We are all airheads."

I stood until the sun rose up, still.

Everything around me seemed to be vague. Some were scolding, some were explaining, some were asking and some were comforting ... Leaders of the bureau were here, silent. All commanders and captains were here, working with others in the crime scene. Xuejing was here, holding my hands and weeping, and even Cao Fa was crying ... People were walking, back and forth, taking photos, setting up warning lines and collecting evidence.

The sun rose up and a new day began. The crowd come and the cars go. No one ever knows who died here last night. A most vicious soul killed a young law protector in the most violent way.

But I know.

I knew what happened here. I could never forget this symbol of life. I also knew that no matter who did this, he's already a dead man! Kill right at the gate of the division office? He's a dead man! Kill a cop? He's a deal man! He killed Jiang Lan, my partner, my colleague, my friend. I will take him down! By all means!

You are dead.

Asking one of my colleagues to send Xuejing out, I turned around and looked at Bin, who's been here all night with me. "Can you help?"

Bin nodded.

Wang Rui was the fourth training partner I've beaten down today.

Before he fainted out, he insisted as long as three minutes under my attack, which set a new record in the gym. Actually, they were not bad at all. Most people came here to practice and relax — using a feint or a kick to take some advantages, or punching out and kicking at the same time to defend. Slow pace, low intensity. It was normal to fight and chat at the same time. After all, no one wanted to show up with bruises the next day and it was not worthy for the training partner to fight at full split with us policemen.

But today, he met me.

Considering his colleagues who cannot bear my attack just now, Wang Rui took me very seriously. Although he was on the back foot, he fought back forcefully. Of course, it was because I took attack as defense and I wore no protect clothing. He was taller than me, so he tried to keep distance with me by kicking. I was sliding to the side and used my right swing to beat him. And due to my rash advance, I have been beaten on the face by his right punch. The tears and blood running down from my eyes and nose almost made me fainted.

Probably excited about his success, he lifted his foot to kick my waist and stabbed close with his right punch. I faltered a bit and raised my right foot. He was quick. He lowered down to grab my left leg with his left hand.

But this was my speciality — a "fake kick real swing" as what Iron Mike[1] did. The purpose was his unprotected face because his left fist was about to punch out.

I didn't use my full strength when I hit his face. Although there's protective clothing and insurance, it was still inappropriate to cause real damage.

I was about to check on him, but it seemed that he wouldn't be awake in a short time, so I asked other training partners to take him out. I gave my face two punches, beads of sweat falling down from my hair, splashing out onto the ground. The pain from all over my body made me really excited.

"Wanna try?" I asked Bin.

Bin was watching all the way through my fighting. He waved a case file at me and said, "Officer Cao sent some files just now. When you calm down, come and have a look."

---

1 Mike Zambidis (1980 —), Greek kickboxing boxer. He is 7 feet 7 inches and therefore is nicknamed as "a condensed charge". He has won many so many boxing competition. His favourite strategy was to perform a fake kick but then swing the opponent down.

All medical examiners, including He Jingcheng, refused to take part in the autopsy. So the files I got was a blend of on-site record and the autopsy report from the City Bureau.

From what I've got, yesterday at 10:21 in the evening, the surveillance camera showed that Jiang Lan left after she worked late in the office. And then, she stepped into the last 50m in her life. She must have been fetching her bicycle outside the south wall, and was murdered right beside her bicycle.

The murderer held the weapon with his left hand, which was a sharp tool with serrated edge.

The first stab was a shallow one on her abdomen. Jiang Lan was a qualified cop. This little girl defended violently before walking to the end of her life. Besides the three defensive wounds on her right arm, there were bruises all over her body above the waist. The fatal one was the knife wound going through her heart. And the wound on her throat, everted on the edge and so deep to expose the bones inside, meant it was cut after her death by the murderer. For now, we didn't know whether he was to enjoy the pleasure of cutting or to make sure she was dead.

There were at least nine exits extended from the crime scene in the direction of west, south and north. People living nearby didn't see anyone suspicious during that period of time. Someone reported some abnormal sound but it was not worth to dig into.

I was confused. "It's too close to the yard of the division office. Just a wall in between. Why didn't she ask for help?"

"Maybe she didn't have time. It all happened too sudden."

"This was not the one who attacked us. I mean the murderer was not only holding the knife with his left hand, but ..."

"For these two criminals, the right-handed one was clearly better than the left-handed one."

"Yes. But why would he kill Jiang? Does he still want to live a life when he has killed a cop?"

"Why was he wandering around the division office? That's what we have to think about." Bin looked at the autopsy photos again and again, which was something I couldn't even bear to take a glimpse. "Was he following her?"

"Follow a cop?"

"It doesn't have to be connected with being a policeman or not. Just like it doesn't matter whether the victim is left-handed or right-handed. And Jiang Lan is right-handed." Bin put a photo close to his nose, as if he could sniff the smell of blood on that. "That night we were attacked, I didn't

195

finish my talk. This perpetrator of rape has at least two MOs."

I followed his lead. "Policemen and hookers. Low-risk victims and high-risk victims. He attacks two distinct types of victims."

"With two different MOs."

"A hunter when he attacks high-risk victims he met at random, and a follower[1] when he attacks low-risk victims who he took as his target of sexual fantasy, which means ..."

"Although you've got the wrong guy in Chi Shanshan's case, that doesn't mean you are walking in the wrong direction."

"The murder is someone within their lives. He knew them!"

"That's all I can tell you." Bin put the photos back to the case file and handed them to me. "Then it's your job. Cross-check whether the two victims have some connections in their lives and pay more attention to the details. Have they taken photos in the same photographic studio? Did they like to go to the same fast food restaurant? Were they using the same brand of makeup? Have they been to the same place to check on a house? Did they share the same insurance agent? ... Those are not difficult to find with the resources in your hand."

"Right on that!" I picked up my phone and found that it ran out of power. I fiddled a backup battery from my pocket and opened my phone, murmuring, "Jiang was too stubborn. As long as she ran back to the office, or to the street, she would have a chance to survive. What the fuck ..."

Bin asked softly, as if he was deep in his thought and didn't want to wake up himself. "If you were her, would you run back?"

"If I were he? I came up to peel him!"

"No. I mean, except for emotions like anger and rage, would you run?"

"Err? Ah ..." Having knocked a series of training partners down, I was still in a rage. It was difficult for me to think in a rational way. "Well, probably no."

"But normally, people would choose to run away when meeting with a villain."

"I won't."

"Neither would she."

"Just because we are cops? So there's a sacred sense of duty on our shoulders?"

"When you give your back to him, you are his prey. If you turn around

---

1 Both are different types of serial killers. A hunter is a serial killer to attack the victim at once when he meets the victim. Hunters usually don't plan his attack. A follower is also called an assassin-like serial killer. Followers tend to follow the target they've chosen and get close to them. Once they get a right chance, they will attack immediately. They plan in advance and therefore are the most dangerous type in all serial killers.

to face him, you are his rival. Fight, or escape. The choice is just within a second. Which one you choose actually comes from your personality."

"So your point is the reason Jiang chose to fight with him was that she was too stubborn?"

"No." Bin patted on the back of my hand. "My point is that she was a good cop."

Thanks to those grandmas and grandpas who came out to have walk, what happened in front of the gate of Haidian Division was well acknowledged now. They wouldn't believe that it was them who spread the information to half of the population in China when they described the crime scene to their children or neighbors in a vivid or exaggerated way. In a era of Internet, the speed at which information spreads made the credibility of Beijing police sank to the very bottom.

It was understandable. When police couldn't protect themselves, how can they protect the public?

But surprisingly, Yuan Shi took all the responsibilities of going into the wrong direction this time. It was said that he admitted on a telephone conference that there were more than one killer. The focus on finding left hands also needed to be discussed and the profile he gave before was clearly not accurate. All these have made Haidian Bureau couldn't allocate the resources in a scientific and appropriate way to follow the case.

Bai's point was simple and direct. "I don't care about my post. When the case is solve, I can even take off the uniform!"

But in the end, the City Bureau didn't blame anyone. No more bullshit! Solve the case before the deadline!

With limited manpower, the policemen sent to protect Han Bin were called back. Bin took Yichen to live with his parents. Yuan Shi took four of his assistants to join the task force. I was assigned as the temporary assistance of Liu Qiang, the vice-director of the task force and two of the local teams and twenty policemen from local police station were assigned to the task force. The director of Haidian Branch announced that all staff of the bureau had to cooperate with the criminal investigation division. Orders from the City Bureau was that the technical team and medical center had to prioritize everything related to the case, and if needed, we could communicate in our own communication line and the SWAT team could help us in arresting the criminal.

The murderer couldn't possibly understand that the minute he killed a policeman, his death was sentenced.

The arrangements were effective. In less than a week, the task force has finished the interview for more than thousands of people, and the range has been spread to Chaoyang, Xicheng, Fengtai and Shijingshan district. All criminal scenes has been guarded 24 hours a day, which was a proposal from Yuan Shi. Although it was true that in several cases abroad, the serial killer indeed went back to the crime scene to have another look, I didn't get my hopes up on this one.

However, my assumption didn't work out this time. There were accidental outcomes. And they were big ones.

The other afternoon, I sneaked off to the gate of the division office to meet Yang Yanpeng with his latest information.

"The only record is Song Dechuan and Peng Kang have travelled together." Yang pulled out a name list from his briefcase. "Around 1994, St. Raison Foundation has sent an infectious disease research and medical assistance team to Cambodia. Long live humanity!"

There were then names on that list: Meng Jingtao (leader), Song Dechuan, Ma Xiling, Hua Meiyao, Chen Juan, Kate Dix, Xu Dongfang, Peng Kang, Gao Jianlong, and Gu Fan.

"And five of them were dead. Apart from the two you knew, the other three died in Cambodia. Gao Jianlong was hit by a stray bullet. Chen Juan and Xu Dongfang was died from infectious disease.

"What about the rest?"

"Not clear. I can dig in further."

"Are they all Chinese?"

"One of them is a Chinese American, so basically all of them. Well, it's a little bit strange if you put it in this way. The Americans sent an aid team to help the Cambodians, but why do they find a bunch of Chinese there? Don't forget. The boss of this team is an arms dealer."

"Is the relationship between the United States and Cambodia ambiguous during that period?"

"The Americans are ambiguous with all countries in this world. Besides, they were not there for the Cambodian government."

"What?"

"Oh, that may be not important. They were reaching the Khmer Rouge at that time?"

"Kim what?"

"Get to know something about the international affairs, bro. Khmer Rouge was an armed force in Cambodia around 1960. It was a left-wing force and surrendered to the government in 1998."

"Yeah, I kind of remembered. Is it that thing building S21 camp and killing more than twenty thousand people?"

"Tuol Sleng prison is just one of them. And twenty thousand was just one percent."

"You said their boss is an arms dealer. What do you mean by that?"

"Can't you see?"

I folded the name list and put it in my pocket. "Arms smuggling under the name of medical aid? Is there any green channel for medical aid teams to avoid declaration?"

"Maybe white channel for a medical team. ... I've checked a bit out of curiosity. Around 1994, there was no large amount of money transferred whether for St. Raison Center or for St. Raison Foundation, unless their money has gone to some vendors on Cayman Islands. These people are not Henry Bethune. Maybe they were just the first group to negotiate with local people or give out free testers. ... Anyway, the Khmer Rouge was on the fall in 1994, and if they ever wanted to stage a comeback, the arms dealer would be very much welcomed."

"I'm afraid that's where the connection is."

"What connection."

"The skill called 'Tiger Bite' you told me last time, is it favored by left-wing people overseas? This Khmer Rouge, is it a left force?"

"Err ... I'm sorry to say that they didn't use skills like this. And I've noticed what you said so I've checked that specifically."

"Follow that lead. I'll go and talk with other people on the list. Do you have some more detailed ..." While I was speaking to him, two police cars were approaching us. The one in front stopped outside the gate. Zhang Qi lowered the window on the front passenger seat and yelled something to me.

I gestured Yang Yanpeng to wait for a second, walked towards him and asked, "What happened?"

After Zhang Qi answered my question, my first reaction was: Is this the April Fool's Day today? But the person sitting in the escort vehicle following has eliminated all possibilities of mischief.

I dialed Bin's number in a hurry. "Where are you?"

"The airport highway." The phone was not connecting well. "I've just sent off my parents. What?"

"Where's Yichen?"

"She's at home. What's up?"

"No. She's not at home." I looked at that slim girl in the car, completely confused. "She was at the crime scene where Xu Chunnan was killed, and now taken back by our people."

When Bin's white SUV rushed into the yard of the division, Yichen wasn't there any longer.

Yuan Shi was told the situation and took her to the City Bureau. "This is to avoid the potential embarrassment, isn't it?"

I was about to stop him, but suddenly, I found Bai stared at me seriously.

Bin was of course not pleased and asked about the situation briefly. When I asked why she was there, he was as confused as me and asked whether he could take a look at her.

Bai refused his request politely. "Take it easy. I can guarantee that no one's going to bully her. After they finished, I'll have someone send her back."

Bin was aware of his intention. He asked me with a low voice before he left. "Are the taking Yichen as the 'research progress'?

"Can't be." I could feel my own blush. "Take it easy. I'll see to it."

"It won't work much to use her as an excuse."

"Don't you think someone's targeting at you?"

Bin's eye corner twitched a bit. "Then let's catch the murderer and get me out of this."

Two days later, Yuan Shi and I was summoned to the office for a secret meeting.

The combination was a bit odd. It was possible that Bai trusted me and disliked Yuan Shi who was still sounding me out. And as for me, I didn't think Yuan Shi was reliable from the very beginning and now, I was not sure about whether Bai was, either.

"That girl didn't talk. She didn't have any expressions or reactions. Don't know what she's thinking or whether she's thinking or not." Yuan Shi reported. "We've sent her to the Interrogation Office in the north yard. My suggestions is that she should be tested on sexual assault."

Seeing Bai was nodding, I felt the situation was beyond my understanding. "What do you mean?"

"I didn't mean anything and I'm not suspecting your friend. But recent cases showed that someone's targeting at him. The reasons to involve her in were limited. Let's check them through and find out the real one.

"Bin was living with her. If you want to know her, you can directly ask him."

"If he is happy to work with us." Yuan Shi shrugged. "I was aware of their relationship in general. Do you think he would answer questions like whether he's been sleeping with his sister?"

"I'd say we should let her go ASAP. After all, running into the crime scene by accident doesn't mean she's the murderer. And she didn't break any law. For now, we need Bin's help. What are these for?"

"His parents have been abroad, and his couple was detained. Although we couldn't get anything between Han Yichen and the murderer, we can take this chance to isolate Han Bin."

"Why would you want to isolate him? Taking him as a decoy? What the fuck! Boss, are you going to ..."

Bai's phone was ringing. He picked it up and burst into great anger. He shouted at the phone, "I'm also selling see view houses! Don't you ever dare to call me again!" Then, he looked down, lighted up a cigarette with a delicate move and took a deep smoke. After dropping the ashes into the ashtray, he gestured us to continue.

I looked at him with a blank face. "I won't be in."

"And I'm not asking you to." Yuan Shi crossed his legs in a cozy way. "The protection plan has just been activated this noon. Two teams. One was staking out downstairs and one was responsible of following him."

I was angry. "Are you staking him out?"

"This is to protect him." Yuan Shi put one hand under his chin. "Around eleven o'clock, my men followed him starting from his company. It didn't occur to us that he directly drove onto the 4th South Ring Road and rushed all the way to the west. And when he got close to Wukesong Bridge, his speed was faster than 140 km per hour."

My heart tightened a bit. "He is getting rid of you ..."

"In a very professional way." Yuan Shi had one eyebrow tilt up and cut in. "A lawyer who can fight a professional assassin and has the counter-reconnaissance ability. Isn't that interesting?"

"You think he knew that assassin?"

"I didn't think anything, only that he is interesting. And we found someone else following him on the way"

"Someone else?"

"A Chrysler with a black plate."

"Foreign license plate?"

"Bingo!" Yuan Shi made a finger snap. "After running the plate number, we've found the car belongs to ..."

I blurted out. "Wales Medical Device Research Group."

He and Bai both looked at me surprisingly. After a while, Yuan Shi stood up and said, "It seemed that we should make more efforts in improving our information communication and resource sharing."

Bai looked at him watch and ended our conversation. "You two can communicate later. Zhao, go to a crime scene at once with him. Lay low and stay away from the investigation. You just go there to check and then back report to me."

"Which crime scene?"

"Shangfeng Apartments at the junction of Chegongzhuang Road and Shouti South Road. You can telephone He Jingcheng for detailed address." Bai put out his cigarette. "Several hours ago, a murder was found there. The Investigation Division of Xicheng Branch was there to investigate. You now go, but don't let them know who you are. I've said to them about your coming. No one's gonna ask."

"Xicheng Branch? But that's within our jurisdiction."

"Do you know there's a Wang Rui working as a training partner in our gym? Recruited outside the system?"

"Yeah, I know him." I frowned. "He's good among all training partners."

" 还好他不算咱们局的正式编制人员，所以你注意别乱讲话。 "

"It's a good thing that he doesn't officially belong to our bureau. So you two, keep your mouth shut."

"He's dead?" I was surprised these things just happen to people I know one after another. "I fought with him two weeks ago."

"The murderer is more cruel than you." Bai told me with a cold face. "He killed him."

"Another right hand died." He Jingcheng lifted the plastic film on the body. "I'm totally confused about this."

The apartment Wang Rui rented was a complete mess. The tea table and sofa in the living room were lying on the ground. The book shelf was leaning against the desk and dozens of reference books of hard cover were threw about on the ground. Broken glass were everywhere, and even electric wire in the corner was pulled out. The lamp was dangling from the ceiling, connecting to the wire system with a single electric wire.

The body was quite near the door. The blood on the ground showed us the route Wang Rui crawling along before he died. A serrated knife was on his body, which is a Spider, C08BK.

"Beautiful shows co-starred with decent killers." After the demonstration, He Jingcheng covered the body up. "The surveillance camera at the gate got Wang Rui leaving at 8:50 in the morning, and came back but we don't know when."

"Death time?"

"Between 9:10 to 9:20. The old lady downstairs filed a complaint to the property management. There must be so much noise for this mess."

"Don't tell me the surveillance camera didn't got any image of people coming in." I've paid special attention to the surveillance cameras. There were several along the hallway.

"Actually, they didn't work at all. Someone sneaked into the surveillance room when the guards were out for breakfast around nine. He turned off all surveillance cameras of the whole building."

Yuan Shi was reading the on-site records. "His bicycle was parking at the gate of the building. He didn't lock it, which means he may be getting back to fetch something."

"And the murderer followed him?"

"The murderer picked the lock." He shook his head, and then nodded. "Maybe there's only one serial killer."

He Jingcheng told us not to walk around. "What I can tell you is that either there are two killers, or he's specialized in fighting as two very different people. There are loads of wounds on Wang Rui's body. I'll have to clean him up to do a count. I've heard that you've fought with him?"

"What? Oh, yes."

"How's he? Is he a fighter?"

"Not a bad one."

"In that case, I would say that there were two killers here, one of which is a left hand and the other a right hand. All the wounds on his body were caused by the same weapon, which is the one on his back. But from the cut, we can see there are wounds caused by a left hand, as well as wounds by a right hand." He pointed at the passage to the bedroom. "The murderer, maybe murderers, picked in and went into the bedroom. And then Wang Rui happened to be back and met him. The fight started from the bedroom door all the way to here —" He gestured a circle above the broken glass on the living room floor. "Wang Rui was clearly not gaining the upper hand, and had broken pieces of glass all over his face. He tried to crawl out when his fourth vertebra was grabbed by the murderer, which caused a wound quite similar to the one on your back. He's done it in a precise way, almost as good as a surgeon. After that, the party was on. The two murderers bullied the victim to a great extent. They even pulled out Wang Rui's pants to poke half of the fluorescent tube into his asshole. I even don't need a autopsy report to tell you that his viscera must be a complete mess now."

"What's the reason to his death?"

"Loss of blood." He clapped his hand. "Probably, he should be ... Well, we'll know whether he was poked before he stopped breathing. The murderer is a cruel one."

"Pick a lock, grab the vertebra, poke in a tube and wounds by both hands. There are two MOs. What's this? A meeting for serial killers?"

"You should see this. The right leg of the body." He Jingcheng uncovered the bottom part of the body. "The angle here shows that his femur is broken."

Frankly speaking, all I can see was that half of tube outside his body, still dripping blood. "What's that?"

Yuan Shi stepped forward carefully. "The femur is the hardest bone of human body. It means that the murderer was overwhelmingly advantageous in strength than him."

"Strength is not the only advantage." He Jingcheng put on his gloves, pressing from his waist all the way down. "Precise attack and huge explosion. That professional assassin must be here too."

"But he won't do something like this, using a tube to ..."

"Unless he wanted to try lightening with a human body," He Jingcheng stood up, "or the other sexual perpetrator was here, too."

Yuan Shi didn't agree with him. "Will that professional assassin work with a sexual perpetrator?"

I also thought this combination was weird. But the fact was right in front of my eyes. Would they work together?

I gave a look at Yuan Shi, involuntarily.

Wang Rui was born in Zhang Jiawan, Tongzhou District. He was 42 years old and unmarried. His parents died early and he didn't have close relatives here. He quit school after graduation from middle school and was hired by several security companies before he worked in the gym in Haidian Branch. From what we could find with his colleagues, he was a kind and genial. So for the reason that the murderer chose him as a target, we've got different opinions. He Jingcheng felt that Wang Rui may have known one of murders and this was to silence him. Yuan Shi thought that the murderer sneaking in beforehand was to find something as several albums in the room was moved and read, from which he thought Wang Rui knew neither of the murderers, but he may have at least one photo that has the murderer's face on it. I didn't agree with both of them.

"Why did the murder weapon left on the scene? To remember their first cooperation?"

Yuan Shi answered. "You Don't Forget Your First One[1]. Do you still

---

1   Said by Jeffrey Lionel Dahmer, an American serial killer who took the lives of 17 males between 1978 and 1991. As a homosexual and cannibal, he was called "monster in Milwaukee". He was arrested on July 22nd, 1991. During the process of identifying the victims, he couldn't remember when he started his first killing, but he could identify his first victim Steven Mark Hicks from scores of photos of missing persons. "You don't forget your first one." he said to the police after he identified Hicks.

remember? That perpetrator of rape took some 'souvenir' from the first victim, Chi Shanshan."

I turned to He Jingcheng. "If it's like what you said, Wang Rui fought with both two criminals after he came back, then it should be Wang Rui on the outside, and the murderers on the inside, right?"

"It should be. There's traces of Wang Rui's defending on the passage wall, indicating that he was standing back against the living room."

"Which means he wasn't facing the door."

"Yes."

"Then why didn't he run? Even though he's confident about his ability, this was still a one-on-two situation. Why didn't he run?

It seemed that this question has never occurred to them.

"Chi, Fang, Xu and Song may not have the chance to run. Peng Kang had tried to run, but he didn't call the police for help. Jiang and Wang Rui had the chance to run, but they didn't. Why?" I was almost asking myself. "Jiang Lan may be bounded up by the duty of a policeman, but Wang Rui can't have been. Why didn't he run?"

He Jingcheng didn't looked up a bit, may be fiddling for some peanuts in his pocket. "Maybe the murderer was too fast. He didn't have the chance to."

"Then at least he could call for help. Is there anyone, his neighbour or staff from the property management, who had ever heard of his calling for help?"

Yuan Shi shook his head. "No. It's a workday today. There aren't many people in the building."

"Then whether he had called for help, at least he didn't run."

He Jingcheng seemed to be aware of what I mean. "Are you saying ..."

"If I were him, I won't run, either." I took a second thought and said, "But that's in a one-on-one situation. Anyone with real experience of fighting would know that it's easy to be outflanked if there are two enemies. As long as you were enveloped, you can never escape. For instance, the attacker to attack Bin and me that night, he's really tough. But even he cannot sustain when we outflanked him."

Yuan Shi and He Jingcheng looked at each other. "Unless there's only one criminal."

It was just a brain twister with a clear answer. The wounded caused by a left hand, a poked-in tube, the Spider, the sneaking into the monitor room, picking the lock and grabbing the fourth vertebra ... There was only one person in front of Wang Rui today — a professional criminal that Bin and I couldn't take down.

And at the same time, he was a really good copycat.

The traffic light under Suzhou Bridge was long enough for you to go to a bathroom or take a fast food. I intended to send He Jingcheng back to the division office first, and then to pay a visit to Bin. The more people died, the less shocking a single case would become. We didn't talk more about the case on the way. I was smoking and he was eating peanuts.

An accident burst out without warning. A lad who was sending out leaflets was beaten by a driver. The lad made a living by stuffing those colorful leaflets under the wiper and in the handle or even throwing them into open windows. The driver, clearly not pleased to his behaviour, got down from his car and beat the lad without saying anything. The driver was tall and strong, beating the lad down on the ground in just several punches and then came on to give him several kicks.

There were many cars on the road. Some drivers lowered their window to see what happened. Someone gave him an applause, but most of the others, including me, were watching silently.

Seeing that driver wasn't going to stop, I called the police.

He Jingcheng was confused. "You are a policeman. Why don't you stop him?"

I hung up the phone and said innocently, "If you were once hit on the face by the leaflets flying through the window while you're driving, you won't try to prevail the justice. At least I called the police. I'm not a pure onlooker."

"They just want to live."

"That's not my problem." I shrugged. "There are tens of millions of people coming from other provinces here. Why do they all come to Beijing? Can't they live back in their hometown?"

"Hey! That's regional discrimination. Beijing belongs to all Chinese people."

"Yeah, so does the earth to all human beings. I bet Uncle Sam thought the same when they were killing the Indians along the Mississippi River, so Lewinsky must thought the President belongs to all Americans. It's OK for her to sleep with him."

"They were just here sending out some leaflets. You don't have to be so mean."

"They can also come to kill."

"Come on, Beijingers can also rape and kill. There's no difference."

"It's in our nature to hurt people." My anger came out of nowhere. "Fuck! How does the world come to this!"

"Though you've suffered a lot due to those leaflets, you can't say they deserve to be beaten like that just because they send out leaflets. There's no one to stop the fight!"

"Yeah. They've got reasons to litter everywhere. And the one who beat him into shit also has his own reason, maybe due to a bad night last night. Is that enough? Should we go on to find its roots from the national strategy or from sunspot activities?" The traffic light turned green. I let the clutch in and the car moved forward. The fighting was still there. The onlookers behind suddenly found the road was blocked and turned to honk their horns. The applause now turned into dissatisfaction and protest.

He Jingcheng was irritated, frowning tightly in silence. He will be like this every time he's angry, and don't count on him apologizing first.

I took a soft tone first. "All right. It's none of our business. What's our bicker for?"

"I'm not angry with you." He turned to look at the side mirror. "We've argued about it, but we didn't come down to do anything for him. You called the police, and I though I wasn't able to stop him. ... We both have the reason to be an onlooker. Yes, we will always find reasons to rationalize all the absurd.

I pressed hard on the accelerator, shook my head and heaved a sigh. "There's nothing we can do. It was the ultimate end of the progress of human mind."

He Jingcheng lowered his eyes and looked up at me. His face told me that he was blaming himself. "It's said that the world is violently sick."

"And it's beyond recovery. Shit! Beijing was not like this when I was a child. ..." I didn't dare to looked back, as if he were a mirror and could reflect my ugly face at the moment. "People turn bad these days."

"Were they be better?" He kept staring at me. "I couldn't remember."

Having parked the car, I walked to Building No. 5 in Zhaolinyuan Yard along the boulevard and passed the place we were attacked that night on my way. The sight reminded me of the moment that Bin saved me from death. In that split second, I thought a lot.

The fact that Wang Rui was working in Haidian Bureau would be found out and became the focus sooner or later, which means Bai couldn't stay long on his position. Two serial killers, two distinct MOs. A white collar, a hooker, two doctors, Jiang Lan and Wang Rui, the murderer was getting closer to us but we didn't know what to do. At the last of the last, I had to come to him and ask for an answer.

Bin stood on the balcony as if he knew I was going to come. Seeing me approaching, he raised the little the coffee cup in his hand to me. Out of all the things he's been through — suspicion, attack, surveillance, being followed up, even separated with his families, he could still stand in the sunlight and face and world in a frank way.

Looking up to his calm, I finally realized that the distance between us was the distance between upstairs and downstairs — after chasing for so many years, what awaited for me ahead was the same old scene.

A perfectly natural one.

"How's Yichen doing?" Bin put a backpack on the sofa and said, "I'm going to Shenyang tomorrow to attend a hearing of an opposition to execution. I'll be back on Wednesday. I hope that I can see her at home when I come back."

I put my coffee on the railing of the balcony. "Don't worry about her. I can assure you that she's safe in the bureau. No one's gonna lay a finger on her."

Bin gave me a bitter smile. "You can assure me when you are promoted to a director. ... What's up?"

I spent almost an hour telling him what I knew in detail. Bin listened attentively, without questions and comments. At last, my conclusion was that, theoretically, it was not possible for these two serial killers cooperate with each other.

"Then there's a copycat." Bin glanced at a white van with civilian plate downstairs. I knew, Yuan Shi's guys were in that car.

"Up until now, I thought there were two serial killers. A psychopath obsessed in sexual violence and a professional assassin with outstanding imitating skills." Leaning on the balcony railing, I leaned back for nearly 90 degrees. "The question was, who can imitate that sexual perpetrator so vividly?

"It seemed that you've got a candidate."

"Right ... You can say so."

"Am I one of the candidates?"

"Yes, but not in the final round." I turned around and said, "First, this man must be a fighter. Second, he knows every detail about the cases, at least about that sexual perpetrator. Third, he has a good counter-reconnaissance ability. Fourth, he is likely to be well acknowledged of how the police system runs. And fifth, he may come from overseas and knows who you are especially ..."

"Know who I am?"

"He not only knows where you live, but you're potentially threatening to him."

Bin held his cup up to his mouth. "There are few people who meet so many requirements."

"Exactly speaking, among all the people I know, only three people meet those requirements."

"Which three?"

I patted him on the chest. "Two of them are standing here."

Bin laughed out. "You are bragging and flattering me. I don't think I'm that capable. You suspect him?"

"Frankly speaking, the more I think about it, the more I feel it was him."

"Your requirements are too vague. You need evidence for a suspicion."

"I started Sanda, so I don't often lift my leg above my knee. Speaking of this, I was always wanting to ask where you've learned your fighting skills." I moved close to him and lowered my voice. "Normal people cannot break a thigh bone just by kicking ... I've heard that people who learned taekwondo are specialized in kicking."

"I even didn't see his face clear that night. If you say half of him is an angel, and the other is a demon ..." Bin lighted up two cigarettes and passed me one. "Will it be such a cliche?"

"Half a moron and half a demon may be more suitable. I don't feel he's that capable from the very beginning ... But if we cut in from a different angle, it is also possible that he just acts as a moron."

Bin hesitated for a while but didn't talk.

I simply leaned on the railing and enjoyed the most beautiful sunshine in a late summer sunset. The gentle wind and the soft rustling of leaves surrounded me. How nice it would be if time can pass more slowly.

After all, my accusation was too bold. Cautious as Bin was, he must be analyzing and balancing. Maybe he was considering whether my "half moron half demon" comment demonstrated a certain subjective prejudice that can affect my judgment, or whether my point of "cutting in from a different angle" can hold its stance.

On the left plate of my cutting-in-from-a-different-angle scales, there were wounds caused by a left hand, objects poked from the outside, a Spider, sneaking into the monitor room, picking and entering and the fourth vertebra ... and on the right plate, there was the well-dressed Dr. Yuan.

A different angle?

Shi Zhan stepped into our circle without fear; Hao Jianbo buried his wife with great grief; "Pang Xin" opened her door and smiled to me; the light reflect from the Spider shed a cold glow on Jiang Lan's face. I believed that if there's a chance to overturn everything, they would make the same choice, because a leopard never changes its spots and choices decide the future.

They chose their fate, an unchangeable one, in every tiny little movement.

"The choice one made comes from his own character."

Likewise, in that tiny little movement of mine, I opened my own door of fate.

"A different angle?" Bin seemed to be confused. "Any other guys in your talent show?"

My mind twisted once and again like a Rubik's cube. "No, I'm not talking about that professional assassin, but that sexual perpetrator."

"Oh? The cross-check I talked about last time, is there any progress?"

"No. But I probably know who the murderer is."

Bin looked down on the ground and the looked at him curiously.

"It was Wang Rui!" Suddenly, I found the setting sun stings me. "Wang Rui was that sexual perpetrator."

Bin moved his neck out of tiredness. "I'm sorry. What you are talking about ... This is beyond my comprehension."

"That murder weapon left on the scene can be considered as a symbol to make himself famous, or a mockery at getting both the murderer and the spoils. The reason that Wang Rui didn't run isn't related to the number of killers on site. Like Peng Kang, he's up to something." My mind was getting clearer as I was speaking. "This moronic sexual perpetrator has only two MOs: finding some high-risk victims within his safe zone, or killing his target of sexual fantasy out of pure impulse. As a training partner, he gets in touch with Jiang Lan often. That's how Jiang Lan became his target. As for Chi Shanshan, the people who can get in touch with her must include the security guards in Changxin Building. Before he came to the gym of Haidian Bureau, he was a security guard. I don't remember whether we've let the guards there identify his photo when we were working on that case, but he may worked there before. It's not difficult to check."

Bin stopped me. "Don't speculate. Where's your proof?"

"It's simple." I took out my phone and started to dial. "Compare their DNA and we'll know. ... Ah yes!" Dialing halfway, I suddenly recalled, "Wang Rui was left-handed. He was a left hand impersonating as a right hand!"

Bin nodded calmly. I continued, "On that day we were fighting, he naturally returned the normal mode to use his strong hand as the back punch when we fought the most fiercely in the end, before he was knocked out. The back punch must come from the strong hand, a very basic common sense in fighting."

It's him! It must be him!

Bin looked at me for a while, his eyes blinking, and finally got what I was saying. "That makes sense. You'd better let the medical center retrieve some DNA samples and send to the City Bureau to test."

It's rare for me to think ahead of Bin when talking about cases. I started to dial the numbers, my hands a little shaky out of happiness. "Hahaha! Bin, is this a Waterloo's defeat for your?"

It's right. I can see what you see.

In an instant, I was frozen.

What you can see, I can see as well.

"Bin ..." I murmured in a daze.

As if I were surrounded by a flashlight, I looked around but couldn't see anything. A kind of isolated numbness crawled down from the back of my head to my forehead like a serpent. The color of the sky and my lost thought became clear once again.

If I could see, how couldn't you?"

"The one who saw him using his left hand as the strong hand is only ..."

No! You didn't see it Bin. You've ignored that. You must have!"

"Only ..."

"A lawyer who can fight a professional assassin and has the ability of counter-reconnaissance."

"You, and me."

Bin's voice came from behind me.

"When the Hundred Days' Reform failed, why did Tan Sitong have to die?"

"Because human beings share the seam weakness. Mr. Tan is a human."

"You're not answering my question."

"You didn't get the answer because you don't think. Although the Hundred Days' Reform failed, Mr. Tan still believed that 'Every reform in every country involves blood. As for China, if there has to be blood and sacrifice, please start from me.' That's his belief."

"We cannot simply say that it is his death that brings the success in the end? That's not as simple as that."

"It's true that he chose to die, but that's not because he's insane. He is not that innocent to think that the minute he died, Cixi would die also, let alone he actually supported the imperial family. He didn't know whether the reform or revolution in the future would be successful, but it's sure that he cannot see it with his own eyes anyway. He must have been clear, however, that his death won't change anything at that moment."

"But he chose to die. What's the connection with human weakness?"

"Many people, maybe everyone of us, would face something like this in some special moment. He's very clear about what he's gonna do, or whether it's meaningful. But even if he knows that his choice doesn't make any sense, or worse, it's actually wrong, he won't change it."

"Many things are limited by loads of objective features. It's like a 'maze'. When you're in, you may not be able to find the way out. So you'll have to choose the only way in that maze. What you said just now is too metaphysical."

"Most of your so-called objective features are more likely to be excuses to whitewash your subjective moves. The 'maze' you've talked about does exist, which is called Nimitta or Karmavarana in Buddhism. We are all in it all our lives. What's cynical is that people could figure out it's a maze most of the time, but it doesn't stop them from making the wrong choice."

"From you point of view, does Tan Sitong die as a joke? Well, if you say so, you're sure to receive reprimands and rebukes.

"I'm not qualified to comment on the choices and achievements of people before. But I admire the most Tan's grace and dignity. He chose to die voluntarily. How will I mock at him? Tan was honorable and respectful. He can chose his own death and wait for the future to comment on him. It's a pity that we mortals won't have that chance. What we choose, no matter right or wrong, cannot be commented by the future."

It was a conversation happened long time ago in front of the tombstone of Mr. Tan Sitong, located in the suburbs of Liuyang county, Hunan province. We were new acquaintances back then, and both single. I was out on a business, and he was out to deal with some cases. We met, we were introduced, and we went to the Shao Mountain together to pay respect to the ancestor born hundreds of years ago.

I could still remember that it was a good day that day, sunny and clear. The tomb can be vaguely seen among the verdant grass, in which some white and yellow flowers were blooming vigorously, growing into a desperation of vitality in flaming sunlight.

And now, eight years have passed.

How I hoped time would stop.

A blow hit on the back of my head bemused me for half a second. An arm locked my neck like a ghost and I leaned backwards along with its move...

Bin!

I pressed my chin hard in case I was strangled and took the nightstick from my back with a backhand pull. I poked backwards before I could draw it out, but he dashed away. In an instant, he was by my side, putting his foot under my leg, trying to trip me over. While he was pulling my hair to bump my head on to the railings, my left elbow hit his ribs or abdomen, my right foot circumventing from between his legs. Roaring, I pushed him to the other side of the balcony with simply brute force.

While stepping backwards, he still wanted to kick me out with one of his legs. I didn't have enough time to pull back my arm, but to move my chest backwards and lower my chin. Bin fell out. My left cheek was hit badly by his knee. I stumbled back for several steps and leaned against the wall.

A shadowy figure rushed at me. My right wrist moved bottom to top, and the nightstick was drawn out, but was locked hard by an elbow half way. My arm was bent over to my chest and another elbow hit on my left cheek. I lowered my waist, raising my left arm subconsciously to protect my head.

The last hit was on my face.

When I fainted out and fell on the ground, I felt I was tamped down into the ground like a deadman by a big iron hammer.

Bin ...

4

"It's lucky he didn't crack you head open on his first blow. He must have shown you some kindness. He cannot make the decision to kill you." Yuan Shi pressed the transceiver in the van open and shouted, "Faster! Follow him!"

I sat in the back seat, at a complete loss. A female colleague of mine helped me to stop my nose from bleeding and deal with the wounds on my eyebrow and left ear, and put an ice bag wrapped with a towel behind the back of my head.

Bin, what have you done ...

"Thank you."

Yuan Shi turned around. "What?"

"Thank you for your arriving in time." I put the ice bag on my legs. "And please tell the men you sent that they have my gratitude."

"One of them broke two bones and was sent to the hospital and the other was still unconscious. But they didn't tell me anything. Who knows your fighting in the balcony was because of the cases of just due to you two arguing with each other. After Han Bin collected his things and got down, they even didn't have the chance to tell me."

"Then why were you here?"

"That's because Dr. He found the lost earring of Chi Shanshan when he aided the medical team of Xicheng Branch to examine the body. The X-ray showed that there were something in the deltoid of Wang Rui's left shoulder. They sent Wang Rui's DNA for test to see whether it can be matched with the murderer's, and the answer is yes. So he is the killer who killed Chi Shanshan, Fang Wanlin, Xu Chunnan and Miss Jiang. Dr. He thought it was Wang Rui himself who put that earring into his body. It's a miracle that he didn't had septicemia. Probably he's too obsessed with the sexual pleasure the constant pain brings."

"So you know it is Han Bin who killed Wang Rui?"

Yuan Shi murmured something and turned back. "Actually, after locating your position from your cell phone, we were coming here to take you."

I puzzled for a few seconds and then got his meaning.

"A person who is a fighter, well-acknowledged of the details of the case, with counter-reconnaissance ability and hates the murderer very much. You're the most qualified." His voice was low, but with a little resentment. "This was a reasonable speculation."

After all, I have suspected him with a similar theory. I nodded and agreed with him sincerely.

"What's strange is that Han Bin didn't left any trace in those crime scenes. If he didn't confess, we have no proof that he's the one who killed Wang Rui." Yuan Shi passed me a earphone. "He didn't care about the lie detection. Will he be afraid of being questioned? Why did he attack the police and run away? This is to tell us that he is of great suspicion.

I tried to put on the earphone, but the great ache stopped me. "It's obvious. Because all the male victims were killed by him."

"You mean Song, Peng and those ..."

"Everyone besides those women." I took out that list of medical team Yang Yanpeng gave me. "Once he was suspected or monitored, it will be hard for him to continue killing."

Yuan Shi snatched the list from me. "Who else does he want to kill?"

"On that list. Except for those five I crossed off, you'd better hurry to find the others."

"Where do you find these names?"

"It's a long story." I closed my eyes to regenerate some energy. "Anyway, go run those names. And then you'll know whether my guess is right or not."

Report came from the transceiver. "A white Honda SUV was found on Xueyuan Bridge on the 4th North Ring road with a plate number EW7368. It's driving from west to east. Please identify."

"That's him!" Yuan Shi pounced back to the transceiver.

Liu Qiang ordered, "Intercept him! Now!"

"The road is good. Our car is approaching Zhixin Bridge. And the nearest roadblock has to be set around Wangjing Bridge."

Xueyuan Bridge, Zhixin Bridge, Anhui Bridge, Wanghe Express Way, Wangjing Bridge, Siyuan Bridge ...

Bin, where are you going?"

I put the ice bag on my ear. "No. There's an entrance to Beijing-Chengde Highway before Wangjing Bridge. He has to be intercepted before reaching the entrance."

Yuan Shi pointed at me. "Do as he says."

Liu Qiang got some concerns. "It's too risky to intercept on a ring road. The cars are driving too fast ..."

"Do as he says!"

"People from Chaoyang Branch was approaching, but it's too late and they can't ..."

"Do as he says! Or let someone else to take the lead!"

I shook my head to Yuan Shi and said to Liu Qiang. "Liu, is there any of our guys around?"

Liu Qiang cursed Yuan Shi with a low voice and glanced at the screen. "Yes. Two cars from the Patrol Force are about to reach Wangjing West Bridge."

"Tell them to drive full force to Anhui Bridge, and, by all means, enter the main road from west to east before reaching Wanghe Express Way. And the stop all civilian cars and block the road to force him leave the car."

When Liu Qiang was making the arrangements, Bai called me. "What happened?"

"Han Bin's got great suspicion. We are not hunting him."

"What crime did he commit?"

"He might have killed Wang Rui and ..."

"Wang Rui? That son of bitch who killed Jiang?"

"You've known that?"

"He Jingcheng has just sent me the report. Who's taking the lead?"

"Commander Liu and Dr. Yuan." I noticed that a piece of information came from the transceiver: The team from Patrol Force has reached Anhui Bridge. They are setting roadblocks."

"Is there any evidence to prove Han Bin is the killer?"

"No. But he has also attacked police."

"Attack police? Who did he hit?"

"Me. And two men from the City Bureau."

Bai was silent for a while and then said, "Be careful about him. Just take him back and do nothing else."

That's not easy.

"The target has driven out of the main road from Anhui Bridge exit!" Is he planning to enter the downtown?

215

Yuan Shi shouted to the microphone, "All units! Surround the target! Control all roads nearby!"

"Yes, sir. I've got a situation. I got to go. Talk to you later."

It was probably the first time I didn't give him an exact answer.

Just as what I thought about, after Bin left the main road of the 4th Ring Road, he rushed to the downtown. City downtown is the best place to hide in. The more prosperous the city is, the easier for him to get away from us.

"Target is driving south. Less than twenty meters away from us."

"Set roadblocks on the road from north to south before Andingmen Bridge. The target has passed Anzhen Bridge!"

"He knocked down the road fence!"

"Team Two report! The target drives in the wrong direction and rushes pass the roadblock. Please send backup!"

"Here's Chaoyang Patrol Force. We are not driving towards him along Jiaodaokou South Street."

"Roger Team Five report. The roads around Andingmen Bridge on the 2nd Ring Road have been blocked both ways ."

"The target passed Andingmen Bridge. He drives south!"

"Chaoyang division arrived at Jiaodakou. Roads around Jiaodaokou East Street and Gulou East Street have been blocked both way. We will take him down on Jiaodaokou!"

"The target abandons the vehicle! Acting Squad report! The target abandons the vehicle!"

"He left the car crosswise! The roads are blocked! Acting Squad, leave the car to chase him! Now!"

"He runs into the lanes. All units! The target is wearing black short sleeve shirt and black pants, carrying a brown backpack. He is now moving towards southwest starting from the lanes to the north of Jiaodaokou. All units! Get off to get him!"

......

Around seven o'clock in the eventing, the van arrived at the hunting scene. Bin was surrounded by hundreds of police in the South Luogu Lane in Gulou East Street. As one of the oldest blocks in Beijing, there were at least sixteen lanes in the South Luogu Lane, which extends almost as long as one kilometer, causing great trouble to us.

Liu Qiang asked me, "He was attacking you from behind. Can you take him down if you came upon him from front?"

Although I didn't want to admit, I still told him the truth. "Not possible."

"Three as a team. Search the area outside-in." Noticing my head shaking slightly, Liu Qiang said again, "Four people a team. Get me the image of the surveillance cameras set by Jiaodaokou Police Station."

"Where does he want to go? Is he feeling panic because there's no way to go?" Yuan Shi stood in front of the digital map, supporting his chin with one hand. "No visual of him in the security cameras. That's his usual style. But where does he want to go?"

"The west is Houhai Lake. But if he wants to get here, he has to pass Di'anmen Street. We've got all roads there blocked. He cannot go though it without being caught." Liu Qiang pointed the marked map. "Chao Yang Patrol Force was guarding the outside. Even a fly can be noticed as long as it steps a foot on Jiaodaokou South Street."

"Then he has to run south. The south is ..." Yuan Shi became excited, "the direction of Jingshan Mountain?"

That was just meaningless. "Yeah. Two more steps and he'll reach Zhongnanhai. He won't even touch that area unless he's got his head hit."

"What?"

Idiot! The southern part of Ping'an Street was not the problem of "downtown". The reason why there were only hundreds of people chasing him was because most of the manpower was in the south of the city. If we let Bin pass through our blocks and got into the area where leaders of the government and Central Party Committee lived in, all leaders of all levels in the police system could be prepared for early retirement in advance.

"Will he have some safe houses here?"

"It doesn't matter." I stared at the map and said, "Anyway, they were all ranch houses with low walls. He can just jump in. In this way, all the houses in these blocks are his safe houses. Now that he's not in the surveillance camera in each lane, then either he's hiding in some of these yards, or moving through these houses. Of course, he can also go underground, using tubes and sewers. But from the structure of the sewers in this area, there's no suitable exit for him. The only several which can be used as exits are already controlled by us. He won't stay long in this area. He will eventually show up."

Liu Qiang wasn't that optimistic. "It's a complicated area with to many people coming in and out. And there are also many tourist groups from abroad. It's difficult to find him. If only we had him blocked in advance! We're not lucky enough. Shit!"

I pressed a iced bottle of water on my head and said, "No. It's not a problem of luck ..."

Yuan Shi agreed with me. "Yeah. Han Bin knew us too well. He probably has the place and timing he will be surrounded figured out the minute he attacked Zhao and ran away. The reason he chose this area must be that he believes it's a good place to get rid of us. And he's right. It's too close to the sensitive area, so the police cannot be gathered effectively. There are too many people from different places, so it's convenient for him to hide. The road can lead him everywhere, so there's more than one direction to run. It must be an approach he had thought about."

Report came from the police monitoring the surveillance cameras. "The target appeared at Shajing Lane in the east. He entered into a clothes shop. Team Seven! Look back! He's just there, less than one hundred meters behind your back!"

"Block both entrances! Team Seven be quick!" Liu Qiang shouted to the microphone. "All the other units ..."

I snatched the microphone and shouted, "All the other units stay put! Team Seven! Go!"

Liu Qiang got my idea and nodded to agree with me. Even Shi Zhan knew how to sell the dummy, we couldn't make the same mistake this time.

"Team Seven report! The target's not here! The owner says he took a red coat, a blue shirt, a black hat and a pair of brown sunglasses, and then ran away through the back door after leaving some money."

"Fuck! Go fucking chase him!"

"Already on it ..."

I said while studying the map, "Let our guys in Heizhima Lane in the north to surround him. Tell every body that he may have changed his clothes. I ... Fuck!"

A red coat and a blue shirt! The search range multiplied by two at once!

As excepted, all units reported that there were "suspected target" everywhere.

Liu Qiang shouted. "Stay calm! Narrow the circle to the area around Shajing Lane!"

Report came from the surveillance team: Bin appeared at the Front Gulouyuan Lane, which is to the north of Heizhima Lane. How did he get through!

Yuan Shi mumbled a "Shit" and ran out with a police transceiver.

"The target showed up at the center of Gulou East Street. He didn't change his clothes. He intended to run into Baochao Lane and was blocked back."

"We didn't get him. We've met with Team Eight. Where is he?"

"Let Chaoyang division send someone to protect Dr. Yuan. He's out of the van!"

"The target ... He's in the west! At the gate of the Hospital of Traditional Chinese Medicine in Dongcheng District!"

"Team One report! The target may have entered the sewer at the gate of the hospital. We are about to get down. Please send some backup!"

"There are several sideways down the sewers. Request to split the team. Van, please ..."

"We're checking the structure. Wait for a second!"

"Figure out their ends first! Control all the exits!"

Get down to the sewers after exposure. Waiting to be caught? I talked to the microphone, "Wait! Is he running into the sewers or natural gas pipelines?"

Liu Qiang was talking to a policeman. Hearing my question, he turned to me and answered, "It's the telecommunication ..."

Oh my god!

"He ..."

Before I could finish my sentence, all surveillance cameras turned black all of a sudden.

Liu Qiang was shocked still. "He's broken the power lines for security ..."

"Not only the power lines of security," I looked out through the window, "and also power lines for transportation. Tell the traffic police to add manpower. There's going to be a big traffic jam."

Expose yourself, purchase clothes, break power line, break down all surveillance cameras and create big traffic jams ...

Bin, what are you doing?

"Team Six arrived at the second exit. The lid was open. No visual on the suspect."

"He must have been here! Continue searching!"

"Send someone to repair power lines!"

"The traffic light of Gulou crossing has broken down. The road is blocked!"

"Team Six report! Someone saw him walking towards the west after coming out of the tunnel. That is the direction of the Gulou three-road junction ..."

"The backup from Dongcheng Branch has arrived."

"The traffic police has arrived at the Gulou crossing. They are directing the traffic."

More and more police arrived — he was creating chaos.

I put on the earphones and left the van, walking towards west along Gulou East Street.

We have lost he surveillance images. Did they have any special meanings to him?

In such a junction of traffic, the broken of traffic lights brought about immediate effects. The traffic was completely congested. All kinds of vehicles were lining on the road, and there were also some parking against the rules or driving on the bicycle road. In this way, it was impossible for the police on-site to drive, which means ...

"Liu, this is Zhao Xincheng!" I rushed towards west. "The junction! The Gulou junction! He was trying to drive out from Gulou junction! Our cars are blocked within this region. They cannot chase him! Block all roads from Gulou junction! Set roadblocks to check all passing vehicles!"

"That's impossible. That'll bring too much pressure to the traffic. Our people has arrived. Di'anmen Police Station has the old Gulou Street blocked. They can intercept in any minute. Is there any way to know where he's going to get a car?"

Clothes of different colors. Bin never did anything meaningless.

"He wanted to disappear in the crowds! The tourist group!" I took a glance at one of the tourist bus blocked on the way. "Many of the domestic tourist groups are wearing the same clothes. He must be waiting for the tourist group wearing red or blue clothes. Let our guys in the junction intercept all tourist buses!"

"Report from the traffic police! One of the two tourist buses let go just now were full of tourists in blue ..."

"Go after it! Commentate civilian vehicles if ours are all blocked!"

"Di'anmen Police Station has it intercepted on the old Gulou Street!"

"Acting Squad! Go and help them! Search the bus! The others, stay put! Keep your position! I repeat! Everyone keep your position!"

I ran straightly to the crossing to the northwest of Gulou and saw a white bus parking in the middle of the street, surrounded by our people. Loads of police were searching it. My instinct told me that Bin was not on that bus, or in other words, from what I knew of him, I couldn't believe he would be caught so easily.

"He's not on that bus." Yuan Shi's voice came from the earphone. "Guys from Chaoyang division and I have found what he bought in the greenbelt in the square to the north of Gulou. The two garments, a hat and a pair of sunglasses, they are all here."

Up until then did I find out what was wrong. "Which car did Di'anmen Police Station use to intercept him. The plate number of this car tells me it belongs to our Patrol Force."

After a mess in the communication channel, I heard someone saying:

"Is that the car belonging to the Acting Squad coming to help?"

"It's our car."

"What? Where's ours then?"

"What? I thought there were two of them parking in front of the bus ..."

Heaving a sigh, I took off my earphone. Nothing could be done. We've lost him.

Chapter VI

The God of Death

1

Leaning against the windowsill, I took a deep breath of the city, of home.

How long does it need to know somebody well?

Living under the same sky, different people make different choices. Bin and I were like this, being poles apart.

I've known him for as long as eight years, but I didn't know him at all.

In my mind, Bin was an ordinary person.

He was born in Beijing in October 1970 and grew up with his grandparents. Since his father worked in Renmin University, he went to the Elementary School Affiliated to Renmin University. Being a good student, he was awarded as the merit student when he graduated, and then was recommended for admission to the High School to Renmin University. During his elementary school, all his teachers praised him as a smart and diligent student. They said he was polite and responsible. Knowing right from wrong, he wouldn't cross any lines but was considerate. The comment from his classmates, however, were poles apart. Some of them admired him and thought he was the pride of the school, and the others scorned him, regarding him as a son of bitch who was a rat and toady.

After he went to junior high, he started to demonstrate some features of adolescent rebellion. He loved sports, and was sensitive about his reputation. He drank, fought, fell in love with girls and talked back to his teachers. Of course, his grade dropped dramatically, barely enough for him to be admitted into the senior high of Renmin University. During his three years in junior high, the comments from his classmates and teachers were alike — hypocritical, cocky, and pompous. He wasn't interested in study, and put all his attention in flirting with girls, and spent most his time with some yobs, not building proper classmate relationship.

Unpopular as he was, he, surprisingly, turned into a nice guy in senior high school. His grade was normal, his attitude towards his teachers were normal and he had normal relationships with his classmates. It seemed that everyone's impression towards Bin was vague. He could play basketball, and football as well. He was able to score within his capability, but not good enough to get everything under control. He was kind, but he's got temper as swell. He would curse sometimes but not unacceptable. He fought, but not the kind who causes trouble. His academic record was not very good, but not bad at all. He liked to help others, but not that kind of knight who would sacrifice himself to help others. Like most of his peers, Bin learned to be sophisticated, mature and mediocre.

I'd like to believe that if nothing happened, he would live a normal and happy life like all mortal beings in this world.

In the summer of 1990, Bin broke up with his girlfriend, who then had been together with him for five years. He decided to commit suicide by dosing himself. Fortunately, He Jingcheng happened to pay him a visit and sent him to hospital. But after that, Bin quit school. His misery started from there.

"Every time I went to see him, I felt he's not bored with the world, but not believing it." He Jingcheng said.

Since we couldn't reach Bin's parents because they've been abroad, we could only get information by interviewing his neighbors and friends. They told us that from January 1994 to December 1997, Bin wasn't here in Beijing. Friends said that he went on a trip alone, but neighbors told us that he just left home. And we could find nothing about him in all records from the justice departments and governmental facilities.

Bin has disappeared for three years, which changed him significantly.

In early 1998, Bin came back as a different person. He was not that old misery young man any more, but a open and cheerful one. Through Professor Han's "effort" and "help", Bin got his degree and the lawyer's license in a short time. Then, he began to work and his life came to a normal one. All his teachers in the Law School in Renmin University, colleagues who have worked with him, friends, old and new, his clients, judges, and even the lawyer defensing for the other side in court — all the people who have met him thought he was kind, sincere, generous and calm. He could social with good and decent manners, thinking from the bigger picture while being considerate.

So, three years, what have changed you, Bin?

Somebody called behind me, telling me Bai wanted me in his office.

I met Yuan Shi at Bai's door. He was rushing out, tears in his eyes. Although I smoke, but what's like behind him surprised me a lot.

Bai was sitting at the desk in the clouds, holding that gun-shape lighter in hand. "Zhao, because of your relationship with Han Bin, you cannot take part in the investigation. You'll be working with the consultant group under Dr. Yuan's leading. Now tell us more about Han Bin."

I caught Yuan Shi running back with a suffocated look with my sideways glance. "Han Bin is ... was ... whatsoever, my friend, a real good one. In my opinion, he's not that special, which means he seems to be more calm or cautious than most of us. He did run away from a big hunt, but he is no genius. He's not that clever. He's ... ordinary ..."

"No really, Officer Zhao." My "current leader" cut in without any hesitance. "I cannot agree with your comment."

"The one who we are dealing with, is a genius in crimes."

When Bin stood against the law publicly, Yuan Shi finally restored his confidence. There was an abnormal obsession in his high and exciting pitch. "Han Bin is one of the best killers in mainland China throughout history, one of a kind! He is the perfect combination of organized criminal and a unorganized criminal. He is a standard serial killer, and an uncertain mass murderer. He combines the characters of a prowler, a predator, a wanderer, a field type and an invasion type. The most hideous thing is, he could find out the serial killer you've chasing for half a year only by a few indirect clues, which shows that he's an outstanding criminal profiler!"

"What a genius!" I bet Liu Qiang didn't get his meaning, but his loud and heavy irony represented what most of the people present were thinking. "According to your comment, we can just give up. Don't waste time here."

"Mr. Liu, is there anyone else in your division to can beat Mr. Zhao Xincheng?" Yuan Shi compelely get back his typical cold face as a overseas expert. "I'm telling you the most practical situation. You must be aware that how terrifying the criminal we're dealing with. He knows all your approaches, and has the ability of counter-reconnaissance. He is careful and meticulous. He can even beat one of the best guys of you down in less than a minute! He can get rid of our chase in less than five minutes and runs in and out in a hunting operation involving hundreds of people! Jesus Christ! Mind is power. In which part can you defeat him?"

Liu Qiang didn't respond. Regardless of whether Yuan Shi was being reasonable or not, the failed hunting operation was the best proof. Although Bai looked as usual, I still felt his pose of holding the lighter resembled the gesture of shooting to a great extent.

I had to come out and mediate. "I agree with Dr. Yuan. My comment to Han Bin as "an ordinary person" is to remind you to pay attention to those most "appropriate and suitable" details when searching and doing interviews. He will avoid being noticed. I don't think he'll try to impersonate somebody, including wearing wigs, or covering his face with sunglasses or facial masks. That's absurd. And also, don't count on him running a red light or expose himself when dating some whores in a night club. He won't live in an hotel, pay bills with his credit card, use phone numbers registered to him name or log into his own email box. He knows too well how to disappear in the surveillance system and makes himself ordinary and normal, perhaps easily to be forgotten in that sense. This is also what Dr. Yuan wants to remind you all. Han Bin knows us too well. He knows what we will pay attention to and what we will ignore. He probably knows that we'll be sitting here discussing those details easy to be forgotten at this moment, and he'll find some ways to deal with it. What he knows about us is way much than what we know about him."

"What kind of a son does Professor Han have ..." Bai swept around the conference room. "Are there any searching directions?"

"Now there are three — the name list, the assassin, and Han Yichen."

Actually, there was also Wales Medical Device Research Group."

"What name list?"

I glanced at Yuan Shi and realized this part hasn't been told to everyone. "It's something from unofficial channel."

"The name list means a lot." Yuan Shi looked down at his notebook. "This medical team to aid the South Asia is little weird. Gao Jianlong, Chen Juan, and Xu Dongfang were already dead. Song Dechuan and Peng Kang were killed here in Beijing. Apart from them, in the remaining five, the leader Meng Jingtao went missing at the end of 2001; Ma Xiling fell down from a cliff by accident when he went on a trip to Mount Qingcheng in Sichuan province; Hua Meiyao was hit by a missing Audi in Huaihai West Road in August 2005 and Kate Dix also went missing when she attended a business negotiation in Hong Kong in April 2006. We are now trying our best to find Gu Fan, but whether he's alive or not, what we know till now shows that this name list is actually a death list. Someone ... and that someone is very likely to be Han Bin, is killing them designedly."

Bai may be a little unwilling to accept the severity of what Yuan Shi had said. "Did it say where Han Bin hide on the list?" He asked.

"According to a relatively reasonable analysis from Mr. Zhao, I thought we have proof to believe that Gu Fan is still alive. The reason Han Bin chose to attack the police and run away when he was only suspected is that he wants to continue his killing."

"Do you know how serious your accusation is?"

"Director Bai, I knew Han Songge is a good friend of yours. But do you know how good his son is?"

The other colleagues present in the conference room were annoyed. "What do you mean?"

Bai's phone was ringing. He looked down to glance at the screen, one eyebrow tilt up. "Who wants to buy a sea view house?"

We all looked at each other. The boss sneered and hung up his phone. "Go and find that Gu Fan. Zhao, what are the other two directions did you say?"

"Han Yichen, who's currently under our detention, and that assassin, who attacked Han Bin and me on August 12th. The former is either Han Bin's accomplice or a sacrifice who has been used. The latter may be an accomplice, may be not."

Zhang Qi asked, "Who would he be if he's not an accomplice?"

An assassin with the same killing skill with Bin. "Gu Fan? Or a killer hired by Gu Fan."

"Your meaning is that these people felt Han Bin's movement and now want to kill him before being killed?"

His girl was in the holding cell, and now he sent his parents abroad. I looked up at them. "Probably. Han Bin's now being chased by them."

After the conference, Yuan Shi and I exchanged our information as usual.

"It seemed that the background of Han Bin and his cases were not normal ones." Yuan Shi was still much too excited. "Have you thought about that up until now, besides attacking the police and damaging public security, we don't have any proof of his killing?"

I was completely at his opposite, being extremely lethargic. "I've heard that the stolen police car has been found?"

"He didn't drive it far, just a little pass the Deshengmen Bridge, and lighted a fire on it by the moat. A lot of people were there to see, causing a traffic jam, so it's easy to find."

"He doesn't have to light a fire in broad daylight if he only wants to eliminate his trace?"

"It's an approach to show off his power. Can't you see? He's just challenging the system! Most of violent criminals like to light a fire."

Maybe, but Bin's not like that. Just as what I said, he won't do anything meaningless.

"Whatever, Wang Rui's death can be a close to many of the murder cases. The pressure on Bai's shoulder should be lighted up a bit. ... How's Yichen?"

"I was about to take her to check whether she has been sexually assaulted, but she went into shock from hunger and dehydration. She is all right after some treatment but if you want to question her, it'll need more time."

"You can go to Zhang Beitong. He's a partner of Bin after all."

"Yeah, I've been there. He isn't be able to provide anything useful, only telling me that if Han Bin were a killer, he must have his own reason to be one. And ... they are not partners. Han Bin has given all his shares of the cafe to him before the Spring Festival."

Immediately, I recalled that the night when Xu Chunnan was killed, Bin and Zhang Beitong was discussing at the bar with some papers in front of them.

"In addition to these, according to Han Bin's office, he withdrew all this shares at the end of last year and attended to few cases these two years. His home is clean. Everything was in order except we found that all this photos were gone and the hard drive in his computer was disassembled. All his debit cards and credit cards were canceled and he withdrew all his savings, probably tens of thousands of yuan. His car is now under Han Songge's name. In my view, he has been planning to run way before now, so he settled every loose end."

"How about the last name on that list?"

"This name is too ordinary. Regardless of people with that name in other provinces, there are more than forty here in Beijing. We are searching one by one. You know most of Han Bin's friends. Ask them here to talk with us. We must know him first."

I shook my head.

After Bin ran away, the reaction of all his friends were almost the same: unbelievable — no comment — refuse to cooperate. Bin was too good in making friends. Even Xuejing asked me once and again seriously, "Are you sure it's not a mistake?"

And what they knew about Bin was no better than me. They didn't know anything about his missing three years, which, in my opinion, is most likely to be the most important in finding out the truth.

Seeing me keeping silent, Yuan Shi switched to another subject. "By the way, that 'Wang Rui' was a fake one. We took his photo to the old neighbors of his family living in Zhangjiawan, Tongshou Distritct to identify, and they didn't know the person in the photo."

As excepted, this was similar to "Pang Xin", who didn't have an identity.

"They told me that the son of Wang's family has went south to work several years ago, and didn't came back home since then. The manager of the security department of Changxin Building identified that he was working there around the middle of 2006, which was before Chi Shanshan was killed. But he's not using a name as 'Wang Rui'. Although we can close the case since the DNA test results match, I'll still let he City Bureau find out who he is."

There was no need to do so since there won't by any results.

"Actually, the MO of this killer is not complicated. When he chose the target randomly, he would look of a left hands specifically, but if the target was someone he had been followed for a long time, he didn't care about whether that's a left hand or a right hand. Of course, maybe he didn't even care about it at all ..."

Yes. As long as he wants to kill, he'll find himself an excuse.

"Han Bin must have analyzed that the killer is a left-hander impersonating to be a right-hander. From his MO, he can see that the killer should be connected with Miss Jiang in someway, and your fighting with him that he happened to see ... So he sneaked into him home to find some evidence."

It's a pity that he exposed himself, just like that case in Haidian Hospital.

"This 'Wang Rui' happened to go back home half way, or his hunch told him something was wrong. Han Bin may have found the murder weapon before 'Wang Rui' entered the room, or may not, it doesn't matter ..."

When two murderers met, they knew what to do.

"It was possible that Han Bin wanted to find some smoking guns and give them to you, or simply killer him all by himself. But in fact, the minute 'Wang Rui' opened his door and saw him, he couldn't let Han Bin go."

Now that Bin's exposed, he couldn't leave 'Wang Rui' alive. He could kill three witnesses outside the west wall of Haidian District, would he care about a fake training partner?"

"This may be his only mistake — to gild the lily. He must have been in great uncertainty when he was setting out the crime scene. He thought too much. On one hand, he wanted to use this criminal, who had been dead at that time, to cover him and confuse you; but on the other, he knew too well that he couldn't cover his trace of killing 'Wang Rui' with his right hand."

Or, it was me who shouldn't have been thinking too much.

"As for both Song Dechuan and Peng Kang were left-handed, it's just a coincidence, I should say."

So I could imagine how embarrassed Bin would be when he knew Yuan Shi was asserted that there was only one killer committing crimes with both of his hands.

"I agree with this part you've said: When Han Bin found he was suspected, he attacked you and ran away to commit more crimes. If we were right about the name list, he may have killed at least ten people in the past several years. So ..."

So the conclusion were the same: Finding out of the last survivor on that name list was our top priority.

Yuan Shi put forward a hypothesis at last. "What if Han Bin had Gu Fan killed before we find him?"

I smiled in a most helpless way. "Then there's no chance for us to find him."

2

Before I could take a glance at the files at hand, I hurried to ask him, "Don't you believe he is a killer?"

Yang Yanpeng looked at me indifferently. "Yes, I do believe."

"Then what do you mean by this?"

"He said because you what to take Han. No one's happy about this. The workshop now exists in name only."

"Then what? Should I take all of you to help him run away or commit a crime? Don't listen to He ..."

"No, No ..." He took off his glasses and took a good look at it for a long time. "Just like you, I didn't know why Han would like to kill ... do these things. But I'd like to believe that he has his own reasons for that."

"Yes, I do, too." I patted on my chest. "Yang, we were both in the business. We should know where the boundary is."

"I can understand you, but I cannot support you." Yang put on his glasses again, "You didn't expel me when you first took over the workshop. Did Han Bin stop you?"

"But I am the one who makes the final decision. What? Does that deserve your pay back?"

"Although I don't think such little information can get you him, but if there's a chance in a million, in a billion that it was his protection of me that leaded to him getting caught ... Well, do you think that's a little bit ironic?" He tapped on the file case in my hand. "Anyway, it's my last time to help you. If you want me to look into Han Bin in the future, take your detention warrant and cuff me at my place."

Seeing Yang Yanpeng leaving, I felt what I lost was not only Bin.

But all the people around me.

The value of the last batch of information was beyond my imagination. It gave me the information I desired the most: what Han Bin did from 1994 to 1997.

About "Tiger Bite": It is a kind of skill that is still be used in the Special forces of the People's Army in several Asian countries, Regiment 861 and the Marine Corps of Vietnamese People's Army.

About that "Medical Group": They arrived at Cambodia in early 1994 and was greeted by Binson, the Commander-in-Chief of the National Revolutionary Army of Khmer Rouge.

In 1997, the Vietnamese government sent the a Task Force named Naga, which belonged to Regiment 861, to Cambodia for a decapitation strike. The destination was Anlong Vengm[1]. The operation was named Kill Son. According to the information above, it was likely that their target was Binson. On June 11th 1997, the whole family of Binson was killed at their residence in Anlong Vengm. But the Vietnamese government haven't said anything about this up until now.

And also, on November 22nd 1997, a Task Force arrived at Anlong Vengm for rescue. One of the hostages was saved and no one died of this. It was said that the hostage was named Huang Feng, and was a survivor of that Naga team.

The information also included some people I could interview.

Huang Feng, survivor of Naga. He was born in Tianjin and now living in Minzheng Street, Sidao Town, Guangxi Zhuang Autonomous Region.

A name list of that Task Force, with 32 names on it.

Ruan Xunsong, captain of Regiment 861. He may be the officer in charge of communication in Kill Son operation and lived in Móng Cái, a small town on the north Vietnamese border after retirement.

Shi Tian, may be an alias, Chinese, or a mixed blood of Chinese and Thai or Chinese and Vietnamese. A famous "agent" in South Asia. His residence address was not acquired, but it seemed that he knew well of Naga.

---

1 Anlong Vengm, a border city in the northwest of Cambodia. It was the last place where Khmer Rouge authority located before 1998.

My first feeling was that direct witness Huang Feng was the easiest to find and to get information from. And the one involved in the operation was the last one to be interviewed. After all, a policeman didn't have any say in the area controlled by the army. And for the rest two, well, better than nothing.

However, when I looked into the map again and checked the name list of the operation once more, the former decision of mine was completely changed.

The first place to go, Hangu, Tianjin.

I have been working as a policeman for more than a decade, but it was the first time I knew that Chadian Prison was under the jurisdiction of the Beijing Prison Management Bureau, and a special branch bureau was set for its management only. Probably because the it's close to the Yingcheng Reservoir and Bohai Bay, although it was clear and sunny outside, and there was no air conditioner in the interrogation office, I could still feel gentle breeze going through, making me quite comfortable.

I lighted up a cigarette and looked up. I intended to toss the cigarette and matches to the other side of the table, but, after a second thought, overlay them together and pushed them forward.

"How are you these days?"

Shi Zhan squinted out of the window and didn't even care about me and the cigarette before him.

There was a familiar desolation in the room.

"Sorry didn't stop by to visit after that." I said softly. "But don't misunderstand me. I'm not coming to provoke you, I just don't know what to say."

Shi Zhan looked back at me and smiled. "You are not looking good by the way."

My hunch told me my way of asking may not be wise enough, so I said, "Maybe. I'm coming to ask for your help."

He sat there in silence for a few seconds, seemingly to guess my intention to come. And then, his eyes turned soft. He asked, "Where was Ying and the child buried?"

"Well, sorry about that, but I don't know ..."

"Then I'm sorry too. I cannot help you." He then, again, turned his head to the window.

I finished my cigarette and opened a yellow file before me. "You were sentenced eight years for racketeering, two years for intentional injury, all together eleven years spent behind bars. Just because your

231

case is too difficult to deal with, the highest court gave an official written reply especially to explain your case. If you can help me, I can send your commutation proposal directly to the district court and if you're lucky, you'll be out of bars after six or seven years. Do you want to come out early?"

It seemed Shi Zhan thought this was a boring condition, too boring that he could even laugh at it. "No, I don't."

I closed the file and took a deep breath. "The tomb of Cai Ying and the child, I can ask for you. I can even call here, in front your eyes. Don't you want to come out early to see them?"

"I do want to see them." His answer was calm. "But I cannot think of any reason to help you."

Such confrontation wouldn't lead to any result.

I opened another blue file. "In September 1997, when you were participating a investigation rehearsal in Dadugang Military Base in Guangxi, you were asked to take part in a special operation. You and your team members stared from Jinghong, and then sneaked into the north of Cambodia through Laos. You were then serving as the point."

A slice of surprise crossed Shi Zhan's eyes.

"In the public part of the file, the process of the operation was hidden. But he result was good. You were successful in rescuing a hostage and none of you were left behind outside the country." I bent forward towards the table, gazing at him. "Shi Zhan, the man named Huang Feng who were rescued by your team, who is he?"

He still shook his head smilingly, his eyes calm and determined. "I don't know what you're talking about."

"There is a name list, Shi Zhan! Don't you dare to say you didn't take part in that operation?"

"Yes, I did."

"On November 22nd 1997, you struck where Khmer Rouge located in Anlong Vengm."

"Yes."

"Did you rescue a man named Huang Feng?"

"Yes,"

"Then tell me who that guy is!"

"I don't know."

"No, you do. Tell me!"

"I won't even if I do."

"The file has gone public. There's nothing you can't say."

"The part that didn't go public is what I cannot say."

"I'm not asking for national secrets. I don't care a shit about politics. I only want to know who that Huang Feng is. Is he a member of the Vietnam Communist Party? Do you know anything about that Naga team? Or Binson? Or the Kill Son operation? What do you know about them! Tell me!"

Probably because some ancient memories were awaken, Shi Zhan's face lighted up a bit. "Your name is Zhao Xincheng, right?"

"Yes."

"Zhao Xincheng, did you ever make a promise?"

"Probably. Why?"

"I have made my promise in front of the national flag that I will be loyal to the team."

"How lofty."

"Keeping a promise is a personal choice. It has nothing to do with laws or moral standards."

"From what you've done, you are calling yourself a patriot?"

"No, I'm only keeping my promises."

"Keeping your promise as long as you know Cai Ying was using you?"

"I made her a promise, and I kept it."

"At the cost of ruining half of your life? She sold you out!"

"That's her choice. I cannot force others to choose for the sake of my choice." Shi Zhan pushed my cigarette back. "I do admit that I was disappointed. But now that I chose to make her that promise, I cannot let her down. Do you know what disappointment looks like?

I lowered my eyes. "I don't know."

"It's simple. Go look at yourself in the mirror."

It was said that if there's no hope, there's nothing called disappointment. One can only be disappointed when he got something to hope for. The hope for others, mostly, come from trust and once trust is lost, the feeling of disappointment will rise along, lingering forever.

Yes. I had to admit that I was really disappointed.

"I'll let you know about where Cai Ying and the child is." I pushed the cigarette back and collected the files on the table. "But what I want you to know is, that child ..."

"He's mine." Shi Zhan cut in. "I brought him into this world. He is my child."

I was surprised. "You knew?"

"No. I know nothing." Shi Zhan reached out his right hand. "But thank you all the same."

As I was about to shake his hands, an idea flashed crossed my mind. I took out Bin's photo and passed it to him. "Have you seen this man before? I mean, when you were in that operation, did you ... You don't have to tell me anything. If you haven't seen him, you can just remain silent."

Shi Zhan took over the phone and gave it a glance. The next second, he fixed his gaze on it, obsessively, with an expression of hesitance.

"This ..." I could hear the sound of his gasp, "I cannot say ..."

"That's all right. I won't force you." I stood up and pretended to leave. "That's it. You take care. I'll come to see you if ..."

"No. My point is ... I don't know whether I've seen him before."

" 什么？ "

"What?"

Shi Zhan pinched the photo between his thumb and index finger, his thumb rubbing it unconsciously. "Maybe that's him, or maybe not."

A complicated feeling started to occur in my heart. "What do you mean?"

He turned the photo over and looked up at me. "Is this the man who makes you disappointed?"

It seemed that there were a mirror erecting in front of me. "Yes."

"Then you'll have to pay attention."

"You've seen him?"

"I don't know. I mean ... I'm not sure." Shi Zhan turned the photo up and gave it another look. "Around three o'clock in the afternoon on the twenty-second, we changed out plan ..."

"You don't have to say ..."

"It was not what we planned. It was a complete accident. This man ... It was raining hard in Anlong Vengm ... Well, it was raining cats and dogs in the whole basin. The rain stopped on the twenty-second, but it was extremely foggy. The weather is advantageous in launching a strike, but the operation was still settled in the evening to make sure its success."

"You said you've changed the plan."

"Yes. Because at three in the afternoon, an armed attack was launched at Anlong Vengm. In order to guarantee the safety of the target, we had to take part in the battle."

"Some other forces were there? Who were they?"

"We didn't know. It's true. We didn't know. Back then there was a troop pretending to attack from the west with many people and strong fire, and several attacks were at the southeast. We got into the camp along the east fence and arrived at the location the target was held, but found the guards were all dead and the target went missing."

"There were others to rescue him? But the record says it was you who ..."

"Yes, it was us. We thought the operation failed at the beginning, and retreated from the coming route. But it didn't occur to us that we came across the target on the way back, as well as the the guy to come to rescue him."

I pointed at the photo and asked. "Was that him?"

"I was the point, so I've fought with him." Shi Zhan stared at the photo, seemingly to recall with a big effort. "The fog was heavy and he was wearing camouflage. I cannot be sure that this is the face I saw."

"But you said 'maybe'?"

"That's because his eyes. If taking the eyes as the only concern, I can tell you that it's him for sure. I haven't seen a — how to say — a pair of eyes like this. They are so dark, too dark to be alive."

"And then?"

"He gave Huang Feng to us and then left."

"Huang Feng didn't call his name?"

"I'm not sure. The others and I were guarding the temporary line of defense while the captain was speaking to them. But anyway, if he is the one you're dealing with, you'll have to pay attention."

"I've fought with him before ..."

"I've fought with you before. That guy is better than both of us." Shi Zhan gave me back the photo. "If it's not the QBZ-95 gave me away ..."

"You fought with him?"

"Yeah. We met face to face in the heavy fog. He must have run out of resources. He didn't even have a gun at that time."

"You didn't shoot him?"

"Holly shit!" Shi Zhan gave me a bitter smile. "He didn't give the chance to."

The second place to go, Móng Cái, North Vietnam.

At the border crossing in Dongxing, I spent two hundred yuan hiring a translator, and his motorbike as well.

My request was: This was my first time to Vietnam. It was better to have a translator and guide.

Vice-Caption Sun of the border station said, "The level of the translator isn't the top priority. The personality outweighs all the others."

This translator, driver and guide's question was simple. "The Ha Long Bay?"

I considered it as an argot. "The Potala Palace[1]."

---

1 The pattern at the back of the legal currency in China and Vietnam. Could be considered as the currency for trade.

Well, we were both open to each other. Deal made!

"男人绿帽头上戴，女人围巾脸上盖，三个老鼠一麻袋，十个蚊子一盘菜，摩托跑得比车快，东面下雨西面晒，背着孩子谈恋爱，花钱要用大麻袋。"

"也许兼职是个很暧昧的概念，至少为主业副业的频繁变换提供了理论基础。一路上，驾驶摩托车的翻译阿关经常会顺风送来一些类似的贯口，显得颇为敬业。

Seeing is believing. Actually, Móng Cái doesn't have any more differences with the cities in the southwestern border in China. Vietnamese was not that dark and the girls were not as beautiful as I've imagined. There were so many motorcycles, and much more slippers. Many people spoke Chinese. Vendors could be seen here and there, but the street was too narrow. The big houses were much more luxurious, while the small ones were very shabby, the differences between which could be used to do public service advertising. The only thing that could make you feel it's Vietnam were the many French style buildings, which were more like a miserable irony from the history.

The other thing aroused my attention was the hostility floating on the streets.

Vietnamese were generally small. I am not beefy, only 1.75m in height and 70 kilos or so in weight. But I was really the Triton of the minnows there. Along my way, I could see many people gazing at me, a distinct newcomer. Although I didn't see any spits or middle fingers, I didn't see any smiling faces either.

"The street's not well these days" Guan told me. "The 'Street Gang' from Guangxi was competing with Dung Ha[1]'s son for the business in the casino and the brothel. Naturally, the newcomers could beat the local boss, but who knows Zhou Qinian was coming to play a part. Well, those are just words on the street. You see now few tourists come to play, or I won't charge you only two hundred yuan."

Now that he was talking about this, I asked directly. "Do you know Ruan Xunsong?"

"Hey! I do have a dark skin and my family name is Ruan. But I'm not his father. I am born in Pingxiang[2] ..."

---

1 Dung Ha, a famous female gangster in the criminal world of Vietnam. Born and raised in Trạng Trình street in Haiphong, Dung Hà was a high-ranking criminal member at the port city, and during her peak back in the 90s, she and Truong Van Cam were considered as the two great mafia bosses of the Vietnamese underworld. On October 2, 2000, Dung Hà was assassinated under orders from Truong Van Cam, who had previously been in a feud with Dung Hà in Saigon. After Truong Van Cam was arrested, the successors of Dung Ha took over his place.

1 Pingxiang, a border city in Guangxi province, is an important trade hub in bilateral trade between China and Vietnam.

I reached out my hand to his face from the back, twiddling a green note. "Help me find him."

Guan squinted at the money with one eye and at the road with the other. "Er ... What does this Ruan Xunsong do?"

"I don't know. But he was a soldier."

"That's simple. Go and ask in Tuberose. That's a place where former soldiers get together. Móng Cái is a small place. It's not hard to find a person."

"Tuberose?"

"Yes! It's from the song of Teresa Teng. Have you heard of it? Like this: Tuberose, I'll sing for you; Tuberose, I got to miss you. Ah — Ah — Ah —, I ..."

I stuffed the money into his pocket. "Shut up and get me there!"

In about the minutes, the same song floated into my ears. But it was the original version of Teresa Teng. Tuberose was a bar located by Chagu Lake, with wooden house of two layers, and seemed like a furniture shop selling rosewood furniture from outside. You could only discover the real service of it after you pushed in.

The bar was roomy, with at least dozens of tables. There were many people there but few of them were Chinese. All the tables were so loaded with empty bottles and ash trays that I couldn't even find a place to sit down. Later, Guan told me that I could sit by any table without people since the bartender there only cleaned them once a day.

A man carrying a cigarette in his mouth walking by my side and said something. Seeing me with no reaction, he asked in Chinese again, "Chinese?"

Seeing Guan a little panic with my side glance, I took out a note of 20 yuan and gave it to him. "Two bottles of bear."

"Saigon or Dai Viet?"

None of the brands on the bottle was familiar to me. Apart from some squiggle foreign characters, I could only understand some numbers. "333."

The man took the money to the counter and brought back two bottles of beer, along with two notes of Vietnamese dong, one of which was 10,000, the other 5000. I took out 20 yuan and gave it back along with those two "big" notes. "I want to find a person. Thank you."

Guan translated my words in Vietnamese, but I could tell that he could understand Chinese.

He didn't took a glance at the money at the table, but asked, "Who?"

Yuan Xunsong."

He frowned a bit and turned to Guan. Guan translated immediately. As expected, the pronunciation was different from Chinese. And when they started talking. I didn't understand what they were saying, but I could tell that Guan was very cautious while he was talking, and the man was taking the lead.

I took a sip of the beer. It was freezing cold, with a taste of corn. 333 beer, well, perhaps it would go well with 555 cigarette and 999 cold remedy granular. Probably because the boss, or most of the customers here were in favor of Chinese old songs, most of the music played here was songs of Teresa Teng and Chow Hsuan, and other singers that I couldn't even tell. Sometimes, a song of Chin Tsai coming out of the player would make me feel fashionable. By a table near the counter, someone was singing along with it loudly.

Actually, I've noticed him the minute I stepped into the bar. He stood out from the crowds with his clearly whiter skin than others, and his big figure, all of which differentiated him from the surrounding Vietnamese. He was holding two local girls in his arms. His rap, mixed with Vietnamese, Chinese and English, was loud. But the locals didn't care about him at all, and sometimes smiled at him.

Guan leaned towards me. "He said that Ruan Xunsong haven't been here lately. If you want to find other brokers, he can introduce for you."

"Ask him what a broker is. I mean what do they do here."

Guan opened his small eyes as large as he could. "You didn't know? A broker is a middle man. You can buy anything from them. Women, children, drugs, organs, guns, information, even lives. As long as you have money, there's nothing you can't get."

"A paradise for commodities." I blew a whistle. "Then ask him to find me a broker who can take me to Ruan Xunsong."

Guan talked with him another around and translated to me. "He asked that whether you want a junior one or a senior one. The prices are different."

Those two names made me laugh. It turned out that brokers here have the same kind of ranking system as in other careers.

Feeling a little stuffy, I took a sip of beer to cool myself down. "Is there a 'menu' to choose from?"

It was definite that Guan didn't dare to translate my words directly.

"He said the junior one only takes the money on the table, but the senior one can cost millions of Vietnamese dong."

Although I didn't know the exchange rate, but the price made me thinking about the hidden meaning behind it. "How much is that? I mean in RMB."

"About four or five hundred yuan."

"That's not a problem." I took out my wallet and put 600 RMB on the table. "Two more bottles of bear. Take me another brand."

Guan was translating, but the man understood what I meant the minute he saw the money on the table. He gave me a sneering smile and said in a slightly awkward Chinese. "I'm only an introducer."

I nodded and waved the empty bottle in my hand. "Don't forget my beer."

He laughed, took the money on the table and stuffed it inside his belt. Through his lifted shirt, I could see a dagger with a leather sheath. I leaned back a bit to feel my nightstick, trying to relax myself with its existence.

And then, he pointed at the big white guy who was singing some soft tunes with his gruff voice. "Siqian[1] ..."

I tightened up in an instant. Paying no attention to his words, I glanced at the exits of the bar silently, and put my right hand on my waist ... until Guan said, "He said that man is the most famous senior broker."

Oh. That was easy money to make.

"Then he said 'Siqian'?"

"No, no. He said that man is named 'Shitian."

What a coincidence!

"Shitian?" I directly sat in front of him, "Dong Shitian?"

Humming a song casually, he looked me up and down coldly, caesious stubble around his mouth. His long and thin face was turned into a square one in the process of walking into his middle age. Having finished this song, he shrugged at me, head leaned to one side, one eyebrow tilt up.

I lifted up ten yuan and snapped to that "introducer". "This one is on me."

"Sorry." Shitian shrugged again, his shoulders as wide as a gorilla. "Do I know you?"

I pointed at Shitian and gave the money to the introducer. "How do I call you? Dong? Or just Shitian?"

Shitian called the introducer back, took that10 yuan note, split it into two and tossed at me. "Who said you can sit here?"

I started to suspect whether "Siqian" was his Vietnamese name.

Bearing his rudeness, I pointed at the "introducer" and said, "He said you are the best broker, a senior one. I want to buy some information from you..."

"I don't think a Vietnamese Chinese can afford my price." He raised his voice and the other eyes in the room were focused on me at once. "Get out!"

I turned around and saw Guan's legs were shaking. I smiled at him,

---

1 It means "tear the money apart" in Chinese and sounds similar with "take him" , so the hero here misunderstood that they wanted to take him down. Actually, he was calling that man's name, which also sounds almost the same with "Shitian" in Chinese.

"Guan, wait for me outside. It's nothing." When I turned back, there were several people standing behind Shitian's back.

"Want a smoke?" I didn't even give a glance at the surrounding hoodlums but took a cigarette out. I passed Shitian the box, he didn't take it. I took a smoke myself and fiddled with the lighter. "I had a friend whose lighter was carved with NAGA, he said ..."

Suddenly, Shitian raised his hand to stop me from saying and the others from coming in. "Is he introducing you here?"

That was a chance. I nodded, "Yeah, I was a friend of NAGA."

Shitian stuck his hand into one of the girl's top, and said with great interest, "No one is still alive in Naga. Which one do you know?"

I had to guess in this way. "Well, it seemed that I was a friend of two dead men."

Shitian's pupils suddenly contracted. "Which one told you to come?"

"I've told you, two dead men."

He seemed relieved. "How should I know whether what you've said is true."

I pulled out a photo on the table from my pocket. That was a photo of Yichen, Bin, Xuejing and I. Shitian pulled out his right hand and heaved the photo very close to his eyes. He examined it very carefully and then said, "Your wife's got a big breast. I'm wondering how it feels like."

"Be careful with your words!"

"Or what?" Shitian tossed the photo back to the table. "You should feel lucky that it isn't a fake one. If it is, your wife should be a widow by now. I'm telling you, son. People who can talk to the two of them at the same time were no more than two. One is me for sure, and the other is definitely not you. It's lucky that the one you knew can save your life."

The phone in my pocket was vibrating, I didn't dare to take it. I felt sweat running down along my back and my heart stood still. Calm ... calm down. He was not buffing, but he didn't dare to do anything about me. Right, he didn't say anything about Yichen and didn't tear the photo apart like he treated that 10 yuan note. Did it mean ... he didn't dare to offend Bin?

I put my bottle of beer by my mouth to cover half of my face. "Han Bin said if there's something I want to know, I can come to you."

"Is he?" Shitian looked at me aggressively. He took up the phone on the table and pressed some numbers. "It doesn't matter. Let's see if you're talking about the truth this time."

I was more nervous. Digging myself into a hole. I was laying up trouble for myself.

The phone hasn't been picked up. I was so lucky. Shitian squinted his eyes, tapping his own front teeth slightly with the phone, and shouted to the bar counter. The music stopped.

Seeing him dialing again, I was almost stifling.

This time it was picked up. Shitian was talking Vietnamese in a low voice and glanced at me vigilantly. I started to regret why I let the translator go just now but had to put on a careless look. I moved the chair backwards a little bit and prepared to get the drop.

Suddenly, Shitian hung up his phone and laughed. "Well, you're not a little liar, but a big one. From the first day I was in this line of work, you are the first one who dares to tell a second lie in front of me."

I didn't respond. His words were not pleasant, but he didn't intend to kill me.

"Lucky you!" As expected, he was a little disappointed that he couldn't put his threat into practice. "There's someone want you alive, so you're lucky to be the first one standing here after lied to me twice.

Having my guess proved, I gloated and talked back insatiably. "The whole room is waiting for your order. You're definitely on the call about whether to kill me."

Shitian gave me a cold smile and suddenly threw his "left hand" on the table. It was an artificial one and I didn't notice before.

"Don't worry. Wanna die? Chances are so many."

If he really contacted Bin, it was unwise for me to lie to him again. And the next hours of drinking with him made me feel that he was a good one to talk with if we could talk honestly. He seemed curious about the relationship between me and Bin and finally got me to tell the story at the cost of not getting me sodomized by a bunch of Vietnamese gangsters.

"It's hard to imagine he should live a life like that." Shitian was humming some unknown tune, eyes flushed by the alcohol brimmed with satisfaction. "Three years of leaving ... You must want to know what he was doing during that three years. But it has nothing to do with your final aim. You want to take him, right?"

Taking another smoke, I didn't say yes, nor did I say no.

"Are you disappointed when you find out that a buddy you knew for over ten years is actually a stranger?" He hummed for a while and turned to me. "Do you think that's a big case when he killed several people in mainland? No, that's nothing. You don't know what he's capable of. He had killed so many, so many..."

"Bin went missing in 1994 in Beijing. Nobody could find him. Did he come here?"

"He did, as far as I know."

"What was he doing here?"

"Not sure. No one knows."

"And then?"

"The People's Army was recruiting back then. He was taken to the army before he could realize what happened. Back then, he was put in Brigade 126, a Battery. There were many Chinese Vietnamese there, one of which was the man you've met but didn't know."

"You mean that assassin."

"They were buddies. I even heard that they've killed an officer together in the army."

"They are friends?"

"They were. But something happened later. Coincidentally, the General Secretary of Vietnam at that time especially talked about the union with socialist countries on *People's Army*, and something like to support foreign soldiers from the very beginning, or because the publication of the *China-Vietnam Joint Communique* ... Anyway, they weren't sentenced to death, but were sent to Regiment 861 at a Military Base in Hanoi."

"Regiment 861 ... He was in that Kill Son operation?"

"Why would he be in Naga if not?"

"The lighter he often used ... There was 'NAGA' caved on it. Is that how it reads?"

"That is the Naga Queen in Cambodia myth. The serpent goddess. Those Vietnamese are much less qualified in naming."

"Who are they killing? Binson?"

"Well, you do know things. It was said that the director of Khmer Rouge intended to surrender. Maybe Vietnam supported the other side, so they went there to interfere."

"What do you mean?"

"Nothing. Anyway, it was said that on June 10th, a team of assassins sneaked into Anlong Vengm at midnight. The whole family of Binson was killed. I was doing business at the New Golden Triangle[1] at that time. That was a big attack. All areas in the north part of Cambodia were influenced. Linwang, the Commander of the Royal Union Army, thought it was Pailashasian, the second son of the Shamarle family who did the trick, but Khmer Rouge considered it as the revenge of some force while Pailashasian insisted that it was because the interference of some foreign

---

1　The New Golden Triangle refers to the region where Cambodia, Thailand and Laos border on. This is a region under nobody's jurisdiction and is named after the old "Golden Triangle" located between Myanmr, Laos and Thailand.

forces. The result was awful. Different forces met in the north of Cambodia and the region was swept over. Munitions, hard drugs, arms dealing ... none of the businesses was available."

"How did you know them?"

"Several days later, the survivors of Naga showed up at the New Golden Triangle. There were only two of them left."

"Bin and ...?"

"One of them was your friend. But his name was not Bin."

"He used an alias? What is that?"

"This, I can't say."

"Why?"

"Because their names were forbidden to be spoken of in the area of Cambodia and Vietnam."

"Bullshit."

"Well," Shitian leaned forward to pull up his belt and then sat down again. "At last, the reason of Binson's death was attributed to Pasoulwate's clearance of his own people. But who knows ... The problem is, whether it was Naga killed Binson, plenty of classical files were lost along with their coming in and out — very important ones.

"Naga took them?"

"Or one the Nagas took them."

"Was that Bin?"

"I don't know, and I'm not interested. But in order to get those files, which probably were only about some box news about Khmer Rouge, many people still made great efforts to find the survivors of Naga. If I dare to tell you even one name, you'll have a chance to speak it out some time in the future. Then those people would swarm to you and torture you to get a location. But you didn't even know about him. So why ask? Don't get yourself into trouble."

"Then you're not afraid of those people swarming to you?"

"I'm special, the most special one in the specials." Shitian stuck out his tongue to lip this mouth, seemingly quite proud of this. "No one would want to be the enemy of the world on the ground and underground in South Asia."

Whether he was bragging or not, I didn't want to be his enemy. "Does that mean the old comrade-in-arm of Bin was chasing after him."

"Only one of them can survive."

"Why?"

"No why."

"Hey! Are you a senior broker?"

"Yeah. That means you didn't have to know."

"That's not a decent thing to do. I told you everything about me."

Shitian laughed in a quite rude way. "Decent? You've gone on the wrong way to find decency."

I started to think about some other ways of getting information from him. "By the way, can you find a man called Ruan Xunsong?"

"You are asking me to run such little errand for you?"

"I just hope I find the right man this time."

Guan was at least right about one thing. It was not difficult to find a man in Móng Cái as it was such a small place.

Walking down south from Tuberose, we entered into a shabby block after a few steps. There was a small barbecue with a dozen of Vietnamese men squatting or sitting around. They were topless, tattoos winding on their arms. Seeing us there, they gazed us fiercely together. I could tell they were different with the retired soldiers drinking and singing in the bar. They were real desperadoes.

I took a glance at Guan behind me. He was paler and more shaky.

Shitian didn't care at all. He pointed at a hunched figure in the corner and told me, "That shit is who you are asking for. Ah, by the way, he's not speaking Chinese."

I told Guan to come with me. In no more than two steps, four locals came forward on our way. Although the highest of them was only the height of my nose, he was really fierce. I looked back at Shitian. "Give me a hand?"

Shitian shrugged as usual. "Do I know you?"

I passed my bag to Guan and stepped forward. Regardless of whether they could understand me, I murmured with my head lowering, "Excuse me ... excuse me ..."

A hand was against my chest and pushed me back.

I reached back for my nightstick.

Shitian reminded me with a cold voice. "Like I said, there are so many chances for you to die."

I stared at those four, and looked around those many hiding in the dark. Removing my hand off the night stick, I stick into my back pocket and took out a roll of notes.

Shitian mocked at me from behind.

Ruan Xunsong was unexpectedly small. He's got a big nose and there was a scar on one of his eyes. His wrinkles obscured his age, but his strong arms and fingers could somehow show his past of joining the army.

I was planned to buy him some drinks to get him talk but the pinholes between his fingers changed my mind — he probably wanted cash more. I asked Guan to tell him to answer my questions. Ten yuan per question.

The most I wanted to know was what on earth happened between Bin and Naga team.

After listening to my question, Ruan Xunsong identified with me by sticking out his ten fingers. I nodded and asked, "Who were the team members of that Naga team sent for the 'Kill Son' operation in 1997?"

The memory of this drunker and drugster amazed me. He gave me the names of the team members: Yaojiang was the leader, Wu Hongshan and Ruan Ba the first task force, Huang Feng and Feng Cai the second task force, Ruan Xiongyong the sniper, Yang Xin the deputy sniper, Pan Guangcheng the medic, and Piao Xing the communicator.

Maybe afraid of me thinking him making the money too easily, he continued before I even asked. He told me that Naga team headed to Laos through Liaobao and then arrived at Banbeisong passing through the south of Laos. They sneaked into the north of Cambodia along Biandan Mountains and arrived at Anlong Vengm at around eleven o'clock on 10th. They started the operation at midnight.

我丢过去十块钱，追问道："后来呢？"

I threw him another ten yuan and asked, "And then?"

His answer became vague. In less than half an hour after the operation, Naga contacted the direction center on the scene and Yao Jiang, the leader, reported that Binson family were all died, and requested to retreat since they were surrounded and attacked.

Knowing that he would continue to talk, I held ten yuan in my hand and looked at him.

As expected, he continued to tell me that the direction center approved their retreat and told them backup would meet them in fifteen kilometers north from Preah Vihear[1]. The breaking out battle was tough. More than half of the team members died.

I threw him the note. "I knew Hang Feng was captured. What about the others?"

Ruan Xunsong blinked his eyes more quickly. His answer was more vague. According to him, forces from different parts wanted to get some benefit from this fight, so Naga was back injured. The retreat failed. Yao Jiang and Ruan Ba was the only two left. They changed the route and went to the new Golden Triangle.

---

1 A place located at the junction of Northern Cambodia, Thailand and Laos.

I mapped out quickly in my mind. "No, that's not possible. The new Golden Triangle was to the east of your meeting place. If they chose to go there, then they'll pass the meeting point. Why didn't they come across the backup team?"

His seemed to be on the verge of being sober, waving his hands hysterically and said that they must have been lured by some force and betrayed the team.

I gave him a punch on his face. He fell on the ground. There was a slight sensation around. Right, good. A carrot and stick policy could serve as the deterrent to the others, a stone to kill two birds. I didn't spare my effort so Ruan Xunsong was beaten to the ground and couldn't get up. I took out 50 yuan and put it under an empty beer bottle. Knocking the table with my finger joints, I said to Guan, "Get him up! Answer my question if he wanted the money."

Before Guan could finish his words, Ruan Xunsong was attracted back by the note, eyes on that 50 yuan note. He grinned in an expression of greedy and flatter, his yellow teeth revealing themselves from his lips. I pressed my hand on the bottle and asked him, "Do you know Han Bin?"

Ruan Xunsong's eyes were both on the money. He even didn't notice my question until I asked Guan to ask him again. But he shook his head in a blank face.

I pulled out the photo and pushed it to him together with that 50 yuan note. I pointed at Bin and asked, "Who is this? Yao Jiang or Ruan Ba?"

He pulled out the money quickly, mumbling something indicating his satisfaction. And then, he glanced at the photo. On that glance, he was attracted just like Shi Zhan.

He murmured something with a shaky voice.

I asked Guan, "What does he say?"

Guan said, "He's saying that it's something of Anlong Vengm, something ..."

Ruan Xunsong was still chewing these words between his teeth and seemed to be more and more terrified. Suddenly, Shitian sat beside me. I was startled, and then found that there were several people approaching us from different directions.

"How careless." Shitian put his fake arm on my shoulder. "This one must have been dulled by drugs. How careless for him to say so."

"What did he say?"

"What he said means the God of Death in Anlong Vengm."

And the next second, a click of metal came into my ears.

I was not bragging. I have worked in the investigation, and then the interrogation, the social crops and back to the investigation again. In all these departments, there were so many hardships and obstacles, dangers and threats. I've always chosen to deal with them in tough manners. I've met spectacles and horrifying situations, and lived through those tough times. But when Ruan Xunsong fell down on the ground along with a boom, apart from the sharp echoes in my ears, the only feeling I had was an unbelievable shock.

A man who was talking with me just now died right in front of my eyes in broad daylight. There was no hurling abuses, no intimidating threats, no violent fights, nor a gun pointing at the back of his head as in the movie. After the the sound of the knell, everything was over.

The 7.62mm bullet pushed Ruan Xunsong onto the table. He then fell on the ground like a puppet without its strings. At the same time, that gun slightly turned its direction and pointed at me.

I thought there would be the sound of a firing pin knocking at the primer in no time. That would be the sound of my knell.

Someone pushed me away. Up until I came back to myself did I found Shitian was standing in front of me, sheltering my chest with one of his shoulders. I then found the one holding the gun was a male youth with a black poppy tattoo on his chest. He was shouting at Shitian and waving his weapon at him, as if telling him to go away.

I heard the sound of turning bearings. Shitian shrugged shoulders and spread both his fake and real arms in a practiced and harmonious way. He talked back in Vietnamese. Although I couldn't understand his words, I could still get his meaning.

The gun turned at him at once.

I pulled out my nightstick and was ready for a real fight. There were three people standing in front of me, and over half a dozen around. If I could take down this one and snatched his weapon, there was a slight chance for us to survive.

But to my surprise, Shitian stood up. He put his right hand on the table and leaned forward, pressing his head near the gun without scruple. Squinting his right eye, he looked into the bore, said something, and suddenly spit at the gun.

The black poppy was very much insulted. He swung the sputum off with rage and then pointed the gun at Shitian. He was furious and scolding, but Shitian was standing still like some sculpture, erecting between me and that gun.

After a while, all the others came up and pushed that black poppy

247

and his two companions away, saying something I couldn't understand. Noticing that all of them were taking weapons, I couldn't help feeling lucky that I didn't act on impulse.

Shitian didn't stop staring at the black poppy until he put the gun away, and then stood straight up to say to me, "Come on."

The backpack was thrown on the ground. Guan was nowhere to be found. I picked up the backpack and found that there were some drops of blood on it. I looked down and found my clothes being the same. Shitian was between me and that bunch of guys all this time, and told me in a low voice. "Don't walk too fast or too slow. And don't run. Try not to look back."

I stood up without a word and passed through under Shitian's arm. On my way out, I took a glance at Ruan Xunsong. He was lying on the ground. His eyes were wide open, watching his blood flowing in front of him unconsciously. His left hand was still holding that photo which cost him his life and his right hand was by his pocket in a awkward way, as if to protect that 50 yuan note with one corner sticking out.

Unaware of how far I walked away, I suddenly felt I was going to faint and couldn't support myself. Being unable to stand up straight, I could only lean on the wall of a residence by the road and have a rest. While I was pulling out the cigarette, my hands were shaking. Shitian also took one and lighted my cigarette up for me.

I breathed heavily, my sweat running down profusely. The first smoke choked myself. Shitian still looked calm and careless, but I could tell some anxiety from his eyes. "It's not a good place for Chinese to come these days. I'll walk you to the Ka Long River[1]."

"They ..." I finally got my rage back. "Should we call the police?"

"Do you know him?" Shitian spread his hands and shrugged, blowing a set of smoke rings. "Early death gets him another life earlier than us. That's not bad."

"'The God of Death in Anlong Vengm.' Yao Jiang and Ruan Ba, are these two names prohibited to be spoken out here?"

"The recent situation here in Móng Cái is quite delicate and subtle." Shitian didn't give me a direct answer. "You can choose to get your guy if you think you're capable, but don't step into these old resentments."

I didn't plan to give up. "Is Bin that God of Death in Anlong Vengm?"

Shitian patted on his fake arm. "I don't know how to explain that to you ...

---

1 Ka Long River is a river of Guangxi Zhuang Autonomous Region in southwest China and Quảng Ninh Province in northeast Vietnam. It runs roughly along the last stretch of the land border of the China-Vietnam border.

but on November 22nd 1997, I saw this arm of mine flying out right in front of my eyes. The God of Death was everywhere that day."

"You were there?"

"A lot of people were there that day, but only few of them walking out alive." Shitian fiddled the cigarette between his right hand fingers. "Later on, the Death of God in Anlong Vengm became a spiritual symbol in the underground world in South Asia. Yao Jiang and Ruan Ba, they are the Buddhas in the shrine.

"Which one is Bin?"

Shitian thought for a little while and shook his head. "You'd better not get in between them."

"Now the other one is chasing after Bin and wants to kill him. What on earth happened between them?"

"Hard to say. Probably the fate."

"Bullshit! Fate or not, it's people's choice after all."

"You can't say it's your luck that saved your life just now, can you?" Shitian squatted down, laughing arrogantly. "Do you think saving your life is my choice and the reason I made that choice is because those lunatics don't dare to kill me? Aha! That's exactly what's in your mind. Exactly! But have you thought about what if they really fired? Or the gun discharged accidentally? Or they took me down together, and then raped and killed you right in front of my eyes? All those coincidences put together lead to your survival. You choose, I choose, they choose, all the people were choosing. We are choosing our fate, and the fate is choosing us."

"You mean they will finally ..."

"Maybe." Shitian stood up and reached out his right hand to me. "Three years of hard training can produce a killing machine, but that's definitely not enough to survive in a battlefield with flying bullets."

Pulling me up, he turned around to look at the direction of the Ka Long River. "That was a foggy day. The heavy fog turned Anlong Vengm into a white maze. The only thing you can do is to grope and wait to come across the God of Death around the next corner."

"Yao Jiang and Ruan Ba both went to the rescue of Huang Feng, right? They both went back to Anlong Vengm on November 22nd! And they walked out alive ..."

"They are no ordinary man. Or I should say, they are not human at all."

"You mean Fate has chosen them?"

"No. They probably don't need to wait to be chosen by fate." It seemed Shitian didn't care about that at all. He shrugged again and gave me a weird smile. "Did you hear them just now? They are the God of Death who controls fate."

It only took me three hours to walk in and out of Móng Cái. I couldn't reconcile myself to the little achievement I got but did aware of the danger of continuing to stay here. Shitian refused to tell me more about Bin's past on our way to Ka Long River and that disappointed me a lot. But apart from that, I suddenly thought of another puzzle we've got — that medical group sent by St. Raison Foundation.

Shitian must have known something about that because he said, "Yes, I know them. I've done a lot of business with their leader. He asked me to pull some strings for him not too long ago this year. That man was something. I can tell on my first sight. He is an genuine son of bitch rarely seen."

I searched in my memory and asked him with doubt, "This year? But Meng Jingtao went missing a year ago."

"First, I didn't make even the slightest mistake for my business." Shitian tapped his fingers on the corner of his forehead, squinting at me. "And second, who is Meng Jingtao?"

"Meng Jingtao is ..." I took a second thought and answered, "his alias. What's his real name?"

Shitian shrewdness embarrassed me. "His name was nothing. I'll tell you for free. His name is Liang Xiao."

My face must have blushed. "Right. So what ... what did he come to you for?"

He used his typical shrug to answer, showing the "career ethic" as a "senior broker".

Getting on information, I chose to go back to my former subject and asked him, "Then why did this medical group came here to reach Khmer Rouge in 1994?"

"Must be to heal the wounded and rescue the dying."

Of course I couldn't believe this answer. And then I noticed Shitian's expression and found out that this was something that I didn't have to know.

"Bin almost killed all their people."

"If he really does something like that, he must have a reason to do so."

"Those the people went to Cambodia as early as 1994, but Bin chased and killed them up until now. Why would he do that? Spending more than the years on things like that? What for? Shitian, you must know. Please tell me."

"I don't know, indeed." Shitian's tone of talking made it difficult for me to tell whether he was telling the truth. "Frankly speaking, I'm also curious about this one."

"You never asked him?"

"I did after a wild drink."

"He didn't tell you?"

"What he said," he shrugged again, "has nothing to do with you."

"Now it has everything to do with me. These people met Binson in person. Naga went to assassinate Binson in 1997. There must be some connections between them!"

"Maybe because he's a humanitarian fighter? Haha ..." Shitian took a sniff and turned away. "You knew one normal part of him, and I knew the other normal part of him. But who actually knows him?"

When we arrived at the bridge of Dong Xing port, Shitian stopped and waved his fake arm at me. "Right. I'll leave you here. Go back to your wife. She seems to be a good one."

I then realized how much favor I owed to him. I took out my wallet and said, "Thank you for you help. This ..."

Shitian took the wallet out of my hand swiftly. Having looked it through, he pulled out a 10 yuan note and put the wallet back into my pocket. "That's for the drink."

Looking at this fellow countryman who travels through the underground world, a weird feeling welled up in my heart. "Can you ... can you tell me your contact information? I mean, I'll really buy you a drink if there's another chance."

"Very much appreciated but no." As expected, Shitian refused my request. But he explained to me, "I don't have a long-time residence and my phone number will be frequently changed. You can't get to me even if you got my phone number now. And you've seen very clearly that Móng Cái is not a good place to go. Zhou Qinian thought he may take some advantages in the chaos, but he doesn't understand that no matter how powerful he is, he can never beat the local boss. I can only tell you that don't come here ever again. No matter for what, don't come here."

"Just because the mafia gangs are fighting with each other?"

Shitian stared at me. "Do you know what I saw in Anlong Vengm on November 22nd 1997?"

I searched in my memory and answered, "You said that you saw your left arm flying out right in front of your eyes."

"That's just something about me." He stroked on his fake arm, as if it could feel his touch. "What I saw was running like hell."

"Running like hell? Run for what?" Were it not for his disability, I really wanted to imitate his shrug. "The enemy's running? Or the bullets are running? Or you're running?"

He didn't answer.

I looked back at Móng Cái and then at Shitian. Taking out a piece of paper and a pen, I left my phone number to him. "If you were to come back to China, remember to call me. I owe you a favor, dude."

He showed all his generosity. "You don't owe me anything. If you do, it's your friend who you owe your favor to."

"Did he ask you to do this?"

"He asked a lot of people. Well, regardless of what you think, I still feel that he's taking you as his friend."

I couldn't help but asked, "Are you saying ... that I shouldn't be chasing him?"

"That's a different matter." Shitian scratched the back of his head. "You two are friends. That's true. But you have different things to do. If someday you do have to fight with each other, there's nothing you can do about it."

"Let's hope that day never comes." I was a little upset. "Take care, Shitian. By the way, I wanted to ask from the beginning about your name. Are you named Shitian with a family name Shi and a given name Tian? Dong is not your family name?"

"Name? Are names important?" Shitian didn't expect I would ask him this. "Someone has told me that names are only codes, but humans are not. From what I could recall, people call me Tian. In the new Golden Triangle, they call me Brother Tian. When I went back to my hometown, some of my so-called old neighbors asked me 'Is Feng from Dong's family coming back? I remembered he had been sold to somewhere else.' ..." His voice was faintly mocking. "In the end, I was still unaware of my name. So what? I don't care! No matter what you call, I know you're calling me."

"That makes sense." I laughed out in a relaxed way for the first time today. "We'll meet again in the future."

"You'd better not ..." Shitian should seem to be a little genial in the rosy glow of the setting sun. "And by the way, in the middle of 1994, the Khmer Rouge indeed purchased a bunch of automatic weapons of various brands. I now can recall there's SG550 or SG551, maybe AN94 of Russian style. You probably don't know, but these are top-notch at that time.

"But that St. Raison Foundation didn't have much money transferred in. Was the Khmer Rouge able to afford such large amount of money?"

"I don't know." Shitian shrugged once again. "After all, there's no such thing as a free lunch."

The third place to go, Sidao, Guangxi province.

Sidao, a town about 30km to the south of Jingxi city, was close to China-Vietnam border. There were few ways to get there, only tractors could take me in. Ever since I set foot on Guangxi, it was raining all the time. I spent a lot of effort to get a ride on a tractor, which cost me 5 yuan and half a pack of cigarette. But there was no ceiling on a tractor, I could only accept the harsh welcome of nature.

Fortunately, I could still get telephone signals though the place was remote. I called Yuan Shi back on my way. His big interest to Bin has completely diverted his attention from the lately dead "Wang Rui". After speaking highly of my terrifying experience in Móng Cái, he told me that the number of names on the search list for Gu Fan was narrowed to three. He also told me that Han Yichen was adopted from an church orphanage in Pianma of Yunnan province in 1999 and advised me to visit the orphanage as I was already in Yunnan. And at last, he gave me another important piece of information.

"You've focused on the living too much, and ignored the importance of the dead. Do you still remember Chen Juan? She died of illness in Cambodia in 1994. We know she was the girlfriend of Gu Fan, but do you know who's her ex-boyfriend?"

At that moment, I saw scenes overlapped one another: Anlong Vengm by the river, and Xiaoyue River in heavy fog.

Bumped on the muddy path for more than two hours, I finally reached the destination like a drowned mouse. Upon jumping off the tractor, I was tripped over by a sloppy puddle and fell on the ground. When the driver drove away with a speed faster than rushing to the crematory, the muddy water split by the tires washed me down from top to toe with the essence of the land.

There were no more than 600 residences altogether in Sidao town, making it easier to look for someone here than in Móng Cái. Half an hour later, I was standing in front of a small convenience shop by the only asphalt road in the town. "Convenience shop" was what this little shop called itself, but it actually was a stall selling fruits in the owner's home. Few people were here to buy things partly because of the rain, so the owner was sitting in an armchair, drinking and enjoying his leisure time.

Right in front of my eyes was a middle aged man nearly 50 years old. He wasn't tall, and wore long pants with low crotch and a short sleeve shirt. The shirt wasn't tied up, so I could see a little of his chest, black and strong. The muscle on his arm filled the sleeves up and showed his strength. The left leg of his pants was empty, but this wasn't the most severe damage in his body. The most severe damage was his eyes, or I should say, was where his eyes should be. On the place where his eyes should be were now two red-and-black polyps intertwined with each other, as if two centipedes crawling out from his eyes. They were so terrifying that I even turned my eyes away.

Standing by his stall, I put my backpack on the ground and asked, "Hey, how much is the jackfruit?"

He picked up the wine cup with a smile. "Hey dude, do you really want to buy the jackfruit?"

A short embarrassment came out between us.

"Only two kinds of people come here to buy my fruit. One is the locals who wear slippers, and the other is the tourists who wear sports shoes. None of them would wear leather shoes like you." He pointed at his "eyes" with pride. "It's true that I couldn't see, but I'm not blind."

I was convinced in the first place that this self-contradictory theory could somehow make sense.

"You're Huang Feng?"

"You must be Zhao Xincheng then."

We laughed together, knowingly.

I directly sat on the ground and took a cigarette from my pocket. "Then you should know the reason I come to you."

"You are either coming to ask for a snub or coming to find yourself a path towards death." Huang Feng refilled his cup while he was talking to me. His action was too precise and agile to make me doubt that he actually had no eyes. "Now that Shitian let you go, son, why come here instead of going back?"

"A couple paid for one night on No. 27 Minzheng Road from December thirteenth to eighteenth 2006, and the male of them was named Han Bin." I gave him a cigarette. "If I'm right with the number here, you're their witness, right?"

Huang Feng raised his hand and took my cigarette. It's said the natural blind always have sharps ears, but it was the first time that I met someone like him, someone who have their eyes damaged after but can still tell things apart with ears.

"December 2006 ... Well, it was true that someone paid to stay here. The man said his name was Han Bin. I was quite cooperative when the police came to ask me. What?" Huang Feng's answer was as rascally as I could expect. "You can't count on me, a blind, to identify."

I cast my eyes on the roads in the rain and asked, "Why would you move here?"

"My wife's here. My child is going to school in Dongxing." Huang Feng leaned back on the walk and said leisurely, "Everywhere is the same as long as I can live a life."

Probably because he has been living in the south for such a long time, Huang Feng's accent changed a lot. Only a few words could reveal that his birthplace was actually the province by the Bohai Bay.

"Han Bin's ex-girlfriend Chen Juan died in Cambodia in 1994. She has met Binson. In the same year, he showed up in Vietnam. In June 1997, Bin joined the Kill Son operation together with you, whose target was Binson. In the years later, he almost killed all the people who have been to Cambodia with Chen Juan. I've already figured out his reason of killing those people, but there are a lot other things I don't know." I leaned forward towards him and added with emphasis, "Answer my questions, or you'll say goodbye to your life here."

It was raining more heavily than before. Down came the raindrops with a rustling noise, and soon became straight lines. The tapping and knocking of raindrops on this isolated small town echoed within distant mountains and surrounding buildings. We sat there silently, listening to the rhythm of the falling rain. People tend to lose the sense of time in such an environment in which silence and noise can co-exist harmoniously. I didn't know how long had passed, but when Huang Feng took out another wine cup, filled it up and gave it to me, the rain had become smaller and the sky dimmer.

I reached out for his wine cup, but to my surprise, he didn't let go. Holding the wine cup, I could felt his body suddenly turned extremely tight like an open strong bow ready to shoot at the only target in front of him. I didn't know what to do. I could neither snatch up his cup, nor could I just let it go. The only thing I could do was to kneel down on the ground and waited for his move.

I could feel his intention to kill sweeping through the air. After a while, he finally let me go. I took the cup back and drank up all the wine inside, and then the bumping of my heart came into my ears.

He was not listening to the rain; he was waiting to see whether anyone's passing through. Nor was he meditating, or asking me to drink the wine, but pulling me close by giving me the cup to kill me. He was the tiger, and I was his prey.

"You're a policeman. Focus on your case, and don't ask about. They are none of your business." Huang Feng frowned a little bit and continued, "I won't be sitting here but for Jiang and Ba. Don't count on me to sell any one of them out."

I put the cup on the ground. "I'm not asking you to sell them out. All I want to know is what my best friend really did in the past?"

"You best friend?" He mocked at me. "Your best friend to be chased by you now?"

"Bin has killed a lot of people."

"Then those people must have their reasons to die."

"That's not new to me. I've been told this several times by different people." I heaved a sigh and said, "He has his reason to kill, and I have my reason to track him down."

"I don't know where he is."

"Like you'll tell me if you know."

"Then why are you coming here to find me?"

"Shitian said that Yao Jiang and Ruan Ba were best friends who can trust the other with their lives. Why would they end up like this?"

"I don't know. And this is what I want to know."

"I've heard that they were chased all the way to the new Golden Triangle. Will that be the reason? Like they have nowhere to go so ..."

"So they sell each other out?" Huang Feng shook his head with a smile. "You know, Kill Son was never a simple assassin."

"What do you mean?"

"Before we leave, Ruan Xunsong asked me to come to Colonel Wu's office alone and gave me a secret task."

I guessed his meaning at once. "To let you kill each other."

"Haha, quick guess."

"It's possible that every one of you has got this kind of 'secret task', right?"

"Jiang told me later that his task was to kill everyone of Naga on our way back. And my task was to kill the spy Jiang."

"Yao Jiang is a spy?"

"Do I look like James Bond?"

"Err ... How about Ruan Ba? Was he asked to kill anybody?"

"No. Maybe the boss thought him inexperienced. He didn't have any secret tasks."

"The others?"

"Xing, Cai and Guangcheng all died on our way out. I lost my leg." Huang Feng was talking in a calm manner. "But on our way to the meeting point, Wu, Xin and Yong died. I don't know how they end up like that, but they did."

"Yao Jiang killed them?"

"Even if he did, he didn't kill Ba."

"Do you mean that now that he didn't kill Ruan Ba but fled to the new Golden Triangle with him, that means their relationship was so good that that they couldn't betray each other?"

"Nothing was impossible at that time."

"Yeah, I know. But he were apart at last."

"Yes, they did. Jiang killed a leader of the local armed force there and recruited some people. Ba went back to Biandan Mountains to avoid being killed. But after that ..."

"After that, they both chose to rescue you in Anlong Vengm on November 22nd."

"I lost my eyes there." Huang Feng was still talking calmly, but was clearly more upset than before.

"I heard a lot of things happened on 22nd."

"Yeah. Well, I was really flattered."

"Speaking of this, I've always want to ask. Why would there be a special rescue operation for you?"

"Do you think it was out of pure good intent for Regiment 861 to train us and send us out to kill?"

I wetted my lips. "They would plant this on you whether you were killed successfully."

"Naga was built to sacrifice. We were all chess pieces."

"But the Khmer Rouge was about to surrender. They would rather choose not to give the Vietnamese the chance to impute at all than to bicker for you."

"I can't think that far. Chinese save Chinese, that's what should be done."

I asked a key question. "Who found you first?"

"Ba." He didn't notice my intention. With his cup empty and refilled again, excitement and pride of recalling his glory days showed up on his face. "I was locked up alone. There were several guards outside, and a patrolling one ... I didn't even notice someone's approaching before they fell down on the ground. Hey! That guy was like a cat!"

"Did Ruan Ba take you out?"

"He held me by the arm and we ran out. It didn't take us long before we met Jiang and the team. It was until then that I found out they didn't get along with each other."

"What did they say?"

"Say what?" Huang Feng shook his head. "It was too foggy that day and the meeting wasn't a planned one. Ba shot several of them down and said nothing. Ah, and there was one who only lost a arm. That was Shitian. He was just nobody at that time. Not like him now."

"He didn't shot at Yao Jiang? Or ..."

"Jiang called my name when we met, so he should be within the visual range. In this way, he must have avoided the shot. Anyway, Ba shot half of his team down at the beginning and then ran away. Then Jiang put me on his back and continued to run out. All his men died there — it's lucky that Shitian could run away from Anlong Vengm considering his condition. He's so lucky."

"Yeah ... And then you met the rescue group ..."

"Yeah, I was lucky, too."

"What was the reason for their conflict?"

"I don't know. They came to see me after that, but none of them spoke of that, so I didn't ask."

"Yao Jiang didn't chase after Ruan Ba after Ruan Ba killed so many of his men?"

"How come!" Huang Feng coughed a little bit and spat. "Who is able to directly confront with Ba in Naga? Although Jiang's got a team, they didn't dare to chase after Ba in such a heavy fog."

Knowing that Huang Feng couldn't see, I didn't cover up my bitter smile.

At last, Bin, I knew who you are.

After a few drinks, our conversation went on.

"They both came to visit you after that. Have they asked about the other one?"

"Of course they have."

"Did you tell them?"

"Of course not."

"That's because you don't want them to kill each other."

"That's not for me to decide." Huang Feng refilled his empty pot once again. "And now they are fighting with each other all the same."

"Actually, you knew what happened from the very beginning." I took a smoke and blew the smoke into the rain. "I know you do."

He seemed to be displeased and didn't say anything.

"They ran together from Anlong Vengm to the New Golden Triangle. But in the end, Yao Jiang couldn't help but choose to sell his buddy out. What a pity."

"You know nothing!" Huang Feng raised his head, smiling with scorn. "Have you ever killed a man, son?"

His meaning behind words alarmed me again. "I will if there's a need to do so."

"That's easy to say ..." He rubbed his amputated limb, "For most of people, killing is way much more difficult than being killed."

I had to admit that I had no idea about his words, as I had little chance to face the choice of whether to take a person's life.

"You can't have enough time to think about whether to kill somebody in the battlefield. You die, I survive. That is an assassin training camp. There are only two options: kill or to be killed. And there is a king of people who can kill for you, and die for you. They are called comrade-in-arms." Huang Feng was talking seriously, "Jiang and Ba, they are both my comrade-in-arms."

From the relationships of Shi Zhan and Zheng Bai, to Ruan, Yao and Huang Feng, I could faintly get another point of comrade-in-arm. Huang Feng didn't even care whether Yao Jiang had sold out or killed his teammate, or whether Ruan Ba would seek revenge for Yao Jiang. Their business was their business. He didn't care. For him, they were both his comrade-in-arms. They were an indispensable part of his life.

But I still hope to hear that from his mouth. "Bin came back to Beijing after he ran out of Anlong Vengm. What about the other one? Going underground? Or being an assassin? Well, they are not that different anyway."

Huang Feng was refilling my cup again. "Don't ask around the bush. What do you want to say?"

"Bin and I joined hands couldn't beat him. The top-notch of Naga do earn his reputation ..."

"Hahahaha!" Huang Feng laughed out. "Do you think you can be taken equal with him?"

"With whom?"

"With 'your best friend'."

"He should be better than me. At least he has the experience. Anyway, he is the 'superhero' who can kill three yobs in a row ..."

Probably taking that a taunting at Bin, Huang Feng, no, the two centipedes in Huang Feng's eyes shook several times. He passed me the cup and said, "It's nothing for him to kill some yobs. You are ... you really know nothing!"

I reached out for the cup and answered, "Yeah, I know. They both have the capability to do so ..."

But I didn't get the cup. The cup was not in my hand. Upon looking up, I found it not in Huang Feng's either."

His shoulder seemed to move a bit. I said 'seemed' because I didn't even saw his shoulder moving. Suddenly, I felt my right elbow numbed, and then my right shoulder. In an instant, Huang Feng controlled my elbow and moved himself by my side together with the armchair taking my body as the axis. When I realized what had happened, he was already right in front of my face. I could see the two red-and-black centipedes shaking 5cm away from me, as if ready to dash at me at any minute.

The cup fell on the ground and smashed into pieces.

No matter how relaxed I appeared to be, I was was always on high alert for any physical contact with him. But what I didn't expect was that, although he lost two of his eyes and one of his legs, he was still agile and swift.

我骇然，这个瞎子甚至没给我惊慌的时间。

"Kill some yobs? No matter Jiang or Ba, as long as he was once with Naga, that's not difficult." There was a playful ferocity in his expression. "Be it yob or policeman, there's no difference for us. You really know nothing!"

4

The last place to go, Pianma, Yunnan.

Probably afraid of her three-floor wooden house not enough to impress me, the landlady of Tonggu Hotel started her propaganda campaign, trying to persuade me out of all my disappointment as I saw this old building. Being a Nu ethnic minority, the landlady was really talkative. "Although we're not big, a lot of tourists choose to say here. The service here is good! Really good! We have cool rooms with big windows. And there's also a fireplace if you feel cold at night. And there are girls if you want to. They can come to serve you in the evening. Girls ..."

Her words left little impression on me, but I didn't have much choice since I was foolish enough to pay the fare myself. Arriving at the guest room on the second floor, I found that although the room was small and old, the furniture were all in good condition and cozy enough to made me feel home. Well, it deserved my fifty yuan.

After settling down, I started off to the local police to check the locations where the local Christian churches opened their orphanages. The policemen greeting me happened to have been trained in Beijing, so he was very nice to me. After checking with him, I found out although there were many Christian churches here, there was only one of them that had an orphanage under its name. That one was called Nanluo.

"They have had big new!" His telling was way more than vivid. "The father who used to run that place was named Zhang Bianlu. He adopted dozens of children. But I've heard that one was actually a monster. He used those kids as dick babies ..."

"What babies?" I was asking him that question not because I was too curious, but because this name which sounds too much like some adult products seemed to be really odd.

"They say that fake father was a pedophile. He not only did you-know-what with the kids, but also used them to do business with some foreigners who passed across the boundary frequently. Since guys from the Civil Affairs Bureau would come to do physical examination for the kids every year, he didn't dare to ask them to really have sex with those people, so he asked them to do the blow job." As he was saying, a strong aversion appeared on his face. "Many of the foreigners came straight there, and they call it 'Dick Bay Club' ..."

"When did this happen?"

"Sever or eight years ago? Or maybe earlier. But something happened later on. There were six girls. They chose to kill themselves by cutting their wrists. Two of them died. Guys from the Civil Affairs and hospital came to investigate and found the kids there were talking in a terrified manner. So they called the police. ... That father? He ran away long ago! Then there came a sister called Ma Li. That sounds to be a foreign name, but she's a Chinese. A really beautiful one!"

When I met Sister Ma Li in the ragged warehouse, or I should say, a warehouse-turned orphanage, I was really stunned.

From her, I could understand "beautiful" from another aspect.

Ma Li was not that beautiful. She was about 30 years old, and had normal features and dark skin. What impressed me was her height. I noticed that she was wearing a pair of flat shoes but still half a head taller than me, who was 1.75cm then. The height was not usually seen in ladies, especially in ladies in the south of China. It was a pity for her to not get on the stage to be a model.

I showed her my ID and told her why I came for her. She answered with a sweet voice. "Right. Do ask me. I'll tell you what I know."

I was still afraid of her not being willing to cooperate, so I decided to talk about the life there to get familiar with her. "How many children are there in the orphanage?"

"Thirty-eight, currently." As she was answering my question, she asked two other local women to hang up the washed clothes. "Maybe six other will be sent here from Beidian next week. I don't know whether there will be new adopted families in the meeting this weekend."

It was a sultry summer afternoon. I could see sweat running down along their cheeks.

"Then how many people are there to look after them?"

She smiled, helplessly but brightly. "They are all here, sir."

Three vs. thirty-eight. I looked at those dangling house behind her and sighed with emotion. "How difficult your life is. Supporting so many ..."

"We have donations from the church and the fund from the Civil Affairs. Children here have enough to eat." She hang up all the clothes in the basin quickly and rubbed both of her hands on her dress. "If there's a chance to sell them in a good price, we could even get some money to buy some furniture."

"Sell ... in a good price? Sell the children?"

"Haha! Does that scare you?" She started to hand up another basin of clothes, and glanced at me in between like a mischievous kid. "Many of the adopters would like to donate some money when they saw the condition here. I will tell the introducer from the church that don't just focus on whether the adopted family is kind or not. It's better to have a rich and kind family. In this way, I only have to cooperate a little bit with the children, and that will bring about some unexpected outcomes!"

Right. I started to feel that she was a bright girl, as bright as the sun.

"Well, if you say it like this, I can also donate some money to offer some help."

"Welcome!" She put the clothes in her hand back into the basin and reached out her right hand to me.

I stepped forward to shake her hand. Her fingers were long but rough, thin and strong, with very short fingernails. Anyway, it was not like women hands. After I put my hand back, I found Ma Li was still holding her old gesture and tilted her head at me.

I tilted my head at her out of confusion.

"The help, sir." She waved her empty hand at me. "Welcome to donate."

I laughed. What a warm and bright sunny day.

"Yichen was a quiet kid. I found she was heavily influenced by that issue the first day I arrived here. So I paid much attention in choosing her adopted family." Walking into the room, Ma Li checked the money in her hand, twice, and gave it to another clergy. "She was such an adorable girl who can get others' compassion. There were many people then who wanted to adopt her."

I looked around. There were nothing in the room except for three bamboo beds and several wardrobes. On the wall hang many photos, reminding me of the bedroom belong to "Pang Xin". Well, this must have been the sister's bedroom.

"So the adopted family you chose for her was one of a kind."

"Mr. Han? He's predestined."

"Predestined? Are you a Christian or a Buddhist."

She took out a box in the wardrobe. Having flipping them over, she passed me a stack of files. "Here are all the documents you need. They've gone through all necessary procedures. "

I took them and had a look. There were copies of IDs, household registers, application of adoption, letter of authorization, character certificate, property certificate, and health certificate, etc. Nothing special. And there was also an adoption agreement. "The adopter Han Songge ... Sister, as far as I know, it was not the adopter himself who came here to take Yichen, right?"

"You mean Mr. Han's son, don't you?" She pulled a basket of celery from outside and sat on the bed to clean them. "He has left a really good impression on me. Yichen liked him too. Oh yes, and he's very generous."

I stared at the files at hand. "Yichen, is this what she was called?"

"Yes. At least when I came here."

"Is Yi a family name?"

"We also have Tao, Zhen, Yangyang, and Minmin. Names are only codes. It means nothing before they find a home. It's life that God gives us and life that God cares about."

Sounds familiar, those words.

When she bent down to pick up some celery from the basket, the cross on her necklace fell from her collar, revealing her skin. I looked away in a hurry and asked, "What, what you said, 'that issue' just now was .."

"Zhang Bianlu." She stopped and heaved a sigh with her eyebrows frowned. "I don't even want to speak his name out. Every time I think of him, I would regret why I didn't come here earlier."

I comforted her. "It's not you to blame. If there must be someone responsible for that, it's your God. It's him who forget those kids here."

"Why? He doesn't forget them. He has a very good memory." Ma Li looked up at me, this time with a pleased expression again. "You see, he sends me here to help them."

Maybe the image of her was too impressive. I could neither nod or shake my head, but to go back the old subject. "That suicide. Is Yichen one of them?"

"She is one of the survivors." Ma Li went back to deal with the celery. "Wenwen, Liu Ying, Liu Yazhen and she survived at last. And fortunately, they were all adopted by good families later on."

"Where did Yichen come from? Is she an orphan? Or abandoned."

She opened her mouth out of confusion and uttered a short "Ah."

"That was beyond what I know. She was adopted by Mr. Han not long after I arrived. You'll have to go to the church for things before I came."

Actually, I didn't expect she would know. "Are there any other kids who's good with her at that time?"

"Maybe Zhen ..." She took a second thought and continued, "That should be Zhen. Wait for a second. Let me get her documents."

"Thank you so much." Taking a stroll in the room, I looked at the photos on the wall and picked up the *New Testament* to read. "You said Yichen likes Han Songge's son?"

She nodded for sure. "Yes. Yichen was usually afraid of adult males, but Han Bin was not one of them. At first I thought whether there would be a problem as Mr. Han didn't come himself, but after I met his son, I knew Yichen has found a good family."

"Han Bin ..." An idea suddenly struck me. "It seemed that you're quite familiar with him."

"He's a big donor." She stopped for a while but didn't look at me. "And his name is on the authorization letter of Mr. Han."

I pretended not to notice and asked, "Why would Han Songge come a long way here to adopt a kid."

"I don't know. Probably he took part in one of the meetings." Her voice lowered a bit. "Or his son took part in one of them ..."

"Sister," my smile was a little more serious, "your Christians are not allowed to lie, right?"

She turned around to look at me. Her face told me she wasn't very glad about my question. "Why do you say so?"

"With due respect, what I mean is that your Christians will eventually pay if you tell a lie, won't you? I'm just worried that whether your memory is right, or you hide something from me accidentally, that ..."

" 'All a man's ways seem innocent to him, but motives are weighed by the LORD.' It's nothing ..." Ma Li crossed her hand in front her chest, "The law of God comes from his natural mercy and kind. Amen." After that, she even stuck her tongue out at me.

Now that I couldn't do anything with her, I switched to a tone of joking, but the words I spoke out were not joking at all. "Do you know that big donor who impressed you most has killed many people?"

Apparently, Ma Li couldn't accept what I said. She sat there like a statue, shocked, her eyes wide open as if to fall out on the ground.

"I said that in the years after he took Yichen away, he killed many people." I watched her reaction quietly. "Of course, he has killed more before you knew him."

"How come ..." She couldn't believe what I said, "He, he shouldn't be a bad guy ..."

264

"Bad guys won't tell you they are bad guys." I looked down on the book, "You see, your Lord has said that you shalt not kill; and whosoever shall kill shall be in danger of the judgment:."

"Verse Twenty-one, Chapter Five, Mathew." Her reflective respond quickly calmed her down, "Then you should read Verse fourteen, Chapter Six."

I didn't open the book but asked, "What?"

"The Lord also said that for if you forgive men their trespasses, your heavenly Father will also forgive you."

The speed she restored herself astonished me. I almost could find out there's a strong heart hidden beneath her healthy and lively appearance.

"Mr. Han Bin is not a bad guy, just like you." After mocking at my offer to teach a fish to swim, she continued with her business with celery. "If he really killed someone, he must have his own reason."

"Whether he is a bad man or not, at least he did something bad. Killing is not right, no matter what the reason is. It is not right." I put down *Mathew* and tried my best to sound forgiving, "If all the criminals have to be forgiven, your Lord would have been worried."

In fact, I really hoped that she said what she said to me when she first met Bin.

As I was turning around like a dog chasing its own tail, a black-and-white photo on the wall attracted my attention. At first, I just glanced at it, but then an uneasy feeling dragged me back to look at it again. I stared at the photo for a long time and asked, "He ... Who is this guy?"

Upon my question, Ma Li stood up, her hands rubbing several times on her dress. She walked by my side and took a glance at the photo. "Oh, that's a group photo taken when the place was first built. Actually I didn't like it at all. But it was the only one left, so I put it in the corner."

I didn't pay much attention on her explanation but pointed at an old man in the photo. "Who is he?"

"Which one?" Ma Li leaned forward to take a closer look. Her eyebrows frowned again. "Oh, that's Zhang Bianlu. He was one of the founders here. Do you know him?"

"Emm ... yes. But when I knew him ..." This was really the biggest achievement of my trip to the Southwest. Another piece was put in the right place of the jigsaw puzzle. "When I knew him, his name was Zhang Mingkun."

Chapter VII

Cooperation

1

"Were you and Bin both there the night Zhang Mingkun died?" He Jingcheng's speed to chew his peanuts slowed down. "You two have many secrets. No wonder Bai reassigned you away."

Upon getting back to Beijing, I was summoned to No. 16, Meishuguan East Street by Yuan Shi. He said I was there to report what I found, but we both knew that I was coming to exchange information. To my surprise, I found He Jingcheng was there to, seemingly to come to report.

"Yichen was well before she was taken into the holding cell, only a little bit dehydrated, which is caused by you guys. She's also suffering from anemia and her liver is not that healthy, but that's not a problem. She has been checked whether she has been sexually assaulted, and you can't depend on me finding any trace of that on a virgin." He Jingcheng glanced at Yuan Shi disapprovingly. "We found there were scars caused by suicidal behaviors on her left wrist. Now we knew how that comes according to your story."

Yuang Shi leaned on the police car, appearing to be very confident. "Funny. When can we question her?"

"She hadn't been eating or drinking anything ever since she was taken into the holding cell. She was put on a drip today and sent back to the north yard this noon. You'd better wait for a day or two before continue your question."

"Sorry, I don't mean to sound harsh." Although he talked like that, he looked really like a cat holding a mouse in its mouth and showing off in front of her master. "But questioning her is the most urgent work."

"That was actually what your investigation guys should take care of and I'm not supposed to say anything about it. But I have to remind you

266

that Yichen has already beyond custody." He Jingcheng, who didn't mind Yuan Shi's feeling at all, stepped on right the tail of the cat. "Even if her adopted parents are abroad and Bin is nowhere to find, we cannot keep her like this just because there's no one to fight for her ... That's breaking the law, right? Xincheng?" He glanced at me after saying this, making me very much ashamed.

Yuan Shi must have wanted to switch a subject because he then said to me, "Zhao seemed to have many information to share with us. Let's listen to his experience first."

I didn't let him down, telling them all that I saw in the past two weeks. He Jingcheng's attention was not that easy to shift, but Yuan Shi was so attentive that he even forgot to cut in with his comments and his favorite foreign quotes.

Frankly speaking, the information that Shi Zhan, Shitian, Ruan Xundong and Huang Feng gave me was quite limited. They either couldn't say much, or didn't want to, or wouldn't like to tell me the truth, or didn't have the time to do so. But combining all their words together, I still learned Bin's past in general.

About the story between Chen Juan and him: They broke up in 1990. After that Chen Yuan went abroad and joined that medical group sent by a foundation controlled by an arms dealer in 1994. She came to Cambodia and met the Khmer Rouge government, whose contact was Binson. In this operation, she died of some infectious diseases. I had several assumptions about her death. First, Chen Juan's death was abnormal. Although it's always what we know that gets us into trouble, it sounded absurd if a medical team couldn't prevent and control a infectious disease. Second, if Chen Juan was murdered, it was quite possible that she had contacted Bin before she was killed. Third, Bin ran away from home immediately after Chen Juan's death and came to Vietnam. It was possible that he wanted to sneak into Cambodia and find out the reason of her death. Fourth, after the boss of that St. Raison Foundation cut a deal with the government, most of the people in the medical group was sent back. And from the name list we could see that Bin almost killed them all, which in turn proved that Chen Juan was probably murdered in Cambodia in 1994.

About Bin's "missing": Bin came to Vietnam the year Chen Juan died, probably trying to sneak into Cambodia through Vietnam. I had two assumptions: First, he knew Chen Yuan was in danger and came to rescue her. Second, he knew Chen Juan was dead so he came to find out the reason. Anyway, he was grabbed and forced to join the Vietnam People's Army so his plan was temporarily suspended. If all the information provided by Shitian was real, which wasn't possible, we could know that Bin was put in Brigade 126, a Battery and met a guy in his days in the army, who had, allegedly, killed an officer together with him. So they were really good friends. Later on, they, out of some reasons, were reassigned to Regiment 861 at a Military Base in Hanoi. They joined the assassin operation planned directly by Hanoi Military Region in July 1997, whose target was Binson, the director who the medical team Chen Juan belonged to came to contact with.

I clapped my hands. "Therefore, he was not a superman born in planet Krypton, but an assassin created by the army and war together.

As for the operation named Kill Son, the operation itself was not helpful to us solving the case. Maybe there were some political conspiracies or plans to cast them away after they had served their purposes, but it had nothing to do with the serial killing after Bin got back home. Binson's death was the same. We didn't care whether he was killed in a decapitation strike or by Pasoulwate because of his betrayal. The only thing we cared about was that Bin may have attained the truth of Chen Juan's death through his operation.

In comparison, the battle happened on November 22nd 1997 in Anlong Vengm was more than interesting. Bin and his comrade-in-arm suddenly became enemies on their way out, but they both joined the strike to the Khmer Rouge and the rescue of Huang Feng on 22nd. In that heavy fog, Bin and his comrade-in-arms, Huang Feng, Shitian and Shi Zhan, killed out from that damp and hot forest and continue to fight in the same battlefield. According to Huang Feng, Bin's comrade fought with him ferociously after they met, and considering the secret tasks they received in Naga, Bin probably sold his comrade out on their way out. And then, his comrade, that mysterious assassin who came to attack Bin and me on that night, appeared in Beijing for some reasons with great rage and hate.

Yuan Shi nodded and said. "Right. This should be the connection to another clue."

He was right. After all these years, Bin's comrade came for a reason. After Bin came back from Cambodia, he took all his patience to check and plan, and finally killed most of Chen Juan's team members of that medical team. It was possible that those people found things weren't right and started to find out who's the one trying to kill them out. Peng Kang shouldn't know Bin's face, but he did find out someone's following him, so he ran into the hospital, which meant that those survivors of that medical team had already found out Bin's identification. They knew who Han Bin is. But that was of no use. I didn't know how well their professional skills could be, but these doctors won't last even a minute in front of Bin. So they found him a rival, a man who could fight with him equally or was probably better than him. That happened to be his comrade.

"The one Peng Kang turned to, also the one following Bin, is likely to be the boss of that assassin." I was pretty sure about my assumption. "The one who cut a deal with the boss of that St. Raison Foundation is the boss of Wales Medical Device Research Group. These two bosses were the third connection."

Whose idea might it be to find Bin's enemy against him? I had had several assumptions. First, one of the members of the St. Raison medical group who had been killed; second, Gu Fan, or Liang Xiao with an alias named Meng Jingtao, who were both survivors of that medical group; third, the Wales Medical Device Research Group

"After analyzing the information we had at hand, I think ..."

"I can tell you now that cannot be Gu Fan." Yuan Shi pointed at a tower building behind us. "Or you can come up to ask him. And if Meng Jingtao's real name is Liang Xiao, you should also know that the CEO of Wales Group has the same name."

2

Gu Fan was more calm than I thought.

Probably because I knew Bin first, I chose to take Gu Fan as a filthy little ratfink, or at least a specious toy boy who would definitely be scared to shit after he knew someone's gonna kill him, maybe full of tears and worshiping supernatural beings — just like a cockroach rushing helter-skelter in the room.

But I was wrong.

This was in fact a ridiculously mistake. It was not Gu Fan I underestimated. It was Bin. The second boyfriend of a woman who Bin had fell in love with crazily couldn't be a man like this.

Gu Fan was standing in front of the window, his strong figure almost blocking all the sunshine out. I walked close and what I saw was a middle-aged man with big eyes, thick eyebrows, a straight nose and a big mouth. He turned around and nodded at me, his eyes quiet and tranquil.

Being a single man living in Beijing for so many years, Gu Fan had a really tidy room. Even the stacks of books was piled neatly on the floor. The room smelt of an intangible aroma of sandalwood could.

"Hello. Zhao Xincheng from Haidian Investigation Division." Saying these chicle as the introduction, I reached out my hand.

Gu Fan shook my hand. His hands were thick and powerful, tidily manicured. His skin took on a fairly healthy tan. I didn't smell smoke on him, nor did I see marks of smoking on his hands. His hair was combed behind, a little bald from the tip. He was wearing gray trousers and a white silk shirt French cuff shirt. Only that pair of Gucci cuffs may be able to afford the whole set of my clothes.

"I've ready answered the questions from you police." Gu Fan was polite, his thick voice being a good companion for his strong figure, only a little bit hoarse. "Anything else I could do for you?"

"We've made thoughtful plans to protect you. You don't have to be afraid." Yuan Shi told me while we were walking upstairs that they have sent three groups of people to protect Gu Fan 24 hours a day and got the entire No. 16 under control. "But you can't be hiding here all day long. If you want to restore your normal life, the best way is to help us to take Han Bin down."

"I don't want to hide here. It's the police don't let me out. Of course I know you're protecting me." Gu Fan's stop before the last sentence told me that he knew fully well that he was the decoy. "Actually you don't have to do this. There are so many cases outside for you to deal with. This is a total waste of resources."

I saw He Jingcheng talking with a policeman on duty. Yuan Shi was viewing the painting on the wall with his hands clasped behind his back, which, in my opinion, was more like graffiti in ink since they were so abstract. Gu Fan put his weight on his left leg, his right foot tapping the ground, clearly urging me to cut into the point.

"Do you mind if I smoke?" I looked around and found no ashtray.

Gu Fan wasn't annoyed at all. He walked by the bookshelf and took out a small color glazed bowl. He passed it to me and said, "Help yourself."

That bowl was so delicate that I was a little embarrassed to use it as an ashtray, so I repressed my craving for tobacco and asked, "Do you know Han Bin? Or ..."

"I've answered the question before. I've never seen him in person, but his name was all around my ears." Gu Fan seemed to be more than generous. "Juan always spoke of him. Maybe she thought facing the past honestly is the best way to walk out of it. But, well, the results failed her."

"Did Chen Juan talk about Han Bin much? In front of you?"

"Yeah. As a men, that's a little difficult to accept."

"Then do you know why Han Bin's coming to you for revenge? I mean he came to all members of that medical group of St. Raison Foundation.

The year 1994, Cambodia, Khmer Rouge ... Remind you of anything?"

Just as what Yuan Shi told me, Gu Fan answered, "Yes." His expression was the same as Yuan Shi told me. It could be interpreted as: I know but I don't what to tell you.

I looked quietly over the doctor dressing like a foreign company boss. Yuan Shi told me that he didn't get anything from him after days of questioning. His leader, teachers, classmates and schoolmates were all called here to talk with him, but clearly, Gu Fan didn't want to tell anyone anything.

"Why?" I asked reflectively.

"What?" Gu Fan seemed to be confuse, tilting his head a little.

"You don't worried about being killed, or don't hope Han Bin was caught?" I put the little bowl on the tea table and took out my cigarette. "Your information could be our first lead to him. He has killed almost everyone of your medical group. I don't think he will stop, unless you and Liang Xiao died."

Gu Fan took a white mug from his desk. He put it by his lips, which seemed to be a gesture to test the temperature of the content inside. "I do have a doctor degree, but I'm not a nerd."

"Liang Xiao found someone to go against Han Bin, didn't he?"

"Peng talked about it once on the phone. But I couldn't remember exactly."

"Do you think the one Liang Xiao found could deal with it?"

"Actually it doesn't matter. Well, it's true he has some advantages as we don't know where he is but he know where to find us, but I still don't believe a men more violent than Han Bin could stop him."

"Han Bin is seeking revenge for Chen Juan's death. At least I'm right on this one, right?"

"I've answered that too. 'I believe so'. After all, I haven't asked him. I can't be sure that's the reason."

"So that means Chen Juan's death wasn't an accidental one."

Gu Fan took a sip of whatever inside the mug and kept silent. I could see his Adam's apple moving.

When I wanted to beat about the bush from another direction, he started to talk. "Well, in fact, we should all die there. Juan died there, as well as Gao and dongfang. But no matter who died there, that's not accidental. That's the final destination for everyone of us."

I didn't know when Yuan Shi came by our side. "Did you kill Chen Juan?" he asked.

Gu Fan smiled out of embarrassment. I saw a slice of contempt on the corner of his mouth — a real contempt with no conceal whose target was the one asking this question. It was clear that he felt it's beneath his dignity to answer this question or even respond to Yuan Shi's way of asking that question.

He didn't kill Chen Juan.

Yuan Shi didn't care about his attitude. He was more likely to talk to himself. "You have a wall full of Hang Faji[1]'s paintings. It was his abstract color ink diptych. I don't know whether they're fake, but I know this set. I found them familiar the last time I came. They are his *The Inundation and Confession of Original Sin*, right? What sin do you confess for? Gluttony? Greed? Sloth? Wrath? Pride? Lust? Or envy? You killed Chen Juan. Why? Out of envy because she still had connection with Han Bin? Or out of pride because she was better in profession skills? Or out of wrath because you had some disagreements? All your survivors had taken part in the murder, right? I'm telling you ..."

Before I could break into his random and arbitrary assumptions, I heard a chaos outside the door and then Liu Qiang rushed in. "Han Bin! We got visual of Han Bin!"

"Han Bin was in Longfusi pedestrian zone in the west. Some of our local patrol officers happened to see him. They didn't take it for sure at first so they followed him for a while, but were attacked in Qianliang Lane." Liu Qiang got on the car and continued, "He is absolutely insane! He attacked the police with weapons, stabbing two of our guys. One of them was still conscious at that time, so he activated the emergency button to call for help from the direction center. He told us that Han Bin was now running away along Meishuguan East Street to the south. Bai just learned it and backup is on the way. Now Dongsi Police Station is controlling all roads from Longfusi to here. Longfusi Police Station and Longfusi Hospital are coming here to save the injured policemen. Since it's emergency, the direction center wanted all man around to surround the region from Meishuguan East Street to Kuan Street!"

The emergency channel is an orange button on the top of the police transceiver. Once it is activated, all stations in the channel can only receive messages in order to ensure a clear communication between the emergency part and the main station. This is not a button frequently used. Only when a policeman is under serious attack could he activate that button. And once

---

1 Hang Faji (1945-), born in Dangtu City, Anhui province, is an independent artist. He is now national first class artist and the member of China Artists Association.

it is activated, the direction center can locate that transceiver with GPS. All policemen around must come to help.

"How many people do we have?" Yuan Shi asked.

"Twenty-one apart from you three." Liu Qiang started the car and switched on the alarm whistle. "I told them to leave one team here. Two teams were heading for the crossing at Kuan Street through Ping'an Street to set roadblocks. The other one was coming with us in the car following behind."

I was rather familiar with Dongcheng District. "What about Liangguochang Lane?"

"Jingshan Police Station will come from that direction. The Social Order Crops of Dongcheng Branch is responsible for the rest of the main road."

It was clear that Yuan Shi was satisfied with the arrangement. "Have they completed the encirclement?"

"They suppose so."

He looked at me. "It seems that Han Bin has chosen a wrong time to visit Gu Fan."

I didn't say anything.

There was an awkward silence in the car. After a while, Yuan Shi started talking. "OK, I give up. I knew he's not as simple as that. What do you think? Come on and share with us."

I took a glance at He Jingcheng.

"I'm a forensic doctor. I know nothing about investigation." He refused and stared back, watching me to play chameleon."

Indeed, Bin shouldn't haven exposed himself like this, nor should he stab the police following him like a idiot. Of course, may be he was insane. Anyway, he really did this, didn't he?"

"I didn't have anything to say, only that we're lucky enough." This was half true, because I really didn't figure out what the plan was behind all these.

Liu Qiang asked with the communicator in the car. "How are those two policemen?"

The answer came back through the communicator: People from the local police station were there, but the ambulance from the hospital hasn't arrived yet.

He asked again, "How about our guys?"

Our car rushed passing the red light of Meishuguan East Street crossing. After a sound of currency, everyone heard the answer, "We haven't found them yet. We are now searching."

Reports from every unit came back through the communicator. All of them told us that they haven't found them yet.

As I was sitting in the back, I had to sit straight and put all my attention to the things coming through the communicator to enable me to tell what they were saying. But soon, I found myself gazing on the ground, confused. At first, I thought I didn't know what I was looking at or why I was in a daze, but soon enough I figured out something.

Yes. All things, all the things Bin had done was on purpose.

"Does this car belong to our division?"I asked.

"The one following us does." Liu Qiang just got back on the main road from the bicycle lane and was pressing the horn hard. "This one is a patrol car lent to us by Dongsi Police Station. It's way better than our Santana."

I mumbled. "Well, then the car Bin took also had a communicator, right?"

Yuan Shi turned around immediately. "The police car from Di'anmen Police Station! It's also equipped with a communicator! He burned that car ... Damn! He took the radio on the car! Liu, turn back! Contact the team on the scene! Han Bin is heading to Gu Fan!"

Liu Qiang didn't know what's happening, but he slowed down the car. "What?"

Yuan Shi was about to take the steering wheel. "Nobody was hurt! And no one has seen him! He took the communicator after he stole the police car. It was him who activated the emergency button which brought all the police there!"

"Contact those who were guarding No. 16. Now! It's possible that we were played." I glanced at He Jingcheng as I spoke, uneasily. "And identify whether there's anyone who has seen injured policemen there."

Liu Qiang turned the steering wheel hard, swinging me right at He.

"No one was found on the scene and we found the lost communicator!" I heard Liu Qiang telling us the answer from the communicator right after I took my seat. He was driving the car in a s-shaped route, making me worried about whether the car would top over before we arrived at No. 16.

"Then contact the guys back there!"

"I've been contacting them." Yuan Shi was holding the transceiver, his body swinging with the car, "But no one answers."

From what we saw on the scene, Bin's action could be like this:

First, he chose a high point in which he could observe the surroundings of Gu Fan's residence and spent some time identifying what the police's plan was. Then he used that radio he got from that burnt police car to create a fake emergency twenty minutes ago.

In order to ensure most of the police in No. 16 were reassigned somewhere else, he first activated the emergency button in an attacked police's tone, and then called 110 with two phones. The rest he had to do was to wait for us leaving.

And of course, he may have been monitoring all the calls in the police channel.

There were five policemen left guarding No. 16. Two of them were in the police car at the gate of the building, one in the security office located in the main gate of the yard, one was patrolling and one was guarding in Gu Fan's room. Bin couldn't have entered through the main gate, and he asked the direction center to inform the guys left to change the communication channel in Liu Qiang's name. Up until then, he has successfully isolated all police guarding in No. 16 from everyone else.

This kind isolation was a temporary one. It only took us less than 15 minutes to drive out and back. But it was still enough for Bin.

According to the kiosk in the yard, Bin bought a can of milk tea there. He used it to crack the window of the police car when he suddenly appeared at the left of the car. And then he found that the car wasn't locked. The driver was hit on his head by the can, or maybe a punch or an elbow, and passed out. Bin opened the door, dragged him out, got in and locked the door. The guy on the front passenger sit who was busy with dealing with Bin failed to call for help, which gave Bin a chance to lock the car with central control. At last, when the policeman found he was no rival to Bin and prepared to break off, he couldn't pull the door open. Bin strangled him from the back, giving him a "livelock", which means to press his carotid sinus with his arm to cause insufficiency of cerebral blood supply. Therefore, the policeman passed out in just several seconds.

Up until then, Bin has cracked all guards downstairs. He went upstairs.

There were two doors in Gu Fan's residence, but the outer one wasn't locked. This was normal, not a mistake. Bin pulled open the security door and knocked on the inside door. The policeman in the room came to answer, but was kicked back by Bin with the door together. The bruise on the back of his head should be caused when he fell and hit the ground. The reason of his passing out was a heavy punch on his left chin.

So to speak, Bin lived up to Yuan Shi's expectation. All these actions and choices were swift and delicate, accurate and effective.

What I couldn't understand was: Had he really planned all these ever since he broke out from the encirclement in Gulou? There was a period after he stole the police car to take the radio and before we found Gu Fan. Why didn't he attack Gu Fan before the police could even implement protective custody? Why did he do this when all the police was searching for him? Attacking the police in broad daylight, he must have known what that means. What on earth did he want to do?

And what baffled me the most was: He spent all the time and efforts, even at the cost of going against the whole Beijing police system, but at last, he didn't kill Gu Fan.

The living room which was tidy twenty minutes ago was now a mess: neither the tea table, the bookshelf, the chairs or that set of *The Inundation and Confession of Original Sin* were at all in their original places. Gu Fan was sitting on the sofa which was just put right, and someone was binding up his wound. A fierce fight not only forced him to recollect the room but also collect himself. I saw his forehead was bleeding.

When I teased with Yuan Shi, saying that I appreciated the decoration style of the room now, I had to admit that I had always hated Gu Fan.

Gu Fan's clothes was torn up, but his manner was still graceful. He told us that Bin kicked open the door, hit the police and announced to him that this was the day to seek revenge for Chen Juan.

I rubbed by chin and said, "You don't happen to be a member of that so-called USTU, do you?"

Yuan Shi didn't mind my question, but his voice raised. "It seemed that he didn't succeed."

Gu Fan shrugged to show us the scene in the room. "I ... I would call that a reflective reaction."

"And then?" I asked back, "How's the result?"

Gu Fan gave me a straight look and forgave my rudeness. "I'm not his rival."

I tended to ask back, but people around tried to stop me with their eyesight. Well, I didn't mind them at all and continued, "Is that so? Then did he run happily with the winner's belt after he beat you down?"

Finally, Yuan Shi turned around to look at me, impatiently.

"No. He didn't intend to kill me today." Gu Fan's works pulled all of us back. "He said if he let me die like this, that's too easy for me."

"What?" I glanced at He Jingcheng. His shoulder was shivering, but he seemed to focus on the wound on Gu Fan's head.

"Then what does he want to do?" Yuan Shi asked eagerly.

Gu Fan swallowed for several times, his eyes turning red. "He said that he wanted me to suffer for 24 hours. At this time tomorrow, no matter how many policemen were here to protect, he's going to come and kill me."

After these words, we were all speechless out of astonishment.

My first reaction was that it was totally unbelievable, and without any rhythm or reason. It was true that Bin must have been here. He created that emergency to distract the protection, attacked the guarding police and broke in. He really did these. But the question was he spared so much effort just to make an announcement, to turn a simple personal revenge into a violence to the national judicial system. Was he mad?

"Is he ..."

"Oh and Officer, he also told me to tell you something." Gu Fan cut in my question, and then my thinking. "He wanted me to ask you that whether you still remember what he said to you that night."

"If I really want to kill him, you cannot even stop me."

Holly shit! He's really mad.

Director Bai has arrived at the gate of No. 16 along with the direction center and called us out to have a meeting. After I came out, I asked He Jingcheng, "Did his wound ..."

"That was not caused by beating. It should be caused by his falling down since his brow ridge wasn't hurt."

Yuan Shi who seemed to be full of worries. I turned to him and said, "Do you really believe what he said?"

Yuan Shi didn't say anything at first, but he then stopped when we got downstairs. "It's possible that Gu Fan was provoking us, and trying to put Han Bin against the police system. But who can tell me why Han Bin didn't kill Gu Fan?"

We looked at each other, lowered our heads, and then looked up at each other again.

He Jingcheng started first. "Maybe it's not that complicated. He's just hating Gu Fan too much."

I disagreed. "Then why didn't he take him away and find some isolated place to dismember him?"

"We came back in time so it's hard for him to take a hostage out ..."

"Taking a man like Gu Fan as a hostage is indeed difficult." Yuan Shi agreed with He and pointed at me. "But if he just wants to let Gu Fan suffer from the fear of death, why didn't he tell Gu Fan that he will kill him someday in the future. An uncertain date can not only prevent us from protecting him, but also intimidated him forever."

He Jingcheng tilted his eyebrows. "What's the point of talking about this one? The most practical problem now is whether he's going to come tomorrow."

I took a second thought and said, "He's not."

Yuan Shi disagreed with me as always. "No, he will."

In my opinion, Yuan Shi's idea was like some mysterious master stroke that didn't always work well. He was good enough to serve the function as a criminal profiling consultant, but not as a leader of a criminal investigation team.

"Do you believe he's such an idiot?"

"He's being more dramatic." Yuan Shi didn't answer my question. "If he's not in mainland China, he's likely to be another controversial legend like Jesse[1]. Don't misunderstand me, I'm not saying you're Coward Bob[2]."

"Come on! Do you have PTSD? Are they anyone who are more legendary than you?" Anyway, I didn't know any of the the foreign names he was talking about.

Yuan Shi didn't care about my slander at all. "We've done plenty of researches during your days in the south. We almost found out which stall Han Bin went to buy his magazines. But everything in his life was normal, even more than normal. Do you know what that means?"

I knew. He could live a normal life and commit a violent crime at the same time. That was a typical sociopath.

"Han is not a killer hiding in some mountains or psychopath down in a basement. He has families, friends, and colleagues. He goes to work and lives a normal life. He goes to convenience stores, attends court sessions, lines up at ticket offices, pays taxes and fines. He is a man with living traces in this society. But for such a man who really lives in this world, we don't even know him. We don't know his motives to kill, his reasons to kill so we don't know why he had killed so many people. And of course, we don't know why he let one of them go."

"Unless," He Jingcheng cut in, "we know why he kills."

I didn't take it as a difficult question to answer. "Regardless of his three years in the army, there are only two kinds of people he kills: the one who he thinks is guilty and the one may hamper his next crime."

Yuan Shi asked, "Was he seeking revenge for Chen Juan?"

"Oh. I take Zhang Mingkun in, although he didn't kill him in person."

He Jingcheng asked, "Then why he didn't kill Su Zhen?"

"Because Su Zhen didn't go to Pianma, Yunnan ..." He Jingcheng's expression told me I'd better leave that part behind and Yuan Shi continued

---

1 Jesse James is a bank and train robber during American Civil War. He is ferocious and foxy. Wanted by both above and underground world, he was sold out and shot in the back of his head by his gang member Robert Newton Ford.

2 Robert Newton Ford, best known as the "dirty little coward" that killed Jesse James, was a member of Jesse's gang. He was then killed by a shooter who claimed to seek revenge for Jessie and kill the cheater on June 8th 1962. After the shooter was sentenced guilty, the government pardoned his guilt as more then 7000 Americans signed to make a plea. Compare with the legend Jessie, Robert the traitor was much more looked down upon, so he was called Coward Bob.

to ask, "What about Wang Rui? Help the police to prevail justice?"

"Maybe he didn't want to see beautiful girls die one after another. Or maybe Jiang's death made him feel he had to help me. Or maybe he just wanted to confuse me by that chance. Who knows? Anyway, killing Wang Rui was his biggest mistake."

"At least he didn't kill any good guys."

"But I don't think those three little ones outside the west wall of Haidian Hospital are so guilty as to be killed."

Yuan Shi murmured thoughtfully, "Those three deaths are the most weird ones."

"Like I said, those are witnesses hampering his next crime."

"Did you see the assassin's face that night you and Han Bin were ambushed?"

"What's that for? I've said it was dark that night, and ..."

"I've seen the records. You didn't describe his features in detail. And I've known the situation. That was a complete accident. It's normal you didn't see or remember his face." Yuan Shi walked back and forth. "I believe you know that as well. But ... you know that and I know that, too. Is there a chance Han Bin didn't know?"

I seemed to have a crack in my head.

He Jingcheng said, "Maybe he was desperate to get away from the scene, so ..."

"Then why didn't he kill that boy as well? You can't say killing three people helps him to restore calm?"

"Then what do you think? Why would he kill those three people?"

"I think this must be connected with those years he spent in South Asia. What are you thinking, Zhao Xincheng?"

I didn't want to answer him so I asked back, "Will you be clearer than me about those years?"

"I won't." Yuan Shi raised his voice, "But I could guess the consequences. And ... you didn't tell me what you were thinking about."

I smiled, my body relaxed a bit. "I was thinking that I won't meet Bai with you later. Time waits for no man. I'm planning to meet that President Liang of Wales Group."

Yuan Shi kept silent for a while, gazing at the direction of Bai's van. "OK. We'll talk after you come back."

"And about tomorrow," I said to him while I was asking the policeman on duty downstairs to find me a car, "I still insist that he won't come. You, or He Jingcheng, please tell Bai my opinion."

He Jingcheng nodded, but Yuan Shi still disagreed. "Are you so sure?"

"I'm sure. He's not some serial killer with different characters, a miserable past and burdened fate. He's not that legendary."

"Then Gu Fan was lying. Did anyone else know what he said to you on the night Zhang Mingkun killed himself apart from Han Bin and you?"

"No, only us two." This part of Gu Fan's speech should be true. Not only in the content, but the way of speaking which accorded with Bin's style. "But Bin's always thinking ahead of us. He knows what we would think and do, and takes actions according to that. Now that we will focus on this region, he won't come."

Yuan Shi responded with a kind of pleasure indicating that he had seen through what I thought, "So you think he's going to attack Liang Xiao?"

He Jingcheng murmured after, "Which means we should go and protect Liang Xiao?"

"According to Zhao's theory, if we go and protect Liang Xiao, Han Bin's going to come here and kill Gu Fan, isn't he? Is he always thinking ahead of us?"

"Then we protect them both." He Jingcheng laughed. "Put more men. That's our typical play."

"I knew that will be Bai's choice before I even waste my time to think." I saw the car coming and turned around. "Remember to tell Bai my theory!"

Yuan Shi was shouting behind. "Where do you think he'll be tomorrow? Gu Fan's or Liang Xiao's?"

I shut the door and put down the window. "Idiot! Neither!"

3

According to what we knew, Wales Medical Device Research Group was a big shareholder of Zhongde Building, so they not only occupied the whole 25th floor, but put a neon light box more eye-catching than the name brand of the building. I took the elevator to 25th floor but didn't find any surveillance camera, which was a clear violation of security regulations and a demonstration of the special position and background of Liang Xiao, but it told us that his business may not be so legal as it appeared to be.

In the nearly 200m² president's office, Liang Xiao stood out the most with his short but strong figure. But I couldn't help to notice those big strong body guards who may serve as something to stuff this empty room besides their own work.

It was hard to believe Liang Xiao was nearly fifty years old judging by his appearance. He was wearing a casual knit cardigan, and had a fair complexion and a young face with short moustache and mid-long hair like an artist, which in fact was the only concrete proof of him being a male. Frankly speaking, he would be a pretty boy that could attract those Thai talent scouts at first sight decades ago. But of course, that was when he didn't stand up. Although he sat in a leather armchair from the very beginning, I still believed that there was no chance for him to be higher than Maradona.

"Nice to meet you." Before I started my greeting, Liang Xiao smiled at me gracefully. "Have a seat, please. Coffee? Or tea?"

I took a step forward to shake his hands. "Thank you but no. I won't be here long."

He didn't stand up from his armchair, just leaned forward to shake my hands and said, "There's no need to hurry. Have a seat, please. Sophy ..." He said to the secretary who showed me in, "Un cafe, l'espresson italien, merci."

He spread both his hands apart after I sat down and asked with a smile, "How can I help you?"

"President Liang, it seems that you have acquired more than we know about the situation." My instinct told me that he was difficult to deal with and talking around the bush would be a safer way to deal with him. "But I'm not here for Han Bin or your murdered colleagues. I come here because of Shitian ..." I saw the corner of his mouth moving a bit. "Shitian told me the deal you've done before ... Well, he believes that you're satisfied with it. But later on he was in trouble. You know, for people doing his business, network is very important."

He was surprised about my sounding out, but his answer was an old cliche. "I'm sorry. I don't understand."

"It was Yao Jiang and Ruan Ba who I was talking about. Shitian was very close to them." I was very confident about my analysis and speculation these days. "It didn't occur to me that you find one of them to kill the other. Shitian was annoyed about the fact that you didn't tell him the truth and hoped you would stop whatever you do. As police, we also think what you have done has violated the law. Although you are a Frenchman, but the law of the People's Republic of China applies to all people on its territory. I'm sure it's not asking too much to ask foreign friends to obey to China's laws on its land, isn't it?

Tasting how much of my statement was true, he didn't admit at last. "Well ... I pay full respect to China's laws, after all it was once my home country. But I still don't really understand what you were saying since I didn't even know these names."

"We all know Chen Juan's avenger was wandering outside. I can understand your concerns about safety." I glanced at those body guards deliberately, "But the extreme approach you're taking right now is not legal and received so much complaints from the underground world. So I come to advise that it's better if you can stop this."

"La haine, c'est la colere des faibles." Liang Xiao murmured. He was a little pleased after he saw I didn't understand French and said, "I don't even understand a work about what you're saying, so I don't know what I can do to help the government."

"Let's put it straight." I put my phone on the table and unbuttoned my suit and the shirt inside, indicating that I didn't have any bugs or recording devices with me. "Han Bin's going to kill you and we will be responsible to protect you and take him down. I hope you can get that assassin of yours under control because if he were to killed, not only the threat from Han Bin cannot be resolved, much more resent from the underground world would come along with it. But if he really kills Han Bin, we'll have to turn to him and you'll get into trouble. No matter who you are — foreign friends or with arms dealers behind you — you'll have to remember that this Beijing, the capital of the People's Republic of China. Your president will be fined if he spit in public."

Liang Xiao was getting unpleasant as I talked, but was teased to laughter by my last sentence. "You are humorous, Officer." He paused a bit. His secretary came in and put the coffee down and then he continued, "But do you think you've make it so complicated?"

It was good that he wanted to talk, but I didn't think he would give me any valuable information.

"What do you mean?"

"A maniac was hurting my former colleagues due to some eccentric feeling and may be threatening my security now. I believe that you, the police, are trying your best to solve the problem but I can still receive my old friends' obituaries. So I have to take some actions to protect my own safety and I don't see any wrongdoings in that. Of course, by actions I mean ..." He gestured and eyed at those body guards around us, "And if a certain friend of mine plans to protect me or to confront with the threat that put me into this situation, that's not something I can control. And I hope the police can understand that."

I pretended to take a gasp. "You've asked an assassin to fight with another assassin and criminal here in Beijing. Well, as a law enforcement officer of this country, I can hardly understand your way of dealing with things."

Liang Xiao shook his head a little at me while he was sipping his coffee.

A sense of déjà vu suddenly struck me and I turned my head strongly out of subconsciousness. The door was ajar nor far behind me, and there was no one there. But I remember I've heard the door closed when that secretary left. I took a quick glance at those body guards around me and felt a slight sense of sneer in the air.

"It's simple." Liang Xiao dragged me, who was looking around then, back to the conversation. "Someone is trying to find me some trouble and I'm trying my best to avoid getting into it. At the same tine, I fully believe that the Chinese government is capable of capturing that dangerous criminal. But from the perspective of personal security, I have to say that if my friend can help me get rid of that trouble, that's good to not only me, but also the company, as well as the Chinese government. Then, tu fais semblant de ne pas le voir. That's not difficult for sure."

"Sorry, I don't speak French."

"Sorry about that. What I said was that I hope we didn't interfere with each other."

Knowing the conversation with this old fox wouldn't lead to any conclusion, I stood up and said, "Han Bin has entered Anlong Vengm several times. It's possible that he had already known the truth of Chen Juan's death. He may also acquired the evidence of the conspiracy between the medical group and Khmer Rouge. Killing a insider may be a useful choice of covering what you've done, but my suggestion is no. No one really knows Han Bin, or the complicated relationships between the team members of Naga. Your choice may not be a wise one. Beside, don't forget this is a legal state. Please give it a second thought."

"Thank you for your suggestion. But we cannot get everything we want, can we?" Liang Xiao showed the same passion and polite to my leaving as my arriving. "There's nothing I can help. After all, c'est la vie."

I went back home to put my luggage away and had dinner with Xuejing, and immediately got back to Gu Fan's residence. At the gate of No. 16, Liu Qiang walked towards me from the police car guarding there. "Director Bai asked why you didn't answer your phones."

"He called me? I didn't hear them." My excuses were really bad. But on a second thought, I smelled something special. If Bai asked for me at this moment, there must be something wrong.

"Wait, wait!" Liu Qiang stopped me from getting inside. "Bai's order. He wants me to take you to him."

"Hey, it's almost midnight. Tomorrow, tomorrow I'll pay him a visit." I dodged behind him and continue to walk in.

"Hey!" Liu Qiang yanked me over. "Bai's waiting for you in the van right now! And he said that anyone who has a past with Han Bin isn't allowed to see Gu Fan, especially you."

"What? What do you mean by that?" I stopped and stared at him.

Liu Qiang put his hand back. "Dude, that's an order. You can speak to Bai if you have your own ideas. Do me a favor, OK?"

While I was hesitating whether to quarrel with him right at that moment, I saw Yuan Shi walking out of the yard. "Yuan ... Yuan Shi!" I shouted. Now it was I who wanted his help, so calling his full name would make us seemed more closed.

Yuan Shi walked to us, confused. I patted on Liu Qiang's shoulder. "I now have very important clues to verify with Gu Fan. You see, with the current leader here, what fuss can I make? He is the expert from the City Bureau. You have to believe him even if you don't believe me."

"With Bai's orders, you can't go in whoever is accompanying you." Maybe Liu Qiang was really worried about me causing any trouble. But the more responsible he was, the worse I felt.

"Dr. Yuan, please don't misunderstand this ..."

Yuan Shi glanced at me and figured out the situation vaguely. He asked me, "Important clues?"

"Significant."

"Bai has been asking you for a while. You can go to him first and then come back to verify, or you can tell me what you want to verify with him ..."

What he said made sense, but I didn't feel right at all. "No, I have to see Gu Fan right now. This may be the only way we could find Han Bin. There are only dozens of hours left. The earlier we get the lead, the more chance we have to nail him down."

Bin's name was like heroin. Yuan Shi was attracted the minute I spoke it out. He asked, "Are you sure?"

I didn't answer him directly but said, "Well, sure or not, Commander Liu don't let me in now."

He turned to Liu immediately. "Commander, we came in with him to question Gu Fan together. If we can really get some important lead from him ..."

"But ..."

Yuan Shi was talking with an absolutely unchangeable decision. "You can come with us. With everyone here, there's no problem. I'll explain to Bai about all this. That's it."

Pulled out from bed at midnight, Gu Fan gave us a rather bitter smile.

"Officers, if you continue to treat me like this, I'd rather let Han Bin kill me."

I put all the greeting words aside and asked with a low voice, "Gu Fan, we know what you're trading when you were doing business with Khmer Rouge in Cambodia in 1994. You guys impersonated as a medical group but sold munitions instead. Now I want you to tell me what they paid with you for those weapons."

Gu Fan's bitter smile was frozen on his face.

"Khmer Rouge didn't pay you in cash and Chen Juan, Goa Jianlong and Xu Dongfang didn't die of disease or accidents. I've seen Liang Xiao. He isn't sending that killer out to protect his own security. He wants to kill Han Bin as he obtained the evidence of your deal in Cambodia at that time. Maybe Han Bin just wants to seek revenge for Chen Juan, but you guys won't let him go since he has something important to ruin you all! Now tell me the truth, Gu Fan, what on earth did they pay you with? Or pay your boss Steven Barrett with?"

"Sorry, I don't want to ..."

"Chen Juan didn't die of disease. She was killed because she knew something she didn't have to. She was murdered by you guys! Now it's the same with Han Bin. You want to kill him!"

"No, I didn't ..."

"Were you there when she was murdered? Or it was you who did this? Did she turn to you for help? Were you standing there and watching her to die?" I told him an impromptu lie. "Now we've found the remains of the three of them through diplomatic approaches. The results of medical examination would tell us everything! Aren't you going to hold it all to yourself?"

"You listen to me ..."

"I just want to listen to the truth! What did Khmer Rouge give you!"

There were tears in Gu Fan's eyes. His face turned dim, his hands rubbing his knees. I continued in almost a whisper, "Gu Fan, which side are you standing with?"

He gazed at me, his expressions changing so rapidly that it seemed he couldn't decide which one to put on. After a few seconds, he swallowed a bit and said, "Back then ... everyone in the team was indeed a medical researcher, everyone except Liang Xiao.

He answered no questions. That was too crappy a skill in shifting subjects. "I'm not fucking asking you this!"

"No. What I really mean is that we were there to do medical researches." Gu Fan seemed to be relaxed a bit. "Juan was chosen to join the team because she was so talented in the research of infectious disease."

"And you killed such a talented person. Why?"

"Because she was too kind, so kind that she couldn't accept what we were doing at that time."

"What were you doing?"

Gu Fan was in a daze. He kept silent for a while, and when he started to talk again, his voice was back to normal. "You've asked me what Khmer Rouge paid us with?"

"Yes, and you didn't ..." Looking into Gu Fan's eyes, I trembled all of a sudden.

"Khmer Rouge was a extreme left force rising in about 1960, and they were armed ..."

"The one who built a S21 camp and killed more than 20,000 people, right?"

"S21 was only one of the camps. 20,000 was just a tiny bit of them."

"Yeah, in the middle of 1994, they didn't changed a batch of automatic weapons. You may not understand, but those are top-notch equipment at that time."

"But there was no big amount of money transferred to St. Raison Foundation's account at that time. Could Khmer Rouge afford such an big number weapons? They didn't have that much money ..."

"Right. There's no free lunch in this world."

"Back then, everyone in the team was indeed a medical researcher except Liang Xiao ..."

"Around 1999, Barrett was recruited by Lockheed Martin and became a shareholder, and was assigned as the CEO of Biochemical Technology Development Department."

"Maybe because he is a humanity fighter? Hahaha ..."

"In fact, we should all die there."

...

Oh my god! It couldn't be possible that what they got was ...

Gu Fan gazed at me for a period long enough for me to finally affirm me assumption, and he was sure that I've got the real answer.

"Beasts ... You're all beasts ..." I felt all my blood frozen at that moment and didn't know what to say. "You are the one who should be dead! Fuck you! You all should die ..."

Gu Fan nodded, dead as a doornail.

Liu Qiang suddenly cut in with his transceiver. "Zhao, Bai wants to speak to you."

I got back to myself and turned around to look at Yuan Shi, who was all confused. Taking the transceiver from Liu Qiang, I turned back and said to

Gu Fan, "By the way, I have one last question for you ..."

Before my next word, I smashed the transceiver onto Gu Fan's head. It fell on the ground with his hair and blood. Before anyone could react, I dragged Gu Fan up from the sofa and tossed him on the ground. A scream came from behind. I turned around and elbowed Yuan Shi away, and then kicked Liu Qiang on the ground. As Gu Fan stood up, I punched him strongly on his ribs and face. It was clear that he didn't fight often. He couldn't even defend himself, let alone avoid my attack. I beat him heavily like a sandbag, until numerous hands pressed me onto the ground.

Along with the chill the cuff brought, I felt extremely pleasant and satisfied watching Gu Fan lying unconsciously on the ground with blood all over his face.

Well, I've got his answer to my last question.

The feeling of satisfaction was real, but the cost was real, too.

Perhaps because he was too busy, or outrageous, Bai didn't even speak to me this time. It was Liu Qiang who came to see me after I was cuffed in a police car for almost an hour.

"Hey, dude. That's hard kick. I can't stand your fist, man." He pulled me out of the police car as he complained. I noticed Yuan Shi and He Jingcheng's presnce.

"I can uncuff you. But you stay still, OK?"

I apologized sincerely and nodded. Liu Qiang released me and put the cuff back in my hand. "Take this. Put it on when you go to see the boss. He doesn't tell me to uncuff you, so don't sell me out. Now, give me your ID and cellphone. Bai asked to take those for the moment."

If I didn't take the final results into consideration, this was quite a tolerant arrangement. I gave him my ID and cellphone without saying anything, and patted him to apologize.

"What does the boss want to do with me?"

"I don't know." Liu Qiang avoided my eyes deliberately. "But the boss says you're on suspension for the moment. And you'll have to say with Mr. He until the morning after tomorrow. You cannot step outside his house, contact with anyone else, or leave his visual. In a word, give yourself a detention. He'll talk to you after the hunting tomorrow evening. ... Well, if you ask me, as long as the operation tomorrow ... oh my it's about two o'clock in the morning ... as long as you don't come to mess up the operation tonight, and criticize yourself sincerely in front of him after that, he will let you go ..."

That was why He Jingcheng was here. I sighed, "That's big trouble."

Liu Qiang frowned at me. "We all know that Bai's good to you. But you're too indulgent to fight with our own guys more than once. If there's someone talking behind your back, how could the boss do? Han Bin's case has cost him most of his energy. Now you've ... Come on, listen to me once. At least stay still today, OK? Stay with He and have a rest. And think about how to apologize to Bai." He turned around and took a glance at Yuan Shi. "Dr. Yuan just put in so many good words for you. Go and apologize to him. I have to arrange the operation. I'll see you around."

After Liu Qiang left, I stuffed the cuff in my waist and asked Yuan Shi, "What now?"

Yuan Shi wasn't happy at all. "Can I take that as an apology?"

"Ah! I'm sorry. So sorry about that. So what now?"

"That should be the most sincere apology I've ever heard."

"Don't know you take it as a so-called sincere or so-called apology. But anyway, it doesn't matter. Do you know that operation plan?"

"Have you known that before?"

"Right. Do they stake out Gu Fan and Liang Xiao together?"

"That's No. 16 and Zhongde Building, to be exact. Liang Xiao and his body guards haven't left the building for several days. And by the way, your suspension is for sure. Even if you didn't beat Gu Fan today, you'll be on suspension all the same."

"All people related to Han Bin has to be avoided in order to keep the operation plan secret?"

"That's part of the reason. The other part is the minute you stepped out of Zhongde Building, the branch received a complaint."

I didn't expect this. "It's not Gu Fan foresee me beating him from some crystal balls and called 110 in advance, isn't it?"

"No. It was Liang Xiao complained about you through the French Embassy and Wales company through the American Embassy. They say you didn't show any IDs and hindered their normal business operation. And you questioned them through threatening and intimidating ... blahblahblahblah. But I don't believe you've done this. And yes, I don't feel strange if you really did this."

"Now I just regret that I didn't do this."

"So, putting you on suspension is at least a gesture to respond to their complaints. And of course, what you did just now gave Bai enough reason to do that. The situation is getting more complicated now. Do you know guys from the Ministry of State Security had come?"

"Yeah."

Yuan Shi didn't expect my response. He paused and then continued, "So you're not surprised."

"I will if you say this to me 24 hours ago." I fumbled in my pockets but didn't find any cigarette. While I was thinking about whether to search the car, I said to him, "It seems that the information has been sent out ..."

He Jingcheng didn't join our conversation from the beginning. Now he said in an impatient tone. "I'll wait you in the car."

Looking at the back of He, I opened my mouth but didn't call him. I turned around and asked Yuan Shi, "What are the State Security guys doing here?"

"I don't know. They didn't say anything. They just took the background information about Han Bin. I thought you might know something."

"I guessed, to be exact." I found myself half a pack of cigarette on the dashboard but there was nothing to light it with. "Han Bin has something really important in his hands and somebody has leaked the information out. So now he is the target. All people above and under the ground in and out are coming to find him."

"Those documents of top secret of Khmer Rouge?"

"What does Han Bin want to do with those documents?"

"Donate to the World Court, sell them to Linwang as a bargaining chip, or put them on the floor when painting the wall ... who knows. I don't think he'll have any interest in those documents. He was just there to figure out the reason of Chen Juan's death. It didn't occurred to him that he'll get those."

"This ... was an added bonus."

"An added trouble perhaps." I was fighting with the cigarette lighter several times before I realized the car wasn't started. The key wasn't there, either so I had to give up. "So how he is both the hunter and the prey. You, me, Liang Xiao, his comrades, the State Security, all the police in Beijing and all other people related to this issue in and out this city, all of them want to find him first."

"Do you think he'll keep those files by your knowledge of him?"

"If you were fucked by a Martian, do you think those scientific manics would only mind whether you are pregnant?"

Yuan Shi looked down on his tiptoes. "So you mean he is as valuable as those files,"

I looked up to the night sky for a while. "Well, he's much more valuable than those files."

After that, Yuan Shi introduced to me in detail about the operation plan. There were backup forces from Chaoyang, Xicheng and Dongcheng Branch. The SWAT team from the City Bureau stood by 24 hours a day. People from our branch were all out. Guys from the social orders and interrogation were no exception. There were no less than 300 people monitoring Gu Fan and Liang Xiao. Even a fly couldn't sneak in without our notice.

"All right. Anyway, I was of no use now. You're responsible for the things left." The cars and police walking in and out the yard were so conspicuous. "Do you think Han Bin's going to come under such circumstances?"

"What do you think? Will he come?"

"I don't know. But I could tell you that dividing his IQ by two could increase one percent of possibility of his coming."

"And you said you had something significant to verify with Gu Fan."

"Yes, and it has been verified."

Yuan Shi smiled mockingly. "At least this kind of violent questioning is unique."

"Ha! Anyway, I don't have the chance to report to Bai, so you'd better listen carefully." I asked a light from one of the policemen guarding there and finally get to take a smoke. "From my personal view, I want to make clear what the deal was between Khmer Rouge and those Americans selling munitions. And I've got what I want."

"It seems that it is the only thing you've verified."

"No, I ... well, I've verified my second speculation in a unique way as just you said. Gu Fan cannot fight, you know. Frankly speaking, if Bin is considered a normal fighter, Gu Fan is an extremely feeble pushover. Do you get it?"

"I only get that if you put it like this, you are not a feeble one."

"No. You see, Gu Fan couldn't even defend when I fight with him, let lone fight back. I bet Bin could take him down with a finger. What did we see when we hurried back to his house? A mess, right? But do you think Gu Fan can fight with Bin in that way and created such a scene?"

Yuan Shi tried to hide his sudden enlightenment. "Do you mean Gu Fan had faked the crime scene? He didn't know how good Han Bin is ... Oh my god! He didn't know because Han Bin didn't fight with him at all! If it's true ..."

"That's right." I took a smoke and reached out my hand to let him see my wound. "You see, this was resulted from a fight with a pushover. No matter how good you are, when you fight, you can hit on any place, teeth, buttons or zippers, and you will be hurt by any of these. But Gu Fan's got none of them, not even a small cut, a defensive one. He wanted to fool me by a wound on his head? That's not even possible."

"But Doctor He didn't mention it when ..."

"He's a medical examiner whose profession is to cut bodies, not a doctor. It's normal for him to ignore this." I looked at afar subconsciously and found that He Jingcheng's car was parking alongside. "But this cannot fool me. Han Bin did hurt some of our guys, kicked the door open and met with Gu Fan. But he didn't fight with him, let alone wants to kill him."

"Then what's he doing there?"

"I don't know. This is my guess, or speculation if you want it to sound more professional. Han Bin came to Gu Fan for the last name. The biggest chance is that Han Bin didn't find out who Meng Jingtao is. I get that name from Shitian, but Shitian didn't know Meng Jingtao is Liang Xiao, or he won't help to bridge the gap to let the two Gods of Death in Anlong Vengm to fight with each other. Gu Fan may be the most direct, or the only insider that Bin can get into."

"Wait. When Shitian knew this from you, won't he tell Han Bin?"

"He may or may not believe what I told Shitian. He needs to verify."

Yuan Shi nodded. "Which means Gu Fan saved himself by selling Liang Xiao out, and in order to cover the relationship between he and Liang Xiao, he faked the scene to mislead us to believe that Han Bin will come to kill him 24 hours later."

"Talented." I breathed out a wisp of smoke. "But it still doesn't make sense in some way."

Having looked down for a while and had a thought, Yuan Shi looked up at me and said, "Yes. Even if Gu Fan gave out who Meng Jingtao really is, Han Bin can also kill him."

"Yes. And I think besides Liang Xiao, Han Bin should figured all the others out earlier enough. Then if I were him, the first one I want to kill is the son of bitch who have slept with my ex-girlfriend and killed her, directly or indirectly."

"Maybe he worried that the relationship between Gu Fan and Chen Juan would give him away too early?"

"That's possible in theory. But at least I won't let him live till the end, or just like what you said, exempt him just because he sold out Liang Xiao."

"Makes sense ... So Gu Fan didn't play a part in Chen Juan's death, and that's why Han Bin didn't want to kill him from the very beginning."

I trod out the cigarette and hoped he got my real point.

"If that's the truth, then unless ..." He didn't let me down. "Jesus Christ! Coopération..."

Yuan Shi looked at me, hoping to verify what he got from my expression. I tilted my eyebrows and said, "Well, what I want to tell you is, when a French word come out from Liang Xiao's mouth after no more than three sentences he spoke, I really want to beat him down. Do you want to try?"

"I mean, they were ... well, they may be cooperating with each other."

"Smart!" I chose one from my limited English word bank to praise him and pretended to slap on my face at the same time. "This is the second thing I've verified with him. In a nutshell, Gu Fan is the person most likely to know where Han Bin is. Do you want to find Han Bin before anyone else? Then go upstairs and interrogate that son of bitch!"

Yuan Shi was no doubt one of the main directors in this cross-district operation. His phone was ringing constantly while we speak. I knew there's not much time for me, so I said, "I'll go and find He. You go first. Please go and ask Gu Fan ... please. Haha! I never thought that one day I have to count on you on a case."

Shi seemed not to care about my tease at all. He said calmly, "Gu Fan was protected by Bai's guys. I don't know whether I can get close to him before the time limit. But Zhao Xincheng, there's a question I've always wanted to ask you."

"What's that?"

"According to the law in China, if Han Bin were to be arrested, he would be sentenced to death, right?"

I looked around. "Maybe."

"Then why do you chase him down with all your efforts? Do you want him to die?"

"I'm not the only one who spares no effort to chase him down." I crossed my arms in front my chest. "You are one of them too."

Yuan Shi didn't respond. He just looked at me and said, "Maybe we don't like each other. But I don't think you are the one who would betray your friends with no reason, especially a friend like Han Bin. For you, he is your teacher, your brother, and your family."

I didn't respond to his comment, either. I just asked back, "How about you then? Why would you want to chase him down."

"In my two years at Quantico, I met so many special people, experts in criminal psychology and serial killers with outrageously high IQ. In my years of dealing with cases, I have issued eleven criminal profiles, helped the bureau nail down five suspects, in which four of them was convicted and one being one of the ten most wanted suspects in the United States. My accuracy rate is always higher than 80 percent."

"Nice."

"I don't do this to keep a good profile."

"I know. Just like serial killers like to kill, you like to chase criminals." I blinked at him, "Most of the serial killers and murderers are maniacs who believe they are super beings beyond human. They believe they can control other people's lives. And if you can control their lives, you've proved you're standing on the top of the food chain. Am I right?"

"I just want to challenge myself with every case."

"You never failed?"

"Yes, I did. But no matter experts or criminal, I've never met someone who is really better than me in the field of criminal profiling."

"Until you met Bin."

Yuan Shi smiled in panic, his head lowered. "He sat opposite to me that day, with the polygraph, no more then two meters. He was always smiling, that kind of normal, tolerant, even sincere smile ..."

I could understand him. "But you felt you were seen through."

Looking at me surprisingly, Yuan Shi nodded. "Well, it seemed that we felt the same."

Suddenly, I was touched my his frankness. "Do you think catching him can help you surpass that old self of yours who had failed?"

"May be not. But I don't want to withdraw."

"Then come on! Dr. Yuan! I believe you this time."

"That's because you don't have a choice." Yuan Shi squinted at He Jingcheng's car. "And you haven't answer my question."

"Me? I just want to ask him something?"

"What is that?"

"Why does he want to kill? Maybe why he keeps me out all the time. And ... maybe there will be other questions. I'll know them by then."

"And then?"

"And then what?"

"If you can find him before anyone else, what will you do after you've asked your questions?"

"I don't know. Maybe I'll see what answers he gave me. Maybe I'll kill him, or help him escape. Or maybe I will be killed by him. Who knows? Well, if there's no other choices, I may cuff him back to the bureau and let Bai deal with him."

"You just want to see him." Yuan Shi's smile was full of compassion. "Actually I could feel out that you are much more like Han Bin now."

"You scared me!" I patted on my chest, "I'll have a nightmare seeing you running in front me naked."

"Isn't your dream to be him?"

I don't want to drive away the topic. "The time we spent talking about him can be used more wisely. If you can get something from Gu Fan, that's perfect. It no, continue to work on that list to see whether we've left somebody out or someone of them didn't actually die. And also, contact Guangxi Police and asked them to pay attention to Huang Feng, but don't try to control him. Disabled as he is, he's a killer. Just monitor him and get his whereabouts. Bin's alone now. If he wants to find someone to help him, Huang Feng may be his choice."

"I'll work on something." Yuan Shi turned his ringing mobile phone into vibration and put it back in his pocket. "Maybe Han Bin's buying himself some time to run away. It's a harsh period for him. He must have known that."

"Then he could choose to kill Gu Fan three days later or three months later. Will it be better if he has more time? But he attracted all manpower of ours to two locations in 24 hours. He must have a target we are not aware of." I reached my hand to him, "Some of what I have said just now was just joking. Don't mind them. Now please take him down. Please!"

Yuan Shi also reached out his hand, but grabbed my wrist instead of shaking my hand. He then took a pen and write a set of numbers on my hand. "This is the security line the City Bureau distributed to me temporarily. A mobile phone number. Call me with He Jingcheng's phone if there's anything new to tell me."

I heaved a slight sigh and said, "To be frank, it's the scene most expected since I was a kid, but it didn't occurred to me at all that the other side of the conversation would be a man."

He couldn't help but talked back this time. "Sorry about that, but leaving my phone number to a lady is what I will do as a gentleman ... Anyway, I'll try my best to follow your clues, but we have to communicate. All communication network was locked down by the direction center one hour ago. Expect for some important organizers who have been distributed with security numbers, the special line for the operation won't be opened until noon. So if you want to contact me, that's the only way."

"No wonder people are walking around. Han Bin used the police channel once and we are back to the prehistoric age." I laughed and laughed, and then realized what was wrong with it. "Wait. You mean ... radio silence?"

"That's necessary precautions. We should be aware that Han Bin's capable of hacking into police channels."

That was what he's after. Isolation. Total isolation.

"What? Are you worrying about ..."

"Is the operation this time secret to the public?"

"Of course. Bai is ..."

"He put all of us in an isolated island."

"What island?" It was clear that Yuan Shi had read something from my expression. "You mean the two sites has been isolated in communication?"

"At least the hundreds of people in No. 16 and Zhongde Building won't react in a very efficient way to things happened outside the radius."

Yuan Shi started to lose control of his expression. "That's ... that's his real purpose. So he plans ... what does he plan to do?"

"I don't know. Go ask Gu Fan." I looked at my watch, "Or you can wait for no more than 16 hours. Anyway, he can go anywhere in the city outside these two sites."

He Jingcheng lived in a small quadrangle courtyard in Zhaodengyu Road, which was inherited from his grandfather who contributed a lot in anti-Japanese war. Having worked for so many years, he did have the right to apply for an apartment as an employee benefit. But he didn't want to move out. Apart from his love to his grandparents, the peace and serenity the yard could provide to him could be what he couldn't give up as not many other places here in Beijing could offer the same.

We were both tired and didn't talked much on the way. His wife Jinging not only stayed up to wait for us, but provided us with midnight snacks. While we were gulping our food, she went to collect a north room for me to rest. Apart from admiring He's got a very good wife, I had a faint feeling that this maybe the future Bin had thought about many years ago.

There were many things to check, to ask, and to deal with. But now, I just want to lie in bed and had a good sleep. Even if Bin wanted to do something, that would be in the next dozens of hours. I had to take the time to have enough rest and be prepared to welcome the final round. So after two bowls of Wonton, I took the toothbrush Mrs. He prepared and went into my temporary bedroom before I could say goodnight.

Taking off the coat and getting into the quit, the warmth brought by the fireplace revitalized me a bit. While I was hesitating whether I should take the time before falling into asleep to organize my thoughts, tiredness brought by days of running about struck me just as the current situation — Bin scored and I was out.

When I was pushed awake, He Jingcheng gave me a cup of hot tea. I took a reflective gulp and then found out there was sunlight sneaking through the curtain. I mumbled to him, "What time is it now?"

"You'll have to have dinner if you stay in bed for a little longer." He

Jingcheng put a cold mobile phone into my quilt, startling me up. "Yuan Shi has no choice but to call me. You'd better call him back."

I woke up immediately. Picking up the phone, I dialed out, "You'd better have a good reason for waking me up."

The voice on the other side of the phone sounded to be quite nervous. "What are you expecting? Gu Fan's death or Liang Xiao's?"

"Both. Then Bin could run away and live a secluded life and I got to have my wife sleeping by my side at night. And you can console yourself in front of a serial killer handbook. ... What's happening?

"Nothing, in both sites. Rumor says the State Security moved in."

"Which means you didn't question Gu Fan."

"That's impossible. People with Gu Fan now are not from the police system."

"State Security?"

"Two Buicks with civilian license parking downstairs and there are half a dozen of people surrounding there."

"Yeah, the State Security. Complicated enough. Well, excuse yourself if there's nothing new."

"And Huang Feng's missing."

"What?" I sat up from the bed. "Verified?"

"Just verified. Huang Feng is missing. It's possible that you're the last one who had seen him from the timeline."

I was too shocked. Heaving the phone, I didn't say a word.

"Hello?"

"Yeah, I'm listening."

"Do you think he's here in Beijing?"

"I don't know. Can you pull out the security footage of the airports and the railway stations these days?

"That's beyond my ability now. And he could use other traffic tools anyway. ... That's not even practical. We can only presume that he's here and he'll be Han Bin's powerful helper. Although I don't understand what he'll do considering his physical condition, I still want to believe in you."

"If he's really here, that will cause a lot of trouble."

"Is he a Paralympic champion?"

"No, he isn't. But he's too simple."

"A simple Frankenstein who doesn't mind killing others?"

"No ... anyway, there's no time to think about him. Just leave him alone then. How about that name list?" With so many things in my head, I didn't even know which one to think about first, and everyone seemed a dead end to me.

"We're still working on that, at least nothing new found out in current responses."

"How much time left?"

"If Han Bin is just playing with us, then there's ten thousand years left; if he really wants to do something, then we only have less than three hours."

I found my watch by the pillow and was surprised to find that it was three o'clock in the afternoon. "Six o'clock?"

"About five fifty. That's when he broke into No. 16."

"All right. Better late than nothing. There's not much time left for you to show your talent. Come on!"

"Now it's not time for criminal profiling. We need a practical direction." Yuan Shi's landing onto the earth startled me. "I don't know where I should stake out at, here or Zhongde Building?"

I looked down at my hand and jumped out of the bed. Having found a pen in the drawer, I said to him, "Give me your number again. I washed it off just now."

After an impatient sigh, he told me his number again and verified it with me.

"To be frank, I found that you've got a special talent." I stuffed the piece of paper with his number into my pocket, "It may be enough to explain your accuracy rate more than eighty percent."

"What?"

"Nothing." Actually I was hoping that he could just analyze something out and bump into the right answer. But right now, time was very limited. "Make sure your phone's on. I'll call you in a minute. That's it. It'll talk to you later."

After I washed myself up, I went into the living room in the east and saw He Jingcheng was eating. Several dishes were placed on the table. They smelled good but couldn't arouse my appetite. "Where's Jinging?"

"Her sister has something emergency to deal with, so she went to pick up her nephew. Come and have something to eat." He Jingcheng pointed at the dishes without looking at me.

I sat down politely and pushed my dish away. That was a slight move but it was enough to attract He's attention. He, however, didn't look up at me, only focusing on his food."

"I ..."

"No talking while eating and sleeping. Wait until I finished my meal."

"That's what Bin said."

"That's what Confucius said. Read more."

"Do you want you hear me talking through this meal?"

He didn't answer. He just continued his meal. But after a while, he put it down and looked at me. On his face, I saw total tiredness. In my memory, he hasn't been tired like this even when worked 40 hours by the autopsy table.

"Not sleeping well?"

"Yeah."

"What's wrong?"

"You know it."

"Yeah, you've left something out."

"I did."

"You didn't miss it. You didn't report it."

He Jingcheng uttered a bitter smile, not approving my words but not disapproving it either.

"The fact that there's no defensive wounds on Gu Fan wasn't a surprising discovery. At least it couldn't tell us exactly where Bin is right now. What you did is just to stall some time."

"Whatever you say." He picked up the chopsticks, which indicated he didn't want to go on the conversation any more.

"But you don't deny it until now."

"Go report me."

I was a little angry. "What kind of person do you think me as?"

"What kind of person do you think you are?"

"I didn't tell anybody!"

"Want to throw a long line?"

"No." His attitude made me sad. "I just don't want to lost another friend."

He chewed for a long time and finally lifted his head up. "Do you really want to put him into death?"

I didn't know whether I should shake or nod. "As time goes by, he will be found in the end. I just want to find him before anyone else."

"I don't know where he is."

"I believe you."

"Then what do you want to ask?"

"The other acquaintance of yours." I leaned forward to put two of my elbows on the table, "Chen Juan."

"That's Bin's girl. I didn't know her well. You should go and ask her relatives and classmates."

"They had all migrated abroad. Nothing I could find about her. As for her classmates, they were all busy about daily chores — divorce, affairs, or pulling strings to get their children into a good school. I don't think I can get what I want from them."

"She is a reason, not a clue."

"But I want to know whether Bin's really killing for her."

He looked down, thinking, and said, "Is there any difference now?"

"Maybe." I took out the cigarette and saw He Jingcheng pointing at the matches beside the fireplace. "You, Yang, Beitong, Shitian, Huang Feng, Gu Fan ... maybe Jingjing and those kids at the workshop, oh yes, and the sister named Ma Li in the orphanage, no matter who you are and what you do, almost every one of you is helping him and objecting me directly or indirectly. And the most I cannot understand is, you do believe that he is killing people, but you choose to indulge him by excuses like 'he must have a reason' or 'the people he killed must be guilty and they deserve to die'. Being friends for so many years, I want you to tell me, for what reason should one be allowed to play God and decide other people's life and death?"

"You have to admit that he's never killed an innocent man."

"Define innocence first." I tried my best to control my impulse to fire out, "Should that young man be killed just because he took two yuan from a kid's pocket?"

He didn't respond. After all, it was pure slaughter.

I put down my cigarette, took a deep breath to calm myself down and continue, "I've always been thinking that Bin was just seeking revenge for Chen Juan. He just has to clear some obstacles in the way of pursuing that end or preventing himself being exposed. But is that really the fact? Regardless of those three young men, unless Chen Juan was sexually abused when she was a child, then Zhang Mingkun has nothing to do with Bin's revenge. Don't talk about the importance of Xiaoyue River to him. Yes, Wang Rui deserves to die, but Bin's not the one to decide. He could redirect the attention of the police to him, which, we all know, is his expertise. OK, I just take it that he happened to come across this. But he can easily take him down and send him to the bureau, right? It's also easy to explain afterwards, maybe getting some awards. Is that really necessary to kill him like that?"

He put him hand in front his mouth, and heaved a sigh slowly. "What do you think?"

"Bin's our best friend. He's also the core of our social circle. I don't want to think about him from the worse part. ... But, there's a possibility that we've put the cart before the horse."

He kills for the sake of killing.

"Nonsense. I've known him well for so many years. ... He doesn't have a reason to do that."

"No, he doesn't. He's looking good and has a decent job. His family is good. He doesn't have any debts, and he has many friends. He doesn't fit any one of the features we know in criminal profiling." I lighted up my cigarette, "But don't forget his three years in South Asia. He was sold out by a military bloc, and sold his own comrade out in turn. Lives are nothing in a battlefield. We know nothing about it. Who knows what influence it had left on Bin? Do you think you know him well? Do you really?"

"I don't know ..." He rubbed his face, disappointingly, "But I really don't know where he is now."

"I told you I believe you. But at least, tell me what happened between him and Chen Juan."

According to him, the days past between Bin and Chen Juan was quite ordinary, except that they had fall in love in high school. But it was not a big case, not even cared by their classmates.

Chen Juan was two years younger than Han Bin. Nobody knew how exactly they got into together. Chen Juan was no more than 14 years old then, a kid rather than a young lady. But Bin was a real Casanova at school, flirting with girls and having fun everywhere. Besides extremely good grades, Chen Juan was also a very good girl, gentle and kind, tolerant to Bin's behaviors. But right at the moment Bin started to find her good, which was around Chen Juan's first year in college, she suddenly immigrated to Canada with her family and broke up with Bin.

"She seemed to be a simple one, but she actually thought a lot." He Jingcheng's comment on her may not be that objective, but I still listened on. "No matter Bin or the classmates and friends around, nobody had seen her through. She knew what she wanted, and she knew how to get them. The most cruel point was that in order to get what she wanted, she can sacrifice anything, and anyone, including Bin."

The day they broke up, Bin committed suicide at his dormitory. Thanks to He, who was careful enough to notice Bin didn't went to play soccer with them, Bin was saved. "He never misses PE class." He Jingcheng said. After that, Bin was in hospital and received treatments, and then suspended his college life and went back home.

"I can still recall clearly that the first sentence he said to his parents after he wok up was 'Sorry', the first to me was 'Thank you so much. I was an idiot."

"He regretted that he shouldn't have committed suicide?"

"If you ask me, I'll say what he regretted was that he hadn't found a secluded place to end his life."

And things happened several years later. Bin received a phone call from Chen Juan in Cambodia.

"I saw he was really upset that day, so I asked what was wrong with him. He was very panic and told me Chen Juan was in danger. I asked him what happened, but he didn't tell me. And after that weekend, I couldn't reach him when I called him. It was until I went to his parents did I know he went missing. His family thought he just left home and were really worried about him. Nobody knew where he was, neither did I, but I knew it must have something to do with Chen Juan."

That was three years.

"He did so much for Chen Juan ... Does he hate her?"

"I don't know. But I've never heard anything bad about her from him. I don't like her because she once hurt Bin. But to be honest, she is not bad, at least not to Bin when they were together .... After all, this is a free world. Everyone has the right to live their own life."

Yes, on the basis of not hurting others.

But right now, I didn't want to define their past. "You can't avoid being hurt in a relationship. You know ..."

"I just know Chen Juan had hurt a man she shouldn't have been, and that man hurt so many other people for her several years later."

"Butterfly Effect."

"No." He Jingcheng looked at me coldly, "If you ask me, that is karma."

I took a second thought and asked him, "So you think, in the end, it is Chen Juan who changed Bin."

"No, she changed everything."

4

Time passed quickly in our conversation. I wasn't that angry about He Jingcheng's concealment due to his friendship with Bin. The more I knew, the more I've discovered that I really didn't know much about Bin. People around him, no matter friends or enemies, seemed to know something about him, a part, a piece. I searched around between them with all my efforts, trying to complete the jigsaw, but his life was still vague and mysterious.

He Jingcheng once asked me, "Do you want to find him or catch him?"

I once lied to me that these two were the same. Of course, finding him

301

needed effort, but catching him needed luck — and that also made make sense if it was put backwards. But for me, Bin was a coordination with complicated meanings. Yuan Shi wanted to catch him to prove his ability, but I didn't even know why I wanted to find him.

From the very beginning of our conversation, I knew nothing practical I would get from it, or He Jingcheng wouldn't sit here, chatting with me. But the worse thing was, I didn't know what I was waiting for. It was sure that Bin's action would lead to new leads, but I was somehow hoping he could escape as soon as possible.

The phone rang at a little past six. At that moment, I should not feel any tension or excitement. I was disappointed and it surprised me that I took that for granted.

As expected, it was Yuan Shi.

"He came."

Half an hour ago, Bin paid a visit to Haidian Hospital. He knocked down the guarding policemen in front of the surveillance camera in the east end of the fourth floor and walked by "Pang Xin"'s bed, and then pushed 300mg morphine into her normal saline infusion bottle. It was for sure that when he stepped out of the front door of the hospital along his way in, that iconic figure of Asian female serial killers in Yuan Shi's mind has faded into history because of respiratory failure.

No more cover and scruples, that was pure killing.

Yuan Shi was painful and confused. "What does he intend to do? Anything special between that Black Window and him?"

I didn't know. Nobody knew.

The operations have taken so many people, plus the communication lockdown, that the information couldn't be sent out until a long time after the case was discovered. After the first group of police got there and controlled the crime scene, they reported it to the direction center immediately, who was embarrassed to find out there was no one left to send there to deal with the case. The groups in two operation sites could be reached, so no one could immediately start the lockdown and search within the area. When Bai heard of this in the direction van from the City Bureau Special Case Center, rigor mortis had already set in with "Pang Xin".

"Bai is afraid that he just looked this way and rowed another, so everybody in those two sites was still stand by. Only the sheriff on duty in each local police station took some of the guys to check in the hospital. I'm on my way, too." He stopped for a second, as if to wait for my response. "If you think of something, feel free to call me."

"Why are you going there?"

"He drew something on the wall of the ward."

"What?"

"They couldn't describe it clearly on the phone so I don't exactly know. It seems that it's some sort of pattern."

Bullshit! Such a boring stunt, a set-up. "Don't go."

"What?"

"No matter what he drew there, his purpose is to let us go and see. You go there and step into his trap, so don't go."

"I'm about to get there. I'll go and see and then talk to you ..." A loud noise came through the phone. I asked for some times and found the communication has been cut.

I put down and phone and told He Jingcheng who was still sinking in his thoughts. "He killed another man."

"Who ..."

"It doesn't matter who he killed right now. The point is he can't stop." I lighted up a cigarette, watching the fire swallowing the tobacco inside. "I'm sure that right now, the Ministry of Public Security is putting up his wanted posters, Class A."

"Do you want to find him, or catch him."

"You've asked me for a hundred times!"

"And you didn't answer."

"I don't know. Oh my god! Of course I want to catch him. What do you think people pay their taxes for? For us to sit in this courtyard, drinking tea and chatting?" I was surprised about my anxiety, "Don't understand me wrong. I don't mean to ..."

It was turning dark already. There was no light in the room. He Jingcheng's eyes was shining a bright grey behind his glasses in the dim light of sunset.

"Do you really just want to catch him?"

"I'll know till I see him."

He stood up, with his hands supporting him on the table, and switched the light on by the door. I wasn't used to the sudden light and closed my eyes naturally. I heard him saying, "Let me show you something."

It was a photo album in his hand. He flipped it over and showed to me one page. There were six photos on that page. The first one I noticed was a group photo of some students on the upper left corner as one of the girls who was clearly taller than the others caught my attention.

Out of astonishment, I looked and asked, "Ma Li?"

"Yeah. She was a classmate of Chen Juan. It's a small world, isn't it?"

He pointed at the down right, "But it's this one I'd like to show you ..."

That was a photo of Bin, Yichen and He Jingcheng, with Wuhou Shrine in Chengdu, Sichuan province as the background. He Jingcheng was a thin man than, and Bin was a little darker. As for Yichen ... well, Yichen looked like...

As I was completely puzzled, He explained to me with a pretence of regret. "You shouldn't have left this out, neither should Yuan Shi."

As I sunk in my thought gazing at the photo, I saw Pianma, downstairs of Zhang Mingkun's residence, the coffee workshop, Cambodia, the yard at No. 16 ... I seemed to be rummaging around in different scenes. All people, all issues and all the fragments have been put together and led to a perfect explanation.

Closing the album, I stood up. "Should I beat you down or something to let you explain that you have no choice but to let me leave."

"No, there's no need. Save your strength." He sit down relieved. "Even if you could find him, he is not easy to deal with."

I nodded, took the keys to the car and walked outside. "Thank you for your help. But I was curious to know whether you want me to catch him or find him."

"That depends on your capability." He opened his album, gazing at those silhouettes of his past memories, "I just don't want him to kill anymore."

It was until after driving out for a while did I realized I didn't have a mobile phone. That was a big trouble as it was really difficult to find public phones these days. I pulled over outside Xinjiekou Mall, rushed in to buy a phone and a new sim card. I put it in and found the battery was low. I was in such a hurry. As the sales lady were explaining politely to me that new lithium battery should be charged for several times, and several hours to activate its memory, I squinted her a bit and said, "The one on your neck seems good ..."

Running outside, I dialed Yuan Shi's phone with a fake pink phone, but heard a soft voice saying "The subscriber you dialed is not available. Please dial again later".

Cell phone signals were blocked in wards. What an idiot of him!

Call the police if there's trouble. I chose to call 110.

After I told the dispatcher my name, identity and my number, she told me to wait for a second. After half a second, a man was calling my name in the phone. It was Liu Qiang.

"Didn't I tell you to stay put in He Jingcheng's place? What are you doing outside? Where do you get your phone?"

"Err ... why are you here in the direction center?"

"Bai told me to take charge of coordination and communication. You didn't answer my questions."

"Liu, I don't have time to explain. Now listen to me ..."

"You should listen to me. As friends, I won't report you to Bai this time if you go back to He Jingcheng and stay put. Don't come out again! There are so many things to do now. Go back to He's place. That's it."

As I was about to take the initiative with my imposing manner and loud voice, the phone was hung up. What the fuck! I had to report to the Bureau for such a reception!

After driving pass Jianxiang Bridge, I decided put that later and dialed Yuan Shi's phone again.

It was connected this time.

"Are you still in Haidian Hospital?"

"Who ... Zhao Xincheng? I just come downstairs. Do you know what Han Bin drew on the wall? He drew ..."

"He drew a picture of Mona Lisa and Tokugawa Ieyasu singing together! Don't mind! I know what he's going to do. Can you find me some backup?"

"What's that?"

"He's targeting at the north yard. He wanted to strike the holding cell after two operation sites and a murder scene took all manpower and when we couldn't communicate with each other effectively! He is going to save Han Yichen!"

"Wait! You mean he ran around half of the city like an idiot, just to save that adopted sister? Oh yes, that was his ..."

"She's Chen Juan's daughter." I didn't focused on the road and missed an exit. Pulling over and backing off, I said, "Han Yichen, the names means Han and Chen. That's why Gu Fan chose to stand with Bin against us."

"The kid is the daughter of him and Chen Juan?"

"I don't know. Maybe Gu Fan is the father. But anyway, she's Chen Juan's daughter. That's enough."

"Are you sure?"

"Have you seen Chen Juan's photo?"

"Yes, in the files. But I don't think ..."

"But have you seen her in her fifteens?"

"Similar to Han Yichen?"

"Twins."

"Wow! Dominant inheritance?"

"That's a complete victory for XX no matter from gender or appearance."

"Hey, genetics tell us that gender is decided by the XY. Don't blame women."

"Then your daddy must be very good at straying away from the point. Whether or not can you get me the backup!"

"Genetics also tells us the IQ of a man comes completely from his mother. It has nothing to do with the father. Only the IQ of a woman comes from both her parents. So it's possible that Han Yichen's IQ come from Han Bin and her talented mother. ... I don't any any backup in my hand, but I can call Bai. Where are you?"

"I'm five minutes' drive from the north yard. Stop the bullshit and get me some backup!" I backed off the main road and switched the clutch, "If he really comes, this is out best choice."

Yuan Shi murmured "if" and hung up the phone.

I then called the north yard. Fortunately, my old boss Liao was on duty today. He paid much attention after my report. "I don't have many people on duty here. You'd better come quick. I'll tell the armed policed at the gate let you in."

After a few minutes, I parked in the north yard. The number of the armed police at the gate had been doubled, and there were patrol team walking around. Liao really reacted quickly. Pulling over the car beside the basketball court, I went to the holding cell first. The officer there at the hall told me that Yichen had just been taken out by an officer. I didn't expect this, but then thought maybe Liao wanted to put her in special custody to keep her safe, so I asked, "Who was the one taking her away?"

The officer glanced at me impatiently. He rummaged in his register book and found out a note, squinting his eyes to read it loud out. "Zhao ... Zhao .. whatsoever Cheng ..."

I felt I was suddenly hit hard on the chest. Snatching the note, I saw my name right on the place of the responsible officer.

Bin has taken her.

There was point arguing with him now. I tossed the note down and run directly to the office building. At the same time, I called Yuan Shi, "He has impersonated a policeman and took Yichen out by a faked note. Come on and block the road!" It was clear that Yuan Shi didn't expect the chance has gone so fast. "It still takes at least fifteen minutes for the backup to get there. I'll contact the police station around. You go and search him!"

Normally, there were no more than half a dozen of policemen on duty in the interrogation office. Whether an effective search can be organized was still in question. I ran to Liao's office in a hurry and pushed the door open. "Commander ..."

Commander was leaning on the sofa in a relaxed way — too relaxed.

And a slight sound of door closing came out behind me.

I calmed myself down and confirmed that Liao was in a coma. Yichen was standing by the table. Her prison livery has been taken off. The minute I figured out all these, a strong pressure stressed down on my back. The feeling of danger made me excited. Without any doubt, I crouched down and pounced at Yichen.

But Bin was faster than me.

This first move of mine didn't work out. His hand has grabbed my shoulder and a kick was added on my left pople. As I was about to lean aside and roll forward to avoid him, a strike was punched on my ear. Upon falling on the ground, I couldn't even feel the pain.

In my dizziness, I heard Bin's voice. "No wonder there are more guards and the yard is locked down. You're the last person I want to see here."

I felt my head was about to break, the back of my head aching too much and my throat starting to sore. Crawling for a few steps on the ground, I reached the sofa and leaned on it. Bin was standing in front the window, looking out. I could hardly recognize him in the police uniform.

Yichen walked to me several steps, which forced me to abandon my plan of standing up. She was holding a black Type 54 pistol, pointing my head with a standard pistol shooting gesture.

"Weaponry of both the south and north yard were down at the basement, which I thought was a complete failure." Bin turned around and leaned on the table, "If there's some terrorists rushing in, as long as they control the entrance to the basement, all policemen here could only be trampled upon."

I was still trying to make a judgement. My call was in time. Commander Liao made the order to add guards and arrange patrol teams. Bin found out he couldn't go out after he had taken Yichen out, so he chose to hide in the office building, which made him happen to come across Liao who would possibly go to the weaponry to take a weapon. And then Bin took the boss down ... and then I came in.

At the very moment, I still wanted to believe that Bin didn't want to kill me. But I wasn't sure whether Yichen would as I felt her character was inherited from her mother who, in my eye, was cruel and slippery. So that police weapon in her hand seemed to be more powerful. The only thing I could do was to pray that her right finger was stable enough or she didn't know how to shoot a gun.

Bin couldn't have indulged her in killing, which could assured me to some sort.

I wetted my mouth to the muzzle. "Do you know? You mother is Chen Juan. And Han Bin had killed a lot of people for her."

The corner of her mouth moved slightly. She didn't say anything, but I could tell she didn't even mind what I said.

Bin walked near me speechlessly. Bending down to search me over, he took my phone and the key to the car. I took the chance to observe him. Besides the eye bag making him haggard, his neat chin and hair and his black eyes were all as usual, nothing showing he was on the run.

"Calculating by your age, I believe he is the most probable one to be your father." I was talking to Yichen, but the close distance between me and Bin made it look like I was whispering to Bin. "Although we all thought you were close in another way ..."

Bin didn't look at me. He took my cellphone and went back to the table. And Yichen's answer made me speechless. She said, "Yeah, I know."

Well, then I knew I had no other ways to deal with the situation.

"That's the secret number to Yuan Shi, isn't it?" Bin was fiddling with that pink phone and checked the time with his watch. "You told him, then the backup should be in ten minutes. At least two policemen are needed when escorting a suspect. Send out Yichen with me."

I finally get a chance to mock at him. "Are you daydreaming? Let your daughter shoot me to death then."

Bin put his cellphone in the pocket and then looked at me for a while with that post. "Being friends for so many years ..."

"Have you taken me as your friend after all these years?"

"What could I do? Tell you everything from the beginning? You won't agree with me."

"Of course ... of course not. But at least I could stop you! Chen Juan is nothing but a woman who have dumped you! All right, let's say you love her so very much. Then how many people should you kill to take her back?" I supported myself up, and Yichen stepped back a few steps, but still outside the radius. "Han Bin! Don't play sneak attack if you're a man. Let's fight one on one! Don't let your child pointing her gun at me!"

Bin looked down disappointingly, shaking his head. "Xincheng, if you say so, that makes me upset."

I suddenly calmed down. "You don't know what upset was like."

"No, I don't mean that. I was upset to you because I didn't kill for Juan. I don't know why you could say so." He took one hand out of his pocket and looked at it carefully. "I kill because I want to."

Killing is killing. It is an action to deprive others of their lives. It cannot be purified, beautified or ennobled by any cover or decoration. But at the very moment, I'd rather believe Bin was just unwilling to find an excuse to polish his actions, or talking about nonsense to stay tough.

If not, this would be the answer I was always longing to get, but didn't want to.

"And also, even if I really did it for Juan ..." He flipped his hand, palm up. It was until then did I found out he was looking at the silver little thing in his hand.

My eyesight didn't recover completely so I couldn't see it clearly and nodded subconsciously. Bin tossed me that thing. Two silver lights fell over my view slowly, so did my heart. My courage was gone in a instant. My defense line in my heart collapsed at once.

That was a pair of platinum earrings of rose shape.

I trembled to pick up my gift to my wife at our anniversary. My mind went into total blank. I couldn't even say a word.

Bin was cold and cruel. There was not even a slice of human emotion in his words. "Now it's thirteen minutes to seven. If Huang Feng didn't receive my phone call before seven, I assure you that your wife couldn't see the sunrise tomorrow. If you don't want to remarry, don't stall. Let's go."

"You fooled me. Xuejing is not in your hands!" I said after I started up the police car, and then gazed at the rearview.

Bin didn't respond. He was siting in the back seat to cuff Yichen.

"Let me confirm Xuejing's safe first!"

He tidied up himself a bit and put on his hat. "Start the engine, or get out of the car."

"No. You must ..."

He reached out his hand and pointed out. I turned around and saw the clock on the dashboard in the direction he pointed at.

"Your girl has eight minute left."

What the fuck!

Driving near the gate, two armed police blocked us and came to check. I pulled the window down and passed them the procedure documents Bin gave me ahead. An armed policeman with a round face looked at the document carefully, and the other was standing on the other side of the car, viewing us carefully.

I was in such a hurry that I couldn't help to urge him. "It's an emergency. Commander Liao asked us to transfer this suspect as soon as possible. She may be an important witness of another serial cases."

The round face frowned and said, "Isn't your Commander Liao the one who told us to seal the gate?" His face was serious, so serious that I even wanted to beat him.

"Yes. But now situation's changed!"

Bin seemed to murmur in the back. "Take it easy..."

The round face glanced at all three of us in the car, went across and talked with another armed policeman, and then went back to me, "Wait for a minute. I'm going to call him and check."

I pretended to be careless and impatient. "All right. Be quick you guys!"

Seven minutes to seven. I could only hope Commander Liao wouldn't be awoken by the phone.

It was clear that the phone was not answered. The round face went to check with another armed police. I felt my hands on the steering wheel was numb and my right leg was shaking uncontrollably. I was about to think whether to drive directly through the gate and rushed out.

"Couldn't contact your boss." The round face went back to the car. "Wait here please. I'll go upstairs and find him."

"Hey you're wasting our time!" I reached out my left hand and patted hardly on the door, "The documents are here!"

Maybe my misbehavior touched one of their nerves. The other armed policeman suddenly raised his gun and shouted at Bin from the right side of the car.

"Get out of the car!"

The round face paused a bit and then pulled my door but it didn't open. "Get out of the car! You!"

I pushed the door open angrily and took that chance to move my numb arm. "What do you mean!"

Bin got out of the car and walked slowly to the other side of the car, squinting at me with a cold face.

When the round face was about to argue with me, the phone in the stall rang. In a moment, no one knew what to do. The two armed policemen may be startled and I guessed we were exposed. Bin looked down to look at something. Up until he raised his left hand did I notice the light on his phone was flickering. I then realized: his phone was ringing, too!

Was there a mistake? There was no time?

Bin glanced at me with a complicated look. He put the ringing phone on the front cover of the car and turned around, pouncing at the guard in the police box.

"Now that for my family, there's nothing I can't do."

Without any time to take a second thought, I stepped forward to hold up the Type 79 submachine gun in the round face's hand and pinned his throat with my elbow.

"I believe you could understand this."

"Turn right. Go along the side road of Badaling Expressway." Bin took off Yichen's handcuff and ordered calmly. I stepped on the gas hurriedly, which may be an approach to get rid of the police alarm from the north yard. "Call that blind guy! Don't hurt Xuejing!"

Bin looked outside the window and didn't respond.

"Call that fucking guy! I won't let you go if anything happened to Xuejing!"

He turned around and smiled. "You weren't acting as to let me go from the very beginning."

"I beg you, man! Call him please! Please! I promise you I won't be in your case any more. Please ..."

"Don't worry. I've already texted him."

When I was about to take a relief, I found the strange part. "Text him? Can Huang Feng read ..."

"Stop."

I stepped on the brake reflectively. Putting the clench on P mode, I was hit from the back at the moment I wanted to turn around. Lying on the steering wheel in a daze, the door was open and Bin pulled me out on the ground.

His next words awoke me immediately. "Do you really believe a guy who couldn't even read a text message can kidnap an adult policewoman? ... Get up!" And then I heard the sound of loading a gun.

Supporting myself with the door, I got up on my feet slowly. "You didn't take her ... I should have thought of that ..."

"Go." He directed me with the gun in his hand.

After I stepped into the woods by the road, Bin halted me and tossed me the handcuffs. "Hug the tree and cuff yourself."

Disappointed and tired, I did as he said in a daze.

Bin didn't say anything. I looked at him taking on gloves and cleaning the gun. I was not afraid. There were much more simple ways if he wanted to kill me. He didn't have to cuff me.

Out of curiosity, I asked, "Where did you get her earrings?"

Bin didn't look up. "I happened to pick up her wardrobe when looking for this uniform. You'll have to blame your wife for this. She put things everywhere."

And the foolish regulation that no jewelry was allowed when at work. I took another thought and asked, "What's the connection between you and 'Pang Xin' or 'Wang Rui'?"

He seemed to be puzzled for a second, and then shook his head.

"Then why do you kill 'Pang Xin'?"

"I've answered your question." He took out that pink fake phone with his left hand. "Don't meddle in my things for old times' sake."

"I refuse. Do you want to kill me?"

Bin looked at me in surprise with a complicated grievance.

Looking at the direction of the road for a while, he raised the phone by his ear and said with a panic voice. "Help! Help! I'm around Xiaoying ... Help! Zhao Xincheng! Don't you dare to kill me!"

I didn't realize what he was going at the beginning and then I realized he was calling the police. When I was about to call for help loudly, Bin raised his right hand and shot for several times. In the tinnitus, I saw him smashing the phone onto a tree and tossed the gun into the grass. He left.

Badly hurt in less than an hour, I had to kneel down and had a rest. But an idea occurred in my head. Having looked at my watch to memorize the time, I smashed the watch open on the trunk, broke off the watch hand from the plate and picked the handcuff.

Xiaoyue River has changed a lot through these years.

It started to rain from the second half of the night. The raindrops fell down from every direction with the wind's help. I was almost freezing to death. Clenching tightly, I still trembled in the cold night in totally wet clothes.

If Bin had been standing here in a rainy night, he must have felt such helplessness.

Strolling along the river, I couldn't find anything to enjoy myself. Except for the glistening water in the rain, it was all dark, like Bin's eyes. You could see nothing in it.

Maybe wanting to make me more warm, I tried my best to think about a sunny day with green meadows and chirping birds. A boy was taking a girl's hand, their shyness booming into vital impulse on this vigorous land. Kisses on the forehead and mouth turned into promises, and became what can't be changed with the help of time and fate. I opened my arms, reaching through the spaces between railings and touching the trees by the river. There were smell of mud and plants mixed together. What a primitive and natural place.

"She changed everything."

I was so obsessed that I didn't heard the sound of an engine. Up until I heard someone calling my name with a low voice did I walked out of this imagination.

Yuan Shi, a man who pays much attention to his appearance, didn't take an umbrella with him, which surprised me a little bit. He looked at me in the same surprised look — to my ragged appearance or all the things had happened before.

After I stepped into the car, I asked him to shut off the car light but keep the air conditioning working. Yuan Shi passed me a bag of McDonald. Hungry as I was, I didn't want to eat after I took a bite of the hamburger. At last, I found a cup of hot coco, too hot to drink, but was perfect to keep my hands warm.

"My suggestion is to go back to the bureau and tell the truth."

I gazed at the coffee color liquid in the cup. "Am I being listed as wanted now?"

"Bai didn't publicize it, for the moment." I could feel Yuan Shi was observing me all this time. "But the announcement has been made in the system within the city. You can be taken down with a compulsory measure."

"What about Bin?"

"He is listed on the Class A wanted posters by the ministry two hours ago."

"What level?"

"Can be shot down."

"Yeah ..." I took a sip of the coco and found some taste in my mouth. "How's the operation?"

"Gu Fan has been taken away by the Ministry of State Security and the operation is over. A team was staking out under Zhongde Building. But I still want you to go back with me. Now that you're forced by him, there's a chance to clear you out."

"Yeah, I believe that." I put the up aside and turned to him. "Bin doesn't want to frame me anything. He just wants some days, some days without me."

"Is he running?"

"He doesn't have to stall me if he wants to run. ... Do you have a smoke?"

"I don't smoke."

"What a gentleman. He wants to kill Liang Xiao. If there's anyone he's still in Beijing for, it must be Liang Xiao."

"I agree. From the painting he left in the hospital ..."

313

"Don't talk about the painting anymore. He just wants all the other police in the district to go to a place in which cellphone signals are blocked. There's nothing to do with that Black Widow ... At least he doesn't admit there's any connection."

"Yeah, you saw him." Yuan Shi sat up a bit, "Have you got anything?"

"What do you want to know?"

"Why does he kill?"

I turned around to look at Xiaoyue River, which was totally blocked by the fog and nothing could be seen.

"He said it's for the revenge of Chen Juan. I need a hand from you."

"Why would I give you that hand?"

"Because 'Pang Xin' could cooperate with 'Wang Rui', Bin with Gu Fan, his comrade with Liang Xiao, the police with the state security, so you can cooperate with me, or to say, you have to cooperate with me."

Yuan Shi thought about it carefully. "Why did he kill 'Wang Rui'?"

"Probably because 'Wang Rui' didn't plan to let him leave alive."

"Then why would Han Yinchen be at the crime scene?"

"I didn't ask, but I can guess. The time Yichen showed up in the crime scene and was taken by our people was exactly the same time as we stopped to protect his residence. And at the same time, he sent his parents abroad so I think the most possible reason would be ..."

"He sent his daughter back to the crime scene to be taken back to the holding cell as a protection? Is that insane?"

"That's not a normal choice, but it's the most reasonable one."

"And then he breaks into the jail? Is he mad?"

"I felt his plan was to send Yichen to the holding cell to be protected by us, and he spends this time killing Liang Xiao and dealing with his old comrade. When the time limit comes, we have to let her go. It's possible that he didn't expect "Wang Rui"'s case exposed him. He has to take the risk to compensate. If I wasn't kept out yesterday, if He Jingcheng decided to help me earlier, if Bin didn't found Xuejing's earrings in the wardrobe, if ever you guys could move faster ..."

"He couldn't run out if you didn't 'cooperate' with him."

"Yes. But I could survive without solving the case, without the uniform, I can't without my wife. Do you want to help me or not?"

"What can I help you with?"

"I need some money."

Yuan Shi took out his LV purse and pulled out a thick stack of notes. Pulling two of them back, he passed all the rest to me. "No need to count. I don't count on you to give it back."

"Thank you. I still need you to book a room for me in a hotel near Zhongde Building. Its window must be facing the front door of the building. It has to been connected with all branch bureaus. I cannot book it with my own ID. You've got your ID here, haven't you?"

"I'll see to that." He found a piece of paper and write me a number. "My secret number has been taken back. Call this number to contact me if you need. Any other requirements to the room?"

"Good ventilation. With a tub and breakfast. Room service. Oh, and the bed should be soft. It's better the bottled water in the fridge can be free."

"I'd better call the police or take you back to the division."

"I still need some weapon. Now Bin's cerebellum is much more difficult to deal with than his cerebrum."

"Holy shit! You're not asking me to find a gun for you, are you? Come on! Why didn't you take the gun he tossed on the scene?"

"Are you insane? Run with a gun? Then I wouldn't be wanted within the system. I don't like guns. Daggers or nightsticks? Don't mind. I'll find something myself."

Yuan Shi heave a long breath. "What else?"

"Don't stop the engine. Switch on the warm wind." I touched the adjustment lever under the seat and pulled the back of the seat down. Closing my eyes, I said, "I'm so tired."

Chapter VIII
Running Like Hell

1

I reached out carefully for my cigarette on the windowsill. Xuejing uttered a soft and tired sound in my arms like a cat. "Don't smoke ..." I hurried to put my hands on her back and patted a time or two. Actually, we have never got a chance like this since we got married. Our daily routine was that she was busy with her work and I with mine. In the rarely coming days that we were both at home, we were both too tired to talk. It didn't occur to me that in such a tense moment, we could get some leisure time like in the honeymoon. Well, I didn't know whether it was ill wind.

Xuejing sat up wrapped in a blanket, her eyes still closed. "You go to sleep for a while."

The front door of Zhongde Building was right outside the window. Except for a little dissatisfaction about the facilities here, this was the best stake out site Yuan Shi could find me.

But my work here was rather easy, especially after Xuejing had come. Maybe the fake kidnapping gave her some sort of romantic experience besides being moved. Anyway, she took a clear-cut stand on my side after she received the phone call.

I suddenly realized that the connection between people were as subtle as this. I knew Bin and married with Xuejing, who could actually had nothing to do with me. Xuejing could have been living somewhere else as a spinster or a mother, and Bin could be another fortuneteller or a criminal who was taking bullets in a execution ground. There was no difference, not a fucking difference to me. Their happiness and sorrow, life and death, had nothing to do with me.

"You choose, I choose, they choose, all the people were choosing. We are choosing our fate, and the fate is choosing us."

Shitian was right. Fate is a leotard knitted by numerous choices intertwined together. It was on everyone's body like a parasite. Bin could choose not to kill, Xuejing not to marry me, and I, likewise, could choose to live here with my wife until Christmas, regardless of the troubles outside the window.

"What are you thinking about?" Xuejing must have noticed that I've been in a silence for a long time.

"Thinking about I could actually give up. Go back to the division and be investigated. And then resign to do something else. Waiting at the gate of the kindergarten after several years. And our turtle can live past fifty years old."

She sat there, wobbling into my arms and said, "That was good!" And then, she looked up into my eyes, "You wish him to give up, right?" And then she threw herself into my arms again, "The question is he won't. so you won't either." She looked up again, "But giving up is still a good idea."

"The way human choose their own fate is from his inner character."

So I knew Bin won't give up, just as Xue jing knew my words about giving up was a good idea I was just saying.

"What do you want me to do?" I knew that was a hypocritical question.

"I want to you smoke less and live longer than our turtle." Xuejing turned around to look at the ceiling leaning on my chest. "I also hope Dr. Yuan would work something out to save my husband from this dilemma."

"Yuan Shi is smart enough. Not every doctor who had studied in America would have a profile like his. It's time that he still needs."

"唔，你或韩哥带他十年，他应该有希望赶上我的水平。"

"Yeah. You or Han teaches him for ten years, and then he can hopefully catch me."

"Be kind, lady." I pretended to flick her forehead. "Yuan Shi uses the criminal profiling skills mostly used in western countries to analyze cases, which are based on the land, people, economy, culture, and even political characteristics in western countries. Along with the powerful support from the technical team in FBI, it's normal for him to obtain some rewards."

"Yeah ... And he plays his old trick on everyone everywhere?"

"How tragic." I held Xuejing in my arms. "Give him some time to adjust to his home country and he will have a bright future."

"Can they find someone else to do this?" Her tone changed a bit. "Are you the only person?"

"They need a man who knows Bin well to help Yuan Shi." I held one of her hands in my hand, fingers crossed together. "Unless someone could talk He Jingcheng in."

"Go find Yu. Is his your first pupil in the workshop?"

"He's more dogmatic than Yuan Shi. He won't work out anything. And he hardly knows Bin."

"How about Tong?"

Xuejing's proposal touched me. Tong was Bin's best student and the only alleged girlfriend before Yichen showed up. But ...

"She didn't show up for many years. I don't know where to find her."

"Well, it seems that I haven't seen him since Han left. In fact, we all thought Han would let her lead the workshop back then."

"Yeah! And if she still cherished her relationship with Han Bin, it's impossible that she would help me. Not helping Bin would do me good. And I'm still the one who she isn't in favor of even if she isn't happy with Bin. So there's no chance she would help me anyway."

The cellphone on the nightstand rang. Xuejing passed it to me without even a look. "Here. Your new favor called."

It seemed Yuan Shi took a deep breath first and then said, "Shall I knock now or give you half an hour to tidy yourselves up?"

"Well, we'll need more time if we want to do something else."

"Then I'll stop the nonsense." A strong knock came from the door. "Come on and answer the door!"

Up until I sent Xuejing out did Yuan Shi cast his eyes back from outside the window. "Three days had past. Nothing happened?"

I closed the door and asked, "Anything new from the bureau?"

The next day after Bin broke into the jail, the City Bureau determined that he was planning to escape and started the lockdown and manhunt in all provinces, setting roadblocks in every important junctions and roads out of Beijing.

"No. Officer Pan comes here every day? Are you sure you were doing your job?"

"When did I say I was working here?"

Yuan Shi was a little annoyed. "Am I booking you a honeymoon suit?"

"I was just here waiting for the day comes."

"Which day?"

"The day the rat comes out or the hunter disassembled the trap, just as what Bin did."

Yuan Shi looked at an old Peugeot. "The stake out here is too easy to see through. Han Bin won't like it. At least it should be disguised in a more skilled way."

"But I felt Bai has put so much effort this time." I walked near the window. "This is a secret post which could easily be seen through. And it's the only one with surveillance devices in the groups monitoring the six exits of the building. But I felt there are fewer people in the car than at the entrance."

"Yeah. Han Bin could tell that, too. But Liang Xiao is still alive, which means either he didn't waltzed himself in, or he has given up killing him. Or ..."

"At seven o'clock every morning, if it's sunny outside, there will be a weird reflect light from the left first window on the fourth floor of the dormitory building belonging to the chemical defense of the Joint Staff Department in the north."

Yuan Shi turned around to look at me, seemingly thinking of something.

"And after three o'clock in the afternoon, the same reflect light will show up from the northwest window on the ninth floor of Building 11 in Qiaoxin Community in the southeast."

"Two stake out sites?"

"I could only identify those two from where I am. But Bai loves manpower. I'd say similar sites won't be less than six."

"Are you sure? The division never tells me there are special monitoring sites here."

"Well, the secret has been kept tight. That means much." I opened the window slightly and lighted up a cigarette. "It seems that Bai doesn't care so much about Liang Xiao's life. It's clear that he plans to shoot everyone who walks out of that door."

There was mingled hope and fear on Yuan Shi's face. "Can I expect Han Bin didn't see through this?"

"Unfortunately, no." I took a deep smoke and almost choked myself. "Even if he doesn't have a perfect observation post like me, some cars pulling over regardless of traffic regulations, the security guards who suddenly like to look around, customers showing up at midnight in a 7-11, and Cao Fa, whose fetid breath can be detected two stops away ..."

"And the fact that Liang Xiao was intact until now can all prove that Han Bin doesn't bite the hook?"

"Yes. He's watching."

"Waiting for Bai pull out all the people?"

"Or Liang coming out for a walk."

"Then his waiting is about to over." Yuan Shi looked out of the window seriously. "Reliable information tells that Liang Xiao and his six staffs are about to go back to the United States."

My eyebrow tilted. "Oh? When?"

"At forty past one tomorrow afternoon. UA5455. A non-stop flight to Los Angeles."

"This is what Han Bin painted on the wall in Pang Xin's ward." Yuan Shi pulled out two big photos from his file case and passed me one after comparison.

I looked up and down, only seeing several black dots on a white wall. "Are you sure they are not dead bodies of a bunch of flies?"

Maybe my attitude was just as what he expected. He didn't mind my mock but looked down to find in his pile of documents. "I find the map of Haidian District as reference. After close comparison, the upper left dot coincides with the place where Song Dechuan was killed."

I didn't take it seriously, taking the photo with one hand and the map the other. "Oh my! How about the lower left."

"Chegongzhuang. That's where 'Wang Rui' lived."

I put the map closer. "The one in the middle is North Taiping Bridge?"

"That should be the location where Zhang Mingkun committed suicide. And the one in the middle left was where Haidian Hospital is. From Peng Kang to Pang Xin, he has killed five people there."

"Then the one in the lower right is ..."

"It's around the National Art Gallery. Gu Fan's residence. And the upper middle is the holding cell in the interrogation office."

"And the one below the holding cell?"

"Around Jianxiang Bridge. Maybe there are cases we're not aware of ... The key is this one." He pointed at a rather black one on the upper right. "That's Rigel."

"Vancouver[1]?"

"No." Yuan Shi stared at me, seemingly hoping to arouse my attention. "That's Zhongde Building."

I knew I was talking nonsense. "I thought that suggests Chen Juan who had moved to Canada."

"Apart from crime scenes we know, there are three dots we still don't know. I've been checking on it, but nothing was found yet. But his route ..." He turned the photo in my hand ninety degrees clockwise, "is Orion. Don't tell me you don't know what this is.

Yeah, I know.

"Even if it's like that, so what?" I tried to behave like an eager student

---

1 Rigel Analysis developed and used by the Environmental Criminology Research Inc. in Vancouver Canada is the most authoritative geographic crime profiling software in the world.

who is hungry about knowledge, but actually, I was preparing to tease about his next words. But to my surprise, Yuan Shi just shook his head, out of hopelessness, or regret or sadness.

"I've considered what you said and that makes sense. It may be some dots and Han Bin painted randomly on the wall, maybe to mislead us. What he drew doesn't matter at all. He just wanted to attract all the left policemen into a place with blocked signal." He slumped down in the chair, his right hand rubbing the button on his dark blue shirt. "When I worked out his puzzle, I laughed at myself. I thought of so many possibilities, and even compared it with the classical endgames in chess, trying to find something meaningful from it."

What he looked like made me sad.

"But it means nothing. Nothing at all." As if to add my sense of guilty, he continued, "I can't explain why he drew it like this, or whether he was committing crimes in carefully chosen locations on carefully chosen targets in order to fulfill this pattern. I don't know whether he wants to tell us that he is the hunter, or hunted by other hunters."

"Don't mind too much." I put down the photo, scanning the other materials on the table without a purpose, "I've known him for eight years. I don't know him better than you."

"He is the only criminal that I don't know where to start."

"So what?" I wanted to pat on his shoulder, but took my hand back halfway, "We still got a chance to take him."

"Liang Xiao is leaving tomorrow. Is this the chance he has been waiting for?"

"他在以少打多，就算没有警车沿途护卫，光靠梁枭自己的保镖，他成功的概率也还是很低。""在车底盘或特定位置安放炸弹呢？"

"Will he put a bomb at the bottom of the car or other specified places?"

"He may know how to do it, but he won't do it."

"Why?"

"That's not his principle of killing."

"The principle of assassin?"

I walked back and forth and sat down in the chair opposite Yuan Shi. "Do you know what the friends around frequently said to me after his crimes were exposed?"

"You said to me once. Something like he must have a reason."

"Something like that."

"I see. Placing a bomb will lead to a chance to hurt the innocent. He needs to do it in a reasonable way."

"Reasonable to everybody, including himself." I took out another cigarette and fiddled it between my fingers. "Bin don't want to be regarded as an ordinary killer."

"He is just fond of killing, isn't he?" Yuan Shi pushed the ashtray on the table to me, "No matter Chen Juan or Han Yichen, they are just excuses."

Fiddling with the cigarette, I felt my fingers getting cold.

"So he doesn't kill the innocent because that would make him look inferior. At least if he were to be caught one day, he doesn't want to be in the same group with Joseph Vacher or Peter Sutcliffe[1]. He must have killed more than that."

I crushed the cigarette in my hand, tobacco between my fingers absorbing my sweat.

"He told you in person?"

Peeling off the wrapper filter tip, I put the light yellow core near my nose. It smelled nothing special, but the tip of my nose seemed to be cold, too.

"Yes."

"That's good. At least I don't have to worry that he'll attack the policemen staking out downstairs." Yuan Shi took a cigarette from my cigarette case and then put it back. "But will it fool himself? I mean, he should have known which type of criminal he is, based on his knowledge in criminal research."

"You'll have to ask him if you have chance later." I picked up my phone on the nightstand, and Yuan Shi was puzzled for several seconds. "Don't tell me you know how to contact him."

"No, I don't." I dialed in a slow but firm way, without any hesitation. "But I have a clue about how he's going to get into Zhongde Building."

He jumped at once. "How?!"

I put the phone on speaker and put it on the table. Several dial tones passed but the call wasn't answered. I dialed again, and Yuan Shi was astonished seeing the number. "Are you mad?!"

This was picked up quickly. The other side of the phone said, "Hello?" Yuan Shi couldn't even breathe."

"Who's that? Speak!"

I lipped my mouth and suddenly didn't know where to start.

"You son of bitch!"

I heaved a sigh. "Boss ..."

"Is Yuan Shi with you?"

Yuan Shi looked at me and gradually calmed himself down. "Yes,

---

1 Joseph Vacher and Peter William Sutcliffe are famous serial killers in the history of France and the British respectively.

director. I'm with him." He should be smart enough to realize that Bai could place so many stakeout sites around the building. How could he not check out who was living in the hotel right opposite to Liang Xiao's office? I saw through his plan and he knew where I was. Only that Bin was probably aware of both.

"Want to come home? Then report your case with me to the City Bureau."

"I'm not working with Han Bin."

"Will you still be alive if you are? Come on and get back! Don't fucking stir around there!"

"I will as soon as possible. But ... well, please search the building. Although I don't know whether we would make it ..."

"Search the building? Did you see Han Bin coming in?"

"No. But there's a great chance he's already inside."

2

When we passed by the Peugeot, I saw Cao Fa was sitting on the front passenger, smoking, and looking at us two in a puzzle. Yuan Shi didn't like him either, but was also confused about Bai's decision.

"There are many people around here. Why does he choose us two to be the first group?"

"Because Liang Xiao is French and that Wales Company is an American company. Two embassies' pressure set at the same time, can he let the police rushing in without any consideration? If they can find Bin inside, that's good. If not, maybe the Haidian Bureau wouldn't exist."

"Haha! So you're the perdu?"

"I am a guilty man with a wanted poster within the system. It won't be worse than that. Now that I'm still here, I don't care, and clearly, Bai doesn't care either. Both happy."

"You don't care, that's alright. But why does he ask me to go in with you?"

"Err ... Maybe because you're from the City Bureau. Maybe Bai is thinking about dragging you in if something happens."

"Damm! I don't want to die for you."

"Don't be so harsh, honey. Do you bring your thing?"

"A pen in my jacket and a big dick down there. Are those enough?"

I started to wonder when Dr. Yuan turned to be such a rude guy and was in the mood of imagining his own ability in his sexual behavior.

Stepping into the hallway, Yuan Shi flashed his ID to the barely waking security guard. Actually I believed even if I showed him a member card of a hotpot restaurant, he wouldn't even care. We walked straightly to the elevator. There was only one of them working in the evening and it was on the first floor.

Stepping into the elevator, Yuan Shi asked me, "You didn't tell me how Han Bin came in."

"The most impossible way is often the most possible one. It's just like that I haven't thought I would be in the same elevator with a gay. Really, I'm much too terrified."

It must be difficult for Yuan Shi to talk with me since he had to filter away my mock and tease even assault, then started to think about my real point. But it only cost him a few seconds. "Do you think Han Bin will cooperate with that assassin Liang Xiao had found?"

"He is very good at cooperating with different people. I even believe he is capable of inviting Hoover and Al Capone[1] to play poker with him. Bin can always find the weakness of others and he knows how to use them."

"But that killer is going to kill him ..."

"That's because personal issues, which is his biggest weakness. He, similar to Bai, may not care about Liang Xiao's life. Liang Xiao is feeling awesome with his support from the company and his nationality of being a Frenchman. But in the end, he is nothing but a decoy."

"So that killer will sell Liang Xiao out?"

"The meaning behind Huang Feng's words indicates that they, the soldiers who have fight for the Communist Party of Vietnam, have some sort of complicated relationship within their group, an exclusive one. Something more intimate than being buddies, but not that much as stepping into the field of gays."

"Complicated." Yuan Shi was scratching his left cheek. "Do you want to tell me that Han Bin is going to find that killer and then persuade that killer to help him enter the building and kill Liang Xiao? And then he is at that man's disposal?"

"Except for the last part, which we don't know they will duel to the death or shake their hands, the others are almost like what you said."

The elevator arrived at 25th floor. Yuan Shi lowered down his voice. "Do you know this kind of assumption is groundless?"

"The surveillance to the building includes all entering and exiting of all

---

1 John Edgar Hoover (1895-1972) was an American law enforcement administrator who served as the first Director of the Federal Bureau of Investigation of the United States. He has been in the position for 37 years. Al Capone was the godfather of Chicago Mafia.

people and vehicles. But due to confidentiality requirements, and to avoid being complained, the division can't check vehicles of the Wales. Bin must have found that out. This is the most possible infiltration approach with the lowest risk, whose premise, however, is to have a mole. And then he'll find that it's possible to find one."

"And ..." I pointed at the glass door of the Wales Company.

Yuan Shi looked at the empty front desk vigilantly. "Nobody is here ... But he's got body guards ..."

"No. Look there! There! The lower left corner."

Up until I pointed out did Yuan Shi noticed the upper half of a shoe sticking out of the front desk. The bottom of the shoe was facing up and the angles of its lying on the ground suggested that there should be a leg behind it. He immediately stood up against the wall like a startled gecko. "This ... Oh my ..."

Couching down to sweep over the hallway, I took out my phone. "If that guy isn't have sex with the desk, I think we can call backup now."

The reaction of the boss was quick. The get-together and lockdown was completed in five minutes. I turned my cellphone into silence mode and said to Yuan Shi, "You go down to the first floor to meet them. I'll watch here."

Yuan Shi didn't move. But I can tell he was very nervous, or excited. "You want to go in, don't you?"

I pulled out the nightstick on my waist and stuck it back to the side. "Yes."

"You wanna try whether you can save Liang Xiao?"

I took a glance at him with my head tilted.

And Yuan Shi glanced back. "You can't be going to watch Han Bin killing him."

"I don't know Liang Xiao well. Even if it's quite possible that he is the one who planned and killed Han Juan, I have no right to judge him." My throat went dry, so was my sound. "It's true that He Jingcheng and I don't like Bin killing. But if there is someone who I could accept to be killed by Bin, the first three would be Hitler, Hideki Tojo and this son of Bitch."

Yuan Shi swallowed with tension. "Placing Liang Xiao with those two, are you complementing him?

"Nobody can dispose others' live."

"Then let him be killed. What's the hurry for?"

"I don't know."

"Well, it seems I have to die for you." He took a deep breath and unbuttoned one more of the buttons on his shirt. "I'll go with you."

325

I should think of nothing to go against him. I could only say, "Have you used your skills of Taekwondo in a real fight?"

"In the 17th competition held in California ..."

"Never mind. Come on,"

We has passed five bodies from the front desk to the door of Liang Xiao's office. All the body guards were stabbed to death. The wounds were all in key areas and made in delicate skills with little blood.

Yuan Shi lowered his voice. "The blood hasn't curdled. It wasn't long after they were killed. Han Bin ..."

"That doesn't look like him." I approached that seemingly wooden black door tightly along the wall. "They were all attacked from close range, and there's no trace of them fighting back. It was that inside mole who had killed him. ... I remembered that he is in favor of daggers."

I put my hand on the handle and pressed a little. The door wasn't locked. Seeing Yuan Shi in a worry, I was about to ask him whether he should go downstairs to meet the others, but didn't on a second thought. He wouldn't back off even for the sake of his face at such a point.

"Watch the back of the door." I pushed the door open and dashed into the room.

Night as it was, Liang Xiao's office was bright as usual in the light of lamps. I squinted through for a while and found out the figure sitting in the big leather armchair behind the desk was Liang Xiao. Half of his face was collapsed. One of his eyes couldn't even open, which made the other open one much more terrifying, empty and hollow. However, the wound that started from his chest and down into the edge of the table, which nearly cut him half, assured us that we didn't have to worry about his complaints in any form.

Behind the desk, two men were standing apart in front of the big window. They were not far from each other. The man on the left had his back to us, and the one on the right who was facing the door was Bin.

I didn't know it was horror or excitement, but I felt my body temperature lowered suddenly and my heart beating violently.

Bin was wearing a black hoodie suit, and a pair of sweat pants. Putting one of his hands on the windowsill, the other one by the corner of his mouth, he was simple, quiet, just like what he was like the first time I saw him. In a distance not close and not too far, I couldn't read his face. I didn't know the mood dominating him was calm or sadness.

He adjusted himself a little and said to the man on the left. "They've almost finished gathering. The police will be here any minute. Shall we stay here or find another place?"

Looked like I guessed right.

That man turned around, pulling the edge of his grey leather jacket with his right hand. He took a glance at Bin and then seemed a little upset of just finding of our presence. He looked extremely ordinary, without even an outstanding feature and was barely handsome. Compared with Bin, he was more outgoing, more extrovert. Bin was an observer, enjoying everything around him as enjoying dramas. But this man was more cynic, hating everything around him. He was always wrathful. I've noticed his murderous look, his eyes similar to Bin's in a great way — a vast darkness.

"Let it go, you both." I found my voice being fluctuated. "Liang Xiao is dead and you've fulfilled your wish. And you," I pointed at that man to take the chance for a breath, "Ruan Ba, the former member of Regiment 861, Vietnam People's Army. You've been surrounded."

They glanced at each other quickly, which was a tacit approval of my identification.

I squinted at Yuan Shi to say something to stall, but only saw the sweating taekwondo master shaking in a blank daze, whose eyes floating between the bodies, the alive and the floor under our feet.

Ruan Ba's mouth moved a bit, but didn't say anything. It seemed he didn't want to talk in front of Yuan Shi and me. He just waved at Bin and then rushed at me across the desk. I lifted my left hand to let him stop, my right hand reaching the weapon placed on my waist and shouting, "You! Stay there!"

Bin seemed to say something like "Leave them alone." By then, Ruan Ba was two meters away from me.

Maybe I was blinking or maybe not. But anyway, he was right in front of me the next second before I could pull my nightstick out. I stepped back in a hurry and Yuan Shi rushed out from behind my left with a shout, which I didn't know either was a procedure before his fight or simply for the sake of encouragement. He kicked out one leg after another, flexibly and coordinately, which was indeed handsome and swift.

His first kick, however, didn't reach the target and the second was warded off by Ruan Ba. I didn't see Ruan Ba's move, but Yuan Shi's leg was, against the inertia, forced to be pulled back halfway. When he lifted the other leg, which was raised too high, and tried to hack down from the above, Ruan Ba slipped close and raised his left arm high to ward off against Yuan Shi's leg, freezing him into a statue doing the splits in just an instant.

Surprised as I was, I didn't even realize I should come up to help. Being a fighter for so many years, this was the first time I have ever learned what's a skillful deflection. Ruan Ba warded off Yuan Shi with the normal force, but his hit on Yuan Shi's bottom was definitely forceful. Yuan Shi uttered a short shout and fell down straightly but was pulled back by Ruan Ba who dragged him on his wrist and leg and hit him right on the face in the sky.

Yuan Shi, Black Belt Phase II, on the ground for less than ten seconds, was technically knocked out.

Yuan Ba took one step back after he landed on the ground and got across Yuan Shi's body. Seeing him approaching my side, I swung the nightstick in my right hand to hit his head. Before I could put my arm down, my pit was hit by a fist, which moved upwards and gave my chin another one. Fortunately, I stepped back in advance or I would be finished faster than Yuan Shi.

The sofa stood on my way when I was falling down on the ground. While I was getting on my feet, I saw Bin kicked Ruan Bs's poples from the back and stepped on one of his leg. Bin used his arm to lock Ruan Ba's neck and flashed back as Ruan Ba swung back his fist with a sharp wind. In an instant, a livid dagger was in Ruan Ba's hand. Bin took several steps back, sneaking at Ruan Ba's supporting feet while he was dashing. As Ruan Ba tiled, Bin took a step forward and toppled him.

I darted forward and slipped down on my knees, the nightstick in my hand hitting right to Ruan Ba's face. Ruan Ba tried to ward off his distorted face with the hand holding the dagger but was kicked by Bin right on the wrist. The dagger flew out.

When I swung my night stick for the second time, what happened was out of my imagination.

Bin pounced to me all of a sudden. A kick fell right on my face. The world was suddenly dark in front of me and the nightstick flew out. I was then dragged by the hair aside. Bin pressed my chest with his knee, his silver pendant dangling on my face. He was breathing heavily. "I told you to leave this alone!"

Choked by my blood from somewhere I didn't know, I couldn't answer him but reached out to drag his necklace. Actually, I knew it wasn't strong enough to be used as a hang. Bin tried to control me by clenching my neck but was pounced down by Ruan Ba the next minute. The two of them rolled down and brawled together. Soon enough, Ruan Ba prevailed and pressed Bin down on the ground.

Supporting myself up, I saw a livid flash from the corn of my eye. I took the dagger Ruan Ba dropped, covering the reflect light of the blade with my fist and darted back.

Before I could approach him, Ruan Ba turned back without any hint, dashed to me and kicked right on my focile. I knelt down out of pain. He pressed my head to his knee. I didn't have any choice but to take a risk to bump into him, stabbing him with the dagger in my hand.

But I missed because Bin snatched my wrist; and I wasn't hit by Ruan Ba's knee either because it hit Bin's back. He got in between us, put his leg between Ruan Ba's two legs and elbowed him down, and then gave me an elbow on my left cheek, along with which my teeth flew out. Fuck! Do you really? I thought in great anger. The pain irritated me. I dragged him close with my right hand. Bin was fast enough to avoid my stab and I was kicked by Ruan Ba from the back.

As Bin fell on me, I strangled him with my left arm, pressed him close and crouched on him. Raising my dagger high — maybe I've paused a little, or maybe not — I jabbed straightly at his shoulder.

However, what happened was again out of my imagination.

Ruan Ba grasped the falling blade. His right hand was cut open at once, blood splashing out like the firework blooming in the sky.

Huang Feng was right. Whatever between them was their own business. I was the one who got into them and wasn't welcomed.

On my astonishment, Ruan Ba put one of his hands on my shoulder and gave me a pull. I could only felt a sudden pain on my right shoulder, my right arm dangling down.

Dislocation of my right arm! Shit!

Before I could make any reaction, Ruan Ba released the blade. Holding my wrist, he pushed the blade to my neck from bottom to top. Damn it! Should I be killed by my own dagger? What a disgracing way to say goodbye to the world!

Bin's right hand was holding my right wrist.

Since I was crouching on him, he was difficult to move, his push not powerful enough to change the direction of the knife. But at least he slowed down the steps of the God of Death, which bought me an instant to change my fate. His left fist beating on the right ribs that Ruan Ba couldn't protect, he pushed the blade back as Ruan Ba failed to continue his move. The blade immersed into the chest of his old comrade-in-arms.

Three hands intertwined with each other together. At last, the room went into quite.

Ruan Ba knelt down by my side, his head lowering down as if to look at the fatal attack he received from his comrade. A forgiving smile crept onto the corner of his mouth, and some vague sounds came out from his deep throat. Gradually, the light in his black eyes dissipated.

Just at that moment, someone, I didn't know it was Bin or Ruan Ba, hit me on the right of my head. I felt my body became lighter and lighter.

Looking down, I saw Bin's face backing out of my sight, more and more blurred, slowly and gradually fading into a complete haze.

I was standing by the river, and Bin was standing on the opposite bank.

Under the bridge was the place where Fan Jiajia used to lie on. Only that the water wasn't frozen now. It was breezing that there were ripples on the surface.

I called Bin loudly, but he didn't respond, his eyes gazing on the water.

Enormous bodies were floating along the river.

I saw Chi Shanshan, Fang Wnlin, Peng Kang, and Song Dechua ... I saw Pang Xin smiling at me, holding a jar of honey at hand. I saw Jiang Lan holding the sim card of a suspect as if holding some treasure. I saw Ruan Xunsong rubbing the fifty yuan with his fingers, full of satisfaction. I saw my grandparents lying in the armchair, their hands holding together. I say my father standing outside the maternity ward, his fists clenched tightly with excitement ... There was no blood, no wound, no disease, and no pain. They were alive and happy.

But I knew they were dead.

They were dead and would never come back.

Bin passed me a cup of warm grapefruit tea. I took the cup but turned to find he was still standing on the opposite bank as if he had never left the river. The fog came out of nowhere as I didn't pay attention. It compassed me, touching me gently like a lover's hand.

I called him again.

He finally looked up at me. His gaze drove away the heavy fog on the river, and then landed on the water like a raindrop.

Xuejing's voice came out by my ear, gently and softly. "Don't smoke."

A cigarette was in my left hand and a silver lighter in my right, on which characters of NAGA were carved and a twisting serpent that was making every effort to break through the block of the metal place but failed. I heaved a sigh and took a smoke, but couldn't help coughing heavily.

"What's wrong? Is he choked?"

"He can't breathe!"

"Cut the trachea open! Where's the ventilator? Get him a ventilator!"

I saw Chen Juan.

She stood up from the water and smiled at Bin's direction.

A bright smile appeared on Bin's face. He walked quickly into the river.

Yichen was begging me, holding my clothes with red eyes. "Please! Please save him! Please!"

Xuejing was leaning on my shoulder. "Don't smoke!"

Numerous pouches were landing on me. I tried to rush of while defending them. But more people were blocking my way. I roared, crimson tears falling from my eyes.

Bin disappeared from the opposite bank.

"His leg!"

"He's going into shock!"

"Control him! Someone go press him!"

"The blood pressure is only forty!"

"Got it! Something's inside! Get a pair of tweezers!"

When I sat up with Xuejing's help, I knew without looking into the mirror that I was like a wrapped mummy. She was reading me my case. My right shoulder was dislocated and my right pinky was broken. The right sphenoid bone was slightly fractured and the left meniscus was severely damaged. I had a broken nose and lost four teeth on my left side, one of which went into my windpipe and nearly killed me. On top of that, three of his teeth came loose and a small piece of my tongue was bitten off by myself. And there were also cervical ligament injury, mild cervical spine injury, and three subcutaneous soft tissue injury together with numerous cuts and bruises. And then, of course, the concussion that kept me unconscious for nearly twenty-four hours must be included.

Well, I really needed to rest this time.

"Is Yuan Shi alive?"

"A little concussion I heard, and something like inguinal ligament hurt. But it's nothing. He seemed to be out of hospital now."

Noticing that the unhurt leg of mine was cuffed, I uttered a bitter smile and gazed at Xuejing for a while. Her lips were dry, and her hair was dirty. Guilty as I felt, I clenched her hand.

She put the other hand on my hand and heaved a sigh.

"You may not want to ask, but they didn't catch Han Bin. The guys from the division was there minutes after you called, but they haven't found him until now."

"Yeah, I know." I tried to move my right arm but only felt a great pain. I could do nothing but abandon this effort. "He's in the river."

It was said that Bai was furious, the reason of which was clear. When the backup arrived at the crime scene on 25th floor, what they saw was two idiots who were passed out and Liang Xiao who was probably meeting with God with one eye open. And then the whole Zhongde Building was controlled and all roads within two kilometer radius were blocked. The building was searched, vehicles checked and the entire block rummaged. But nothing was found.

And more unexpectedly, Bin wasn't breaking out alone. He took Ruan Ba's body with him.

At daybreak, a team scrutinized the splendid neon light box reading "Wales Medical Device Research Group" under the big brand reading "Zhongde Building" on the edge of the rooftop. They found traces of blood and people hiding there. Going through the tunnel of imagination, I almost could see Bin, hiding in the shade of those splendid lights in the chilly wind in deep autumn, holding the body in his arms and sensing it turning colder and colder in the chilly wind in deep autumn.

Bin has once hidden in midair. But how he got away with his comrade remained to be a mystery.

I was kind of glad that he wasn't found then; otherwise for him, I believe, being arrested or death, it was never a choice. I've heard that after Bai knew it, he was so angry that he said that those policemen who were in charge of searching would rather jump down from the roof.

Actually the stakes were high. As long as he couldn't make it, the cost would be high too. What's more, he, always cautious, was forced to rely on luck this time. If the shelf of the light box couldn't support the weight of two grown men, if anyone of the policemen was cautious enough to look down, if Ruan Ba's wound wasn't wrapped good enough that the blood fell down on the nose of one of the policemen down below ... He could have escaped alone, at least with a higher possibility. But he must take Ruan Ba with him, and pushed he himself to the edge of death.

I couldn't help to wonder how would someone like Bin sell his comrade out?

He didn't abandon anyone by his side, no matter Chen Juan or Han Yichen, Huang Feng or Ruan Ba.

No matter the alive people, or the dead soul.

Two days later, the division sent a specialist to the hospital to take a record. Bai also came to visit me, which moved me a lot. After I've answered the routine questions, I was told that the decision on my punishment would be announced after it was discussed by the City Bureau. Learning that I wouldn't be sent to the prison, I cared nothing else. I asked Bai to stay for a while. I wanted to talk with him alone.

To my surprise, Bai didn't yell at me when there were only two of us in the ward. He even told me that he wanted to reassign me to a team in Social Corps that wasn't in popular demand and recommended me to find some local police stations that wasn't too busy if I didn't want to stay in the bureau.

I was much too grateful. "Boss, there's a favor I need to ask from you."

Bai knocked at the cuff locked on my wrist with one of his fingers as thick as a cigar. "You look well in this one."

"Err... It's not that." I tried to grin but failed as my missing teeth prevented me. "Do you still remember that Shi Zhan?"

"What?"

I knew he did. "That kidnapping case of Cai Ying ... You see, I've promised Shi Zhan, who was in prison in Chadian now, that I'll let him know where Cai Ying and her child buried. Well, I know you're too busy to deal with things like this. But you see that I wouldn't be able to get out of hospital in a short time, so ...

"Do you fucking think you are not close enough with those criminals?" Bai's reaction wasn't a surprise to me. "Have you got any plans about the police station you want to be after this? I can pull some strings for you on that. Now, do stay put."

Seeing Bai wanted to leave, I was anxious. "No, boss! I have something more to report to you!"

Bai didn't even look back.

"It's about the call Han Bin had once made to Zhang Mingkun ..."

Bai stopped at the door and glanced back at me. It was no secret that a call from Bin had forced Zhang Mingkun to jump from the building. It was only that they didn't meet each other when the crime happened, and we couldn't know what they were talking about at that time so it was impossible to charge him even as the crime of insult. Zhang Mingkun's death was considered as a suicide in the end.

But Bai finally turned back, pointing me with his chin to tell me to go on.

"Bin at least made two phone calls that night. One was to find someone to get the phone number of Zhang Mingkun's residence, and the second turned him into Peter Pan." I made a slight move on the bed, within very limited range. "Then I began to wonder how he get the phone number because it didn't show up in any of the case files.

Bai stared at me, stone-faced and speechless.

"I checked Bin's recent calls the next day. The first call he made was to our division, and then the called was switched to one specific person. I didn't know who." I paused on purpose to check Bai's reaction, but there was none. Bai was still expressionless. "But what was coincident was that the record showed someone had checked all information about Fan Jiajia at that time in our division. The log in information showed that the log in ID was BYS. Who you know whose ID it is?"

I sat up and lowered my voice. "Director Bai Yinshang."

Bai stared at me motionless for a while, making me worried whether he could lase out from his eyes.

"What's your point of all these?"

"My point is that, actually, every one of us is doing something we think is right. It's nothing as long as it doesn't hurt anybody. So my favor, no, Shi Zhan's favor ... well, please do him this favor."

"Don't think I don't know what you want to do!"

"I only want to do something I think is right."

Bai took a step toward me, angrily. I couldn't move, so I have to give him an unflinching look.

After half a minute, he had no other choice but to calm down. "Don't be too hard on our own men."

"I know, boss."

"Are you sure you've really thought it through?"

"It's the best thing I've ever done to work for you since I joined the police system." I reached out my right hand, slowly. "Thank you so much for your help and support these years."

Bai's face showed he was moved a little bit. He pressed my hand on my chest and heaved a sigh. "You take care of yourself."

"Then Shi Zhan ..."

"I know." After these two words, he walked out of the ward and didn't looked back.

On a morning of the next week, Yuan Shi came to pay me a visit. I was so shocked about where he was hit could disable him that I hurried to put on a face of sympathy and comfort.

"Nothing about that!" It was clear Yuan Shi's aware of what I was thinking about. The bruises on his face was almost gone, only a small scar left on the corner of one eye. "It's just a little malposition of my hipbone."

"Oh my! I was so worried that you've been changed to the other gender buy that punch!"

"Are you the right person to mock at me?"

"Yeah, since you're here to visit me."

"Come on! That punch made me pee blood for a whole week!"

"Look at you! Such a panic! Don't worry. You'll be used to it when you see that coming once a month ..."

We've been beating the breeze and didn't hit the point until Xuejing went to get us some lunch.

The whole city was searching for Bin ever since he escaped like a legend. The searching was delicately done. Even all members of the criminal research workshop were all under monitor. Both of us agreed that Bin wouldn't try to escape at such a sensitive time. He needed some rest and had to figure out how to deal with the dead body of his comrade.

Of course, Bin didn't show up and neither did Yichen.

Several days ago, Huang Fang showed up in his residence in Sidao, Guangxi, alone. The policeman in charge of staking him out came to question him and he just play dumb.

"He would escape to the south, Cambodia and Vietnam."

Yuan Shi sat by the bed and put his chin on the top of his walking stick, nodding. "Yeah. The selva, leeches, fruits, dysentery and personal arms ... What a perfect comfort zone." He continued after thinking for a while, "He will disappear forever if he has crossed the borders."

"No." I took a glance at the door lying on the bed, from where I could see the guarding policemen standing at the door whose number was reduced from two to one after Bai's visit last week.

Yuan Shi was generous. "I'm willing to offer a reward! A reward for whoever can get me him."

"Prepare the money, then. I'll go."

The third week was hard.

The message of me getting into the hospital was spread out. He Jingcheng, Yang, Beitong, Cao Fa, Liu Qiang and all members of the workshop who didn't even speak to me before this, and my classmates and colleagues from the division and the branch bureau, even the City Bureau, all came to visit me. Well, I was well aware that some of them were coming to see me, and others were coming to see whether they could get some information about Bin from me. And most of them were coming out of both reasons above.

Later on, there were also some young policemen I didn't know. Some were coming to admire me as an idol, and there were also some people who gathered at the door and gossiped about what I've done. He Jingcheng told me that I was a celebrity inside the system. At first I couldn't take it, but then I felt well relieved. I was the perfect negative example as I was hunted inside the system due to suspected conspiracy with a serial killer and received complaints from different embassies because of breaking into an international enterprise. I beat a citizen called Yang Yanpeng right before the armed police first, and then beat the victim, Gu Fan, right in front of my colleagues. And then I beat some armed policemen who I didn't know with the suspect. I was really typical.

My story was exaggerated and put on the internet by some busybody who knew a little of something about this. There were even two versions of it: "The best undercover broke in to a jail", and "The jail-breaking man closely connected with the suspect". But it didn't last long. The next day, the story of mine was replaced by things more attractive like "A 19-year-old mistress showing off half naked" and "Beautiful master finding a boyfriend".

In the rest of my time apart from dealing with these visitors, I've been persuading Xuejing.

She probably have known what I was thinking long before I talked to her since she didn't say anything after hearing my words. Xuejing was too smart. She knew that the difference between people in understanding the same issue was unable to coordinate. So she just take it. She had a theory: Half of what men do is for women, and the other half is inexplicably insane. When I was that man, she didn't care what I do as long as I didn't do it for women besides her and my mother. And as for the second half, well, it was normal for me to do something ridiculous. The point was whether I could be stopped in the right time.

But now, she knew she couldn't stop me.

When women is thinking, terrible things happens. It's common for them to put the most ridiculous method into practice after the brainstorming. It's lucky that I knew Xuejing wasn't going to chop off my feet, or added a dose that would put an elephant to sleep into my dinner. Nevertheless, I still felt flustered when I saw her meditating silently this week.

On the evening of Saturday night, she finally asked me, "Cheng, will you die?"

"Of course." I didn't have a lot of merits, but not considering my wife as a child or idiot was one of them. And of course, switching to another subject was my next merit. "No one can live forever."

"Being attached for no reason, and then hurt by Han, and then was hunted within the system and now get in hospital." She said, fiddling with her hair, "I know I married with a brave man. You're not afraid of the authority, nor the mobster, Han, or death. I couldn't think of anything and intimidate you, Cheng. You are afraid of nothing. But what you've done, what you have done was to let the person who cared about you most live in worry and fear."

I reached out my hand and touched her hair. And then, I put my hand on her shoulder. "Honey, believe it or not, I've made up my mind when I entered Zhongde Building. Whether the hunt was successful or not, I won't be a part of it. Because I think if Bin was really insistent about Liang Xiao's death, he must have been killing out of revenge. Maybe he will stop killing when these people are all dead. Or maybe he will hide in a small temple somewhere and do nothing evil when that day comes. So whether he is to be caught in the future has nothing to do with me. Just like He Jingcheng, I just don't want him to kill anymore. As long as he stops killing, we'll let him go. There are so many policemen in this world, we are not the only ones who are responsible in protecting justice."

"But he won't stop, right?"

"Yeah, he won't"

"Why are you so sure?"

"Because I finally know the reason he kills, his motive as what we used to speak of in the workshop." I took the hands of my lover, tearing welling up in my eyes. "And I was the one more likely to stop him."

"Is he a killer or an avenger? Why does he kill?"

The forth week was good. I could leave the bed and stand on my feet after the stitches were taken out and splints removed. All was well expect for some missing teeth. Yuan Shi showed up as he promised me last time and brought what I asked for. One of the good things about having a backup like him was that I didn't have to worry about money or fashion style. Holding a LV razor in my hand, I start to think if I could ask him to change my phone into a blackberry one ...

"Hey! I'm asking you!"

"What?"

"I was asking you why Han Bin has to kill. Do you know his motive?" Yuan Shi didn't need to depend on a walking stick to walk, but he couldn't stand long. He took off his light blue woolen suit and put it on the back of the chair, tidying up the legs of his trousers, and then sat down, as if there would be some bacteria crawling onto him and continued to hurt his miserable wound which had already been cured.

"We've talked about that hundreds of times, OK?" I pulled out some CK underwear and put in the changing clothes of mine that Xuejing prepared for me.

"Hey! Those are new!"

"Yours are too small for me. And ... can you stop being nauseous?"

The sunscreen cream and Ray-Ban sunglasses were tossed out by me, relentlessly.

He was clearly unhappy with my choice. "You'd better call backup the minute you have visual on him, or it's just a waste of time."

"Don't worry. I'll mange."

"I was confident like you until I have to depend on a walking stick."

I laughed. "We are different. You see, if Bin wants to kill me, I would have been died hundreds of times."

"Yeah, yeah, yeah. I forgot you were gay staying together."

"What?"

"Or actually you were brother-in-laws with different father or mother, or you were the descendant of some aliens who deliver you guys with some of the wormholes. Anyway, anytime he sees you, he'll beat you to shit, but he won't kill you. Is that right?" He even tilted one of his eyebrows dramatically, which could drive out anyone's impulse of beating him to shit.

As I was zipping my bag, I said, "Yuan Shi ..."

"What?"

"He won't kill you either."

"Yep! Because that's not his logic."

"The so-called logic was just things outside. We didn't know the things inside. What's his motive?"

"Wait a minute." Yuan Shi put two of his fingers on the tip of his nose. "If he won't kill without any reason, then it doesn't matter who's after him, right? He doesn't have any reasons for killing them. In fact, he didn't kill any of the policemen till now!"

I nodded, glancing at the dozing policeman outside — a young lad who has newly graduated from the police academy.

Yuan Shi crossed his legs carefully without touching anything around him. "But you insist."

"Frankly speaking, I want it to be me.

He licked his lip and asked after a second thought. "The old question, his motive. What's his motive?"

"He wants to die."

Yuan Shi held his breath, and after a while, he suddenly took a deep breath like someone dived out of the water. "He ... Well, when Chen Juan left him in 1990, he did commit suicide. But didn't he give up the plan later?"

"Maybe for a while, or maybe he forced himself to accept the fact that he couldn't be together with the only woman he loves."

"But he cannot accept his lover's death."

"I don't think he'll accept that." I said coldly.

"But he can't choose to die at that time since he has to take care of the only daughter of Chen Juan." Yuan Shi stared at me as if he wanted to find some answers on my face. "But he couldn't stop him from the idea of committing suicide, so he ... Christ! Does he kill to feel death?"

Xuejing's eyes full of tears appeared in my mind. I looked at her, and then looked at Yuan Shi. I felt I couldn't be more confirmed. "From the very beginning, Bin is finding some substitute for his own death."

"What can be a substitute for death?"

"Another death."

"So he won't stop killing." Yuan Shi put down his crossed leg and leaned by the bed. "Unless ... you're not going to take him back."

I nodded, trying my best to give him a forced smile and dreamed that it would cover what I was thinking. "I hope I can help him."

The night nurse came in to change my bag for the first time around nine o'clock. After she left, I called the plainclothes standing outside in. Every time I wanted to use the bathroom, they should be the one who took off my cuffs and accompany me there and back.

"Yes, Mr. Zhao." That was a boy, wearing a light green sports jacket and light blue jeans. His neat hairstyle and gloss on his face told me that he was a young lad in his right years. I couldn't help to heave a high. I was looking at myself decades ago.

"Excuse me, I want to ..." As I was saying, I pointed to the direction of the bathroom outside the door.

"No problem!" He took off my cuffs quickly and hang the bag on the mobile shelf, so quick as if he was afraid of being blamed by some rigid instructor. "Take it easy, sir. I'll get the shelf. Mrs. Zhao didn't come today? Is she on duty?"

I put the quilt aside and sit by the bed, listening attentively of what's happening outside. At the same time, I pulled off the needle and stretched myself lazily. A month of lying in bed would kill me for bedsore.

It seemed that the young boy didn't notice me pulling off the needle. "Oh, your ... I'll go get a doctor."

I grabbed his right wrist with my left hand. "Don't worry, buddy. Sit down, please."

He didn't struggle, but seemed to sense some danger.

I said with a comforting tone, eyes squinted, "I said, sit down."

He sat down slow uneasily, the right hand which was in my control raised high on purpose, afraid of me using some legendary witchcraft in the novels and turned him into some sitting duck.

I stood on my feet and put on the slippers. Leaning on the bed, I let his wrist go.

"What's your name, buddy?"

"Jin Yonggang." He didn't dare to look up at me. He could only stare at my needle hole which still got blood oozing from it. And then he added politely, "Just call me Jin, please."

"Jin, do you know who I am?" I pulled out a piece of napkin from the box on the nightstand and cleaned the blood on my hand, and ripped off the bandage.

He was about to answer, and then paused. After a second thought, he got what I meant and gave me the same answer. "Yes, I do."

"That's good." I pressed his shoulder with my left hand, and leaned forward to take out the cuff from the leather sheath tied around his waist. He flinched a bit, but I pressed him hard, whispering, "Don't move, buddy. I don't want to hurt you."

I cuffed him to the bedside and reached out my hand, "Keys, the transceiver and your cellphone."

To my surprise, he was very cooperative. Like a child who's got his hidden snacks found, he gave me everything I asked.

I put those three on the windowsill that he couldn't get, closed the door and took out the bag Yuan Shi had prepared. As I was packing, he couldn't even look up at me nor asked anything. I walked back to the bedside when I finished packing and asked him, "I've never seen you before. How long have you been in the division?"

He could finally peep me for several times, and looked away every time we had an eye contact. "No, no more than a month."

"It's a tough job, police." I patted on his shoulder and pointed to a red button on the wall. "Press this and the nurse will come. Of course you can go get the keys dragging the bed, but I hope you can make your choice after an hour, if that's possible."

"Mr. Zhao, you ..."

"I'm going after Han Bin. And tell the division when they come to find you that I'll report what I find if I really find something. Oh, and tell the bosses that there's no need for them to consider how do deal with me. I don't plan to wear this uniform after I come back." I patted him to tell him look up, and then pretended to cut my throat with my hand. "See? Here on the position where the carotid artery is, pinch some bruises with your fingernails and tell them it's me who strangled you from behind. That will save your ass."

He looked at me attentively, not my hand, but me. I looked at the Cartier watch that Yuan Shi offered and realized that even though the division wouldn't spare no effort to chase me down, I didn't have much time. I had a plane to catch.

As I was walking out, Jing Yonggang called me, "Mr. Zhao!"

I turned around and looked at him with my head tilted.

"What?"

"I thought ... I will report truthfully. I am ... I am not a lair. But ... I will do that an hour later." His embarrassment almost make me guilty. "You ... you keep safe. Please keep safe. Oh my, how, how could I ..."

In that instant, I didn't know I should say something polite or just comfort or encourage him. The passion and zeal of a young man almost burned me.

Son, this is a career that has nothing to do with safety.

Nothing.

3

Sidao town didn't leave me with a good impression from the very beginning. It was raining heavily when I last came here, and it was still raining this time, only not that heavy. The drizzle accompanied me when I set foot on that only asphalt road and as I stepped forward, the rain became frost and then turned into snow flurries.

Yuan Shi probably needed to launch a satellite to make a phone call to such an isolated barren mountain. When I heaved my phone to answer his call, I was even afraid of my evil past would get me struck by the lightning. My escape this time didn't cause a sensation this time. I assumed that the bosses were used to this and didn't want to bother themselves with my case. There was only a wanted poster within the system, even without the authorization of coercive measures. Of course, this was another way of telling me that there wouldn't be any punishment inside the system because this would be the end of my police career.

The latest news from Yuan Shi: Han Yichen had left the country.

No more than 24 hours ago, a model like nun took her preaching tour group to leave the country from Dongxing, Guangxi. After checking the surveillance footage, Han Yichen was found in the group. And Yuan Shi was furious about why she wasn't listed as wanted after she broke out of prison.

The Ministry of Public Security was quite embarrassed on the case of Han Yichen. Due to over custody without enough evidence and official charges, the big bosses wished everyone related to this case remained silent, or the administrative litigation and state compensation involved was well enough for the online media to throw a party.

I wasn't planning on chasing that clue, or I would be at Yunnan to wait for her. As the only child of Chen Juan, Yichen lived a miserable childhood. Giving her hard time would only let me despise myself, let alone Bin would chase after me to the end of the world and pinned my on the cross upside down.

And I was sure that on the other side of the boundary river, there must be a lone wolf who was good at shrugging to back him up. If I must go there, it was quite possible that Shitian would lead his international team and rush into Guangxi to cut me into pieces.

So in this way, it was almost impossible for Bin to show up there. I've check the border map, there were too many towns on the long and twisting border line. Finding a location and heading to the south, he could be out of the country after a couple of miles of mountain roads, even easier than a tour trip. Bin was not so stupid as to break off the border alone.

I met Huang Feng again in his own yard. He was working in his jasmine garden. Hearing the sound of me waking in, he didn't even lift his head.

"It's not a place that snows often here. As far as I could remember, there was one in 1998, and another in 2000, and then 2002, and then the January two years ago. Snow every two or three years, well, how lucky you are."

Huang Feng's yard was pretty much like that body garden of Pang Xin's. Actually, most of the privately-built lose-rises were pretty much alike, with a yard in which some flowers and vegetables were grown there, only the source of the fertilizer were a little bit different.

I wasn't blind, so I couldn't tell why Huang Fang could tell I was here. But at least I knew it wasn't something I should be perplexed with. Walking close to the garden, I smelled a slight aroma of jasmine, and felt the warmth that came from the earth. Huang Feng was wearing a short-sleeve army green shirt and a pair of dark green trousers. The empty leg was tied up, and a khaki plastic slipper was on his right foot. There was some soil between his toes. I stood behind him, slightly aside, and put all my attention onto his big back muscle that even made the shirt tight.

"Has Bin ever came?"

Huang Feng turned back slightly, in an angle so precise that I thought he had some mystery power to help him. But he didn't say anything. He just utter some faint sneer and went back to his work.

"And he must have told you that I'll go after him. Any message for me?"

"Well, you're just reckless." He finally put down the tools in his hand, reached a white mug beside his foot, and gulped down for several times, white smoke coming out of his mouth. I tried my best to sniff. It was not water.

He took out a cigarette out of his pocket, tidied it up a bit by his mouth and lighted it up.

"Smoke less. This will kill you sooner or later." As I was sayting, I actually would like to have one for my own.

"Are you more hurry seek your death than I am?"

"I looked into the mirror every day and saw a man could live forever." I took a step forward on purpose, "Bin won't kill me. The man who is capable of killing me is either died or running away. Huang Feng, do you think you can succeed considering your condition?"

Huang Feng clearly puzzled a bit, and then became furious. He yelled at me, "Are you insane? Your idiot!"

"You don't believe me?" I put my backpack down on the ground and took half a step back. Standing aside, I said coldly, "Shall we try?"

Huang Feng supported himself up with his hand. His movement was swift. With the support of the walking sticks, he leaned a little forward. I can see the rubber head of the walking stick stabbing into the mud deeply.

I pulled out the nightstick and tossed it onto the backpack. "I will fight you bare hands. Can't let others say I'm bullying you. Don't worry. I'll keep you alive."

"There's no need." The muscle around his eyes were twitching. He changed his barycenter while talking with me. "My wife is able to handle the kids."

I didn't mind fighting with him, but still wanted to verify before he started his attack. "Come on! If you died, who would be here to guard the tomb?"

His tendency to attack paused a bit, but was still in the mood. "What?"

"You came to a place thousands of miles away from your home town and even have a family. Is this what you're busy with?" I pointed at his garden — of course, he couldn't see it, but I would take that he could — "Well, it's funny that people like to bury dead bodies in their backyards right? Do you feel weird about this?"

Huang Feng turned to where I pointed, and seemed to get my point halfway. He laughed, "Do you think he ..."

"She, maybe more precise." I cut in his words and his chuckle. "The tomb of Chen Juan was here. You have been living here for such a long time. Your task is to find, deliver, bury and guard her body."

343

His mouth opened a bit and then closed. His body was still in the mood of fighting, but the muscle on his face was relaxed. Snowflakes fell on him, and smelt into water the next second, disappearing into nowhere. I even believed that if they had ever had the chance to choose their own fate, they would rather bypass him.

The missing body of Chen Juan was initially a trivial missing piece of the puzzle, not important at all. But it was to Bin what the shroud of Jesus was to Vatican. When I found out everyone was helping Bin, it suddenly occurred to me that for a limp and blind man who would sacrifice his life to Bin, this may be the best task, let alone he was quite familiar with the area.

"But it didn't occur to me that you really put all your life to this in order to repay him. You earn my respect." I lowered myself, all junctures of my body being sore and aching. "Come on. Be practical. Ruan Ba and Yao Jiang couldn't take my life with joint hands. Do you think you'll have the chance?"

If you can beat me down, this will be the end of my chasing trip. Or it will encourage me to fight with Bin the next time without thinking about letting him go.

Anyway, I really wanted to have a fight.

But he didn't took another step forward. I didn't see disappointment and sadness appearing on his face until he sat down. He moved a little, rubbing the edge of his injured limb, but his words were still tough.

"I'll let you go."

"Where's Bin?"

He smiled like a bad boy. Well, I still felt he was much more normal when he didn't smile. "You won't catch him."

"Catch him or not, I want to find him. Anyway, I have to find him."

"I don't know where he is."

I took a second thought and asked, "Does that mean that he didn't tell you anything because he knew that I will come here to ask you, or forced you to tell me something? That's ... not very possible. You won't take that. Oh, I know. He was afraid of you would be tricked to tell me something, so he didn't tell you anything, did he?"

Huang Feng frowned. This was probably very close to his limit of intellection. "Do you think ..."

"I also think he must have been persuading you not to fight with me. And he's telling you that's because he's afraid of you hurting me."

Huang Feng was silent. The snowflakes falling down made me tremble with cold. But I still said coldly, "Yes, you think you're his friend. You are grateful. You're helping him. But you're also an idiot! You didn't even know what he was doing. You don't know him, and you cannot understand why he did this. You didn't even try to justify his actions. You think that all you can do is to help him or to remain silent before the police. But you're wrong. Bin trusts you, just because you're an idiot who doesn't even know how to think. You don't ask for reasons, and even don't asked for whether it's right or wrong. You call your blind loyalty friendship. But you know what, what's between you and him is never friendship, or help between friends. It's just he giving orders and you obeying them. You're not friends. You're captains and soldiers!"

Huang Feng was astonished, and that made his gesture stiff, and his square chin becoming more and more rigid. "If you trust someone, you're not going to ask him why."

"Do you know how long Bin had asked him the same question? I've been always asking myself, too. He couldn't get an answer, so he kills. But pathetically, killing cannot provide him with an answer."

"He knows what he was doing from the very beginning. You don't have to ..."

"Is he? I doubt it. His answer to himself just provides him with a ridiculous logic: He wants to be with Chen Juan, but he can't. So he uses other people's death to feel what death is like. If you ask me, that's fucking insane!"

"Will you remain calm if your wife were to be killed?"

"I don't know ..." I swung one of my arms violently.

Why a man in want of a grandson so much would bully his daughter-in-law so much? Why would a bullied women would kill her own child? Why would a men fell in love would sacrifice himself voluntarily? Why a young kid who didn't know anything apart from surviving would tell such a big lie and a husband who was ready to welcome a new life would discard his late wife? Marginalized people without an identity were frantically taking revenge on society. A yard of bodies couldn't stop a driver from bullying right on the street. The murder weapon could be traded with human lives. ... All of us thought we were doing the right thing. Well, we did have a natural gift to justify everything.

"I don't know. But Bin's killing regardless of seeking revenge of following his ridiculous logic. How many lives would he like to take to compensate Chen Juan? Because he wants to seek revenge, because he wants to find a substitute for death, because the victim deserves to die ... Will a murderer earn other's sympathy just because a random excuse? Everyone understands him and supports him. Even a nun could betray her God in order to cover for him. You are all fooled, including Bin himself. Chen Juan's dead. She won't come back even he kills hundreds or thousands of people. She's dead, buried under our feet. Every day, numerous people die. And the only thing for the ones left to do is to look forward and keep moving on. I believe no one could replace her in his heart. Likewise, no one could be that substitute. If he couldn't look forward, he might as well choose to die!"

Huang Feng asked after a long silence. "Do you want to kill him?"

"I have to take him back because I'm a policeman. And I can also help him since we are friends. Of course, I can kill him, which is the dream he has been dreaming of. Anyway, I would have my own reason for the path I choose."

"I couldn't see the difference of killing me and taking him back."

"He won't be sentenced death for sure if he turns himself in or is arrested." I have just thought that out. "Binson's secret files are too important. Once Bin was taken, the State Security will surely take the case."

Huang Feng grinned at me. "Aha! Actually you don't even know why you want to find him."

"I do. Where is he?"

"Indeed, he doesn't tell me. Try to find that kid. He won't be too far away from her."

"Bin must know what I thought, so he couldn't be with Yichen before he leaves the country. Save your plan on borrowing knifes. I know what Shitian is capable of around here. As long as I'm not after Yichen, he doesn't have a reason to pinpoint at me."

Huang Feng turned to me with a sad smile. "OK then. I see I have to stop you here."

"In fact, I'm not sure that I can take you down." I walked slowly to the cottage by the garden, feeling warm the minute I stepped under the roof. "Of course, I believe you cannot be sure either."

It seemed that Huang Feng was thinking about whether there's any bragging or taunt in my words. After a few seconds, he uttered a self-deprecating laugh. "You're right. I'm not sure. You're somebody."

I took my backpack and put away my weapon. Lighting up two cigarettes, I passed him one. "I still want to go to the border to take my chance."

"What a stubborn man."

"Just check there. If he really leave the country, I'll let him go. Bin is also very important to me. I don't have to push him that hard. Anyway, I'm border with my police career. I'll go back home, have a family and find something easy to do in some security company. It will be good to come to you and Shitian and have a drink, and listen to some stories of that Kill Son operation."

"That's interesting." Huang Feng reached out his hand suddenly and held my right arm. I was used to his abnormal location ability so I didn't doge but to keep relaxed. He grabbed my arm and murmured, "Well, it's really hard to say ..."

"By the way. I do have some questions that I want to ask you."

"Be my guest."

"Someone like Bin ... I mean according to what I know about him in the past eight years, he doesn't look like someone who would sell his partners out." I said, fiddling with the cigarette between my fingers, "Then why would he sell you guys out back then?"

He turned to face me, taking a deep smoke. As he was thinking, he even dropped the ash carefully outside the garden. At last, he shook his head. "No. He didn't sell us out."

"All right. Leave that alone." I didn't want to spoil the friendly atmosphere by something too far away from now. I stood up and asked, "Has he really been here lately?"

"You should go out and ask those people who are staking out. Do they see anybody else here?"

"Right. I'll go and ask them. I'll come back and have a beer with you if I can't find him." I put on my backpack and reached out my hand. To my surprise, his super power didn't work this time, probably because he couldn't sense any hostility on me.

"Wait and have dinner with us." Huang Feng raised his arm a little, as if he was not sure whether I moved or not. "My wife will come back with my kids today. She's a good cook."

Unexpected kindness really moved me a little. "Yes? You wife's back? The kids having a holiday?"

"No. There seemed to be some fights between us and the Vietnam in Dongxing. Something about taking up Nam Cam[1]'s area in Móng Cái. To many people and too dangerous. So I told them to come back for some days."

I didn't feel good. The words Shitian had warned me occurred to me suddenly.

"If Bin's not here, will you take care of Chen Juan's daughter?" I asked while packing in a hurry.

"There's plenty of people queuing for that. I'm not even in the queue." He asked as he heard the sound of me packing things, "Won't stay for dinner?"

---

1 Truong Van Cam (1947-2004) Truong Van Cam, a godfather-like figure for Vietnam mafia. A number of corrupted officials was involved in his case after he was arrested. He was charged with several convictions including murder, and was sentenced to death on June 3rd, 2004.

"Next time." I didn't have time to show him my courtesy as I was in a hurry.

"Hey son!" He called me and said, "He really didn't sell us out."

I'm not in the mood of finding out right or wrong. I just nodded and rushed out, leaving his talking to himself in his small yard.

"He didn't sell any one of us out."

"You provoked him and we can still be talking in the same world?" Yuan Shi's voice seemed to be very twisted. "Don't explain. I know you must be seducing him to earn a chance to survive."

"He is a disabled man. Don't look down upon me."

"T800 is the terminator even if he's got a leg broken. You are not as handsome as John Conner. Do you need medical treatment?"

"I need some backup. And the medical treatment can be prepared for my future need when I come back to you."

"I think it is the time to give up. Entering into an area in turmoil where we don't even have the right of jurisdiction without a concrete lead, you are courting death, pointlessly and meaninglessly.

"Bin will be there."

"There's another question, maybe not important." He switched to another subject, "About Yao Jiang and Ruan Ba. As what you thought, Yao Jiang, the one who sold his guys out, is Han Bin."

Actually I did have thought about that from another angle, so I didn't respond.

"From what Huang Feng told me, the toughest fighter must be Ruan Ba, and it's logical when he seek revenge after he was sold out." There was some noise in the phone so he paused. "But have you thought of this: actually Han Bin is Ruan Ba, and the man you killed together in Zhongde Building is Yao Jiang. Han Bin has been living a relatively normal life ever since he came back from Cambodia and Vietnam. It's possible that Yao Jiang will change the balanced situation if he was really living as a killer these days."

"It could be possible." I couldn't help smiling holding the phone, "But what's the evidence?"

"No evidence at all. In my opinion, if Hand Bin can commit suicide, kill others and leave his home country for a woman who didn't even love him, he, a paranoid, won't stand his own behavior of betraying. Let's put it this way, if he is a kind of man who would sell his team members out, he wasn't even likely to go to South Asia after his suicidal behavior."

I just wanted to tease him. "Then why Yao Jiang came to kill him? "

"It's easy to understand. Because in his mind, Hang Bin will come to seek revenge one day. Yes, Han Bin may or may not come to him when he's got time. But the point is Yao Jiang is going to worry about this his whole life. If he ever wants to take a sound sleep, he will have to kill Hand Bin."

"Yeah, maybe. But there is a possibility that Huang Feng and his lot didn't tell us the truth. Who is Yao Jiang and who is Rua Ba? Maybe A did sell B out but B is actually C, and then it would be C selling A out... Who knows? And as you said, it's not important."

"Yeah. It's nothing important for me or for the case. But you'd better figure this out for your own good. If Hand Bin is Yao Jiang, he will kill you. If he is Ruan Ba, it's also irrational to provoke him. Look at those who have done that, they are dead or driven nuts."

"Don't worry. No matter who can survive between us in the end, my nerves are stronger than yours. I'm not that easy to be driven nuts."

"If he's here, he'll tell you that don't seek for the chances to hurt yourself only because of guilty." Yuan Shi hesitated for a second and turned to be more serious than before, too serious that is, "No matter where you are in the end, there's always a distance between you and him."

"Oedipus complex?"

"I didn't say that. But you won't find him anyway."

"It's not a right time for Yichen to go there. No matter how many people there to protect her, Bin will be there to keep her safe."

"Maybe. I can get you a binocular and a loud speaker. You can just blare to him from far away. Just as what I said, take this as the end. Stay in Dongxing and I'd love to arrange you back to Beijing."

"This is our last chance." I covered the phone and coughed, "At least let me get his promise that he would never kill any more."

"You come such a long way just for this? What about he promises you? Would you believe him?"

"I'll make my own judgement. And I need some weapons."

"You don't even have a time for judgement. Móng Cái is a small place, but you can't take a step forward if you go there now."

"I could go and find Yichen first. Ma Li and her group could easily be remembered. It will not be difficult to get their trace."

"You really believe in Huang Feng, don't you? It is great if you find Han Yichen, and even if you find her, Han Bin will still kill you. No matter who he is, he'll blow out half of the solar system for Chen Juan's daughter if he has to. What on earth do you want? Do you really want to kill him?"

"Yes. I will if that's the only way to stop him killing."

"Then what's the difference between you and him? You can do whatever you like with a life as long as you've got a good reason?"

I was not at all in the mood to discuss with him the universal moral standard or the sacred law. "Just take this as the last time you help me. If there's no backup, at least get me some weapons."

Yuan Shi asked with an edge to his voice, "What if I refuse?"

"It's up to you. I'll go anyway."

There was a long silence on the other side of the phone. In the end, he heaved a sigh. "All right, but you must promise me one thing."

Thinking about whether I should gave Xuejing a call, I said, "I'm not sure whether I could be back alive."

"I'm not either. Or you could say I think you won't. But please promise me, if he cannot promise not to kill any more, take him back. But if you can't, then let him go. Under no circumstances will you kill him. Please, under no circumstances. If you kill him, you'll be him forever."

This was once my dream. It didn't look too bad now from a certain angel.

Not only he, Deputy captain Sun of the frontier post also tried to talk me out of it.

Dongxing was closed two hours ago. Even if Yuan Shi didn't cover my back about the wanted posters within the system, I could still tell that their dissuasion was for my own good.

At the same moment, Móng Cái, just one street away from Dong Xing, had already been a battlefield.

It was said that after the street gang went there, they formed a balance with the former troops of Truong Van Cam, although fights and conflicts were frequently seen. But nobody had foreseen that Zhou Qinian, the monopolist who controlled the leather business in Yunnan and Guangxi provinces, should aligned with the street gang, which broke the local balance. This had upgraded the local fights into a regional conflict, which was unexpected to all parties.

The foreign affairs departments of both China and Vietnam said nothing about this, a sign to let them run their own courses without affecting the promising future of both countries.

Under such circumstances, the local situation was completely out of control.

Therefore, when I crossed the border with only a nightstick on my waist, people in the frontier post were looking at me with a compassionate face. They probably thought I've got some suicidal tendency. For me, a policeman who was going to take off his uniform, this was a significant and passionate send-off.

Standing on the border bridge, I saw that classmate of Yuan Shi who was beaten to the ground by me. He didn't wear any splints anymore, so I thought he must have recovered from that case. But we were still a little embarrassed for this meet. It was clear that he was still angry with me, but seemed to believe that I was a man walking towards death, so I could see obvious compassion on his face.

I was quite curious to know that how an elite like Yuan Shi could have a classmate doing gray business and could show up in front of me in just a couple of minutes. But after Bin's case, that didn't last long. I saw him pulling open a black duffel bag, uncovering the newspaper on the surface and presenting me three pistols.

Out of a QSZ 92, 5.8mm for military use, a Glock 21 with a big clip and a pistol I knew nothing of, I chose the Glock. Although he recommended that MP446, which was the Russian one I knew nothing of, I still couldn't trust my life with a gun I was completely strange to. I haven't used the Glock either, but I had long heard of its convenient safety device that could keep live ammunition loaded. In a word, I was a really bad shooter, missing the target nearly every time in the shooting practices in college. Well, it was a total waste of my teacher's guidance. If I had to fire a gun today, it was better to have an M61A1 produced by Liang Xiao's boss, or at least, I was holding something which could fire at any time.

He warned me repeatedly that the long clip was added after and used metal instead of plastic in order to be loaded faster so one side of the gun was lighter than the other and I needed to aimed lower when firing. That was not a problem, I believe, since I would have a chance to test it soon enough.

Checking the backup clips, I asked, "What's the situation down there?"

He turned around to look at me, and then shook his head, puzzled. "Do you really ..." He stared me for several seconds and then continued, "Don't shoot unless you really need to. Otherwise it'll cause a chain effect."

I stuck the gun into my belt. "I know."

He was still shaking his head, not likely to believe that I was really going there. At last, he passed me a dagger for military use which was big enough to cut a watermelon and anything as the size of it.

"If you have to shoot, then don't hesitate."

I didn't respond this time. That depended on who I was aiming at.

"Meticulous as the plan may be, it's a complete waste if there's no luck."

Yes, Bin had planned everything, and he's got good luck. But ever since he set foot on this land on which he and his team members were sold out, Lady Luck had gave up on him. No matter Liang Xiao and Chen Juan, or Ruan Ba and Yao Jiang, these elites who had lost the protection from their own country, were destined to be the puppet of some hegemony. So far for Bin, his well-planed escape route was completed out of use because of the sudden turmoil in Móng Cái that had become the center of a huge storm. His plan couldn't be carried out successfully.

But the time of passion was short. Soon enough, I found my plan couldn't work out either.

When I was in Dongxing, I thought it was only a mob fight about some gray business worth billions of yuan. But up until I stepped on this land did I realized that the fight for control was just a beginning. Conflicts between different peoples, clashes between different cultures, huge gaps between the rich and the poor and the issues accumulated after such a long time ... People may not need a reason to fight. The instinct of hurting each other would naturally push things through. I could saw fire in the direction of the fair. There were slippers, hats, remains of bicycles and motorbikes on the streets. I was running quickly after I crossed the border and saw scores of brawls on my way. Hundreds of people were involved, but not a single policeman were seen on the scene. It was said that hundreds of government officials were involved when Nam Cam was arrested. What a demonstration of power of Vietnam gang! Shitian was right, Chinese mafia without a "support" behind would get nothing here.

I was hit by things from God knows where on the way. At the gate of the fair, I saw two men beating a corpse. Noticing that they seemed to have tendency to switch their goal to me, I fought them back. When I passed the Waizhai Street from the outside, a half-naked woman rushed out from a small shop by the road, swinging the hammer in her hand without any reasons. I couldn't understand what she was saying, so I had to run away. I also stunned a fellow countryman who wanted to smash his face with a slipper and helped a woman to salvage the body of her dead child from the sink in a fish market. Increasingly, I found that this was not a simple fight between Vietnam mobs and Chinese mobs. It seemed that no one cared about who he was beating and killing. The whole street was filled with craziness and insanity.

I wanted to go back, really. I was terrified.

I once imagined that maybe one day, I would sacrifice myself for the country as a policeman. But it should be an occasion when I was facing fierce criminals and after a strong and remitting resistance. At least, I should be in my own country, on the land on which I was raised. I didn't want to be turned into an unknown body lying in a gutter on a foreign land by somebody I didn't even know of due to some ridiculous reasons he himself even didn't know.

I didn't even have the translator Guan with me this time. I could only grope my way to Tuberose myself. Without a motorbike, it was very difficult for me to struggle through the groups fighting with each other. Going through lanes and alleys between cottages and shelters, I tried my best to move to the Southwest of Móng Cái. After half an hour, I've got a general idea of the people wander in this region. One of them were plain civilians, most of which were staying at home or being bullied by some of the mobsters. One was new to this area, most of which were Chinese and could be calmed down by a short greeting like "Hey! Chinese too!". And the third belonged to local mobs who came out to fight with Chinese on their first sight but would leave the local civilians alone. The last were ruffians and hooligans ranging from teenagers to middle-aged grown-ups. They formed gangs and did all the evil, but were cowardly bullies, just like the twin of the New Nazis in South Asia.

I knew I was followed when I was in Gualan Street. I could see the red railings on the second floor of Tuberose just rows of lose-rises away when half a dozen of Vietnamese popped out from a mango stand. A short man with short hair was yelling some Vietnamese at me, holding a cheap hacking knife in his hand. Naturally I pretended that I didn't hear them and walked my own way at my normal speed. However, the irregular sound of running forced me to quicken my steps. Luckily I was wearing a pair of leather shoes that had full advantage over slippers. The followers didn't show up when I turned out of Gualan Street. On the sight of scores of barrels for industrial wastes piled on the east of Chagu beach, an idea suddenly stroke me and I hided myself in.

It would be the best that Shitian was in Tuberose, and that was my only clear plan. But what if he wasn't? What if there was only Ma Li with her kids? I couldn't hope those drunk Vietnamese veterans would give me a hand, let alone believe Ma Li's preaching would move them.

Now that I was not certain, it was better not to let a wolf in. In order to keep safe, I decided to beat them down using the little maze formed by these barrels.

But I didn't expect to fight with a bunch of idiots. After they chased me out, their eyes swept over the empty Chagu beach. Without a look at the barrels in which I hided, they rushed directly into a residence built with gray bricks opposite. Eight in, six out. I tried not to think about the reason why the other two weren't out and force myself to focus on the rest who were standing less than 20 meters away from me. It turned out that after a discussion, they shouted like maniacs, swinging their hacking knives like some Indian soldiers. And after that, they rushed into Tuberose.

That was completely out of my expectation.

All of a sudden, my mind went blank. And then I realized what a coward I was to stay there like this. I got out of the barrel and ran to the front door of the bar when there was a small chaos in that gray residence. A bastard walked out along with a faint cry. He was mocking at the other one who looked a little disappointed while putting his pants on. But both of their faces went wildly horror when they saw me.

I didn't want to waste time so I pulled the gun out.

Those two bastards cooperated quickly. They raised their hands high. One of them raised only one hand as the other one of his was holding his pants.

This was something difficult to deal with. They were not bad enough to be killed, but if I let them go like this, there was a chance that they would be my trouble in the future. I took my finger out of the trigger and tapped the gun slightly. The time was running, and I was getting anxious.

I should shoot. I should not hesitate.

In such a predicament, a short middle-aged Vietnamese woman rushed out of that residence. She was wearing a large grayish shirt. The lower edge of her dress was torn out. I raised my gun at once and put my finger on the trigger, not only to prevent her from taking me as a mobster, but didn't want those two guys to hurt her again.

But she didn't even look at me. She just rushed into the man holding his pants. He was bumped down as he was couldn't even fight back. And then I saw a hacking knife. That woman stood up from his back, pulled the knife which was stabbed deeply into his body and looked at the other man.

The other man was completely shocked. He must have been tasting horror again and again between my gun and her knife as his feet were moving backward out of instinct. I could see where this would go, so I put away the gun and pushed into Tuberose.

And then I nearly bumped into a cheap hacking knife.

Raising my backpack soon enough, I slid to the right and swung my fist to the back of the head in front me. At the same time, I kicked on his knee, pulled his head close and banged it to the wooden door. At the first bump I heard the sound of knife falling on the ground, and at the second bump, I felt the body between my arms suddenly sunk and lost support.

As I turned my head out of this man, I saw a home to veterans out of recognition. Tables, chairs, bottles and records were scattered everywhere. Half of a chair were on the counter and people were lying around. Some of them were on their backs and some were not; some eyes were open and some were not; some were familiar to me, and some were total strangers.

The guy who had brought me a bottle of 333 was leaning against the door of the bar, one hand holding the neck of half a bottle and the other pressing his thigh, blood spewing between his fingers like a small fountain. The floor under him had turned black. The guy confronting him was a guy holding a chopping knife. Undoubtedly, my appearance distracted him a lot. And now he had turned his face to me.

We were the only two people standing in the room.

I pulled out my nightstick and strode to him, my left eye twitching again out of my control.

When he found out his speed of stepping back was not as quick as I stepped forward, it was too late for him to run. Obviously, he found out that too. He yelled out and rushed towards me, raising his chopper high. I raised my nightstick to fight back. Well, it was not just a matter of speed. My nightstick is longer than his knife so it could reach his head before I rushed within his range of attack. His hand stopped in the air, stepped back and fell on the ground. His eyes became gray. I took a step forward, kicked out his knife that he couldn't hold tight, and gave him another nightstick at his neck. He passed out.

At the same time, 333 collapsed.

I hurried back to him, took out the mini emergency case from my backpack and tried to stop him from bleeding. But my effort was in vain. Warm and thick liquid flew across my band. Nothing, nothing could I hold tight. Nothing.

He put his fingers on my wrist to remind me to look up. I saw a face with bitter smile. He shook his head disappointingly, and murmured some words I couldn't understand.

I held his hands and asked, "Where's Shitian? Shi-Tian! Si-Qian! Yes! Yes!"

His eyes were about to close, nodding now and then as if he was sleepy. "Siqian, Siqian ..."

"What? What did you say?"

His shoulders lurched and he slid slowly to the left. I held him and shouted, "WHAT? What did you say? It's me! Hey! It's me! Look at me! It was you who gave me that bottle of 333. Look at me! Look ..."

There was a moment that I though he was gone. But suddenly he opened his eyes and grabbed my collar. He said to me in that awkward Chinese of his, "Children ... Children ..."

"Children! Yes! Children! Where are the children? Where!"

His eyes turned to the counter. Looking at the direction he was looking at, I saw a small door inside the counter on which a leather curtain was hanging there to cover it. My hands felt a little lighter. I looked down and found out he has gone. My hands felt heavier all of a sudden.

I put him down and checked the room to identify Shitian wasn't in one of the bodies. And then I walked into the small door, went through a long and narrow kitchen and left Tuberose from its back door.

And then, I saw the nun who was once beautiful and lively, and Han Yichen who was crying on her body. It was the scene I didn't want to see at all.

Ma Li was wearing a black-and-white church robe, but it was clear that her identity as a clergy couldn't earn her the respect she would have been given. The white part of her robe became red and the black part was now a dirty purple. Yichen cried out loud, trying her best to drag her on her feet but only left a winding line of blood on the ground. A girl who looked no more bigger was waving half a burning stick, making every effort to drive away laughing thugs — don't count on me giving another description for people with tattoos, needle points and hacking knives — around them. They were laughing and teasing, stepping back a few steps and then forward.

Many more bodies were placed in the vicinity, one of which was a kid I've seen in the orphanage, and the rest were all children at their six or seven or teenagers.

My mouth was wide open, but I couldn't make a sound. I was so terrified. I hated my hesitation outside the bar, hated all the killings I've encountered in the past one hour; I hated Bin and Chen Juan, the people who had created all this; I hated myself and what I was going to do...

"We are choosing our fate, and the fate is choosing us."

Yes, it was what I chose. I hated it, but I chose it. "

"Your choice actually comes from your personality."

What I was going to do was what I believe was right.

"All a man's ways seem innocent to him, but motives are weighed by the LORD."

These murderers didn't even spare the least effort to justify themselves.

"It's said that the world is violently sick."

No. The word has never changed. It was us who were sick. It was human.

"People turn bad these days."

Greedy, furious, hypocrisy... We were beyond recovery. We hurt our own species and all the others we could only to satisfy our own desire.

"When you give your back to him, you are his prey. If you turn around to face him, you are his rival."

Yes. They've given us a sufficient reason, a reason for me to turn around.

"Will you run?"

Will I?

My left eye was twitching again. I came across Yichen and Ma Li and rushed out to them and protected that little girl behind my back. As I swung my nightstick with my right hand, it was obvious that the man in the middle wasn't expecting this since he even tried to avoid. The nightstick hit right on his head. He fell down on the ground without even making a sound. At the same time, a white flash dashed out on my left. Without thinking, I turned to confront him. Sparks flew out as my nightstick hit his knife and I felt there was a rhinocero striking my waist. The strong reflective power made my stomach ache. Before I could fight back, my right shoulder was hurt by another knife and a kick on my right hip. I flew out.

Falling on the ground, my stomach was writhing so hard that I couldn't even feel the agony. I crawled up and swung the nightstick to the crotch of a man rushing to me holding a big knife high. I spent so much effort that the head of the stick was pressed back. That son of a bitch uttered a muffled sound and curled up like a dead shrimp, writhing on the ground in agony. A kick came out from my left. I pulled my dagger out from my waist and stabbed into the outside of his thigh, warm blood spurting out on my face.

Seeing this, the last one turned back to run, but was caught up by me and swung down. A stab followed into his heart.

Crawling up, I found myself covered with blood. As for whose blood it was, I didn't know, neither did I care.

It was my first time to kill, but I didn't have any strange feelings.

Yichen and that girl looked at me, shocked in still. I looked back at Yichen and knew she had recognized me. But I'd rather she hadn't. They were just kids. They should not face this, not the mostugly respect of humankind.

A burst of footsteps and dozens of people appeared before me. They each got a stick or knife at hand, pointing at this side and shouting, looking just like the defective goods produced by some filthy factory, being the same filthy, ferocious and ugly.

Come on! Gave me the same reason! Gave me the reason to kill you!

I walked to Yichen. Near her, the man who was stabbed on the crotch was writhing on the ground. I asked her gently, "Where's Bin?"

Yichen closed her eyes and shook her head, weeping.

"Leave her here and go find Bin." I shook my head to the other girl, "I'll take her back."

The animals on the ground were crying loud, and the monsters nor far were approaching.

I stuck my dagger back, holding the nightstick with both of my hands.

The head of the stick touching the back of that guy's head, I posed as to swing out when playing golf.

Can I?

They were approaching, tramping the bodies of the kids.

What the fuck! Why not!

I gave it a hard swing.

When I reached out to my gun, I heard someone called "Don't shoot" with a low voice, and then three figures dashed out from behind me. These were skillful guys familiar with this. They were short, wearing a vest and holding the same bayonet. Their brown shin was shining in the air. In less than half a minute, six of those approaching monsters fell on the ground and the rest were running away.

But it didn't cost nothing. We had one man down, too. One of the guys with short black hair had a knife cut on his throat. He was lying on the side in the crowds and didn't get up again.

Turning back, I saw Shitian held up Yichen, eyebrows frowned tightly. His light pink shirt and khaki pants were all clean, which, along with his square face, were way more eye-catching than ever in a place like this. A man as strong as the champion of UFC was standing by his side, sweeping around with his eyes wide open.

Shitian gazed at his dead buddy for a while and then asked me, "Why are you here?"

"You should be lucky I'm here." I cleaned my faced with my hand, and then noticed he and his buddies were all carrying guns with them. "Where's Bin?"

He called the rest two back with some foreign language and gave Yichen and the other girl to them. "Can you get out by yourself? I had to send them away."

I lowered my head, looking at the same direction with Yichen. "How about her?"

Shitian glanced at Ma Li's body, seemingly to be anxious.

That champion of UFC talked to Shitian with some foreign language, which I could tell was not Vietnamese. Shitian nodded. The others then put the two girls and their shoulder and retreated to an alley to the southwest.

Shitian said to me who was gazing at Ma Li, "Come with me if you don't want to take her."

There was no time for any struggle. The dead was dead and the alive had to live on.

We reached Xiongwang Road after passing through the alley. Shitian told me that was a shortcut to the car waiting for us. The situation in Móng Cái was out of everyone's expectation and that was the reason why he didn't show up at the meeting point on time, which lead to so many innocent deaths. I asked him where on earth Bin was, and he seemed to think I was insane. But he still shrugged, indicating he knew nothing about it.

I wondered why they'd rather to have man down than to fire a gun. Shitian seemed to be regretful. "There are numerous guns in this street. But have you ever heard a single gunshot?"

I recalled and found out indeed no.

"No gunshots could be counted as the fighting rule agreed privately by both sides. At least it could control the death toll in some way. It could be accepted to shot Ruan Xunsong to death as he was nobody, but hundreds of people shooting to each other, that's something else. And once there is a gunshot, the local police could no longer keep their hand off."

"But we don't belong to any side."

Shitian took his phone out while walking. "Then following the rules is more necessary. Try to fire a gunshot, and then you'll know the reason. And you'll soon be the reason, too." He talked to the phone briefly in Vietnamese and looked around, seemingly to describe our location.

I didn't know what's going to happen to me but couldn't prevent myself from going on. I could only ask Shitian, "Would you please do me a favor?"

"What is that?"

"If I ... I mean ... If something ever happens to me, would you please tell my wife something? You're such capable. You'll find her. I mean, tell her in person."

"Haha! That beautiful and sexy wife of yours? No problem! I could ..." He looked at me and chuckled, and then the smile faded away suddenly.

"What do you want to tell her?"

"Tell her that I'm sorry ..."

"Only an apology?" His eyes looked like the sea in the moonlight.

I gritted my teeth, trying to swallow my cowardliness back, giving up all my shyness and containing all my memories. "And ... and ... I ... Anyway, that's about it."

Shitian stopped.

He didn't mind the urges from all the others and took out the cellphone he just put back. "Zhao Xincheng, listen to me. If you don't dare to say what you wanted to say to her now, you'd better turn back. We don't have anyone to worry about, but you are no. You can't go on in this way."

I didn't take the phone. I knew if I called Xuejing at that moment, it was sure that I would lost my courage to go on. Like many other things, if you think too much, you don't dare to carry it out.

But this was my first time that I would rather sacrifice my image of a tough man. Something in our life was long been ignored by us. Love and dead, they were both close to me, too close for me to touch, to talk about, but there was no way to elude.

It was probably how human should be. In the most helpless moment in our lives, we tended to think about the closest one to us most. Like most of my colleagues, I was never a good husband. If there were another chance for me to choose from being a good cop or a good husband, I didn't know which side I would tend to, which life I would like to live more. But what I was even less sure about was if there were a chance for Xuejing to choose for a second time, whether she would marry me. I couldn't say what I was up to today was something I could be avoid. That was not responsible. But she was right about one thing: Through all these years in our marriage, I was always making her worried.

The temptation to come home was like gravity, making me distracted and upset. Actually I really hoped that Xuejing would be by my side at that moment, but was glad that she wasn't here to bell the cat with me. Yes, from a certain point I could eventually understand Bin: I could die, but I couldn't bear the one I loved was hurt.

Because Xuejing, I love you.

And then, we entered that narrow shortcut.

A shortcut means efficiency and facility, but hides conspiracy and plot. When we reached the middle of the alley, two groups of mobs appeared on both ends of the road as if they've been discussing about this before. As a result, we were stuck in this narrow alley which could only hold two people passing by.

A nervous feeling rushed up to my mind. I yelled to Shitian to tell them to move forward, and turned back, raising the stick and the dagger high and confronting those mobs from behind. Sounds of shouting and fighting immediately came from the direction we were running at. Arms and knives were intertwined with each other. Girls were weeping.

More and more people were rushing into the alley. The two in the front couldn't stand still and could only rushed to me, knives high in the sky. I pulled out my nightstick and poked it under the neck of the man on my left, and at the same time his knife cut my arm open. I lowered down and slipped near the man on my right, stabbing the dagger into his chest. The blade couldn't move forward halfway as it was stuck between the ribs. The nightstick flew out. I could only give several kicks to the one on my left, who lost his balance and fell down and covered his wound with his hand. I stepped on his neck artery and he passed out. The one on my right was not dead but couldn't fight back. I clenched the handle of the dagger with my right hand, and heaved him in front of me as a shield. The wound on my arm hurt a lot.

Maybe I was tough or maybe they didn't arrange well. But anyway, this worked for a few seconds. But soon enough I realized this was a world I couldn't calculate with normal approaches. A livid knife went through the shield body into my left ribs. I couldn't breathe, so I had to throw him down and took a few steps back.

The same knife hacked at me in no second. I stepped aside out of instinct. My heavily wounded left hand grabbed his armpit. A Glock 21 was pulled out and pointed at his chest.

I stared at him, but couldn't see his face. I even believed I wouldn't remember his face for my whole life. I didn't know whether he could see me but I knew he didn't see the gun. We looked at each other. Furious hate out of nowhere could be seen from our red eyes. As the color became dark, he saw the coming of death, and I pulled the trigger.

As the trigger went halfway, the open of the locker led to a slight vibration, reminding me that I still got chance to go back. But we I didn't. I pulled the trigger to dead end, and the pin collided on the bullet. Something slid through the gun barrel along the rifling. The body twitched hard in front of my eyes. Smell of fire emitted from the gun.

I raised the gun a little higher and gave me another shot. The upper-aiming gun sent the bullet into his collarbone. Fragments of bones crashed out and pinned into my hand like shrapnel. His half body flew backwards. I let go of his armpit, left hand sliding down his arm, and snatched his knife.

And then I took a footstep forward, and pulled the trigger to the points between those eyes, same color with mine, behind me. Once, twice, three times. The crowd didn't step back. I cut open one of the shoulders with the knife in my left hand, and sent several bullets into his abdomen. As I was moving forward, something flying towards me cut my cheek open. I slipped to my right and stabbed the knife into someone's ribs. Up until I put the gun on his shoulder did I realized that it was shot loudly, shrapnel bursting into his dead face.

I saw, I rushed, I kill.

I wanted to stop but I couldn't.

Governed by the rule of the jungle, we are just animals. Getting rid of all constraints, I would be more powerful than them. Giving me an appropriate reason, I could even surpass Bin.

The fact that the trigger couldn't be pulled reminded me that I ran out of bullets, but the enemies were still flooding in. I took off the clip. It dropped on my foot. As I was about to take out a backup one, a sliver dagger showed up out of nowhere. I hurried to brush it aside with the gun. It was pushed away from its original direction and stabbed into my left shoulder. I could feel my heart convulsing. I suddenly lost all my strength and knelt down. Just at this moment, a hand dragged me back pulling my collar. I fell on my back.

A black lightning crossed over me. At last, I saw him.

Even I was about to faint out, I could still recognize that figure dashing out there, quick as a ghost and sharp like an awl. Bin and his comrades had one thing in common — fast, too fast that they didn't seem to belong to this world.

The gun was hot and my fingers cold. I couldn't help but laughing. This was what Shitian saw in the heavy fog in Anlong Vengm on November 22nd 1997.

The God of Death is running like hell.

Epilogue

The slaughter scared most of the crazy people away and the rest was also trembling with fear. Bin bought us a safe distance of several meters full of bodies. He staggered through them and helped me up to move back. Shitian and his guy had killed their way out of the alley.

As we arrived at the end of the alley, he helped me to lean on the wall and coughed heavily. I then noticed there was a film of viscous liquid outside his black shirt and an obvious wound on his left chest close to his armpit was bleeding fast, blood soaking his left leg. He looked down, breathing heavily and briefly. His legs were shaking.

All my ache were frozen at that second. I stood up straight and held him in total flurry.

Bin squinted his eyes to cast a glance to the rest of the guys in the alley. The slow-moving crowd hurried to a stop.

He then turned to me and said, "You came anyway ..."

I looked at Xiongwang Road. Shitian and his guys were nowhere to be seen. Instead, a big crowd was there to surround us inside. They were angry anarchists. Casting my eyes over the furious crowd, I could not see the border line although I was facing the direction to my hometown. The sun had set down, but it wasn't completely dark. I could look infinitely far by the light coming from nowhere.

In the distance, there was my wife, my friends and my colleagues. There were noodles I grew up with and a city I grew up in. There was The Fingerprint erecting in a noisy block and Xiaoyue River in a rainy night. There were Bin's most cherished memories.

Pushing the backup clip in, I tried to support him with my left arm. "Come on. Come back with me."

Bin pushed my away, looked up.

"Xincheng, we ... we cannot go back any more." he said, out of breath. I was even afraid of him falling down the next second.

I looked at him. For the first time in my life, I understood the feeling in his eyes: That was sadness, sadness wandering between humanity and barbarity, and sadness which could never be replaced.

"The most fortunate thing for a man is that whether a woman is in love with you, you can love her either way."

But the most unfortunate was, no matter how much you loved her, you couldn't force her to love you. Love was an unsolvable mystery.

A person who pays too much attention on love cannot live long, and the love that is beyond the acceptance of a man turns into hate.

Yes, Bin. You are chasing for death. That Han Bin I knew eight years ago had his soul go with Chen Juan when she was dead. And the left was only a body that would walk upright.

I took the chance to give him a comforting smile. "In the end, you still tricked me. You are not Yao Jiang. You kill and you save. But you didn't ever sell anyone out."

He smiled back. "What's the difference..."

I asked what I always wanted to ask. "Will you kill any more?"

Bin coughed again, large amount of blood coming out of his mouth. He sniffed and stared at the weapon in my hand. The corner of his left eye was twitching as it was smeared with some Vaseline. He asked back, "Are you here to kill me?"

I felt twitching between my eyebrows. I clenched my gun and looked around, as if hoping to find the answer.

He put his hand on my shoulder as if wanted to whisper by my ear. But the next second, he dashed pass me and rushed to the flooding crowd.

I tried to reach him with my left hand, but failed. This was the last chance. I immediately loaded the gun, held it high against the wall and aimed at him — or the crowd opposite him.

"Bin!"

He looked back and turned around, staring at me with a faint smile as if seeing another himself in another world.

I remember the hint I heard on the border bridge and lowered the gun a bit. My finger pressed harder on the trigger until the lock was open...

How many bullets are there in a clip?

Slowly, Bin raised both of his arms high, both his elbows close to his waist, like a nestling giving up to fly because of congenital disability. He was standing there, as if to welcome his final scene that I brought to him, or ready to be finished by the knives and crowd.

"We cannot go back any more."

Go along by your side, or send you off away.

Squinting my left eye, I identified the target and pulled the trigger to the end.

（全文完）

Exile

Hu Yibiao looked around the the living room: A cloth sofa with single color, a round cane tea table, an open chipboard cupboard, a floor lamp with a parchment cover and a weft-faced plain wave jute carpet. He has known Xia Yutong for three years and he knew it would be the style she's gonna choose — light color, avoiding sharp edges, no glass and few metal, and not a single piece of leather. Everything was quite similar to what he had expected, which made him rather comfortable.

When he saw Xia Yutong for the first time, all his feeling accumulated in the many years playing an undercover, all those anger, violence and loneliness gnawing him over, found their way out. In his mind, this psychological mentor sent by the City Bureau was no more than a self-glorifying delicate princess in fairy tales and he was confident enough to confront her in mind and left with a complete success to enjoy his long paid holiday.

But the reality ... well, we cannot say the reality beat him down because Xia Yutong changed his mind. He didn't want to comfort himself by hurting others again.

"Have you made a full recovery?" Xia Yutong came out from the kitchen, passing him a mug of freshly made black tea. Afternoon sunlight wrapped her slim figure like a astral lamp, and her almost transparent skin was a little dimmed against this background.

"Not easy even if you want to die." Hu Yibiao reached out his left hand with only three and a half fingers and took the mug. Coke with ice was always his favorite, but every time they meet, he was happy about this warm feeling.

Over the past years of his undercover experience, the number of scars was probably on a par with that of his tattoos, his injured left hand not included. This was caused in an operation several months ago conduced with Xicheng Branch. It ended up with a gun fight. He got shot on the outside of his right leg and the back right on his waist. Thanks to his good appetite, the two bullets only took some fat away, not really different from a skin trauma. He attributed to his luck of being beefy and even was happy about the fact that he lost five kilograms. As for his big figure would increase the possibility of being shot, he didn't care at all.

"I met with Zhao Xincheng just now downstairs. He said you quit from the forensic center?"

"You've talked with him, why would you ask me?" Xia Yutong always chose to redirect when coming across the question she didn't want to answer. "And it has been two years since you've finished your psychological mentor. It doesn't matter whether I was still working in the center."

Of course it didn't matter. Hu Yibiao would ask her out frequently. Sometimes it was because of work, but most of the time it wasn't. And Xia Yutong wasn't against this. They didn't have the slightest things in common in their experience, life, and personality, even in their preferences for drinks. They even despised one another when working together. It was actually a wonder they would get along with each other more than thousands of days.

He didn't give up. "Is it about Qin Chi?"

That was a target they both paid attention to in the last operation, who is the vice commander of the criminal investigation division of Xicheng Branch. The operation was a success, but it didn't work well for Qin Chi. He wanted to know whether Xia Yutong was annoyed by his story.

She smiled and turned her head to reach for the sugar jar, more silver ones in her hairs scattering on her shoulder. "I thought his story would affect you more than me."

"No, I'm just used to things like this." Hu Yibiao put two cube sugars into his mug and took the stirring stick passed by Xia Yutong. "We are all like this. People come and people go."

Xia Yutong sat down opposite him. "What brings you here today? It can't be another 'accidental killing', can it?"

The most obvious feature of Hu Yibiao's operation was his high death rate when chasing after a suspect. On one hand, it made him a frequent face in the hearings; and on the other, it led to increasing cardiovascular diseases among the leaders in the Bureau. The compulsory psychological mentor was the last procedure after each assessment, which was also his favorite part.

"No. It's said they've got another one. I'm hopeful to lose that name."

"Is that the one from Fengtai Branch?"

"That guy named Zhou Xun. He's much crueler than me."

Bullshit. Zhou Xun's problem was mostly caused by his strong figure and strength. Frankly speaking, he just couldn't control himself when things got worse. But Hu Yibiao was not. He didn't intentionally, every time.

Xia Yutong looked down. "Yeah, I've heard of that also. He refused to be psychologically mentored, and would rather be put in suspension."

Hu Yibiao looked away too. "He entered the system the same year with Zhao Xincheng. Those guys, each is more impertinent than the other."

It was always like this. When he lied and she saw through him but didn't want to tell, they would both feel embarrassed. Hu Yibiao was living in his lies half of his life, but even if he was just hiding something away from her, he would also blush. Although it was so considerate of Xia Yutong that she chose not to look at him when she saw through it, it still made him panic.

"And you've made your decision about leaving the system." It was normal for her to say something like that as it was actually something they've talked about before Hu Yibiao went on operation in Xicheng. Now that the operation was over, he had to choose a path.

"Yes." It was unwise to tell a second lie. He nodded quickly. "I talked with Director Wang about his, and he gave me another choice."

"The police academy or the training camp?"

"The training camp. They knew I couldn't stand new kids." Actually he couldn't stand anybody. "The training camp's offer is better and they don't have many classes. I could do with it."

Xia Yutong seemed to be much more relieved. "That's nice. The bureau's got you a good offer."

"Nice is not enough for me." Hu Yibiao, on the contrary, seemed to be annoyed. "I refused. I won't be able to do anything there. I could only teach those little masters in the field or SWAT team how to save their lives."

"Is that nice? Just don't teach them how to kill a suspect."

"I couldn't understand that once the suspect confront us in violence, we would have guns and broadswords waiting for us. Then what? We just stand there and wait to be killed?"

"We've talked about this several times. You know my opinion."

In their last mentor session, Xia Yutong onced said to him, "If you do this all the time, you'll be more like a criminal."

Like always, Hu Yibiao couldn't agree with her opinion. "The dead are not good guys. But it's the good guys that they kill."

Xia Yutong thought for a few minutes and said, "Most of the people knew the existence of the law. But why there's always someone who tries to break the law?"

Hu Yibiao leaned back a little, stretched his arms along the backrest of the sofa. "There are always some nuts who lost their mind. I don't study this."

"In a specified situation of under some specific circumstances, people would believe that some of their emotion, need, approach or even luck could go beyond the law."

He had always hated complicated logic like this, even if they came from Xia Yutong's mouth.

But Xia Yutong didn't want to let him go. "I believe that there's must some musts in your experience of killing the suspects."

Hu Yibiao asked back, "But?"

"You know that 'but'. "

"Every time there's supervision, research, hearings, questions and assessments ... If that's not gonna fucking wash me up, is there anything would be?"

He walked tall because results from several researches have proved that what he did complied with the control procedures of Grade VI which could be conducted under the threat of being confronted by the criminals using "fatal approaches to confront in violence".

"Including Jiang Huai?"

Hu Yibiao was stunned. It didn't occur to him that Xia Yutong could ask him that question, or he was afraid that she would ask him that question.

Jiang Huai was a most cruel and ferocious violent criminal who was suspected of several intentional murderers. At the end of that operation in Xicheng, this guy shot one of his partners to death and killed one of the supervisors from the City Bureau. When he fleed to the lane on the south of Building 5, he came cross two policemen face to face and fought with him. Being an assassin in a mafia, Jiang Huai was very good. The two policemen was fought down one after the other. When he was about to kill them with the gun he intended to pick up, Hu Yibiao arrived in time and a gunshot closed all following legal procedures.

The foregoing story was not only proved by the two policemen on the scene, but was witnessed by several residences in Building 5. They all proved that his response was out of question, and the result was something everyone would like to see. After a cross check between different records, the hearings could be saved. Other than the City Bureau did not confirm the meritorious service performance of Hu Yibiao, everything is perfect.

And now, he seemed to understand where the indifferent attitude from the City Bureau.

"It seems Wang Jiang had talked with you before." Hu Yibiao was not happy at all, but didn't dare to put on a poker face to show his feeling.

Xia Yutong seemed relaxed. "Director Wang showed me the records. After you arrived, you first raised the gun high and yelled at Jiang Huai to stop. Under the circumstances that he intended to pick up the weapon and tried to continue his murder, you fired a gun to warm him but the damp primer of the bullet in the chamber deactivated its coming out. The suspect then rushed to gun and you withdraw the chamber and fired a gunshot to kill him."

"That's correct. Is there a problem?"

"No. After I read the files, Director Wang told me there's no problem in it."

Hu Yibiao leaned back again, and he found that he had moved to far from the backrest and only half of his ass was on the mattress.

And what Xia Yutong said next fixed him like that. She said, "No problem, but should not be encouraged."

That's it.

Hu Yibiao reached out for the mug. The tea was not warm any more.

"Director Wang is confident that I would be here to see you, right?"

"Yes."

"And you played like you didn't know anything."

"He just told me that he has some new plans for you, but he didn't tell me specifically."

"What does he want?"

"He wants you to accept."

"What if I still refuse?"

"Then I'd like you to accept."

Hu Yibiao was really annoyed. The corners of his mouth tightened, his nose broadened, and the back of his head felt numb due to a surge of blood pressure. The boundary between the whites and the blackness of the eyes started to become cloudy. He never wanted to look ferocious in front of Xia Yutong but he couldn't control it now. He couldn't control his anger, or his fear.

It seemed that Xia Yutong was about to smile, but what she said was way opposite from her teasing tone. "At beginning of the operation that day, you got a QSZ 92 from the warehouse, but you switched it to a Type 54 with a dective when you entered into the scene. What? Are you afraid of QSZ 92 being too powerful?"

"Jiang Huai was a good assassin. It took a QSZ 92 too long to trigger. If I happen to come cross him, I don't want to die because of short of fractions of a second." A further reason wouldn't be wise, but he didn't want to give up."

"When the driving hammer is open, QSZ 92 was quicker to fire out. It could prove the starting linkage."

"I couldn't let the driving hammer of my gun open all the time. Type 92 was more easy to control."

"Afraid of being slow and miss shot at the same time. How torn."

"We police are torn creatures. I'm used to it." He didn't know when he'd like to say these words. It seemed that the longer he was as a policemen, the more frequent he'd like to say something like this.

"A deactivated primer could be resulted by four reasons, in which a damp one was the last possible inside a warehouse, but the most possible to be caused by human behaviour."

"The bullets of QSZ 92 and Type 54 were all Berdan primer. If I really want to do this, I don't have to switch the gun."

"I'm not saying that you are the one who deactivated that bullet. But it seemed that you think it's necessary to switch the gun."

A feeling of desperation swamped Hu Yibiao. "Like I said, it was because of the trigger ..."

"It was because QSZ 92 has a pull-rod split structure that can achieve the first double action. If the first shot failed, the second one can be dealt with and shot out immediately. But a Type 54 has to be withdrew manually if there's a dud." Xia Yutong took the teapot on the tea table and refilled Hu Yibiao's mug. Several white hairs on her shoulder were more than conspicuous.

Putting down the tea pot, she pushed the mug and her conclusion together to Hu Yibiao. "When you switched into a Type 54, it means you have some 'flex time' brought by the possible manual withdrawal, which could be enough to induce Jiang Huai to take and risk and pick up the gun."

After looked down in a long silence, Hu Yibiao calmed down finally. He didn't care about where the future would end, but just didn't want that push hand was hers. And then he realized that it wouldn't be something Xiao Yutong would do. Her personality forbade her from doing this.

As expect, her voiced lowered down. "Have you thought about that there's a chance you didn't withdraw that dud when he picked up that gun and aimed at you?"

Hu Yibiao held his mug with both of his hands and heaved a long sigh. "We humans have to accept our fate."

"Bin has said that." After a while of lost in thought, she turned back to that unhurried lady who is always taking her time. "If it's Jiang Huai's fate to be shot to death as a violent criminal with several murder cases on him, then Hu Song, you'd better accept you fate with a good mood."

Hu Yibiao didn't look up. He was tasting her persuasion, the one from a person he trusted the most, a person who knew his real name which few people know, a person who could accept his personal identity in his life increasingly marginalized by the mainstream police system

"To be a trainer at the training camp?"

"Whatever, just do what the Bureau wants you to do." Xia Yutong continued when he looked up, gazing at his eyes, "You are a murder weapon, and you'll have to be supervised all the time. That's your fate."

Hu Yibiao was gazing back at her. She was barely more than thirty years old but didn't care about her white hair. She was a genius in criminal investigation and forensics who didn't want to show up in public. She would pass him a warm cup of tea from the tea table, talked frankly about her advice and care, and fill up his loneliness with her softness untiringly.

"Right. You win." He pleaded, "I gave up."

Xia Yutong didn't like to force people, so what Hu Yibiao did seemed to upset her. This topic came into a sudden conclusion and they chatted about other things to relax. Guan Hongfeng from Fengtai Branch quit his job because his little brother was listed as wanted; Zhou Xun should be promoted as the commander, straightly crossing two levels; there was no one sent to Xicheng District but Lu Mingjia was good and Hu Yibiao spoke highly of him; He Jingcheng was not successful to be promoted as the director of the medical center in Haidian Branch but he didn't care about it; why don't you find a man to marry and you didn't have a wife; so what if we two be together in the end and it sounds good.

Before the next refill of that mug, Xia Yutong made him a new cup of tea. Hu Yibiao tapped his belly with the three and a half fingers left on his left hand and asked, "Talk to me. Why did you quit?"

She has to tell him the truth. This was their way of communication. Every time when she revealed the true feeling of Hu Yibiao, he had a privilege to ask her a question which she had to answer with truth. There was no logic in it and nothing to do with equal communication. And the biggest effect of it may be to seek psychological balance.

Xia Yutong was rolling up her sleeves slowly, her head lowered down. Hu Yibiao knew she didn't like lying so the stall was to find herself a mood to tell him the truth. He started to regret his question.

When he was about to make a joke and start another suject, Xia Yutong gave him the answer. "It was Bin who suggested me to quit."

These words irritated Hu Yibiao at once. He swallowed back the dirty words he was going to say, but his face already showed his anger.

"Exactly speaking, he advised me to stay away from all organizations related to the police system." She explained, seeming to comfort Hu Yibiao or herself, "And I wanted to change an environment also. You know, it's a hard job to face you guys all day long."

Hu Yibiao didn't respond. Now that the answer came from Bin's suggestion, than that "also" from Xia Yutong was just an excuse. Han Bin was a lawyer. His father was working as the consultant of Haidian Branch. He was good friends with Zhao Xincheng and was said to be Xia Yutong's teacher. Hu Yibiao had met with Han Bin once, a guy of middle-figure, simple clothes, genial and kind, modest and nice. But his experience of walking through blood made him alert. There was some kind of smell on him, some kind of abnormal, illogical and antisocial smell. He, however, couldn't see any traces of disguise in Han Bin, but isn't the best disguise the one couldn't be seen through? Anyway, Hu Yibiao didn't like him, and was particularly annoyed by Xia Yutong's obedience to him.

"If his words mean that much too you, why not marry him?" Hu Yibiao was teasing and a little bit jealous. It was not that there was something between them, although he really doubted about it. It was no admiration, nor revere. But he still saw her as the manipulator of his fate. This kind of confusion irritated him very much.

Xia Yutong was happy to tease with him, "I just couldn't leave you."

Well, that was enough. More chatting this time and the subject went farther than before, from decoration style all the way to the Battle of Zama between Hannibal and Scipio. At last, Xia Yutong took out a tool whose tip is like a raindrop from the interlayer of her tea table and peeled an apple. Hu Yibiao didn't take he apple, but the hunting knife with two sharpened edge and a slightly curve blade. He looked it over. Although the handle wasn't made from antler, the blade wasn't polished with a typical style and there was no nude lady marks, Hu Yibiao still managed to find something like "DELAWARE MAID" which wasn't neatly carved. He then realized that this was probably the most expensive luxury in this room.

Putting it back on the tea table, he gulped his apple. "I'll have to take it down that I've eaten this here today."

Xia Yutong swept the apple peels into the dustbin with a smile. "Maybe it's a fake."

"There are fakes of Loveless, but they tend to fake those classical ones with a nude lady on it, or with no marks at all. No one would fake his works in the fifties. Experts don't play with fakes, and newbies won't take its appearance. That's not a fake."

"I didn't know you know knives and antiques so well."

"Just a little." Hu Yichen switched the apple to his right hand, rubbed his left hand on his pants and picked up and knife again. He picked it up with his middle and ring finger to feel its weight and then read the carving carefully again. The marks that getting deeper from the edge to the middle told him that this line of capitalized English characters was hand carved before thermal treatment, not a production from the CNC milling machine. "The best of the best, this one. This must be something auctioned from $50,000."

Unexpectedly, Xia Yutong's smile was not natural as before. "I didn't know the price. It's he who thought that I like this kind of knife and gave it to me as a present."

Yeah, that "him". He was everywhere, that almighty "he".

"That one named Han Bin, what does he want to do?"

It was a hint that they'll go back to the old weird atmosphere, but Xia Yutong still let the conversation flow since she was curious about why Hu Yibiao was asking this. It wasn't something he's gonna ask as usual. "Why do you say so?"

"Is he planning to do something? Something illegal?" Hu Yibiao put on a serious face and said with a firm tone. "He's afraid of dealing with you after he was caught so he told you to stay away from the system."

There was a slice of sadness crossing her eyes, but she smiled in a relaxed way. "I don't know. I never think about that."

"Never think about that? Or don't want to think?"

Xia Yutong seemed to be a little upset. Yes, it was impossible that she would never think about it. And it was impossible she didn't come out an answer. But so what? It was just like all the people who came in and out of her office. They were all experts in confronting with criminals. They tried hard, with all their efforts to chase after them, but couldn't ever stop people from hurting each other.

"I don't care about things like this, and you shouldn't have think about it."

"There are enough criminals in the world. I won't waste my time on a lawyer." Hu Yibiao threw the apple core into the dustbin and leaned forward, his hands rubbing. "If he breaks the law one day, there will be someone taking him down. If you want to change your job, I have no stance to persuade you."

But then, the corner of his mouth tightened, and the boundary between the whites and the blackness of the eyes started to become cloudy again. "But if what he's going to do will hurt you, I won't waste my time switching to a Type 54 this time."

It may not be strange for Hu Yibiao who had killed several criminals in different operations to say something like this, but Xia Yudong was still grateful. After all in this world, there was few people who'd like to risk their lives for you. In Hu Yibiao's philosophy, whether his comrade is alive or not was like a switch. Once activated, he would break out any rule or moral restrict in a cunning and ferocious way only to achieve what he wanted.

If this could be seen as a certain trailer, it was a rough and simple one without any editing or special effects. It pointed directly to the result. It was dangerous, desperate but valuable.

Xia Yutong gazed at me, seemingly to see through the other side of the coin. Maybe Hu Yibiao and Han Bin were the same kind of person in essence. They seemed to cared about nothing, but in fact, they paid most attention to their loved ones. They were used to cover their loneliness and cruelty under their mask, and would like to show the world their strength when they had to stand out to protect their beloved ones.

In the end, she stood up, both of her hands put in her pockets. She came across the sofa and stood still in front of the table. There was a market selling flowers and fishes which could be seen from her window. Many people thought it was the old market which was moved here, but actually they just shared the same name, with no connections at all. Although she liked those little ones very much, she had been there only once since it opened. Every day when she came back home, she would close the whole world outside. It was a pity that this kind of solitude couldn't bring her a peaceful life.

"He won't do something like that. I assure you." Xia Yutong knew that in Han Bin's value system, human beings were worthless. But she was one of the few who would be seen as a human by him. But now, it embarrassed her a lot.

Hu Yibiao's voice was as muffled as a gun with a silencer. "It doesn't matter. You can tell him what I say if there's a chance."

Xia Yutong gave him a bitter smile, her voice as low as a sigh. "Did you say we humans have to accept our fate?"

"And you said I'm a murder weapon." Hu Yibiao talked back, "Either live under supervision, or be exiled. As long as I'm still a murder weapon, there's no good end of me."

"Promise me."

Hu Yibiao turned around and then found Xia Yutong was looking at him, her back leaning against the windowsill. The beige curtain dangling down by her side, through which the winter sun could be seen shining on the dim sky outside.

"No matter what happens in the future, we have to accept our fate and let nature take its course. Could you promise me?"

An unfortunate feeling swept over him. Hu Yibiao asked back in hesitance. "What if I don't?"

Xia Yutong shood her head with an understanding smile, as if he was a stubborn kid. "Then at least don't forget to switch a Type 54 then."

"Why mentioning that always. I'm telling you, the switch doesn't have anything to do with Jing Huai's death."

"Yeah, I know." Xia Yutong put her hair behind her ears and said to him calmly, "But I believe you'll need that fractions of a second.

Reprint Afterword

A family of mine left us forever at the end of last year. He really wanted to see me finish the second book of mine when he was still with me. But I was busy with changing my job and couldn't focus on my writing. One version was turned over and then another. At last, I couldn't finish this one in time. Speaking of this now, I cannot say I'm sorry or regret, but it's still something taking up my mind.

Before that, I quit the job I was doing then and would go back occasionally to visit my old leader and colleagues, but not much as time passed by so we are naturally not as close as before. I know I'll go back to visit them when I have time, but I will never go back to the career I have been fighting for 11 years.

After I quit, I stared to grow fond of archery. I've practiced diligently for a year but didn't achieve much. Then the club moved so I took it as a chance to quit, regardless of the new location of the club was actually closer to my residence.

A baby dog, a mixed blood of a Border Collie and other species, came to the cafe accidentally. We decided to give him a fashionable name so called him Espresso at first, but it was a little difficult to pronounce so later on it was called "Yi", which could be understood as "Meaning" in Chinese. Now he grew bigger and became a little cunning. But in general, he is a good boy.

I got my own little dog this summer. He's really naughty so I will give him several slaps when I couldn't control my temper. But then I remembered that I was told several times that I should educate him with positive examples and should not punish him with violence, so I came to apologize to him. Now several months passed and he grew bigger and naughtier. But I started to get used to it. Slaps are rarely seen in our communication.

Another year is almost over. I don't know whether I could make a living in my new career. But I still want to finish my second book as early as possible.

Although it could compensate nothing.

It's weird that for the same item, it we don't have it, it seemed to be short of something; but when we really have in hand, it cannot fill in.

But that's normal enough. Life is always complicated.

"Life is interesting" is a truth that stands under certain circumstances. Some lives are too hard and overstretched, without any spare time to have fun. The so-called "C'est la vie" will finally let some of us down and live up to some of our desires. There will be happiness, and there will be sorrow. There will be dreams fulfilled and problems unsolved. In such a life, we move forward, together, to our final end.

This is to thank all my families, friends, colleagues and readers. Thank you all for building my life, and thank you all for your effort in yours.

November 22nd 2016, Beijing

www.ingramcontent.com/pod-product-compliance
Lightning Source LLC
Chambersburg PA
CBHW020418030726
47495CB00006B/1559